DEATH AT THE BAR X RANCH

A Mary Malone Mystery

Marlene Chabot

Enjoy!
Marlene Micheil Chabot

D1400980

OTHER WRITINGS BY MARLENE CHABOT

DETECTING THE FATAL CONNECTION
NORTH DAKOTA NEIGHBOR
MAYHEM WITH A CAPITAL M
DEATH OF THE NAKED LADY

Anthologies Containing Short Stories Written By Author

WHY DID SANTA LEAVE A BODY
FESTIVAL of CRIME
SWF STORIES and POEMS; VOL. I
COOKED TO DEATH: LYING ON A PLATE; VOL. II
MARCO ISLAND WRITERS STORIES and POEMS; VOL. IV
DARK SIDE of the LOON

DEDICATION

This book is dedicated to my deceased mother Eva Mc Neil, a feisty woman who danced until she was ninety-two. Her active lifestyle, along with two other women, helped me fashion the character Mrs. Grimshaw. I hope I'm lucky enough to experience all the world has to offer as my mother did until the day I too am called home.

ACKNOWLEDGEMENTS

A huge thank you to Angie Sanders for the many hours spent proofing this book. I'd also like to thank Imgrund Motors of Brainerd and the fantastic horsewomen who have helped and encouraged me along the way.

Staci Grattan and Toni Wasilensky — Spirit Horse Center — Brainerd, MN
Kathleen Lordbock — Horse owner and trainer — Brainerd, MN
Dr. Deb MacKay — Veterinary Medicine and horse owner — Crosby, MN
Cindy Murlowski and Joan Pasqua — Bel Meade Stables — Naples, FL
Cindy Schneider — Horse owner and boarder — Crosby, MN
Lara Simonson — Horse owner and trainer — Naples, FL
Cheryl Gilson — for introducing me to *Horses For Dummies* by Audrey Pavia and Janice Posnikoff D.V.M.

~Prologue~

Mary Colleen Malone's my name. I'm not what most people would consider either a girly-girl or a tomboy. I'm more an in between type of gal, in between men, in between diets, in between jobs. It varies from week to week. This week, however, not I, but circumstances beyond my control, shoved employment to the top of the heap.

Teaching's my game, or it was up until yesterday morning when I strolled into the teachers' lounge and spotted a rare, unexpected gift tucked inside my cubbyhole. At first, I thought the hot-pink slip was someone's idea of a joke, but then reality smacked me in the face. I hadn't slid under the unemployment radar after all. With one swift hurricane after another chiseling away at the U.S. economy, teachers without tenure were the latest surfers to be caught up in the storm.

Hmm? Maybe I can sub in Blaine. That's not too far north to drive.

"Aim for the stars," everyone said. *Yeah, right. Fat lot of good it did me.* The aligned planet and stars supposedly assigned to my personal universe imploded on contact. Goodbye lifetime job. Hello unemployment.

To think I was once so elated being the first member of the Malone clan to receive a master's degree. Now, I'm just depressed. While I sit idly by twiddling my thumbs, my siblings continue being smugly employed, including the one who flips flapjacks at the local pancake house just around the corner.

So, what's a smart, single thirty-five-year-old unemployed dame to do? I haven't a clue. Perhaps it'll come to me while I snooze.

~1~

They say there's a wee bit of blarney in me, and if that's the case, I accept it. I have no problem with my Irish heritage. Besides, it's bound to pop up now and again in my profession. I'm an elementary school teacher, but believe me when I tell you, what unfolded shortly after my career went bust didn't have a smidgen of blarney in it.

"Mary?" a wisp of a voice called behind me. "Mary Malone, is that you?"

My fingers immediately stopped fumbling with the spare key to my brother's apartment. The timely intrusion couldn't have come at a better time. I had been fighting with the lock for the past couple of seconds and was on the verge of blurting out words not meant for even a turtle's ears.

I curled my fingers around the key and twirled in the direction of the person seeking me out. "Oh, Mrs. Grimshaw. I thought the voice sounded vaguely familiar."

Mrs. Grimshaw's thin, oval-shaped face, bedecked with a charming pair of silver-colored granny glasses, stared at me in bewilderment. "How could you have forgotten my voice already, Mary? It wasn't that long ago your brother Matt and I saw you at Elaine's party." Her bony, heavily veined hands grasped the sides of her full-length yellow floral apron and flapped it for emphasis.

The woman she was referring to was Elaine Best, my closest friend since childhood. She, along with my brother, his now ex-girlfriend, Rita Sinclair, and I vacationed together this past January in Puerto Vallarta, Mexico, thanks to my dad's overly-generous Christmas present.

Upon returning home to Minnesota's sub-zero temps and mile high snow banks, Elaine convinced her husband Frank that they should host a Mexican-themed party and include her travel companions.

Unfortunately for Matt, Rita had just broken up with him, and he was left with the challenge of finding a last minute date.

Mrs. Grimshaw fit the bill perfectly. A longtime neighbor, she's remained in Matt's corner through thick and thin, rain or shine and even the death of his wife, Irene.

The tiny lady with stately white hair pulled into a bun who was standing in front of my 5 foot 6 frame could easily pass for someone in her late seventies, but I knew she was much older. You see, my brother had shared she was a nonagenarian.

As soon as this mid-thirties female learned of Mrs. Grimshaw's real age, I pleaded with her to spill where she'd hidden the true fountain of youth since I knew the fountain in St. Augustine, Florida was simply a tourist trap.

Of course, the Italian born woman thoroughly disappointed me when she merely said, "Stay active. That's the ticket."

I lifted my thick shoulders now. "I forgot for a split second, honest. When you speak to as many people as I do in my line of work, voices start sounding the same. So, how are you?"

Mrs. Grimshaw's aged olive-green eyes twinkled through her wire-rimmed glasses. "Me? Why, I'm fit as a fiddle. Grazie," she replied as she inched closer to me. "How about you, Mary? I heard the Anoka-Hennepin school district was forced to lay off a substantial number of elementary teachers this spring. You weren't one of those who received a pink slip, were you?"

Bile rose from my stomach when *"pink slip"* resounded in my ears. *Yuk. Why did those two nasty words have to crop up everywhere I go?* Unable to answer without feeling worse than I already did, I shifted my attention temporarily to the pumpkin and pea-green colored shag carpet covering the fourth floor hallway at the Foley Apartment Complex.

How can people stand to look at this crazy carpet day in and day out? So '60's. The owner of this building's lucky I don't live here. I would've demanded that they replace the carpet the first day I moved in.

With a calmer stomach now and nothing more in the hallway to find fault with, I figured it best to answer the elderly woman before she concluded I was a terribly rude person. "Afraid so," I replied, keeping my eyes glued to the carpet, "I had one more year to go before receiving tenure."

Matt's neighbor reached out and clutched my hand. "I'm so sorry, Mary. According to your brother, you're a great teacher."

My head shot up like a puppet's when its master tugs hard on its strings. "Huh? Imagine that. Did he make that comment after visiting my classroom this winter?"

"As a matter of fact, yes."

"Humph." I rubbed my free hand on a pant leg. "Well, all he ever says when he's around me is that I'm spoiled rotten, which I'm not. There are four of us in the family for cry'n out loud."

"Oh, Matt's so very proud of all his siblings' accomplishments," the older woman hurriedly explained.

I raised my hand to my cheek now and rested it there for a while. "Is that so? Then why does he continue to treat me like a dingbat?"

Mrs. Grimshaw's barely-noticeable eyebrows rose slightly. "*Mi scusi. Non capisco.*"

"Sorry. I guess Matt forgot to share foreign languages and I don't see eye to eye. Could you repeat that in English?"

"Oh, of course. It seems the language of my homeland is creeping its way back into my life the more I advance in age. What I said was 'excuse me, I don't understand.'"

"Understand what?"

"Dingbat. I've never come across that word doing crossword puzzles."

"It means idiot," I chirped.

The woman standing alongside of me let go of a girlish giggle. "That's Matt. He usually doesn't permit himself to say what's actually on his mind. He told me 'it's not manly.'"

"Maybe it has to do more with being a private investigator, keeping things under wrap so to speak."

"Hmm? That could explain it. So, Mary, what brings you to the Foley today?"

"In the last call Mom received from Matt, he asked that I check on his apartment from time to time."

My brother's neighbor pursed her almost invisible wrinkled lips. "I don't know what he's worried about. His work in Germany ends next month, and he certainly doesn't have any plants in his apartment to care for."

Matt's apartment key began to take flight in my hand like it was a Mexican jumping bean. "That was the original plan, but things have changed."

"Really?"

"Yup. Delight Bottling Company is acquiring a pop facility in Ireland, so Mr. Welch asked Matt to extend his stay."

The nonagenarian's eyes misted up. She hastily diverted them to Matt's apartment door which my slightly overweight body was partially hiding. "He wouldn't have taken that job offer with Welch if Rita Sinclair hadn't broken up with him." She shook her head. "Did you know he was going to ask her to marry him?"

"No way! You're kidding, right?"

Mrs. Grimshaw twisted her head slightly from side to side. "No. That's one subject I don't joke about." She peered at her slippers.

"Hmm? Surprised my mom and dad never mentioned it either."

Catching how distraught Mrs. Grimshaw looked after hearing Matt wasn't returning as soon as she thought, I wished I could erase that fact now somehow.

We all knew how much the childless woman doted on my brother—making him Italian meals and desserts.

How do I go about cheering her up? "Say, Mrs. Grimshaw, why don't you help me check Matt's place out? You're more familiar with the layout than I am." When I finished the invite, I turned my body slightly and placed the key in the lock again. This time the key worked. *Amazing.*

From the corner of my eye, I caught my brother's apartment neighbor lift her age-spotted hands to her eyes and wipe away the tears forming. "I'll go in on one condition, Mary."

I lined up directly with the elderly woman now. "What?"

"Call me Margaret. Mrs. Grimshaw's too stuffy."

"All right. Margaret it is." I swung Matt's door inward with one arm and extended the other arm out. "Elders first." My brother's neighbor didn't put up a fuss. She simply shuffled her pink and white stripped Isotoner-slippered feet over the threshold and waited for me to follow.

I hastened in and bolted the door behind me. "Might as well check the back of Matt's apartment first and then work our way back here."

"That's fine, Mary, but I have to warn you I don't know what might be lurking in his inner sanctum. I've never been privy to it."

Don't worry. If it's too shocking, I'll warn you." I immediately took the lead, traveling down to the end of the narrow hallway which brought us to two rooms, the bathroom and Matt's bedroom.

I totally ignored the bathroom. No one in his right mind would want to inflict more misery on it. Matt's bedroom, on the other hand, was worth looking into. Who knew what lurked there?

Finding the door to his bedroom closed, I gripped the handle and turned it. Nothing happened. No problem. A stuck door has never stopped this gal's curiosity. When there's a chance to find out if your brother was a neat freak in his sleeping quarters, or a pile-of-junk kind of guy, you go for it.

I lightly leaned my shoulder against the door, hoping it would do the trick. The word *lightly* definitely needed to be redefined. When the door gave way, I flew through the air with the greatest of ease and let loose with the most ear-splitting yelp anyone's ever heard, including the late Alfred Hitchcock. The short-lived ride, when finished, dropped me on a stiff clump of something.

Since the room was cloaked in darkness, I hadn't a clue what saved me from a visit to the emergency room, and at this point I wasn't sure if I wanted to find out. Knowing Matt, I could be sitting on a couple weeks' worth of dirty clothes or a body.

Devious notions flitted back and forth between my brain cells until reality finally sank in. If I was sitting on a dead animal or body, an atrocious odor would've knocked me senseless by now; Matt's apartment had been closed up for several months. Besides, the only animal my brother owned was Gracie, a dog, and she was staying at my folks.

"Mary, what is it?" Mrs. Grimshaw inquired in a deeply-concerned tone. "Should I stay in the hall?"

"No, no." I replied, as I remained on the floor and continued to grope around in the dark. "Everything's fine..." Then I saw it. "Margaret, hurry, flick on the light switch. A red-eyed monster is flirting with me."

Two seconds later the bedroom light came on. It wasn't as bright as I'd hoped, but it served its purpose. "There does that help, dear?" the elderly woman asked as she entered the room and offered me her bony hand.

"Immensely."

"How did you end up there, Mary?"

I pointed to the garments rubbing up against my sandals. "Matt left these darn jeans on the floor."

The little Italian woman let a soft "Ah," escape her lips as she carefully scanned the room in its entirety. When she finished, she said, "I don't see that red-eyed monster you mentioned. Are you sure you weren't just dazed from the fall?"

Now that the room was lit, the maze hiding the monster made it almost impossible for me to see too. A mammoth jar of Vicks, an alarm clock, a box of Kleenex, a box of Milkbones and a stack of paperback spy thrillers completed the list of items obstructing my view. I quickly directed Margaret's eyes to the nightstand. "There it is, in the flesh."

"Oh? Matt must have forgotten to clear all his messages on his answering machine before he left."

"Either that or…"

"Or what?" Mrs. Grimshaw impatiently cut in.

"It's something he never heard."

A slight smile erupted on the elderly woman's face as she pressed her hands together in steeple fashion. "Hmm. That's true. So, are we going to listen?"

I pretended to be outraged by her suggestion. "Why, Margaret, that's invasion of privacy. What's on that answering machine is for Matt's ears only." Then I laughed. I may have performed with great finesse as a trained teacher, but when trying to pull a fast one on a peer or another adult I've never been able to maintain the right decorum.

Joining in the merriment, Mrs. Grimshaw's laughter ripped through the room. "Do you want to press the 'PLAY' button, Mary, or should I?"

I weighed her question for a split second. "Nah. Let's both do it. That way we won't know who's actually responsible for pressing it."

Matt's neighbor reacted enthusiastically. "I like the way you think. Reminds me of Agatha Christie's mystery *The Orient Express*. Ready?"

"Yup."

"One message left at 3 p.m. on May 24th."

"Yeah, Mr. Malone, this is Reed Griffin. I own a horse stable, the Bar X Ranch, out in Cottage Grove. Perhaps, you've heard of it. Anyway, I found your listing in the yellow pages and thought I'd give you a buzz and see if you're interested in a new client. My problem concerns horses. Most days you can reach me at 651-245-9240." Immediately after the number was shared, the tape came to a screeching halt.

I glanced at the expandable silver Timex wristwatch wrapped around my wide wrist. "Today's the 27th," I stated out loud. "He only called three days ago."

The nonagenarian standing next to me didn't seem to be the least bit interested in how many days it had been since the stranger called. She was already on a totally different wavelength. "Horses? My, it's been a long time since I've even given them any thought. I was a little girl back in Italy when I first caught sight of them at a circus, horses and ponies prancing every which way. Several children were selected from the audience to ride in the pony-drawn carts that day."

The caller and his immediate problem shifted momentarily to the back seat for me as I escorted the elderly woman out into the hall and wondered if she'd been one of the chosen children. *Do I dare ask?* "Were you one of the lucky ones, Margaret?"

The little woman brushed the air with her hand. "Good heavens, no. But that same summer, my parents took me to their friend's farm for my birthday, and I got to ride a beautiful chestnut-colored Belgian horse." She smiled fondly. "Ginger was such a gentle horse. I'm glad I got to ride her. What do you think of horses, Mary?"

Why did she have to spoil my day by asking me to recall something I'd rather not?

I fluffed the straight thin hair clinging to the nape of my neck as I was forced to dig up a horrible memory from the deep dark recesses of my mind, an experience I long ago classified as a total disaster. A huge sigh escaped my lips before I spoke. "I rode a pony when I was four. It didn't work out so well, and I'd rather not get into it if you don't mind."

I'd made a pact with myself long ago that I'd never go near those four-legged creatures again, and I meant to keep it. I didn't care who tried to prod me to do otherwise.

The elderly woman honored my request and didn't pry further. Instead, the two of us strolled into the kitchen, the hearth of the home, wrapped in our own quiet thoughts.

The first item Mrs. Grimshaw's eagle eyes inspected was the black and white checkered linoleum under our feet. Maybe she was looking for telltale signs whether Matt scrubbed it with Spic and Span before he left the country.

Too bad it was spotless. She'd have nothing to report to the other Foley apartment dwellers on that score. The woman's eyes soon shifted from the floor to me. "You misunderstood what I was asking in the bedroom, Mary."

"I did?" What else could she have been referring to other than horses? That's all we'd been discussing.

"I didn't want to know what you thought about actual horses."

"Oh?" *She tells me that after she got me all worked up.*

I continued to scan every inch of Matt's kitchen above the floor while I waited for my brother's neighbor to explain further. The room was immaculate. Not one solitary crumb or dirty dish on the counter, table or sink. Too surreal. Was I perhaps dreaming?

Nope. The loud smacking created by Mrs. Grimshaw's slippers when she crossed in front of me let me know I definitely wasn't dreaming. "Mary, did you hear me? I asked what you plan to do about the message."

"Ah, I don't know," I innocently replied. "I suppose I should at least call Mr. Griffin and tell him Matt's not available."

"Yes," the elderly woman said in a low no-nonsense manner as she continued on to Matt's harvest gold nineteen-cubic-foot no-frost fridge that sat in the opposite corner of the room, "that would be the most sensible thing to do, wouldn't it?"

I casually nodded in agreement.

Mrs. Grimshaw cracked the fridge door open and peeked inside. After checking the fridge's contents, she allowed the door to close on its own. Obviously, she didn't find anything of interest, or she would've kept the door open longer.

"I don't know if you've had time to listen to the news lately, Mary, seeing as you've been busy with end of school activities, but one of WCCO's newscasters said thirty unrelated violent horse crimes were reported this month, four of which occurred in our friendly state alone."

I vaguely recalled someone mentioning it at school, but let it slide. You see, I'm not a fan of horses. None of my friends or family owned them, and I was too rattled by my own topsy-turvy world to care.

Instead of letting on I'd overheard a bit of conversation about it I pretended to be totally ignorant. Who would it hurt? "You're right. I haven't listened to the news in quite some time. Why would anyone want to mistreat an animal?"

The elderly woman sighed. "I don't know."

The kitchen had passed my inspection and apparently the nonagenarian's too, so we moved to the last room, the living room, where most people unwind after a stressful day.

As soon as I entered the room, I plopped my plump derriere down in Matt's most prized possession, a chunky black La-Z-Boy chair he inherited from my folks several years ago when they were refurbishing parts of their house. Choosing the comfy chair for me was a no-brainer. An elderly person would find it extremely difficult to get out of. The chair didn't come with the necessary equipment needed to hoist a person to upright position. *Hmm. Pretty comfy. So this is how Goldilocks felt when she sat in Baby Bear's chair.*

Relaxed now, my interest gravitated to Mrs. Grimshaw as she carefully positioned her small frame on the plain brown medium-sized sleeper couch that's been slammed up against the largest wall in this room since my brother moved in ten years ago. "You know Matt's set up isn't as bad as I thought. I could easily settle in to an apartment similar to this for a long, long spell. What's the square footage for a one bedroom here at the Foley, Margaret?"

Matt's neighbor plucked at the tight ruffles on the bottom of her apron. "Why, I don't really know. My apartment's a two bedroom."

"Oh, I just assumed..."

Evidently what I was about to expound on wasn't worthy enough to bother with since Matt's neighbor quickly bypassed it. "I don't mean to interfere in your life, Mary, but without a full time teaching position in sight you may want to re-think where you now live."

Curious to know what path Mrs. Grimshaw might be leading me down, I swiftly queried her. "Do you have something in mind?"

As a matter of fact, I do." She stretched her almost skeletal arms in front of her. Why not move in here? You know me, and you'd be doing your brother a huge favor."

"How's that?"

"Matt wouldn't have to give up his lease. You could sublet the place for the time being."

I folded and unfolded my hands several times while I gave the woman's suggestion serious thought.

Sublet? Hmm? I wonder? Nope. You couldn't possibly afford to stay here, Mary. Everyone says rent in the downtown district is extremely high. "Thanks, but I think I need to weigh other options at this time."

"Are you sure?"

"Ah huh. A person needs too deep of pockets to cover rent for a spot in this part of town."

Mrs. Grimshaw slowly drew her arms inward and cradled them on her lap. "I wouldn't be so quick to leap to that conclusion if I were you."

I felt my eyebrows lift off my face. "Care to elaborate?"

"Few people know what I'm going to reveal, so you must keep it under your hat. *Capisco?*"

"Sure, sure," I agreed barely above a whisper, not knowing what I actually was agreeing to.

"I'm sure your brother's shared I'm one of the Foley's old-timers."

"Yes, he did."

"Not necessarily in age, mind you," she solemnly pointed out, but rather the amount of years I've lived in this building." I nodded politely. "So, what I'm going to reveal is extremely important."

"All right."

"If you talk real sweet to the owners, they'll work with you concerning your income level. They'd prefer to keep their long-standing tenants happy rather than wasting time checking out every drifter that passes through their doors."

"That makes sense. No one wants to spend money on credit reports if they don't have to."

My income and lease both come to an end in a few weeks' time, and I hadn't even given any thought to the consequences yet.

I massaged my forehead while I mulled over what the little woman had told me. "You've definitely given me food for thought. Living here rates better than in the street or back home with my parents."

"I'm sure it does." The elderly woman's thin lips formed a wry smile now as she scooted to the edge of the couch and stood. "Well, I'm glad I could be of help to you, but I'd better get going. I have caramel rolls waiting to be baked."

Caramel rolls? No wonder Matt likes having Margaret as a neighbor. Food and sweets—the one weakness my brother and I share. *If you moved in here, you'd get to taste all kinds of goodies like Matt.*

I stood and escorted Mrs. Grimshaw to the door, ashamed of the selfish thoughts that had swept through my head. People don't move into a place because they know the neighbor across the hall shares her cooking with other tenants. How lame is that?

I gripped the elderly woman's thin hand for a second as she edged out of the apartment onto the ugly hallway carpet. "Thank you so much for checking Matt's apartment with me, Margaret, and for your housing suggestion. I really appreciate it."

"My pleasure. *Arrivederci!*" she said. Then she quietly strolled across the hall leaving me to my own thoughts.

~2~

I closed the door behind Mrs. Grimshaw and scurried back to the cheese, the message machine, to hear what Mr. Griffin had to say one more time.

The second the recording ended, I dug into my small handy-dandy half-moon-shaped blue and green faux leather purse and plucked out a teeny notepad and pen to scribble down what I'd heard. It was imperative that I do this since I no longer forced my memory to be all knowing. As a matter of fact, I couldn't think of a single friend who did. Why bother when you can just Google it, right?

The thick lime-green pen snugly gripped between the fingertips, poised for action, was one of many I kept acquiring from the local establishments around town, a freebie. Although, the stores I shopped at didn't necessarily think so. But that's not my problem.

Look, if they wanted their pens to remain at the location, then a gizmo should be attached to it to reel the guilty hand back when one stepped away from the counter.

"There. Message erased." Only one more thing to do. My index finger hovered over the OFF button waiting for my mind to command it to shut the machine down, but the order didn't want to come. I finally gave up. *The dumb machine's been on several months already, Mary, why bother with it? If someone calls for Matt, I can simply contact them like I'm doing with Mr. Griffin.*

Finished with all that I wanted to do in the apartment, I forced the pen and paper back into my cosmetic-jammed purse, made sure all the lights were off and then skedaddled out of the Foley as fast as my short legs could carry me.

My still rather new navy-blue Volkswagen, which I affectionately referred to as Fiona after my great aunt from the Irish side of the family, was patiently waiting for me on a one-way side street two blocks south of the Foley complex. It didn't look like anyone had tried to force his or her way into it. Now, all I had to worry about was if my meter time had run out. Nope. It hadn't. Five minutes to spare. "Spring Lake Park here I come."

Since my parents wanted the lowdown on my brother's apartment as soon as I got around to checking it out, and I had no plans for this afternoon, even though it was a Saturday, I chose to drive to my childhood home to give an in-house report instead of repeating myself over and over via the phone. According to Matt it was only a twenty minute drive from downtown to the burbs on Highway 65, but it depends on what season it is.

Of course, there were other underlying reasons to pop by too. This gal hadn't had a decent home-cooked meal in over a month, and I wanted to see Gracie. The folks volunteered to care for the mutt the instant Matt announced his European assignment for Delight Bottling.

It had been a couple weeks since I made the familiar trek to my folks' house and I was already feeling the guilt complex creeping in as I rounded the corner to their home.

Oh, I knew they'd be ecstatic to see their baby; they always were, but I was expecting the love emanating from them to be over the top today, especially since they had just learned I'd be out a job in a couple weeks. I hastily envisioned my parents literally tripping over themselves now as they made their way to the front door and welcomed their youngest child with open arms.

The second the "Bug's" tires rolled onto my parents' slightly inclined driveway I laid on the horn, giving fair warning company had arrived.

Surprisingly, the blast from the car didn't do the job. Neither Mom nor Dad flew to the window to see who was here.

"No big deal, Mary," I soberly told myself. "They'll go bonkers the minute you walk through the front door."

That didn't happen either. As soon I opened the front door, Gracie charged outside taking Dad along with her. Okay, I know what you're thinking. I've still got my Mom to give me the much needed hug I had anticipated. Well, rethink that one. My five-foot-five thin-boned French-descended mother had no clue I was there. She stood near the living room with her hazel eyes affixed to the two who just flew out the door, knees locked together and hands resting on her hips while a hearty laugh spewed from her ruby red lips.

Disheartened, I forged ahead and purposely blocked her view. The laughter that had rocked the roof only a minute ago halted abruptly. "Mary? I didn't know you were here. When did you arrive?"

"About five minutes ago. I rolled into the driveway and honked the horn."

"You honked the horn?"

"Yeah," I whined like a spoiled brat.

"Sorry. I never heard it. Your father was using our ancient hair dryer on Gracie. He just gave her a bath, and I was down in the basement doing laundry." She quickly moved around me, walked to the door, and closed it.

I turned to face her. "Mom, why are you bothering to shut the door? Won't Dad be coming right back?"

My mother shook her dark shoulder length hair as she started to stroll down the hallway. "I doubt it. It's time for your father and Gracie to take their daily walk around the block."

I followed behind as she led us deeper into the recesses of the house. "Speaking of Gracie," I said, "How's the babysitting going? Has she been a handful for you guys?"

"Gracie? Heavens, no. She's a peach. I love having her around. Your brother's longer commitment in Europe is actually a blessing in disguise. With Gracie here, your father has no excuse for not getting his daily walks in." Mom's been overly concerned about my father's lifestyle, eating and exercise, ever since he had heart by-pass surgery a year and a half ago. If she continues to watch him the way she does, he'll probably outlive all of us, which is a nice thought.

By the time we reached the doorway of the kitchen, my mother's prattling stopped, which gave me time to absorb what was going on in the medium-sized family dining area of my childhood, including uncovering what delicious aroma had made its way to my nostrils. Whatever it was, it was hidden from view. Perhaps it was in the oven. *Well, if it's not ready to eat while I'm here, I'm definitely begging for takeout.*

"I'm glad you asked about Gracie," Mom said in a quiet tone, interrupting my thoughts. "We'll need someone to watch her when we go on vacation next month. You know, if you volunteered, you could have free rein of the house and a chance to reconnect with the old neighborhood, especially some of your classmates who still live in the area."

"I'll think about it," I lied, dragging on every word. Mom didn't know the classmates still living in this part of town were those I definitely didn't want to mess with: born losers, in and out of jail like a revolving door.

I pulled a wooden chair away from the round oak table, the one that had been passed down to my parents upon the death of my father's Irish grandparents, and sat. As soon as my hand touched the ancient table's smooth surface, I patted it like one does after catching up with an old friend. So many tears shed here, and yes, wonderful times too, including super-duper meals.

No one knows this, but this dearly loved antiquated table actually kept me grounded over the years with its fervent message—life is nothing but one big circle that continues on and on.

Someday, if I ever find Mr. Right, I'll probably inherit this well-worn family gem. It's a well-known fact that my sister Margaret would never want it–her decorating style was modern all the way. And Matt and Michael, my brothers, didn't give two hoots about furniture.

Mom and I had been indulging in sweets and a strongly brewed black mango tea she had recently purchased at a new tea shop a couple blocks from here, when Dad showed up at the back door, huffing and a puffing like the big bad wolf in the *Three Little Pigs*, towing the dog behind him instead of vice versa.

Gracie looked worse than Dad. Her head hung low allowing her long tongue to dangle dangerously from her mouth, dripping doggie drool on Mom's sparkling clean, light-gray star-designed linoleum floor.

My father didn't permit himself the luxury of joining us quite yet, even though his exhausted body definitely needed to park someplace fast. Instead, he took care of unfinished doggie business: unhooking the mutt's leash, patting her on the noggin, and pointing out the water dish. "There's your water. Go get it, Girl."

The medium-sized dog zoomed to her dish and lapped up the liquid in lickety-split time.

"Gracie's such a good dog," I said as I watched her. "Matt was lucky to find her when he did. According to him, if he hadn't walked into the Hennepin Humane Society that day, she would've been history."

My seventy-year-old father pushed aside a clump of sandy-brown hair that had fallen over his eyes when he was busying himself with Gracie. "I agree wholeheartedly. Remember what a basket case your brother was after Irene's death? He could've ended up becoming history too."

Mother's eyes saddened. "Yes, indeed."

"I don't believe it," I said. "Life's too precious to Matt."

Dad joined us at the table, selecting a chair near Mom. "I didn't mean taking his life, Mary. I meant work-wise. His mind was beginning to shut up shop."

"Oh? I didn't realize."

Dad quickly changed the subject. He probably sensed how dumb I felt. "So, daughter, what brings you here?"

"Oh, I thought I'd check on Gracie. Make sure she's behaving herself."

The minute the mutt's name vibrated through the air, she dashed to my side, furiously sloshing water every which way. Her wet doggy fur didn't intimidate me in the least. I was prepared. The blue jeans I had on had already seen miles of better days. I shoved my chair back and permitted her wet head to rest on my lap.

Dad squeezed his squarish jaw and shook his head. "I'm sorry I didn't greet you on the way out the door. If I'd known it was you, I would've said something. I thought the figure I passed was Shirley Nelson, the neighbor from across the street. She'd called your mom earlier and told her she was coming by to show her something."

He thought I was Shirley Nelson? She's fifty pounds heavier than me if not more and thirty years older. "Mom, did you hear what Dad said?" I whined. "He thinks I look like the Nelson lady. There's no way I resemble her."

Mom's cup of tea grazed her lips. "Well, you have to admit you both do have the same color hair, Sweetie."

"Thanks a heap."

"You're welcome," she replied, setting her blue-and-gray-striped mug down before glancing Dad's way. "Archie, speaking of Shirley, she hasn't shown up yet. Thank goodness."

Even though neither of my parents had felt the need to be sensitive to my feelings, I wouldn't dwell on the fact. Nothing would be gained by stomping out. Besides, it wasn't in my best interest to leave. If I did, I would never learn what was in the oven or be offered a taste. I reached out and smothered my mother's hands which were still warm from being wrapped around her mug of tea. "Are you sure an alien hasn't snatched your body, Mom?

"What are you talking about?"

I let go of her hands. "You brought us kids up to be tolerant of others."

"I did indeed. But when one gets older, you realize you're less willing to put up with certain people, including Shirley. The woman doesn't know when to stop talking and go home." Mom raised her hand and placed it under her chin. "I've had it up to here with her, Mary."

Thanks to Gracie's constant begging for our attention while we sat at the table, a great solution to Mom's dilemma came to mind. "If someone gave Shirley a pet, she'd be too busy to chit chat."

"A marvelous idea," Mom mumbled, pushing her chair out and going to the cupboard where dishes are kept. "Why didn't I think of it? Archie, let's head out to the woods behind the house tonight, find a stray cat and drop it off on Shirley's porch after she goes to bed."

Dad raised his thick brown brows. "Enough about that darn woman, Rene. Our daughter didn't drive all the way out here to hear complaints about our neighbor. Right, Mary?"

"Ah, no. Not really."

"Did you hear that, Rene?"

"Yes, Archie," she replied, searching for what I presumed to be Dad's favorite coffee mug.

Dad turned his full attention to me now. "So, what else besides Gracie brings you out here? With the beautiful day we've got, you should be taking full advantage of it, riding your bike around Lake Harriet or Calhoun, or sunning yourself on one of the beaches."

I can understand his biking idea, but lying on the beach in this bulky body. *Come On.* Laughter itched to burst forth, but I lassoed it in. *I'll have to remember to jot Dad's comment down in my journal for posterity. There's no way this gal's robust figure is going to plop down on any beach exposing even an inch of skin until she finds a diet that performs overnight miracles.*

Mom hadn't found what she was looking for yet, so I'd patiently waited till she did so. I wasn't about to explain the real reason for my surprise visit until I had both Mom and Dad's undivided attention.

"You're right, Dad. It's a great day for tooling around on a bike," I said, staring at the fourth cookie I was about to consume, "but I've been busy with other things."

"Oh? Like what?"

Mother finally came to the table. "If I'd known you had used your mug already, Archie, I wouldn't have wasted so much time digging through the cupboards for it." She set the mug in front of him and returned to her chair.

"Sorry, dear. I should've left it by the coffeemaker not the stove." He picked up his mug and filled it with tea. "All right, Mary, let's try again. What have you been up to?"

"You told me Matt wanted me to check out his apartment, right?"

My parents nodded. "Ah, huh."

"Well, I just came from there, so I thought I'd swing by and give you a report in person."

Mom threw her arm around my shoulder. "Thank you. I didn't think you'd have a chance to go there so soon. Did Matt leave a huge mess?"

I braced my mug with my hands. "Actually, I was pleasantly surprised. The place was left in pretty good shape."

Dad cleared his throat. He's known to do that when he has something of significance to say. "Well, I don't know what you expected to find, Mary. You certainly can't classify Matt as a slob."

"No, you definitely can't," I bounced back, "but he's not a neat freak either."

Mother interrupted what could have ended up being another lengthy discourse between my father and me. Neither of us likes to admit to defeat. "I know what you're saying, dear. You thought with Matt's leaving so abruptly he wouldn't have had time to clean as thoroughly as he did."

"Exactly. He didn't even leave as much as a dirty spoon in the sink."

"I'm impressed." Mom passed the plate of goodies to Dad now, making sure the healthier ones were nearest his hand. She was as vigilant about what he ate as she was about his getting his exercise. After Dad took the plate from her, she turned to me and added, "Did you run into anyone while you were there?"

I didn't reply right away. I wasn't sure if I liked where my mother's questioning was headed.

Thankfully, Dad's grilling of mother gave me respite for a few seconds. "Who would you expect her to see, Rene? She rarely goes to the Foley."

Mom's face dialed to a bright crimson. Obviously she was embarrassed to be cornered in front of me. "I... I don't know, Archie, maybe the cute, single, tall blonde-haired guy who lives next to Matt. I forget his name. Help me out here, Mary."

My hands suddenly loosened their grip on my mug. If it hadn't been resting on the table it would've been in a thousand pieces. "You mean Rod Thompson, the computer geek who works for the FBI? You can't be serious, Mother? No way!"

"Why not? When cupid calls, he doesn't ask the fellar or the gal what they do for a living before he shoots them with his arrows. Rod's handsome. He has a reliable job, not like some guys you've dated: the tattoo artist from Arkansas or the human cannonball from Wyoming."

"At least they stick around," I shot back defensively; "FBI agents never know if they're coming or going. One night they're in St. Paul and the next in Fairbanks, Alaska. No thank you. The next guy I get involved with is going to have his work firmly planted in Minnesota."

Dad tried to diffuse the escalating situation. "Now gals, there's more important things to talk about then the dating scene, like politics and where Mary's going to live once her teaching career ends."

Why did he have to say, "Career ends"? My job loss is a temporary setback. Tears sprang to the corner of my eyes. I swallowed hard. *No tears, Mary. You promised yourself that. You're a big girl, and big girls don't cry. Yeah, right.*

Setting my moroseness aside, at least while I was in the company of my parents, I brought myself back to what my father said about where I was going to live once my teaching job ended. Was he about to throw out a suggestion? I remained steadfastly silent, waiting to hear more.

"Don't worry, Mary. Your mother and I have been fretting over what you'll do once your income is cutoff, and we've come up with a darn good solution."

Oh, oh. Here comes the move back with the folks offer. My reflexes went into overdrive. I threw up my hands but not in resignation. "Dad, I don't want to hear it." I took a deep breath and rambled on. "I can't picture myself moving back home after living on my own for so long. It wouldn't work. I've got my habits, and you two have yours."

My mother calmly picked up her blue ceramic teapot and refilled our two empty mugs. "You're a grown woman. We don't expect you to move back home."

"You don't?"

"Of course, not."

I felt foolish. How could I have been so off track? I was positive they'd want their baby to move back home. I mean, what parent wouldn't? "I guess I jumped the gun. What was it you wanted to share, Dad?"

"My sister, Zoe, happens to be in a similar bind."

"You've heard from her?" Some of my most memorable childhood years involved Aunt Zoe. It didn't matter that she was a grown-up. Whenever she was around, she'd join right in with whatever childish nonsense we were up to. "When can I see her?" I hadn't laid eyes on my favorite aunt in about a zillion years. Well, fifteen at least. She and her wealthy husband, Uncle Ed, traveled so much I began to pretend she was a gypsy.

"Soon, real soon," my father softly replied as he ran his hand across his wet lips. "As you know, Ed died a few months ago while they were on safari."

I nodded solemnly. "Yeah, Mom told me. I felt so sorry for her, being in a strange land like that and having no one to turn to for solace."

"Me too," Dad said. "Unfortunately, that wasn't her only problem. When she finally returned to the states, she discovered Ed's bank account wasn't so bloated after all."

"But, but that's impossible. How could that be? Uncle Ed was worth millions."

"That's true, Kiddo, but the stock market fell a couple times, a ton was spent on travels, and what was left, well, that went to Ed's children from his previous marriage."

My jaw dropped to my waistline. "Previous marriage? Are you saying Aunt Zoe wasn't his first wife?"

"Yes, that's what your father's saying. Uncle Ed was married before." Mom turned to Dad. "Get to the point, Jim, she's in her thirties. Stop sugarcoating things."

Oh, oh. Trouble's brewing in the Malone household. Mom only uses Dad's first name when she's upset with him otherwise his middle name is mandatory. Archie was his grandfather's given name, and that's what he wants us to use when speaking to him.

My father hesitated a moment longer. "Okay. It's like this. When Ed married my sister years ago, he neglected to change his will, so what was left of his estate went to his two grown sons from his first marriage."

"You've got to be kidding," I said. "Uncle Ed had children and you didn't feel the need to share that either?" I felt like a foreigner in my parents' home.

"Oh, honey, you were so little when they got married," my father explained, "and as the years went on we forgot to inform you."

"But, but," I sputtered, "Margaret, my own sister, didn't even spill the beans, and we shared the same bedroom for almost fifteen years. I thought sisters shared everything." Evidently I was wrong.

Gracie suddenly tired of my up-and-down emotions. She lifted her head off my lap and found refuge under the kitchen table with all our stinky feet.

Mother's soft hands covered mine. "You know now, sweetheart, so can we please move on?"

I shook my head to clear it. "I guess. Dad, you said you had a solution to my dilemma. What is it?"

Before he spouted off the plan, he glanced at Mom for a second. Maybe to get her *Good Housekeeping* stamp of approval so he didn't end up in the doghouse I don't know. "We, Mother and I, thought Aunt Zoe could help solve your income problems."

I scratched my head. "How? According to you she's down and out."

"True, but you could pool your limited resources."

"What resources? In two weeks I won't have any."

Mother spoke again. "You're so frugal, dear; surely you have a little nest egg saved for a rainy day." I didn't reply. Most of it went out the door when I bought Fiona. "Anyway, we were thinking if your aunt and you lived together, you wouldn't have to leave your cute little apartment."

"What? I don't want to live with anyone else. If I wanted a roommate, I would've had one by now. Besides, I've already started making plans to move."

Mom and Dad tilted their heads so they were aligned. They reminded me of Siamese twins. "Really? When did you do that?" they asked in unison.

"A couple weeks ago," I lied. Heck, if they didn't tell me about Uncle Ed, they sure didn't need to know I made my decision to move a second ago.

~3~

Two Weeks Later

"Okay, guys, pay attention. Around the bend there's a doozy of a corner, and I can't afford to lose any dishes," I warned as my three companions and I stepped off the elevator loaded down with boxes. "Just take five paces to the right and then steer to the left a bit and your home free."

My brother Michael, one of the people assisting with the move, smarted off. "Don't worry, Teach, we kids know how to follow directions. Besides, Alex and I couldn't bear to see you eating off the floor."

After he made his corny speech, rowdy laughter spewed forth from him and his friend and filled the fourth floor hallway.

Hopefully the noise hadn't irritated the other residents as much as it did me. I couldn't afford to be kicked out before I even got settled in.

"Glad to hear it," I spouted back, taking the lead. The corner I mentioned a few seconds before appeared and I made it past without mishap. But would my helpers?

"Hey, Alex, stop goofing around," Michael shouted.

"I'm not."

"Then back off my tennis shoes if you don't want to see me trip."

"Sorry. I didn't realize I was that close to you," came his tired response.

"Stay focused, you two," I chided, "You're almost there."

My new abode was within easy sight and I felt as nervous as a rattlesnake. To calm myself, I began the countdown. "One, two, three. Here it is, Aunt Zoe. Home sweet home." I stared at the closed door within six inches of my nose, but made no attempt to open it.

Was moving here a big mistake, or would this new chapter in my life be a blessing in disguise? Only time would tell.

Standing nearly on top of me, Aunt Zoe busted into my private reverie. "What's wrong, Mary?"

"Hmm? What?"

Not getting the response she probably had anticipated, she inched ever nearer. "We're here. Open the door."

For a mere second, my eyes dropped to the heavy box of books I had loaded myself down with, and then they bounced to the door again. "I, ah, need the key."

"Well, where is it?" she inquired, "Did you leave it in the truck?"

I shook my head from side to side. "No. I think it's in the back pocket of my jeans."

"Oh? Well, I can remedy that. Would you like me to get it for you?"

"Sure." I know what you're thinking. I could've put the darn box of books down and gotten the key myself. Well, that's fine for others, but my motto is why do double duty when you can get it done in one stroke. Therefore, I'd hold unto the box until I walked into the apartment.

My dad's sister quickly set aside the shopping bag she was carrying and stood at attention. "Okay, Sweetie. I'm all hands. Just tell me which pocket the keys in."

I turned to the right. "My left one." The jeans were a tad snug, but I figured she ought to be able to get her pudgy fingers between the two pieces of fabric.

Aunt Zoe slowly glided behind my right side now and poked two fingers in a pocket. The box I was holding was beginning to feel heavier and heavier by the second. "No, no. You've got the wrong pocket. It's the other one."

"Oh, dear, I don't know why I get those two mixed up."

I could tell her why, but I didn't want our roommate relationship starting off on the wrong foot the very first day. "That's okay," I calmly stated, "It's not unusual to get the left and right mixed up."

"But this happens a lot," my aunt moaned.

Just as she began to correct her mistake, an apartment door opened and then closed. All I could think of was Rod Thompson, the geek from hell. I'd never hear the end of it. He'd laugh uncontrollably at the interesting view, one woman digging in another woman's pockets. I hurriedly glanced to the left of me. Nope. It wasn't him; thank goodness.

"Ah, Mary," Mrs. Grimshaw cheerfully announced, "I see move-in day has finally arrived."

"Yup."

Aunt Zoe finally yanked the apartment key out and almost tore the back of my pants off in the process.

"I've got it, Mary," she shrilly proclaimed, dangling the key in front of my nose like a freshly harvested carrot. "I've got it."

"Great," I replied a bit over the top. "Can you open the door?"

"Oh, of course," but instead of doing what I requested, she whipped around to face Mrs. Grimshaw and extended her plump hand towards her. "Hi, I'm Zoe," she said, "Mary's my roommate."

Mrs. Grimshaw looked from Aunt Zoe to me and then back to Aunt Zoe again. She probably had a ton of questions spinning around in her head. Unfortunately, most of what she wanted to know would have to be explained when my roommate wasn't around. The elderly woman graciously accepted my aunt's hand. "Nice to meet you, Zoe. I'm Margaret Grimshaw, but my friends call me Margaret. I'm a long-standing resident of the Foley."

"Mrs. Grimshaw, I mean Margaret, has known Matt for many years," I explained as I repositioned the box of books, using a hip for support. "Isn't that right?"

"Yes, indeed," she replied, using the tone of a librarian.

Aunt Zoe shook her spiked red-crowned head. "Oh? You're the lady Mary told me about. You gave her the lowdown on how to leverage her way in here."

"*Si.*"

Thanks a bunch for that hot tip."

"You're welcome. Now, Zoe, perhaps you'd better open that door like Mary asked. It looks like she's losing her grip on that box."

My roommate got all jittery. "Oh, yes. I got so caught up in introducing myself I forgot, and the guys are closing in fast." She spun towards the abode entrance, shoved the key in its lock, and threw the door open.

"Thanks, Margaret, for coming to my rescue," I said. "I owe you one."

The elderly woman waved her hand in front of me. "It was nothing. I could see you were having trouble." She started to move away, but then she changed her mind. "Mary, why don't you two take a break this afternoon and stop by for a cup of tea. I'll have my double chocolate chip brownies ready by then. They're one of Matt's favorite."

Brownies? *Yummy. That's all I'm going to be thinking about while I'm unpacking.* "Ah, thanks for the offer, Margaret. We'll definitely do that."

As soon as I walked into the apartment, Aunt Zoe said, "Mrs. Grimshaw's one nice lady, Mary. We're lucky to have her as a neighbor. Why, we could've ended up with a real crabby person living across the hall from us."

"Yup. Or a non-stop talker," I softly replied as thoughts of delicious goodies danced in my head. Since the few pieces of furniture we brought were still out in the U-Haul truck, I set my box on the floor in the corner of the living room where nothing else took up space and wouldn't be in the way. "You know, Aunt Zoe, Margaret and you have a lot in common."

"Oh, you mean she likes to travel or she's a widow?"

"Not that per se. Margaret's just a very active person. Besides being involved with the local gardening club, she loves to dance, paint, and cook."

"Dance? Huh? I wonder where she goes. Maybe she'll let me tag along. So, where did the guys disappear to, Mary?"

Michael's voice suddenly boomed through the dry air, saving me the trouble of explaining where they might be. "Hey, Sis, do you want the boxes on the kitchen table or the counter by the sink?"

Just because my brother found it necessary to yell didn't mean I planned to respond likewise. No way. Living in an apartment, one hears every quarrel or conversation that drifts in from surrounding residents, and I sure didn't want to have anyone know about my life so they could share it with others. So, I hustled off to the kitchen and gave him a quick answer. "Matt's table's being stored at Mom and Dad's along with some other stuff so put the boxes on the counter for now. If you have any other questions, I'll be in the living room."

Aunt Zoe sat on the couch with her legs crossed. "If you tell me what to do, Mary, I can do it."

"At this point just stay put. The guys and I can manage the truck."

"How about I unpack the dishes?"

I ran my hand across my forehead. I wasn't used to giving adults things to do, just children. "No, I'm definitely not ready for that yet. I have to clean out what Matt's left in the cupboards first. The box I just brought in has several magazines in it if you'd like to read something."

Aunt Zoe leaned back and stretched her arms in the air. "Oh, like what? *Ladies Home Journal*? *O*? *Readers Digest*? *National Geographic*?"

"Sorry, I don't have any of those, but I do have excellent educator magazines, *Instructor* and *Education Week*."

My aunt's perpetual smile flipped to a frown in two seconds flat. "You know, my eyes are kind of tired. I think I'll watch TV instead," then she reached for the remote control.

Feet shuffled on the entrance's oak floor, meaning Alex and Michael must be done in the kitchen. I put my tennis shoes back on. "Okay. I'll be back soon."

"All right," she half-heartedly replied, finally settling her eyes on a CBS wildlife program.

A nature show? You'd think the woman had her fill of nature while in Africa. Oh, well. At least she'd found something to occupy her time, or so I thought.

I'd barely moved three inches when Aunt Zoe cried out, "Mary."

What now for heaven's sake? I whipped the upper portion of my body in her direction once more. "Yes?"

"The keys for the lobby."

"What about them?"

"You'll need them to get back in the building, right?"

"Yeah, so?"

She pointed to the object on the cushion next to her.

"Oh?" I must've dropped the keys there when I came in. I held out my hands, indicating she should toss them to me. She did. I caught them in midair.

"Good catch, Mary," Michael commented from the sidelines. "We'll put your name on the Twins' roster for next season. Now come on. Time's a wasting."

~4~

I'd just finished tucking in the top sheet to make the final hospital corner on the bed when I glanced over at the radio situated on the nightstand diagonally across from me and noticed the time. Three o'clock already. Good grief. The day had slipped through my clutches too fast. Alex and Michael had left over two hours ago, and I still had barely made a dent in my unpacking. I straightened my back. *Don't be so hard on yourself, Mary. Remember Rome wasn't built in a day either.* "That's true." *And now that your bed's almost made, your body can crash anytime it wants.* "True again."

I quickly spread the lightweight, wine-and-rose stripped hand-me-down coverlet across the bed, placed the sham-covered bed pillows against the headboard, and then staggered the color- coordinated tossed pillows in front of them. "One important task done. Yay."

With the job completed, I stepped back to appraise my work. Whoa. Different bedding made a huge impact.

The once male-dominated room with a dark plaid bedspread had been successfully transformed. I patted myself on the shoulder. "Good job, Mary." Of course, I'd still like to replace Matt's tiny desk with one of my own someday so I can spread my teaching stuff out on it instead of the kitchen table where I'd be in Aunt Zoe's way.

It was she who insisted I occupy Matt's bedroom. With all the traveling she'd done over the years, it didn't matter anymore if she slept on hard-packed earth or a super comfortable mattress in a five star hotel. "Besides," she added, "the working gal in this apartment, namely me, required a good night's sleep." When I graciously accepted her decision, I told her the bed was always available for catnaps during the day.

What should I tackle next? The kitchen or finish up in here? Three blue medium-sized Rubbermaid storage bins stacked one on top of the other stood in a corner of the room begging to be emptied. They contained what little clothing I owned. The clothes won out. Dishes didn't have a chance when it came to wrinkles.

Just as I approached the containers, my stomach loudly complained. "Oh, crap." It wasn't only the afternoon that had slipped away. I'd forgotten about Mrs. Grimshaw's offer of brownies and tea. I zipped out of the bedroom in nothing flat.

Aunt Zoe lay as still as a turtle all spread out on Matt's La-Z-Boy taking a catnap. It's nice to know someone has time for a nap. Not wanting to be blamed for giving someone who just joined the ranks of Medicare a heart attack, I cautiously inched towards the recliner and my aunt's head, and then spoke softly into her ear. "Aunt Zoe, wake up."

The woman's sixty-five-year-old body jerked wildly. "Wha... Huh?" Her grayish-blue eyes popped open. "Oh, dear, I must've fallen asleep. Sorry." She released a huge yawn.

"Don't apologize. My body is feeling the effects of the move too. I just haven't given in to it yet."

My dad's sister stretched her short arms above her head. "Is there something you need help with?"

"Ah, not exactly. Remember our neighbor's invite?" Aunt Zoe's head immediately bobbed up and down. "Well, it's already three. We better get going before she reneges on it."

"Oh, yes. We don't want to ignore an invite our first day here. Just let me freshen up a bit. I don't want to give our neighbor the wrong impression."

"Will that take very long?" I politely asked, not knowing if her version of freshen up included a shower too.

She flashed one of her multi-colored ring-fingered hands in front of me. "Five minutes at the max," and then she straightened the recliner to a sitting position, pushed her five-foot-two frame off the comfy black cushions, and made her way to where her many packed suitcases stood. After examining the suitcases for a couple seconds, my aunt grabbed the handle of the bright green medium-sized one and began her trip to the bathroom.

As I watched Aunt Zoe's slow progress down the hall with the suitcase, I pictured Matt's small medicine cabinet being invaded by nothing but makeup. It sent chills down my spine.

I'm a no-fuss lipstick girl. The lipstick's stored in my purse, so all I required for bathroom space was a tiny spot for a toothbrush and toothpaste. Hopefully, my aunt will leave me enough room for that.

The bathroom door finally squeaked, confirming it had been closed. I plopped on the couch and carefully studied the minute hand on my watch. Never having lived with my dad's sister before, this was the perfect time to see if she'd be ready when she'd said. Late people drive me bonkers, and that includes my friend Elaine. Maybe it's the teacher in me. An educator learns fairly quickly that a classroom doesn't take much to become a zoo, and a late teacher really magnifies the problem.

Four minutes and fifty seconds later, my roommate floated back into the living room looking like an African queen. Three layers of dark beads surrounded her chunky neck, and three pairs of tiny silver pierced earrings stuck to each of her earlobes. She'd tossed off her fancy jeans and blue long-sleeved top to make way for a Dashiki, a long flowing garment I've only seen advertised in a magazine such as *Serengeti*. It was definitely different, but this Irish/French gal wouldn't be caught dead in one. I believed in blending in, not standing out. Her ensemble was rounded out with uniquely designed sandals probably from Africa too. The woven shoes exposed her pudgy toenails that had been painted bright orange to match her garment.

Now that she was standing directly in front of me, Aunt Zoe flung her arms out at her sides and quickly twirled for inspection. "Well, what do you think?"

I sat there dumbfounded. My aunt's choice of clothing and such was over the top, but everything she does is like that. I, on the other hand, Miss straight-laced Mary, have never done anything wild or exciting except for parasailing in Puerto Vallarta this past winter.

"I know; it's great isn't it? And, you wouldn't believe how comfy it is."

I managed a thin smile. I would've loved to have told her what I really thought, but I couldn't.

You see, I'm a firm believer in allowing a person to express themselves in ways that aren't harmful to animals or other human beings. I just hoped Margaret's nonagenarian eyes could handle the bright psychedelic experience. She's too old to have been a flower child.

*****

A lightweight voice addressed us the minute I rapped on the well-worn door across the hall from us. "Come in. Come in." We obeyed immediately and were greeted by our hostess, a hint of lilacs, and freshly baked sweets. When I twisted my head a smidgen, I discovered the flowery smell wasn't from the recent use of perfume like I thought but it came from a vase filled with real cut lilacs decorating a coffee table. And, yes, a plate of goodies sat there too. *Yummy.*

The nonagenarian's face was aglow and so was her body. "I'm so glad you could make it. I thought maybe you two ladies were too tired to drop by." The front of Margaret's short frame was covered with a red-and-white chef-style apron over a dark navy short-sleeved cotton dress. The outfit was a sharp contrast to my aunt's ensemble.

Guilt ridden about our late arrival, I hastily apologized for the delay. "Sorry, we're showing up so late, Margaret. The afternoon slipped by faster than we realized."

A true diplomat, the elderly woman offered a fresh smile. "Dear, there's no need for apologies. I would've understood if you hadn't come. Even though I settled in here years ago, I've seen what a toll moving takes on others as they come and go."

"Oh, man, does it ever," Aunt Zoe said as she edged into Margaret's personal space.

The loss of free flowing air didn't upset the nonagenarian in the least. She merely adjusted her thin glasses balanced precariously on her nose and said, "My, Zoe, what a lovely garment you have on."

Zoe shared a half-moon grin. "Why, thank you. I'm glad you like it. It's a Dashiki."

I piped in with, "She says it's so comfy."

"Well, it is," my aunt went on, "There's nothing to bind me."

I gave my aunt an amused look. Luckily, she understood my silent message. "Oh, forgive me, Margaret. I... I didn't mean to imply I wasn't wearing any under garments."

Our new neighbor put my roommate at ease. "Don't worry. Your words didn't shock me, Zoe. Nowadays, we're so bombarded by quotes from movie stars and athletes telling us how liberating it is to have nothing on underneath. Believe me, for someone my age, it's just liberating to know I still have something there to hold up."

Aunt Zoe and I burst out laughing.

Once we all settled down, Margaret swayed the topic from under garments to outer wear. "So, tell me. Did you find your Dashiki at Nordstrom's?"

This old thing? No. I bought it in Africa."

"That's right," Margaret hastily replied, "Matt mentioned you've been to Africa several times. I'd love to hear about your adventures sometime if you don't mind repeating your stories."

My aunt's hands sliced through the air. "Oh, not at all. I never get tired of recalling my wonderful adventures. Just give me a jingle when you're free and, I'll dig through my storage containers for photos too."

"I'll do that," she said.

The very first words Margaret had said to us suddenly echoed through the room again. "Come in. Come in," but the high-pitched words didn't seem to have been uttered from her mouth; her lips were sealed. Unless she was a ventriloquist, but surely Matt wouldn't have kept that under wraps this long.

My eyes swiftly darted in and out of the two exposed areas: kitchen and living room. There didn't appear to be anyone else around.

Leave it to Aunt Zoe to figure it out. "Why, I just adore parrots. My deceased husband, Ed, and I saw so many varieties during our travels. I've been told they're easy to care for. Is that true?"

The nonagenarian flapped her hands in front of her. "Oh, my, yes. You barely know they're around, nothing like a cat or a dog, and they live sixty years or more." Now she ushered us into her dining room.

My aunt wasn't ready to drop the topic on birds quite yet. "What kind of parrot do you own?"

"Petey's a Blue-fronted Amazon. Speaking of pets, how's Gracie doing? I've really missed that mutt."

"She's fine," I rapidly replied. "As a matter of fact, we get to watch her for a whole month."

Margaret's eyes lit up so brightly one would've thought a switch had been thrown to show off a dark baseball field. "When? Will she be coming here, or will you stay at your folks' house?"

I didn't respond. My mind had taken a sharp detour to Margaret's delightfully decorated dining room table: ecru-colored linen tablecloth, plaid luncheon napkins, and white fine bone china trimmed with a sliver of gold. Of course, the piece de' resistance, a large plate of freshly baked brownies, sat smack dab in the center of the table.

Since I had left Margaret's question unanswered, Aunt Zoe took it upon herself to fill in the gap. "Gracie's staying here starting tomorrow."

Our hostess clapped her hands. "Wonderful. I can't wait to see her. Ladies, make yourselves comfortable. The water's simmering on the stove in the kitchen, and I just have to transfer it to the ceramic teapot."

As soon as Margaret left the room, we pulled out our chairs and sat. "Ah, this feels good," I shared, "after all that zipping in and out of the apartment and unpacking."

Aunt Zoe leaned closer to me and whispered, "You should've taken a nap like me, Mary. I'm ready to run a marathon." I didn't think so but I let it slide. Now she pulled away from me and swiftly turned her attention to the spread laid before us. "Our neighbor is such a perfect hostess, isn't she? There's no way I can do all this busy stuff, and I'm nowhere near ninety. Exactly how far over ninety is Margaret anyway?"

I shrugged my shoulders. "Don't know. Matt never clarified that for me."

"Hmm?" Aunt Zoe said as she lightly tapped her index finger on her lips. "Perhaps he didn't know either."

I was about to change the topic, but then Margaret traipsed into the dining room carrying a dainty black-and-white Japanese-style teapot. "Here we go. I hope you don't mind if I set the pot by you, Mary. Sometimes these old hands get a little shaky."

"No problem."

Before I even considered picking up the hot pot, I dropped my left hand on my lap. No scalding water was going to burn me. No, way. It's better to play it safe now rather than regretting it later. If I didn't, I could end up with a whopper of a burn and a doctor bill to boot like my teacher friend Julie.

She was transferring hot water from a teapot into a larger container when the container slipped and she got second degree burns on her legs. Not realizing the seriousness of her condition at first, she tried to soothe her pain with a hunk of aloe vera the school secretary broke off from a potted plant in the teachers' lounge, but it didn't do the job. She ended up in the emergency room.

Ah, but you left out an important piece of the story, Mary. That hospital visit changed Julie's life forever, remember? She ended up marrying the dreamy doctor who was on call. The couple lives in a mansion on Lake Minnetonka with their three adorable children, a nanny and two wolfhounds.

"Whatever."

"What did you say, Mary?" Margaret inquired. "I didn't catch that."

I lifted my eyes from the pot that had taken me down memory lane and found our hostess sitting across from me. "Sorry. I got sidetracked momentarily; that's all."

My aunt burst into our two-way conversation. "Mary and I had been discussing your lovely table setting while you were busy in the kitchen, Margaret."

"Yes. I said your table presentation reminded me of visits to my Great Aunt Fiona's years ago. She loved to lay out her fine things too."

"As for me," Aunt Zoe added, "the bone china teacups and our visit with you brought to mind something quite different."

"Oh, and what was that?" Margaret politely asked.

"Why, Tom Hegg's book, *A Cup of Christmas Tea.* My husband Edward purchased it for me this past Christmas. Such a delightful story."

"Ah, yes, and a very timely one," the old woman said as she passed a plate of freshly baked brownies to me. "Too many people forget about the elderly, and we have a wealth of information to share. For instance, in regards to table settings, one should make use of her fine china, silver and things as frequently as she can instead of stashing them away for the next generation, don't you agree, ladies?"

Aunt Zoe's generously made-up face tightened considerably. "I most certainly do," she snapped. "My stepsons ended up with my elegant table settings, and what do you think they are going to do with them? Why, sell them on Craig's List or Stella's." Now she took the napkin resting next to her place setting and shook it with great force before dropping it on her lap.

I didn't like seeing Aunt Zoe overwrought. She's usually such a jovial soul. I quickly offered a suggestion. "I'll check the lists on a daily basis for you, Auntie, if you'd like. If any items get listed, you can snap them up." Then I snapped my fingers for emphasis.

"There's one major flaw in that plan, niece. Where exactly would I store my beloved possessions once you got them back for me? Every inch of space in our apartment has been gobbled up."

My eyes dropped to the tablecloth for a second. "Sorry, I didn't think that far ahead. Oh, I've got it. Mom and Dad can make room in their basement."

Aunt Zoe placed her hand on my arm. "Mary, you're so sweet. Your concern for my china and such has touched me deeply, but I think it best to let things lie. They were just things from my past, nothing more. Besides, I have a new life, different surroundings and God willing, plenty of years ahead to bring more modern things to the table."

With that said, the Aunt Zoe I knew sparked back to life. "Forget the old. Bring in the new is going to be my motto. Now pass that plate of brownies, would you, please? I want to enjoy what our wonderful hostess has prepared for us."

Thankful the subject on setting a fancy table had gracefully fallen by the wayside, I gladly passed the brownies. If the discussion had continued indefinitely, I wouldn't have had a nickel's worth to share since I've never been married or had the money to acquire such lavish items for my home. My cupboards held garage sale specials. At least you don't cry if you drop one, and they make darn good ammo when you broke up with a boyfriend.

After chatting about other things for a spell, our hostess requested I add more hot water to everyone's cups. When I finished, she inquired about my job prospects. "Mary, now that your job has officially ended at Washington Elementary, have you found another position elsewhere?"

The fresh cup of lemon tea and second brownie that had been begging to touch my lips would have to wait. "Oh, I'm not quite finished there yet," I hastily replied.

Margaret looked at me in bewilderment. "You're not? But you told me you got a pink slip."

"Yes, but the principal at Washington asked me to substitute teach during their summer school program, so I told him I would." I glanced down at my goodies now. I had more to say, but I didn't know if I dared continue or not. I sided with sharing. "Oh, and, I've ah... got something cooking with Mr. Griffin." Time to attack the brownie. People can't force you to talk when your mouth is jammed. It's not polite.

Boy was I wrong. "Then you called him?" Margaret swiftly quizzed. Obviously this particular nonagenarian didn't care whether I followed Emily Post's advice about food and conversation. I acknowledged her inquiry by simply nodding politely.

Aunt Zoe's voice rose sharply. "Excuse me, Mary. I seem to be missing something here. No one told me there's a new man in your life?"

I tried to rein in a chuckle. Good thing I had swallowed my brownie before Aunt Zoe's questions started, or I'd be choking instead. "There's no new man in my life. Therefore, there's nothing to tell."

"Then what's cooking with Mr. Griffin? Why call him?"

I plucked my cup of tea off its saucer. "The guy left a message on Matt's answering machine, so I called to let him know my brother wasn't available. End of story."

Dad's sister wasn't giving up so easily. "Come on, Mary," she said as she moved closer to me, "spill the beans. You never were very good at hiding things from me even as a little child. I always knew when you had more to say."

"I haven't forgotten. It's like you have this uncanny ability to read minds." I turned to Margaret. "Don't ever play poker with her; she always wins."

"I won't if you fess up," the nonagenarian said.

~5~

"Mary, what are you doing?" Aunt Zoe asked in a subdued tone. "It's 2:00 a.m."

"I've been tossing and turning for several hours, so I thought I'd get up and snack away instead," I explained, keeping my eyes peeled on the bread in front of me. "I'm making a peanut butter and celery sandwich. Care for one? It's nice and crunchy."

"No, thanks. I don't think my stomach could handle it this time of night."

When I finally looked up, I found my aunt standing in the kitchen doorway struggling to keep her narrow eyelids open. Her face was plastered with yucky brown stuff that looked like dog poop. It scared the crap out of me. Maybe that's what brought on Uncle Edward's death. Then again maybe it was something more drastic like her wardrobe. It can shock your heart too.

She was wearing a frilly, full-length neon-pink-and-black silk negligee which clashed sharply with her red-spiked do, as well as, with my two-piece yellow-and-purple striped cotton pajama set. When my eyes had thoroughly scanned her from head to toe, I got up the courage to ask, "What's that gook on your face?"

Aunt Zoe touched her cheek. "Oh, it's an old African recipe that wards off evil spirits and tightens the skin at the same time." Between you and me, from what I've seen of her face during daylight hours, I'd say the recipe wasn't living up to its promises.

My stomach made small churning noises as it impatiently waited for me to finish what I was doing. I patted it. *I know, I know. Enough small talk. Get on with it.*

"Do you need a knife, Mary?"

"No. I've got one." I picked the utensil up and waved it in the air for a moment before I shoved it into the peanut butter jar to collect a thick gob of it. Once the sticky stuff was secure, I jerked the knife out of the jar, smacked it on a piece of white bread, laid the broken bits of celery on top, and then topped it off with another slice of bread. Culinary creation completed. I set the dirty knife on the counter and said, "Well, I guess there's one good thing about a teaching hiatus."

"Oh, what's that?"

"I can eat as much peanut butter as I darn well please."

My dad's sister gave me a questioning glance. "You mean the school can dictate how much peanut butter you eat? Why, that's ridiculous." Her spiked hair stayed in place even though she shook her head vehemently. "No. I take that back. It's obscene."

I grabbed a hunk of hair that was blocking my view and wound it behind my ear. "Not exactly. Let me explain. Nowadays, those of us caring for children have to be extremely careful when handling peanut products. The mere whiff of peanuts can make a child seriously ill. Why, last school year alone, we had three elementary students end up in the emergency room."

"Really? Peanut allergies? Hmm. I must've been out of the country when that hit the news. I'll have to add it to my list. Hopefully I haven't missed anything else. You know, it sure makes me wonder how in blazes I ever managed to make it to adulthood with all these so-called new allergies popping up all over the place."

"Me, too." I hefted my plate off the counter and carried the snack I created to the table, thinking my aunt would join me there, but she didn't. She strolled over to the counter where the open jar of peanut butter was waiting for its lid. Once that was taken care of, she picked up the dirty knife and set it in the sink. "Auntie," I said, "I'm really sorry I woke you."

"Don't be." With nothing more to do, my roommate marched over to the table and stood next to me. "Do you suffer from insomnia a lot, Mary, or is this something new for you?"

I lifted the sandwich off the plate and permitted myself to chomp on a corner of the sticky crunchy sandwich. "No, I don't generally get up. I've just got tons of stuff swimming around in my noggin tonight."

My roommate finally tired of standing and pulled out a chair to sit. "I've got the perfect remedy for sleepless nights. Write down what's on your mind and then pop back into bed."

Peanut butter was sticking to the roof of my mouth, making it difficult to reply. "Ah huh. I've heard that."

"Well, why not give it a whirl?"

"I don't know where to begin."

"No problem. How about if you skip the list this time and tell me what's on your mind instead?"

I ran the tips of my fingers across my forehead. "Too many things. Is Matt safe in Europe with all that's going on in the world today? Am I going to be able to manage my bills without a decent job? Will I ever find another teaching job? Should I have told Mr.Griffin I could help him even though I don't know the first thing about solving a crime?"

My aunt laid her hand gently on my shoulder. "Wow. Your mind is bogged down, isn't it? Unfortunately, I'm no wizard, Mary, so I can't answer your first three questions, but I can the last. Have you ever read the book, *No. 1 Ladies Detective Agency?*"

"Nope," I hurriedly replied thinking only of my unfinished sandwich. "What's it about?"

"A recently divorced African woman is left with a tidy sum of money when her father dies, and she's determined to make good use of her inheritance. So, she moves to a new town and establishes a detective agency, even though she doesn't know the first thing about—"

I cut my aunt off mid-stream. "Wait a sec! I haven't inherited any money, and how the heck does the woman help people if she doesn't know the first thing about what she's doing?"

Aunt Zoe's medium-sized mouth opened wide like an alligators to permit a long overdue yawn to escape. "Why, she orders a book on how to be a detective."

I dropped what little was left of my sandwich on the table and lifted my arms in the air. "That's it!"

"What? You're going to purchase a detective how-to book?"

I let my arms return to the table. "Heck, no."

"Then why did you get so wound up?" she asked as her chin drew ever closer to the table.

"Matt's office on Lowry Avenue. Why, I bet that's where all the cases he's handled over the years are stored. He never gets rid of anything." Now that I knew how I was going to resolve one of the many things on my mind, I stood and gave my aunt a peanut-buttery peck on the cheek. "Thanks for the late night chat, Auntie. It's just what I needed."

My aunt's head immediately righted itself. "Does that mean we can go to back to bed?"

"Of course."

~6~

Two Days Later

Mr. Griffin made it quite clear that he expected me at his riding stable no later than eight this morning, and I didn't plan to disappoint the man. Of course, bringing along extra baggage, namely Aunt Zoe, might put a damper on things, but it wasn't up for discussion. I had no other option.

Okay, that's not entirely true. I could've asked Mrs. Grimshaw, another sidekick. Her wisdom has helped Matt countless times, but relatives are relatives, and there was no stopping mine, especially after hearing the nitty-gritty details.

All right, all right. I know what you're going to say. There was one more card I could play. Simply put my foot down and say "no," but I wouldn't take that route either. No, this gal was twirling in the wind and desperately needed someone to provide moral support.

I glanced at the clock radio on the nightstand. It was six-twenty-five. In less than two hours, I'd be breaking a long-standing pact with myself, never ever get within even a fraction of an inch of a horse's den. My body shivered, and not from lack of blankets. At least Aunt Zoe would never find out about my horse phobia; I promised to keep that little secret hidden deep within myself.

The alarm went off at six-thirty on the dot. Not wanting to waste even a second, I jumped out of bed and rushed to the bathroom to shower first even though my aunt usually rises before me. Being that Aunt Zoe's older and needs more time, I'd rather see her go ahead of me. Last night however, she made a point of telling me her body didn't kick into high gear until she's had her two cups of coffee, which I took to mean I should use the facilities before her. Lucky me. Usually the only two beverages in my morning vocabulary are orange juice and tea.

When I stepped out of the shower, I slapped on a minimum amount of makeup and the same for body lotion. No horse was going to sniff beauty products on this gal's face or any other parts of her body.

With my morning pampering routine out of the way, I slipped back into the bedroom, wearing just bra and panties, and donned the only pair of clean Lee jeans I could find.

These jeans were much snugger than the others I owned. When I bought them, I told myself I'd shed a few pounds, but like every diet I've been on, so far, no fat has dropped off, giving me the suave model figure men so crave. The button above the zipper was determined to have its own way, so I left it undone. Who would notice?

The upper torso would be covered with a size 16 T-shirt emblazoned with *Go Cowboys* I'd found at Goodwill.

I know, crazy shirt signage, right? Here I am with a terrible fear of horses, and I purchase a shirt representing a football team in Texas, a state where 980,000 plus horses roam. Maybe my extra sensory perception factored into it at the time. Who knew. Right then, I was just thankful I didn't own a cowgirl hat or boots otherwise my aunt would never let me leave the apartment without them.

I noticed the shower was blasting away when I left the bedroom to get a bite to eat in the kitchen. Aunt Zoe must've jumped in there while I was dressing. I glanced at my watch. We had exactly fifteen minutes left before we took off. Hopefully, my roommate will be ready to go.

The kitchen cupboards didn't have much in them. I opened and closed several cupboards before finding a half full box of outdated bran cereal Aunt Zoe had brought along.

The toothpick thick cereal looked like mice poison my parents' basement was littered with, except the cereal was brown not blue. I bent my head and took a whiff. It smelled so-so. I guess this wasn't a morning to be fussy especially since my cereal disappeared three days ago along with the orange juice. My chosen replacement for the juice was ice cold tap water. I grabbed one of my many mismatched glasses now and filled it to the brim.

By the time I finished breakfast and piled my dishes in the sink, Aunt Zoe was standing under the kitchen archway ready to roll, and yes, she was wearing bright-red cowgirl boots. They must've been stashed in one of her many suitcases. "Mary, where are your boots?" she shrieked.

"I don't own any," I said, sauntering over to where she stood. "And I certainly don't feel the need to purchase any for the type of work I'll be doing for Mr. Griffin."

Wrong response. My roommate continued to stare at my feet like I had an incurable disease. "Humph. Well, you can't show up at a riding stable with those flimsy sandals. No way. What if Mr. Griffin wants us to ride around his spread? One look at your feet, and he'll know you don't know the first thing about horses."

His spread? Where did she come up with such a hairbrained idea?

The woman actually thought Reed Griffin's horses are roaming all over tarnation like cattle do in Nebraska, Texas or Wyoming. Although by the time we get to Cottage Grove, I'd probably wish they were. *Do I dare straighten her out? Nah. Let her find out on her own.* I flung my arms in midair. "Fine. I'll go put on my scruffy tennis shoes."

"You'll thank me later, Missy," she said as I ran off to the bedroom, "especially if there are piles of you know what everywhere."

"Yuk." Halfway down the hallway, my body jerked to a halt. It had become as rigid as road kill. I already felt fenced in, and this was only day nine of our, what I had hoped would be, compatible living arrangements. *This is no time to dwell on shoe issues or anything else, Mary; you're on a tight schedule. Would Miss Marple let little things bug her?* "No." *Okay, get moving. You don't want to screw up on your very first case.*

The tension buildup in my head finally let loose, sliding off me like baby oil, and I continued on to the bedroom to collect my tennis shoes.

When I caught up to Aunt Zoe by the entrance to our abode, I noticed she was holding something behind her back. "What have you got?" I quizzed.

"A surprise."

"For Gracie?" We'd be getting the mutt later today.

My father's youngest sister laughed. "No, silly, for you," and then she quickly exposed what she had been hiding. "Ta da."

"Oh, no." My hands immediately flew to the sides of my face. "Please, tell me I'm not seeing what I'm seeing?"

"Sorry," she replied. "No can do." After placing the bright-red-and white cowgirl hat on her head, she offered me the fuchsia one.

I stomped my foot. "I refuse to be a part of this."

"Oh, come on, Mary. It'll be fun. You need to lighten up a little. Your schoolmarm charm isn't going to rope any cowboys in with that attitude."

That did it. I grabbed the hat from my aunt and tossed it in the hallway closet. "It's staying right here," I said, using a terse tone, "and that's final."

"Suit yourself. But if you lose a cowboy over it, don't say I didn't warn you."

*****

When Matt agreed to let me stay in his apartment, he said I could use his underground parking space at the Foley as well. Of course, he left it up to me to figure out where to store his Topaz. The idea did occur to me to just leave the clunker on a nearby street. No one in his or her right mind would want to touch it. But then I have a thing about respecting other people's property, so I asked Michael to take it off my hands, which he did the day after I moved in.

Today, however, I discovered Matt left out one teeny, tiny bit of information when he said I could use his garage spot. He never mentioned how difficult it was to get in the car. By the time my aunt and I stepped into Fiona, we felt like we'd missed our calling as contortionists.

"What's with the narrow parking spaces?" Aunt Zoe grumbled as her car strap and buckle duked it out.

"I think it's more to do with how the people on both sides of us park their cars. The space allotted is ample enough."

"Humph. Well, maybe we'll luck out when we return and both cars will be gone."

"Let's hope so. I don't think I can handle a repeat performance."

"Me neither."

With no time to spare, I turned the key in Fiona's ignition and then handed off the garage door opener to Aunt Zoe. I figured if I was steering, she could at least manage the mammoth garage door. Once the door was high enough for the "Bug" to pass through, I floored the gas pedal and zoomed out onto the main street.

The minute Fiona's tires smacked the freeway, my aunt dished out another question. "Mary, do you know where you're going?"

"Southeast. According to Mr. Griffin, his property's situated right on the dividing line between two suburbs, Cottage Grove and Woodbury."

Aunt Zoe turned towards me now. "I meant do you have good directions?"

"I hope so; I don't own a GPS."

"GPS? Is that one of those tracking devices?"

"Yup." I held the steering wheel with my left hand and grabbed the lone slip of paper off the dashboard with the other. The paper held the directions Griffin gave me during our short phone conversation. "I hate getting directions that say 'go east so many miles then go south four more miles'. Why can't men just tell us what landmarks to look for?"

"Because that would be too easy."

  I passed the directions off to my passenger. "Here, why don't you help me watch for the turnoffs."

  She hesitated for a moment. "Okay, but I think I should warn you that your Uncle Edward used to say a tiny tot could do a better job of reading a map. He swore that's why we got lost so often."

  I smiled. "Typical man. He didn't want to admit that he purposely ignored your assistance."

  My aunt shook her head from side to side. "Hmm? I never thought of that. Do you really think that was the case, Mary?"

  "You bet. There are three men in my family and believe me, I know all their tricks."

  My passenger straightened her short body. "Well, I'm sure glad we had this little chat concerning map reading skills. Too bad there's no way I can confront Edward in regards to this matter. His departure from this world makes it quite difficult to do so."

  "Not really. All it takes is a séance," I joked, and then drew serious. "I actually do know someone who does séances for a living. If you like, I can have her set one up? You know when a person dies there always seems to be unanswered questions."

  Aunt Zoe fanned her hand in front of her face. "Oh, no. Absolutely not. I refuse to be a part of a séance. Edward was dearly loved by me for thirty-six years, but I'm not bringing that man back. There's a good reason for the expression, 'Let sleeping dogs lie,' and I'm not about to mess with it."

  I snatched a glance at my aunt to make sure I hadn't dug up raw emotions she'd wanted to keep buried. The grieving process for a lost loved one can take up to three years. Since she seemed to be in control of her feelings, I continued to grill her. "Where is Uncle Edward's body?"

She twisted her head slightly in my direction. "There isn't a body. Edward was cremated."

"Oh, well where's his urn?"

"There's no urn."

My thick untamed eyebrows inched ever upward. "No urn? But...but, I thought that's where a cremated person's ashes were placed?"

"Oh, no. It's not necessary. Ashes can be put in almost any type of container. For example, I requested Edward's remains be placed in a small hand carved lidded bowl he happened to buy the day before he died. He said it was a gift for me. Perhaps he had a foreboding, but if he did, he never shared that. Anyway, the bowl makes it much easier to divvy up ashes that way."

Divvy up ashes? What the—? My aunt's words threw me off kilter in more ways than one. The car swerved and almost connected with an early morning jogger. As I quickly overcorrected my steering, the Ford Focus traveling alongside me almost got stamped out. The Ford's owner, a total jerk, wasn't understanding at all as he laid on his obnoxious horn and gave me the finger salute. I pretended he didn't exist.

"What was that about?" Aunt Zoe asked.

"Nothing."

Once the car was back on track, I thought about asking more concerning my uncle's ashes, but responsibility overrode curiosity. The questions could wait. Two good scares in less than a minute were enough for me this morning. I didn't exactly relish the thought of joining the ranks of females at Shakopee's Correctional Institute anytime soon. Besides, I heard through the grapevine the facilities were already overcrowded.

Fifteen minutes after our harrowing escapade, Aunt Zoe notified me of the final turnoff.

"Take this exit here, Mary. That's it. Then go left on King's Trail. Griffin's place should be a mile down the road on the right."

A few minutes later I stepped on Fiona's breaks. We'd reach the gates leading to Reed Griffin's property. "Super directions. No deviations and plenty of time to spare," I said. "That's what I like." I turned to my passenger. "See, Aunt Zoe, you didn't get us lost."

"Interesting."

"Yup. It proves what I said earlier."

The two of us stared at the massive, black wrought iron gates that stopped Fiona from tooling along any further. Obviously, they were meant to keep unwanted guests out. A two-foot white letter *X* hung smack dab in the middle of the gates, and aged elm trees untouched by Dutch elm disease cloaked the rest of the entrance.

I started to unfasten the seatbelt, so I could get out and see if the gate was open, but my aunt stopped me. "Don't bother. I'll check the gates for you."

My trembling hands lingered on the steering wheel, giving it an unwelcomed bath. "Thanks." An unexpected reprieve is exactly what this gal needed. I flicked on the car radio hoping it would soothe my body, including the heart. It didn't. Nothing but church services this morning.

Fresh air might help. I settled my sweaty fingers on the control button for the front windows. A second later, they slid down. Nope. That didn't do anything either.

By now you've probably put two and two together and figured out I'm a chicken through and through. I enjoy keeping life simple. I don't like trying new things, and yet, day in and day out I'd challenged my students to conquer new things. What a hypocrite, right?

It wasn't that I hadn't been asked by friends to try skydiving, kayaking or even rollerblading. I had.

I'd smile sweetly and agree to go only to take myself out of the equation at the last moment. Make up any lame excuse. And believe me there were plenty. "It's my aunt's birthday." "My dad's sick." "Got a cold." I think I figured if I didn't attempt a new experience, nothing terrible would ever happen to me.

This past winter though, I tempted fate, like I'm doing today. There were four of us staying together in Puerto Vallarta, and I suggested we go parasailing. My brother, Matt, expected me to chicken out at the last minute like I always did, but boy did I fool him. I went up first, and guess what? Nothing happened. But when the last person in our group took her turn, Matt's girlfriend, Rita, things went dreadfully wrong. Thankfully, Mother Nature played a part in her accident, not me. I would've never lived that down.

Why couldn't my hands stop sweating? *Forget about them. Keep your* eyes *focused on the gates. Yeah, sure.* Just what I've always wanted to stare at, property containing my worst nightmare. Yikes!

Well, what did you expect, Mary, when you stuck your neck out? Huh? That you wouldn't have to pay the piper a trillion times over.

~7~

Aunt Zoe finally returned to the car after what seemed like eternity. "I saw a couple men standing at the top of the hill chomping the bit. Maybe that's where the stable is, Mary."

"You could be right. Let's check it out." I quickly shifted the car's gears from park to drive and then crept onto Griffin's private property.

When we were approximately halfway up the hill, I pulled in to what looked like graveled parking slots for roughly eight cars. Wide, lush open field as far as the eye could see began its journey right where the gravel ended, at Fiona's front bumper. I turned the engine off and then told Aunt Zoe to stay in the car until I found out exactly where Mr. Griffin was. She promised she would. With that settled, I left the car and began my ascent.

Good thing it wasn't pouring out like the weatherman had predicted. Otherwise this city slicker would be sliding on her butt all the way back to Fiona.

The rough terrain under my feet definitely wasn't suited for sandals, but I'd never admit that to my aunt. On the other hand, even if boots were the appropriate wear, this gal still wouldn't be caught dead in them. I was never much for watching westerns, and by the time I was old enough to watch TV, Dale Evans and Roy Rogers were long gone. Maybe if they had stayed on the air in reruns, I'd have wanted boots just like Dale's. According to what I've heard, she was the one cowgirl young girls loved to emulate.

The two men Aunt Zoe referred to remained in deep conversation as I drew ever closer. Even at three feet away I couldn't make out what they were saying yet, but my eyes sure appreciated what they gathered in so far, especially of the tall, lean man who I assumed to be near my age.

Definitely hunk material, Mary.

The way his booted feet were clamped to the earth gave one the impression he owned the ground he stood on. He had a younger Clint Eastwood air about him. Think of the movie, *The Good, the Bad and the Ugly.* His skinny sideburns, thin mustache, prominent Adam's apple, tousled sandy hair and clenched teeth helped to complete the look. The only thing missing was a cheap cigarette dangling from his fine chiseled lips.

Something told me this man was not Reed Griffin. Over the phone, I heard a more mature, self-assured person not a cocky, raw one.

Finished with his face, my eyes drifted to his shirt, a navy-and-white striped logo polo shirt with top two buttons undone. The small opening exposed a clump of dark chest hairs. My face warmed considerably. Not wanting to endanger what I'd come for, I shifted my gaze to the older man next to Clint's double.

As I did so, the super-hot guy's voice raised several decibels and I froze.

The young dude's left hand pumped wildly, drawing ever closer to the older man's face. "I told you before, Griffin. Keep those damn horses off my property. If I catch them there again, you'll be sorry."

Crap! I had unknowingly stumbled on to a bad Old West shoot 'em out, except this was the 21st century and I was in Minnesota not Texas or Wyoming. Before I could decide what to do next, Aunt Zoe came rushing up from behind. Glad to see my support person had arrived, even though she had been told to stay put, I turned to her.

"Ah, Mary," she said in an almost inaudible voice, "perhaps you should wait in the car with me until these two gentlemen settle whatever nasty dispute they're having. It wouldn't be too smart to get in the middle of it."

"Too late," I whispered back, "I already am."

A minute later, Clint's double became aware of our presence and immediately stopped the flow of fist and words. But just because it seemed he had nothing more to say, it didn't mean he was finished. His beautiful fiery-blue eyes bore into us now. "Looks like you're getting pretty desperate for help, Griffin. Grandma and the young chick over there ain't going to give you a day's worth of work. Heck, I bet they can't even mount a horse."

My French-cut nails dug into the palms of my hands. "Why you…"

Only my aunt's quick thinking kept my words from being blasted to the South Pole. "Hush, Mary. Remain neutral. It's not your fight."

She's right. I bit my tongue and patiently waited for the older man, my client, to say something in our defense, but those mediocre lips of his didn't budge an inch.

"*What did you expect, Mary? The man doesn't even know you yet. So what? It shouldn't matter if he knows me or not. According to old episodes of Oprah, chivalry is still alive. Well, obviously not at this ranch.*

The nasty dude I'd become so enamored with, only a few minutes earlier, thrust his non-calloused hands into his narrow-legged Calvin Klein jeans, turned on his heels, and stomped off to a bright red and black four-wheeler stationed near the rough-hewn chestnut-colored riding stable.

After the man and his vehicle fled lickety-split down the hill, heavy clouds of dust engulfed us. Aunt Zoe suffered most. She coughed uncontrollably.

Mr. Griffin's unkempt brown brows dug into his forehead making them even more pronounced than before. "You all right, Ma'am?"

"I'll be fine," Aunt Zoe sputtered through her coughing fit, "Just give me a sec."

"Are you sure?" the man with the jutted broad jaw asked one more time. "Cuz it's no trouble to fetch water from the stable."

At the mention of stable water, auntie got control of her diaphragm reflexes mighty quick. I have a feeling she thought Griffin was going to retrieve the drink from a trough not from a fridge full of bottled water waiting to be dispensed. Nowadays, riding establishments provide water out of necessity. They don't want lawyers knocking at their doors because heat exhausted customers collapsed on the trails.

Griffin turned to me. "Sorry about that little incident you just witnessed, Miss. That young man's very ill-mannered."

"It's okay. It didn't bother me," I lied. Sure, I can't ride, but the way the guy said it left me mighty sore.

"How can I help you gals this morning? The riding stable's not open until noon."

"We're not here to ride," I said as I stuck my hand out in front of him. "I'm Mary Malone, Matt Malone's assistant," and then I pointed to my companion, "and this, Mr. Griffin, is our, ahem, indispensable secretary Zoe Rouge, another relative. I hope you don't mind that she tagged along?"

"Shoot, no. That's fine." The man offered a gracious smile as he reached for my hand and pumped it vigorously. "It's nice to see family members working side by side."

Well, that went better than I anticipated.

"However," he continued, "we need to get something straightened out before we go any further.

Oh, boy. "What's that?" I cautiously asked, concerned he had checked up on me and found out the only thing I'd done since college graduation was teach.

"People around here call me Reed."

Whew. I breathed in a sigh of relief. *He wants to be called Reed. I can handle that.* "Sure. That's fine." I pointed to the road leading off the property. "I have a feeling that's the guy you've been having problems with. Am I right?"

Reed Griffin rubbed the edge of his firm jaw with his thumb. "You're dead on, Miss Malone. Been told his daddy was in real estate and left him tons of money. So what—that doesn't give the spoiled son of a gun the right to do whatever he wants to those of us whose lands butt up against his."

Aunt Zoe cast her eyes on the sloping hill. "He sure was fired up about something. Care to fill us in?"

Way to go, Auntie. I reached in my summery blue and white woven shoulder bag and searched for paper, pen, and the mini-recorder my brother left in his nightstand.

The purse had just been cleaned, so it didn't take much effort to wrap my fingers around what I needed. Most days a squirrel can locate his buried acorns faster than I can find one lousy tube of lipstick.

Ready to go now, I quickly awarded myself responsibility for note-taking and handed off an easier duty, handling the recorder, to my aunt.

~8~

"Ever since Clint Russell moved to this area two months ago, there's been nothing but bitterness and hostility brewing between him and those of us bordering his land. I'm surprised no one has knocked some sense into him yet. I've only held back because I didn't want to be slapped with a darn lawsuit. That fella's got the longest chip on his shoulder I've ever seen. Why, it's as long as the Rio Grande."

Whoa! My newly created secretarial duties came to a screeching halt. Clint's double is a Clint? Obviously, something got lost in translation. I mean, the dude does speak with a different accent than true Minnesotans. His has more of an eastern twang to it. "Excuse me, Reed. I just want to clarify something."

"Certainly, Miss. Go ahead."

"That guy who was just here, did you say his first name is Clint?"

My, ahem, client cleared his throat and then spat on the ground. I suppose if there would've been a spittoon present he may have used that. "Yup. I was informed that's the name he was christened with. Supposedly, a relative from way back when had the name, and Clint's momma plucked it from her genealogy charts. Anyway, like I said, there's been nothing but trouble since he showed up this spring. Before that it was as peaceful as a meandering brook winding its way through a meadow all a bloom."

Ah, how sweet. The man has a way with words as well as horses. *Okay, get back to reality, lady. As a teacher you know people tend to remember only what they want to remember.* Before I continued my line of questioning, I jotted myself a note. *Do some digging. See if there were horse-related problems way before Clint came on the scene.*

Finished writing now, I looked up at Reed and asked, "What seems to be the main beef with Clint?"

Reed tugged on the front of his navy-blue Twins baseball cap. "He's constantly filing complaints to the sheriff about those of us bordering his property."

"And with you, it's mostly been about your horses ending up over there, right?"

"You got it. How the heck they're showing up there is beyond me though. My property is totally fenced in. When I give you gals a ride in my pickup in a little bit, you'll see what I'm talking about."

Pleased to hear we wouldn't be riding horseback to check out Reed's land like my aunt assumed, but would be chasing around via an old pickup instead, I could feel some of the fear about horses settling to the back burner, thank God, and offered Reed a genuine smile. "Great. We're really looking forward to seeing how your property's laid out, aren't we, Zoe?"

"Yes, indeed," she replied, batting her thick-glossed eyelashes as she drew her short body closer to Reed Griffin and his ringless hand. "But first, I'm dying to see what goes on in this building here. Is this where you keep your cows?"

Aunt Zoe may be a widow but she certainly hasn't forgotten how to string a man along. Flirtation. It's all about flirtation. A must in my book. Women have used sexual overtures for thousands of years to get what they wanted from the opposite sex, starting with Adam and Eve.

"No, Ma'am. Afraid there are no cows on this property. Just horses," the man with the southeastern accent replied as he quickly stepped in front of us and opened the barn door. "Step inside, ladies, and I'll show you around."

The horse barn was nothing like I expected. "Holy Smoke! I didn't realize horses had such fancy digs nowadays. Makes me a tad jealous." *Especially if the quarters were actually horseless.*

"Exactly how many horses are stabled here, Reed?" Aunt Zoe swiftly inquired before I commented further.

"Twenty."

"Are they all yours?" I questioned. We had just passed a stall where a reddish-brown horse had been watching our every move. "Or do you board as well?"

Reed smiled widely, exposing smoke-stained teeth. "Ten are boarded, and the rest are mine. The owners come out to ride as frequently as they can. If they can't get out here at least once a week, one of my workers takes them out on the trail."

"Do the horses you board just use the trails," my companion asked, "or are they trained for specific shows too?"

The man, who might be a tad older than my aunt and at least ten inches taller, seemed pleased we wanted to know as much as possible about his business. "Both. There's an area specifically set aside on the property where jumps are set up. I can show it to you later if you like."

"Sure," Aunt Zoe and I replied in perfect harmony.

By the time we reached the other end of the building, silence sliced the stable. A perfect spot to drill the man more. "Didn't you say you had twenty horses stabled here? I only counted ten."

"Yup, you heard right. The other ten are out stretching their legs. Maybe you gals saw them when you drove in."

I shook my head. "Nope." If I'd seen loose horses, I would've given them wide berth.

"Oh, that's a shame," he continued. "As you probably know horses can't be pent up all the time. It's bad for their legs. Besides that, being cooped up all day makes for a neurotic horse, and no one wants to work with a horse like that, too dangerous."

"If you were a riding newbie," I said, fanning my hand in an arch fashion, "which breed of horse would you recommend?" Don't worry. I hadn't gone off the deep end yet. It was a hypothetical question. There was no way I was working out my fear of horses today or ever.

Reed rested his thick hands on his hips and thought about my inquiry for a moment. "Well, I'd suggest either the American Quarter Horse or the Tennessee Walker. I have both on the property." He left one hand on a hip and cupped his chin with the other. "Of course, a Polish Arabian's a good fit too."

With our indoor tour completed, we backtracked to the barn's midsection and Reed went over details about his horses and the six people he offered boarding services to.

After sharing what he could in regards to his business, he whisked us off to what I considered a black Ford pickup. Don't hold me to the color though. The pickup looked like it had tangled with a mud pit recently.

The minute the pickup began snaking its way to the back of Reed's property, Aunt Zoe started in with new questions, forgetting that I was the one hired to do the investigating not her. I let it slide. There was nothing to be gained by getting fired up over it. Besides, the two of them were hitting it off so well. "So, how much acreage do you have here, Reed?"

The man driving the truck opened his mouth just wide enough to reply, "Roughly eighty acres," and then he swiftly asked, "Zoe, has anyone ever told you what sharp looking boots those are?"

Her pale face immediately turned the color of her spiked hairdo. "Why, these old things?" she said, lifting her boots to inspect them. "Not that I recall."

"Well, they are. So is that hat of yours."

"Why, thank you, Reed. Right before we climbed in the car this morning, I tried convincing Mary she needed a comfortable pair of boots like mine. Didn't I Mary?"

My eyes had been studying the scenery outside the side window while Aunt Zoe and Reed had kept up their lively conversation, and they continued to do so now, even though common courtesy required my attention elsewhere. You see, if I locked eyeballs with Aunt Zoe, I'd laugh so hard my snugly fit jeans would part like the Red Sea. And no one wanted to see that happen, especially me. "Yes, you did, Zoe."

After a few more minutes of driving, Reed's truck stopped abruptly. Apparently we had reached the area my client wanted to show us, a piece of land that butted up against Clint Russell's property.

Leaving the keys in the ignition, Reed quickly slipped out of his door, came around to the passenger side to help us down, and then made certain our feet were securely planted on the ground before pointing to a specific section of traditional, white wood fence he wanted us to take a look at.

I put myself in sleuthing mode and swiftly moved to the area noted. Once there, I requested my companions to stay behind me while I examined the wood structure. Neither party gave me any grief. They probably appreciated the fact that they were being given more time for idle chitchat.

For me, the most significant thing to establish first was the height of the fence since the ground is always shifting.

Standing as close to the wood structure as was humanly possible, I soon realized both my neck and head jetted above the top rail. Definitely up to code. According to horse Internet sites I had visited the other day, the recommended fence height for average-size horses should be between fifty-four and sixty inches. I peered over my shoulder. "A horse would break its leg if it jumped this high a fence, wouldn't it, Reed?"

"Not necessarily. There are exceptions to the rule. Scared horses are known to be extremely athletic and stallions, which we don't want on our property, could clear it just fine."

I made a mental note to myself to Google horse jumping records when I got home. Like the man said, a spooked one can surprise you. "Did you have to replace any loose fence boards after the incidents?"

Reed slid his calloused hands up and down his Rustler jeans. "No, ma'am."

"Hmm?"

Twice he's been notified that horses he boards have ended up on Clint's property, and no one has the foggiest notion how they got there. *Please. Someone knows something.*

I squatted by the fence post nearest me and stared at it intently. It looked in good shape. No rotting or splitting. No visible signs of chipped cement surrounding the bottom of the post. *Better do a tug test.*

I wrapped my arms securely around the midsection of the post and pulled as hard as I could. Nothing happened. The post was solid. Since there wasn't anything more I could think of as far as testing the stability of the post goes, I stood and meandered over to the other post connected to this same section of fence and repeated the process. It didn't budge either.

With the inspection done, I turned towards the two onlookers. "If someone had loosened these posts to allow horses to get through, there should be pieces of concrete left behind as evidence, especially since the horses' activity took place during the night, but there's nothing."

"I hear yeah," Reed replied in what sounded like disgust. "It's like the horses flew over the fence."

Aunt Zoe laughed.

"Or, they were lifted over with some kind of fancy gizmo attached to a crane," I offered. "But then, more people would be required to achieve the feat, and we all know the more people involved in a crime the greater the likelihood someone would spill the beans."

There was only one other possible conclusion I could come to but I didn't spell it out. I had a feeling Reed already knew, even if he didn't want to admit it out loud. A person he knew was taking the horses over to Clint's property. The big question was who and why?

With no solid leads to go on, we returned to Reed's truck and I inquired about the people bordering his land.

He filled me in as much as he could, and before I knew it we'd come full circle, back near the barn where we began the tour. "Well, there you have it ladies. You've seen all there is to see. Now don't forget about the horses when you're backing up. They're still roaming around out there somewhere."

Darn, I'd forgotten about them. I'm not walking back to the car with horses running every which way. I quickly made up a story about having a sore foot and asked my client if he'd mind dropping us at my car.

As it turned out, Reed's presence was required when we returned to Fiona and it wasn't because of a dead battery.

Picture this, a ginger-colored horse, one of the ten getting fresh air, stood lazily alongside the driver side of my car with his head protruding through the open window. He must've liked what he saw because he wasn't about to move anytime soon. You could say he had taken a real shine to Fiona.

Oops. I bet he has a sweet tooth. M&M's had gotten spilled in the car, and I had never gotten around to retrieving them all. "Oh, crumb. Reed, can horses get sick from eating chocolate?" I only asked because dogs could.

Reed didn't answer. He seemed off in his own world. That didn't deter me. I kept my eyes riveted on him, knowing he'd have to open up sooner or later about what's causing him to be so unsettled.

A few seconds later, one of Reed's calloused hands flew to his head causing his cap to go flying. The other hand swiftly raked it in. Then the words, "Crap," flapped out of my client's mouth faster than a chef could flip flapjacks over a frying pan. *What's with him?*

"I'm so sorry," Reed said, as he barreled out of his pickup. "I should've warned you about the windows."

He headed straight for the horse and swatted him on his back side. "Go on. Get out of here." The animal jolted and took off like his hind legs had been nipped by a German shepherd or a house full of flies.

Once the horse had taken off, Reed saddled up to Fiona and quickly tucked his head and shoulders through the open car window. *Geez, does the man have a thing for chocolate too?* Not knowing what was going on in my client's head, I turned to my aunt and said, "I sure hope he doesn't get stuck."

"Me, too."

"There was no need for him to use the window you know. All he had to do was ask me to unlock the car."

"Do you know what's got him so riled up, Mary?"

"I think he's a chocoholic."

"What makes you say that?"

"I spilled M&M's in the car a couple days ago."

"Oh."

When Reed's upper body didn't exit the car after five minutes, Aunt Zoe became alarmed. "Mary, I think he might really be jammed in there."

I shook my head. "I hope not. I don't want to be the one to call 911."

"Well, if you're not going to check on your client, I am," Aunt Zoe announced rather firmly. She rushed to Reed's side and began tugging on his long-sleeved checkered shirt. "Are you okay?"

I took a good look at Reed when he finally yanked his head and shoulder out of Fiona's window and spun around. He wasn't chomping on anything. "I know you don't want to hear this, ladies," he said as he rolled his eyes, "but I'm afraid the damage is done.

Ah, too bad. The horse didn't leave any candy for him.

"That's all right," I shouted from the truck, hopping out and heading for him. "The next time I drive out this way I'll bring a two pound bag of M&M's just for you. Which kind do you like? Peanut or plain?"

The man had a confused air about him. Maybe no one's ever offered to buy him M&M's before. "What are you talking about, Miss Malone?"

I turned to my aunt for assistance. She flipped her palms in the air. "Candy. Isn't that what you're...?" My mouth went numb. No, I wasn't having a stroke. I just finally noticed what Reed was referring to. "Oh, my God!" I screamed as panic set in. "My steering wheel! The horse ate my steering wheel!"

Aunt Zoe reached for my hands. "Now, now Mary, calm down. It'll be all right. Tell her, Reed."

Before my client had a chance to reply, my loose tongue took over. "It won't be all right. How can it be? I can't drive the Volkswagen home without a steering wheel."

When my information finally sunk in for my aunt, her mouth dropped opened like it was waiting for a golf ball to make a hole-in-one.

"Now ladies, don't panic," Reed interjected. "You can have a lift home in my pickup."

"But... but what about my car? How am I going to get it back to Minneapolis?" I moaned.

"You don't have to," Reed said, "A tow truck will come get it, Miss Malone."

~9~

The overdue rain forecasted earlier for the Twin Cities splattered Reed's truck in earnest as we pulled up along the newly painted curbing outside the main entrance to the Foley. Over the hum of the engine, Aunt Zoe and I thanked our driver profusely for his kindness before adding our goodbyes.

Of course, if one analyzed how our appreciation to the man was noted, you'd discover my aunt's was laid on thicker and lingered much longer than mine. Could she already be smitten with Reed Griffin? That's all I need, a budding romance between my client and Aunt Zoe.

Not wanting to end up plastered on the front page of a crazy newspaper looking like drowned rats; I hastily prodded my aunt on. "Rain's coming down harder. We need to run for it, Zoe."

"Hmm. Oh, yes, of course. Thanks again, Mr. Griffin."

"My pleasure, ma'am. Talk to you gals real soon."

The minute I swung open the truck's door we made a mad dash to the Foley's entrance. Amazingly, even with the downpour, Aunt Zoe and I barely left a trail of rain as we walked across the lobby to the elevator. Hopefully, what made it to the floor won't cause additional mop up work for Mr. Edwards, the caretaker.

Back at our humble abode, my roommate immediately claimed Matt's La-Z-Boy for her respite. I, on the other hand, took refuge in the kitchen where I could mull over the morning's events concerning Fiona while stuffing my face with comfort food. Whenever my nerves get jangled, only the most fattening foods soothe me: candy, ice cream, pop, potato chips, gobs of dip and macaroni and cheese.

Just as I stuck my head in the fridge to get a can of Pepsi and search for something outlandish to eat, there was a knock at our door. Since I was in no mood to chat with anyone right then, I asked my roommate to see who it was.

A rapid reply sweetly volleyed back. "Sure." The bottom of the recliner squeaked now as it got tucked in by my aunt, which meant the door would be cracked open soon.

While my bidding was being handled, I remained hidden in the kitchen waiting for a two-way conversation to ensue.

"Hello, Zoe."

"Why, Margaret, what a pleasant surprise."

"Is Mary around?"

"Yes, she just stepped into the kitchen."

"Is Gracie with her?"

Forget the Pepsi and comfort food, Mary. Nothing made me feel better than talking to Mrs. Grimshaw. If anybody could understand my woes, it would be a grandmotherly soul like her.

I raced to the entryway and greeted our visitor. "Oh, Margaret, you wouldn't believe the morning we've had."

Mrs. Grimshaw's thinning eyebrows had been standing at attention when I first caught sight of her, but now they arched severely as she looked high and low for something. "How so?" she asked.

Even though the old woman's words sounded like she was interested in what I had to share, clearly her mind wasn't. She continued to scan the areas nearest the door. Had she dropped something on the carpet when she was here last? Why doesn't she say what she's searching for? We could assist her.

Eventually she stopped looking around and said, "I can't believe Matt's sweet dog's been giving you a rough time. She never does for me."

I threw my hands in the air and gave Aunt Zoe my special look. She got my drift. Neither of us knew what the woman from across the hall was talking about. Maybe she was showing signs of dementia.

Not finding whatever it was she wanted, Mrs. Grimshaw finally gave up. "Mary, where's Gracie hiding?"

"What do you mean? Gracie's not here." Just as I said that, something finally clicked in my head. I was the absentminded one, not her. "Oh, no!" My hand flew to my forehead. "I can't believe I forgot about her."

"Probably because you were so upset about the car," Aunt Zoe said.

She's right, but what was her excuse. "Margaret, I'm sorry, I need to make a phone call, but I'll be back in a flash."

"Take your time, dear. I'm sure Zoe can keep me entertained."

"Yes," Aunt Zoe said. "We can discuss dancing."

When I rejoined the women in the living room a minute later, I found them sitting on the couch, heads together, exchanging recipes. "So, then you add just a smidgen of garlic to the sauce right before serving," Mrs. Grimshaw said.

"Mmm. Sounds delicious." My roommate said, focusing on my movement to the recliner. "Who did you rush out to call, Mary?"

"Mike, my brother."

Not satisfied with the curt reply, Aunt Zoe demanded to know more. "Why did you need to contact him?"

"See if he could pick up Gracie." I slipped into the La-Z-Boy and directed my attention to our visitor. "Margaret, did Zoe fill you in on our crazy morning yet?"

A hasty reply came, but not from the lips of the elderly woman. "Nope. We found too many other things to chat about, didn't we, Margaret?"

"Yes, indeed," our guest stated, straightening out the hunched position she'd had while sharing recipes. "What happened? Did you visit Mr. Griffin like you planned, Mary?"

My stomach lurched forward and did a flip or two as thoughts of the damaged car floated miserably around in my head again. "Yeah," I responded sourly, "we went there."

Aunt Zoe shot off the couch and paced dramatically. "The poor girl, she's a total wreck."

Our neighbor sighed. "I've noticed. The man you two met up with must've been a real slime ball."

If it had been any other day but today, I would've burst out laughing. The absurdity of the word *slime ball* being used by a woman in her nineties was too much. "Where did you catch that verbiage from, a TV show?"

"Slime ball? Why Matt of course. He said it a lot when sharing tidbits of cases with me."

"Oh, I never thought of that." I turned to my aunt. "I think you should be the one to clear the air regarding Mr. Griffin. You spent more time with him."

Auntie nodded nervously. "If you insist, dear." she said, clearing her throat before she went on. "Take it from me, Margaret; Reed Griffin is no slime ball. The man is one fine gentleman."

I leaned forward in the La-Z-Boy. "It's what went down at the end of our visit that upset me so much," I briskly added.

"Oh, dear." Mrs. Grimshaw scooted her short cotton-clothed body to the end of the couch, bringing her closer to me. "Do you feel up to sharing, Mary?"

"I guess so." Unfortunately, I wasn't as ready as I thought. Tears slid down my cheeks, but instead of hiding them like I would around a man, I let them flow. "I lost the use of my car through sheer stupidity."

The elderly woman's mouth jerked open. "Oh, no! You had a car accident. How awful. How did it happen? Are you both all right?"

Aunt Zoe couldn't contain herself any longer. "You don't understand. Mary didn't bang into another car. A horse and her car didn't see eye to eye."

"A horse?"

"Yes, a horse," I weakly replied. "It found the "Bug's" steering wheel quite delicious, and with the steering mechanism gone, there's no vehicle to drive."

Margaret's bony hand flew to her cheek. "Horses like salt, but I never knew they chomped on car parts. What a dilemma you have, Mary. I'm sorry. If I had a car, I'd lend it to you, but I stopped driving five years ago. Any idea how long your car will be indisposed?"

"Haven't a clue." I wiped my square-shaped face with the tips of my fingers. "All Mr. Griffin said was the car needed to be towed to a shop for repairs."

"How on earth did you manage to get home from his place? A cab?"

My aunt's face grew flush as she eagerly explained. "Why, no. That kind man at the horse ranch offered us a lift in his truck."

Margaret shifted her gaze my way and winked. "Ah. I see. Well, Zoe, Mr. Griffin certainly does sound like a true gentleman. So, when are you going to see him again? Ah, I mean when do you think the two of you will need to go back to the area to do more investigating?"

"I don't know. What do you think, Mary?"

I gritted my teeth. Despite having no car I needed this job. "The sooner the better, I guess. I don't want the case to grow cold."

Our neighbor seemed to have drifted off to another dimension. Her face showed signs of strain as she tapped an imaginary message on her brightly covered lap with her fingers. "Mary, you need to speak to Matt and ask if you can borrow his Topaz. I'm sure he won't mind. It's sitting in storage."

The elderly woman's suggestion made me feel like an elephant had finally been lifted off my chest. "Neighbor, you're a genius. Why didn't I think of that?" I jumped out of the La-Z-Boy and marched over to Margaret to give her a gentle bear hug.

Aunt Zoe moved out of the way. "Like I said before, Mary, you were so focused on the VW you couldn't think about anything else."

"You're right, Auntie. I had a bad case of tunnel vision, but now I see clearly."

I let go of Margaret, started to backtrack to the La-Z-Boy, then stopped abruptly, and spun towards the two women again. "Would either of you know what time it is in Germany?" Not born a procrastinator like certain people in my family, I chose to get the long distance call to Matt out of the way as soon as possible. Why delay what can be done today is my motto.

~10~

Instead of remaining comfortably seated in the living room while I completed my call to Matt, the two women met me between the hallway and the kitchen. Obviously, curiosity got the best of them. "Well, how is he?" they eagerly questioned in unison. "What did he have to say?"

"Who? About what?" I lightly teased.

As silly as my aunt can be at times, she wasn't about to partake in any silliness at the moment. She reprimanded me. "Don't be so childish."

I flipped my palms out like I was holding back a tidal wave. "Okay, okay. Considering Matt had put in a gruesome ten hour work day and was slipping between the sheets, he sounded like one would expect, exhausted. But don't worry, he managed a request. I'm to greet you both and give you hugs."

"How sweet. But what about the car?" Margaret drilled, "Can you use it?"

I balled up my fingers except the thumbs, which pointed to the ceiling.

Margaret's furrows on her forehead grew deeper. "What's she doing, Zoe?"

Auntie gingerly deciphered my actions. "Thumbs up—everything's A-okay. It's a go for the Topaz."

"That's grand. I suppose you mentioned Mr. Griffin to Matt while you were chatting too."

I swiped my hand in front of me. "Nah. Why, complicate things?"

*****

"C'mon, Mary," my brother Michael whined, "I haven't got all day." He was already on the elevator and was keeping the door from sliding closed.

"Don't get so uptight," I spit out as I picked up my pace and finally hopped on, "You know you don't have anything better to do today." I turned around to face the door and discovered that Margaret and my aunt had followed us. "Are you sure you're okay with watching Gracie?" I inquired of them one final time.

Aunt Zoe acted miffed. "Yes, of course."

"Just do what you have to do," Margaret cheerfully added, gently waving me off with the bottom of her yellow floral apron.

Michael released his hold on the OPEN button now, and we were immediately surrounded by four gray sterile walls and silence, the perfect time to ask about Matt's car. "Did Matt ever mention how the Topaz runs?"

My brother shifted his stance a little. "Not that I recall. Why?"

"I was just wondering how dependable his car is. It's more than twelve years old you know."

My brother scratched his thick head of hair for a moment while he thought about that tidbit. "That's right. He bought it back in '93, didn't he?"

"Yup."

"Well, I guess you'll find out soon enough."

"That's what I'm afraid of."

The elevator suddenly jerked to a halt. When its door popped open to let us out, the sun's harsh rays were bouncing madly about the lobby, inducing Michael and I to don our sunglasses before strolling anywhere.

"Mary."

"Yes?"

"I was thinking maybe you'd like me to call around town to see who can replace your VW's steering wheel the cheapest and the quickest? A man usually gets better results talking to car technicians than a woman."

Michael wasn't exaggerating, but still, why did life have to be that way? "Thanks, but I've got time to handle it yet. Summer school doesn't start for another week, and they don't use subs right away."

Our conversation regarding the car stopped when we came upon Mr. Edwards who was preparing to scrub a portion of the floor by the front doors. The seventy-something man's thin, sandy brown hair splotched with grey was combed to perfection, but his brown plastic eyewear sat askew on his nose as usual. Rustler jeans skimmed the tops of his hard-toed black shoes and a chocolate brown short-sleeve shirt exposed his almost pale, transparent skin. One arthritic hand held the wet mop while the other rose slightly to greet us.

The two of us waved back.

"Nice guy," I shared with my brother once outside. "Not nosey—just does his job. A good one at that, I might add."

"You'll get no argument from me about his cleaning thoroughness. Every time I walk through the Foley lobby or ride the elevator, it smells like Mr. Clean has recently visited."

I jabbed my brother in the ribs.

"Ouch! What's that for?"

"For being so sarcastic. The apartment building should smell clean. Why, that man's busy getting things done in the building from 6:00 a.m. till 10: p.m. every day except Sunday."

"Is he married? If not, he'd be a good catch for someone."

"I don't know. I never thought to ask. Maybe he's a widower and doesn't have anywhere else to hang out."

Michael jiggled his car keys in his hand. "That's possible."

Evidently he found room to park close to the Foley; otherwise he wouldn't have his keys out yet. I glanced up and down the street, but didn't see his car anywhere. "Okay, I give up. Where did you hide your little gem?"

"You mean my shiny new Buick?"

I nodded politely. He was being sarcastic again. His car was ten years old.

"Around the corner."

The second we hopped in the car, Michael began giving me the third degree. Mom and Dad probably put him up to it. "What have you and Zoe been up to?"

I was evasive. "Oh, you know. A little of this, a little of that. Chatting with the neighbors."

His head nodded like he understood. "Have you filled out any job applications yet?"

"No time. I've got something else cooking right now."

"Oh? Like what?"

Michael and the remainder of my family would go ballistic if they knew I took a case meant for Matt. "A guy I know is shorthanded at his riding stable," I said as coolly as I could, "and asked if I'd help out."

My sibling shook his head. "A riding stable? I don't know, Sis. I sure hope you haven't taken on more than you can chew. Horses can be quite fickle at times, especially stallions."

Don't I know it. "I've been assured there aren't any stallions around. The males have all been castrated, but thanks for being concerned," and then I carefully segued into a new topic that kept us going until we arrived at his place.

When Michael removed the Topaz from the Foley's underground parking lot after Matt left, he stored it on his property in the pole barn which is surrounded by tall grass. Wouldn't you know I had forgotten that little fact and had dressed inappropriately for tick season.

He took a good look at me now as we pulled into his driveway. "Those shorts and flip flops aren't going to cut it with the tick population on my property, sis. You'd better wait here while I retrieve the Topaz."

Disgusting ticks. Mean buggers. Why did one of the worst arachnids have to live in Minnesota? Talk shows might joke about ticks, but no one living around here does. We take them very seriously. Some ticks are harmless, but others cause major problems like Lyme disease which attacks a human's muscles and heart if not caught in time. I watched now from afar as Michael made his way through the uncut grass leading to his pole barn and quickly disappeared out of sight. *Hmm? How many ticks would find their way up his pant legs? None if he's lucky.*

Within minutes he drove up behind the wheel of the Topaz, parked and jumped out.

Not wanting the car to idle too long, I got in and plopped my size sixteen bod behind its steering wheel. Of course, the next logical step was to set my foot on the gas pedal, but I couldn't do it. I didn't know this car's quirks like I did the VW's.

What if I bumped some tiny gizmo and repeated another close call on the highway like this morning's drive to Reed Griffin's property.

My hands shook. Right this very moment, Aunt Zoe and I could be lying in hospital beds being nursed back to health at St. John's in St. Paul. Yikes! On the other hand, if one of the guys on the most recent poll of sexiest men alive was hovering over me, well, I wouldn't be too unnerved.

A few seconds later, I found I still couldn't shake off my nervousness and instead of backing up I checked the position of the side view mirrors.

Michael had been watching my silly antics all the while leaning against the ancient oak tree at the side of his driveway, but now he strolled over to the car and motioned to roll the window down. So, I did. "What's up, Mary? It doesn't take a rocket scientist to put your foot on the gas pedal and back the car up."

"I know. I know. I just didn't realize how nervous I'd be about driving someone else's car. It's a heavy responsibility."

My brother bent his head down, so we'd be on equal footing. "Look, did you worry every time you drove Dad's car when you were in high school?"

"Are you kidding?" I chuckled. "Of course not!"

"Well, then, just pretend Dad's loaning you his car again for a couple days, and everything will be fine."

I shook my head. "No, it won't. How could it be? I was a teenager then."

The phrase 'ignorance is bliss' made perfect sense when hormones were raging fast and furious through my system, but it doesn't now. I'm a mature adult. With borrowing comes responsibility.

Michael shot back, "In other words, you're old enough to know how much things cost to repair."

"Ah, yeah. Something like that."

"Well, if you don't back out of here soon and head for home, a certain threesome is going to be hunting you down."

I brushed my bangs off my forehead. "Huh?"

"Gracie, Aunt Zoe and Mrs. Grimshaw."

"Oh? Okay, okay, I'm going. Wish me luck."

My brother pulled his head away from the car window now. "Good luck. And, Mary..."

"Yes?"

"Call me when you get back to the Foley."

I held the steering wheel in one hand and saluted him with the other. "Aye-aye, Captain."

*****

There's nothing like being smothered to death with doggie kisses the minute I walked in the door. By the time Gracie finished with me, there were tiny puddles everywhere.

"Sorry," Aunt Zoe said as she reached out to grab Gracie's collar that was cinched around the mutt's neck. "She just emptied her water bowl right before you walked in."

A beautiful young pregnant woman, who was short in stature, stood serenely by listening to our conversation. Her shiny straight black hair flowed down to her waist, partially covering the black and white silk sari she wore.

"It's all right," I smoothly replied. "Next time, I'll call before I enter."

"That wouldn't hurt." Aunt Zoe's so naïve. She had no idea I was being sarcastic.

Since Margaret and Aunt Zoe were in charge of Gracie while I was gone, I ignored the stranger for the moment and listened for the elderly woman. No shuffling feet were coming our way. That was odd. "What happened to Margaret?" I quickly inquired; worried she might have gotten sick while I was gone.

My aunt let go of Gracie. "A friend of hers is dropping by in a little bit, so I figured she'd like a few minutes to primp."

"Ah," is all I managed to say even though I was dying to know if our neighbor's company was male or female. Matt had let it slip quite a while ago that Margaret goes out with a man friend occasionally.

"I really must go, Zoe," the stranger announced abruptly.

"Oh," I said, "I hope you're not leaving on my account. I didn't mean to scare you off."

"No need to worry. It's time for me to prepare supper, that's all." Now there was an awkward pause.

Aunt Zoe glanced at Kamini and then me. "Please forgive my manners, ladies. I just realized I forgot to introduce you two. Mary's my niece."

"And her roommate," I pointed out.

"Ah," the pregnant woman said.

"Kamini, Mrs. Singi, lives in the apartment directly below us, Mary."

My hand stretched out to her. "Nice to meet you, Kamini. If we ever make too much noise up here, let us know."

The woman smiled broadly. Then she politely grasped my nicked hand with her fine smooth one.

"Kamini moved here from India five years ago," Aunt Zoe explained. "Her husband owns the optical store next to our apartment building."

"Really? How convenient for you." The young woman shook her head politely. I removed my sunglasses from my nose and wagged them in front of her. "You know, I've been telling my aunt that the lenses in these glasses aren't as strong as they should be. Perhaps I'll stop by the optical shop tomorrow and have your husband take a look at them."

Mrs. Singi smiled shyly. "Yes, please do. I work there too. Well, goodbye."

"She's a beautiful woman," I said the minute the door closed behind Mrs. Singi.

"Funny you should say that, Mary."

"Why?"

"The Hindu word for beautiful woman is Kamini."

"Oh?"

As we left the hallway behind and headed for the living room, I dropped my humongous purse on a narrow wood table meant to hold small items like keys, wallets and such. The table didn't cave in, so I figured it was okay to leave my purse there from now on. "Auntie, how did you happen to meet, Kamini? On the elevator?"

Aunt Zoe veered towards the couch. "Doing laundry."

"Ah, yes," I said plopping in the La-Z-Boy, that's a great place to meet neighbors." *Especially those of the opposite sex.*

The mutt wasn't sure where to go, my aunt or me, so I helped her along with the decision making process. "Gracie, its cookie time."

She barked a soft, "Wuff, wuff," scrambled over to me, and sniffed for her treat.

"Isn't that cute, Mary? She knows exactly what she wants."

I stifled a long overdue yawn. "Yup."

"So what's on the agenda for the rest of the day?"

"No plans. You're on your own. All I want to do is decompress. Teaching a rowdy bunch of second graders is a piece of cake compared to this morning's stressful activities."

~11~

Only 7:00 a.m., and the sun was working its magic on my behalf, spreading its warmth across my face, telling me it was time to get up. Obviously I'd forgotten to overlap the two curtain panels before I went to bed.

I opened my eyes and shut them again. No sun was ordering me around. Besides, I hadn't gotten the required eight hours of beauty rest yet.

A word of warning to those who like to outsmart the sun—closed eyes alone won't keep the pesky sun at bay.

I raised my head slightly off the pillow, reached for the mauve-colored bed sheet I'd tossed off during the night, and pulled it over my head. Being undercover didn't help either. My body heat was rapidly rising, and it didn't have a darn thing to do with a man sharing my bed.

I discarded the sheet, grabbed the pillow, and put it over my face. Sounds a bit drastic, huh? But if I wanted to succumb to sleep, the pillow was the only sane option left. I didn't own a sleep mask.

In case you're wondering, my lack of sleep had nothing whatsoever to do with too much caffeine racing through this size 16 body at full throttle before bedtime. My brain was simply overtaxed with concerns regarding a new steering wheel. You see, since I don't have insight into the future, like so-called psychics, when I received my pink slip, I sat down, analyzed every possible car-related scenario imaginable, and then I contacted my insurance agent and opted for a much higher deductible.

Obviously, the joke was on me. My so-called thrifty decision had one major flaw. It didn't add a horse to the mix.

Gracie had slept on the floor below the bedroom window last night, and now she pressed her head on the mattress near my head and began to whine.

"Oh, for cry'n out loud, not you too," I mumbled, flinging a hand out. "It's bad enough the sun thinks I should be up."

The mutt was no dummy. She knew who was in control. She whined again and then nuzzled her nose against my hand.

"All right. All right. I'm getting up, but you're going to have to wait for breakfast." I whipped the pillow off my face and slowly drew my sleepy body up.

When I finally got into a decent sitting position, a loud, shrill, beeping noise emanated from outside my room. Gracie went wild. She tried to burrow under the bed. "What the…?"

Fully awake now, I bolted out of bed. A fire alarm was continuing to sound from somewhere in the building and I needed to get Aunt Zoe out of the apartment pronto, no matter what I was wearing. This was no time for a style show. I swung open the bedroom door and made a mad dash down the hall.

"Aunt Zoe! Aunt Zoe! Wake up!" I frantically yelled as I continued down the hallway. "There's a fire! There's a fire in the building."

Just as I reached the kitchen doorway, Aunt Zoe stuck her head out. I almost had a heart attack on the spot. Foam rollers the size of orange juice cans were holding her fiery red hair for ransom while a butter knife and tea towel kept her hands occupied. "What's wrong, Mary? What's all the shouting about?"

"A fire alarm went off. We need to leave the apartment immediately."

My roommate kept a calm demeanor, even after I broke the scary news, and continued to brandish her black-specked knife in front of me. "Oh? That's nothing to worry about. Go back to bed."

"What do you mean nothing to worry about?" Before I could get anything further out of her, the six-foot muscular-framed guy who lived to the left of Matt's apartment, FBI agent Rod Thompson, made his way into our narrow hallway too.

Dressed in a fine navy-blue suit, a solid powder-blue tie and shiny black wingtip shoes, he looked like he was part of an early morning wedding. Of course, I knew that wasn't the case. The man with the tousled blonde hair dresses like this every day when he's on duty. It's mandatory.

The minute Rod's sapphire-blue eyes soaked in the view, me, he let loose with a whistle so earth shattering it could've caused a teakettle to explode. "Oo la la. I love your ensemble, Mary. It beats the heck out of what you were wearing the last time I saw you."

Oh, my God! My hands flew to my cotton bikini-cut Jockey underpants.

Aunt Zoe, bless her soul, sensed my embarrassment and was kind enough to pass me the towel she was holding. I tried to drape it around my bountiful hips without much success.

I was hoping Rod would execute good manners and leave once he saw how uncomfortable I was, but he didn't. Obviously, he didn't care. "You know what you remind me of?" he asked, wagging his index finger at me.

"What?" I stupidly responded.

"A water goddess," he announced.

A low grunt escaped my lips before I shifted my attention to my roommate. "What's going on here?"

Aunt Zoe didn't answer. She simply motioned for us to enter the kitchen.

Rod didn't take her up on her suggestion, thank goodness. "Gotta go. No time for coffee," he shared. "Oh, Mary, make sure to wear that outfit again real soon," and then he winked.

I threw the towel Aunt Zoe had given me, but I missed the mark. It landed on Gracie's head instead of Rod's. She'd followed him to the door.

With Rod gone, my aunt was forced to explain what happened. "I'm sorry the alarm woke you, Mary. I burnt the toast. I'm not used to these new-fangled contraptions. My old toaster had just two narrow slots for bread, and I never had to touch the setting. Now, they've got a hole for bagels, one for waffles, one for toast and even one to warm up leftover pancakes. It drives me crazy. I tried fanning the smoke with the dishtowel, but all it did was set off the alarm. I didn't realize it was so touchy."

"How did you finally get it to stop?"

"Why, that nice man, Rod, took care of the problem. Apparently, he knows some trick to silence it."

I just bet he does.

I cringed as I recalled how Rod's eagle eyes traveled up and down my scantily-clad body and the stupid comments he'd made. What TV show did he glean those words from? No wonder he wasn't married yet.

"What's that frown for, Mary? You're not upset with me, are you?"

"No, no," I lied, giving my roommate a hug to prove it. "It was just burnt toast after all."

"Huh? That's exactly what that young fellow said. Well, now that you're up, do you want to join me for breakfast?"

Breakfast? Who was she talking to? I sure as heck wasn't up to settling in for my early morning routine at the kitchen table when the air quality was hovering towards obnoxious. Think sauerkraut. For me, burnt toast ranks number one. I couldn't possibly eat until something drastic was done to clear the air.

Luckily, relief was only a couple steps away, in the bathroom sat a new canister of air freshener.

I dashed down the hall, grabbed the lilac spray, and returned to the kitchen where I swirled around the room like a twister, diffusing flowery scent in every corner. When finished, I took a whiff. *Ah, much better.*

Unfortunately, what's good for one person wasn't necessarily good for the other party. Aunt Zoe was gasping for air.

Since I hadn't seen her chomping on anything before spritzing the air, I knew I was to blame. Well, not me personally—the freshener. I stuck the can on the counter, approached my aunt who was still stationed at the table, and fanned the air surrounding her. Previous hand action similar to this had provided good results. After roughly twenty vigorous swipes, I let my hands fall to their natural position. "There that should do it."

"If you say so," my roommate squeaked.

"Hmm?" Obviously, it was going to take more than mere air movement to get her voice back to normal. I moved behind her and gently rubbed the top of her back. It was cloaked in a chartreuse floor-length cotton bathrobe. "You'll be fine in a minute, I promise. I just overestimated the power of my hand on the nozzle."

"That's very reassuring," she answered in a voice that had finally made it past a whisper.

The mutt found her way back to the kitchen and begged for attention again. I stopped rubbing auntie's back and moved to the cupboard under the sink where we stored Gracie's box of Milkbones.

"Here's your breakfast," I said, dropping a few treats on the floor, "Now, let me get mine." The dog happily snapped up her snacks. Then she sauntered over to the fridge and plopped down in front of it. Luckily, the carton of milk I'd need had been left on the table so there was no need to disturb her. She could be quite obstinate when she wanted to be.

With both the dog and my aunt nicely taken care of, I rummaged through the cupboards looking for a glass and cereal bowl. It's amazing how long your mind retains the location of kitchen items stored in a previous household, but you can't remember where you placed something in your new home just the night before.

Finally finding what I was searching for, I quickly filled my glass to the brim with juice and plopped down with it and a bowl of Fruit Loops cereal. Since I wasn't on any special diet today, I didn't care what went in my body—tomorrow would be a different story.

"Mary, how come you never told me you had been involved with the man next door? Is that why you rushed to move in here?"

"What?" The spoonful of milk and cereal that had just entered my mouth spewed across the table. "We weren't. We won't," I said, grabbing a napkin and mopping up the mess. "And, no, I won't explain. She didn't need to know about the evening I spent downtown barhopping with a bunch of gals. It wasn't like we set out to get drunk on purpose. Because we didn't. We were simply helping a fellow teacher celebrate her upcoming nuptials.

Of course, brother, Matt, got wind of the details prior to the big night and suggested that his baby sister crash at his apartment instead of driving home on snow-clogged streets, bombed out of her mind at two in the morning. So, I acquiesced to his request.

When I'd gotten to Matt's after the party, I was feeling extremely happy and never bothered with the flannel nightie I'd brought. Instead, I donned an extra-large Twins T-shirt I discovered in the bathroom hamper.

Little did I know my brother would forget about my stay and invite over his nemesis, Rod, for an early morning discussion about a dumb apartment issue. Matt told me later I was hanging half off the couch, snoring away with no blanket covering my butt.

"You can't fool me, Mary," Aunt Zoe said, breaking my train of thought. "I saw that little spark between the two of you." She pointed one of her chunky fingers at me. "Why, you'd be perfect for each other."

The words "No, thanks," burnt my lips as they slid out. "There's plenty of other fish in my pond to fry." *Yeah, right, Mary. In your dreams.*

~12~

Even though breakfast was over, there was no plan for a hasty retreat to clothe my half-naked body. It could wait a while longer. Clearing my mind of stress held top priority. Besides, I knew there was no danger of Rod Thompson making another surprise appearance. He'd left the premises and possibly the state.

I strolled out of the kitchen and headed to the entrance closet, our catchall, where stuff went that had no other home, including the Holy Grail—the Yellow Pages. That thick book could relieve anyone's stress. It contained every business imaginable.

Several boxes had to be removed before I found the tattered book. It had become one with the carpet. Surprisingly, it didn't put up a fuss when plucked from its cushiony bed and carted away.

After spending an hour speaking with a half-dozen body shops, I discovered Paul's Body Shop in Cambridge was my best bet for the type of repair Fiona required.

Money or no money, I had to bite the bullet. Although, Dad's been known to take pity on his baby girl. I suppose I could shed a tear or two in front of him when the job's finished. With the repair scheduled, I moved on to the selection of a towing company.

The convenient maps at the front of the phone book helped me surmise how far Fiona would have to travel from point A to point B, sixty-some miles. "Whoa!" Mike had warned me towing distance makes a huge difference in price, and sometimes the unsuspecting underdog is gouged even more than necessary. Hundred dollar bills flashed before my eyes.

It wasn't like Cambridge or Princeton were connected to Woodbury's boundaries like our Twin Cities—Minneapolis and St. Paul. Woodbury was east of St. Paul, and Cambridge and Princeton were north of the Minneapolis suburbs.

When it came to towing businesses, Carmichael's appealed to me the most. Yes, I'll admit their corny ad, *we've always got your front and rear covered, day or night* could easily be misconstrued, but I went with it anyway. As far as I was concerned, any business that thought outside the box during these tough economic times, including using a risqué sounding ad to get the job done, earns kudos for ingenuity in my book.

It took ten rings before someone picked up. "Judd here. What can I do for you?" an owlish male voice asked. I quickly explained my dilemma to the worker bee on the other end. "Sure. We can tow it for you. There'll be an additional cost, of course."

I almost snapped, *"Isn't there always hidden costs?"* but thought better of it. Instead my stomach did somersaults. Money was about to fall from my piggy bank not theirs. *But you want Fiona back, don't you? Yes.*

I got up from the La-Z-Boy and paced back and forth on the ugly, moss-and-brown carpet, leaving indentations wherever my feet had been. The movement didn't reverse the racing palpitations and headache that began the moment I hung up the phone like I'd hoped. I inhaled deeply and then slowly puffed the air back out. *Calm down. You can't afford to add a coronary to your troubles.*

"What on earth are you doing?" Aunt Zoe inquired. "Is that a new dance your generation has created?"

I stood completely still. "Sorry. Was I disturbing you?"

My roommate dropped the Danielle Steele novel she was reading in her lap. "Not really. The prancing caught my eye. What kind of move was that?" She didn't wait for a reply. "Dancing's good for the body and mind. Edward and I danced once a week no matter where we were."

"Really?"

Dad's sister bent her head slightly. "Um hmm. I bet a single gal like you goes dancing a lot too. Remember when you were real little how you'd dance like crazy whenever a cute tune came on?"

I flapped my hand at her. "That was before I reached puberty. Junior high teenagers are a different breed. They can be so cruel. When we took dance lessons in gym class, they made sure the whole world knew I had two left feet."

My aunt laughed. "What did they know? Sounds like the little rascals were jealous."

I shook my head. "No, they were right. My dancing stinks."

"Niece, you're too hard on yourself. Why, the Malone clan's limberness is a well recorded fact in Ireland."

Facts in a book don't make it so.

Not wanting to insult my dad's sister, I said, "My klutzy ways probably come from my mom's side of the family. You know the French. They're too busy with smooching everyone."

Aunt Zoe scooted off the couch. "Don't give up so fast. I can teach you. Why, there's nothing to it, Mary. It just takes practice. Plus, dancing offers other great benefits."

"Such as?"

"Meeting the opposite sex."

"Ah, I... I don't know."

"Oh, it'll be fun. Tell you what. I'll check out what's going on around town, and then you and I will go some night. Okay?"

I scratched my head. "I'm not making any promises." *Dancing. Yuk! I'd rather curl up in a fetal position in bed than don dance shoes for some dumb Don Juan.*

The topic of dancing expired finally, and I was relieved, but then my aunt moved on to another matter. "Have you found out where you can have the Volkswagen towed to yet?"

I glanced at my bare feet. "It seems the consensus is Cambridge."

"Cambridge? Why, that's quite a distance from here, isn't it?"

"Yup."

"Is that why you were pacing?"

"Partly," I sighed. "I also don't know how I'm going to cough up the money for the repair and the tow job. I haven't started to sub yet, and we haven't done anything for Reed to merit a payment either."

"Dear, a gal with a master's degree ought to figure out a quick solution, don't you think?"

"I guess. Otherwise, I'll have to find another job."
*There's no way this gal is driving the Topaz any longer
than I have to. It's a piece of junk.*

~13~

The morning was about shot when I finally entered the shower to scrub up. As the warm cascading water flowed from the old-fashioned shower head and gingerly rinsed soap residue off my skin, it brought back fond memories of Playa Los Muertos Beach in Puerto Vallarta, helping me forget my woes for a few measly minutes.

The abundant supply of gorgeous, muscle-bound Mexican men ogling every move of mine made me feel sexy. *It would be nice to feel that way again.*

I stared at my left hand. I bet if I had stayed in Mexico just a few more weeks I'd have a big shiny stone on the ring finger, something no male stateside has managed to do yet.

The moment I shut the water off Puerto Vallarta vanished down the drain along with the soap suds. Such is life. Some days stank more than others. Feeling a bit chilled now, I yanked the towel off the shower rod and wrapped myself in it before shoving the curtain aside.

The thick, luxurious plum-colored towel covering my body from knee to neck had been purchased from Kohl's the day before I received my pink slip. It was a steal, half off, so I didn't feel the need to cut corners and return it.

When I stepped out of the shower's confinement, I discovered the rest of the room entombed in thick fog due to the Foley's neglect to install exhaust fans. Not wanting to discard the towel quite yet, I decided to forego my minimal daily makeup regime in front of the vanity mirror.

Instead, I groped for the non-enhanced undergarments I'd left on the toilet lid. I only wear enhanced ones, the type that turns your face blue and causes you to come up for air every five seconds, when attending a special event, like a blind date. Too bad grandmothers, members of the girdle-wearing generation who think it's so easy to get a guy's attention nowadays, don't understand how tough it really is.

What's that? You don't need enhanced lingerie? Well, lucky you. You probably only have a bran muffin and a glass of water for breakfast. Am I right? Ah huh. That's what I figured.

Well, this gal's size-sixteen bod never gets a second glance unless the extra fat is neatly tucked away.

As long as I'm hanging it all out there for you, you might as well know the pull-in-your-tummy lingerie wasn't the only item I passed on. Anyone who knows me can testify it's an extremely rare day when I step out without wearing one of the million pairs of pierced earrings I own. I feel naked without them, and, quite honestly, they make a person look snazzier. But today was different. One doesn't have to dress up for an optical store. The only thing looking at you were 1000 pairs of glasses.

I threw my shirt on and then stuck my legs into my jeans. The minute the jeans closed ranks on my butt, the zipper insisted on playing tug-of-war with me. *Weight gain's not the issue, Mary. It's the twenty times they've been laundered. That's all.*

I left the partially steamed bathroom behind and went to the living room where I assumed Aunt Zoe was since the room served a dual purpose; living room and bedroom. My assumption was correct. She was sitting on the couch deeply engrossed in her novel. "You must be at a really hot spot in that book," I said purposely trying to break her concentration.

"Why do you say that?" she innocently inquired without looking up.

"Your forehead has a million ridges on it."

Unfortunately, my remark didn't succeed in breaking my aunt's eye contact with the pages of her novel as I'd anticipated. "Well, you're right, Mary. I'm at an exciting part. Picture this, war time—World War II—two lonely people keep bumping into each other at a VA hospital. The woman's husband is severely wounded and hasn't got long to live. The man, a doctor, has been a widower for a few months now. Sparks ignite."

"Hmm. Sounds like those sappy novels written by Nicholas Sparks and Nora Roberts. My sister can't get enough of them." Personally, I've never understood what people saw in romance novels or movies. I hate them with a passion. Such utter nonsense. When in our lifetime has a Prince Charming ever come charging in on a white stead to sweep a gal off her feet? I dare you to name one.

"Are their books made into movies too, Mary?"

"I'm pretty sure."

"Maybe you'd like to read my book when I finish. The story could end up on the Hallmark Channel."

Where's the mouth wash? How dare she suggest I read a romance novel or watch Hallmark? "Not right now," I forced myself to reply. "I've recently reached a plateau in my reading, and I'm not sure which direction I want to take next. Perhaps a good mystery. Matt left a few on his nightstand." I removed my overly large bright blue sunglasses from the highly waxed coffee table and perched them on my nose.

My roommate's red head bobbed this way and that. "Isn't Griffin's case mystery enough?"

"It's not the same. One is fact; the other fiction."

Aunt Zoe finally peeled her eyes away from her book and locked them on me. "Hmm? I guess I can't argue with that. I see you finally got dressed. Why the sunglasses? Are you going out?"

"Yes, as a matter of fact, I am. I thought I'd take a walk to the Singi's optical store and see if I needed stronger lenses for my sunglasses. Care to tag along?"

"No, thanks. Perhaps if I was further along in my book."

"Well, I'm off then."

"Ah, Mary."

"Yeah?"

"Are you sure you want to go like that?"

"Why?" I cautiously asked, searching for any telltale signs of toothpaste stains.

"Your top's inside out."

Oh, crap. I had forgotten to turn the shirt back to the right side after it came out of the dryer. I treaded further into the room in case someone came to the door, and then I pulled off my shirt and reversed it. "There. Is that better?"

My roommate smiled broadly. "Much," and then her eyes drifted back to what she was reading prior to my interruption.

Gracie had been laying low while I was chatting with my aunt, but as soon as my hand hit the doorknob leading to the fourth floor hallway, she leaped into action. She loved getting her exercise, or rather she loves making us work out. "Wuff. Wuff."

I flung my free hand out in front of me. "No, Girl. Not now. Later." I felt bad the mutt couldn't join me, but shops around downtown Minneapolis don't permit dogs to roam inside their buildings like other out-of-state metro areas did.

Gracie hung her head and let loose with a couple whimpers before she backed off and ran to Aunt Zoe's side and whimpered some more.

I quickly scooted out the door and left the pleading wails behind.

*****

Shards of sun rays greeted me the instant the elevator door burst open. I'd definitely made the right decision to forget about Fiona for a few measly minutes.

I stepped onto the Foley's newly scrubbed tiled floor with a bounce to my step and quickly cut a fine path through a group of residents to reach the double glass entrance doors which led to the neighborhood sidewalk.

Once outside, I turned right and walked approximately nine feet before stopping underneath the optical store's dark green awning where a medium-sized sign displayed a huge metal pair of eyeglasses.

The store's aged exterior, covered with old reddish-brown Chicago brick, matched the Foley's which helped the two buildings blend nicely together. But there the similarities ended. No ivy vines clung to the one-story building. And this front entrance was flanked by enormous picture windows one couldn't ignore.

Each window was tastefully decorated with display racks showing off the latest in optical wear: Ray-Ban and Oakley sunglasses, funky reading glasses, children and adult eye wear and a variety of optical needs for fun at the beach.

I could feel sweat beading up on my forehead now. If I stood outside much longer staring at the façade, the sun would certainly turn me to mush.

I reached out to grasp the store's door but before the fingers made contact a young woman, wearing a very tight short white skirt, crinkled black sleeveless top, spiked heels and long stringy washed-out blonde hair, flung the door open and paraded out. My stance was far enough back, luckily, otherwise, I'd be short a few teeth and several hundred bucks.

The woman never apologized—too absorbed with her texting.

After she fled, the door waited for no one. I barely managed to squeeze through the entrance opening before I was smacked in the caboose.

A light bell rang as I stepped inside. Kamini, who was situated in the outer office, glanced up from her work behind a long narrow counter and presented me with a wide smile. I automatically flashed one back. "You have come to see us, how nice."

Wanting to comment on the windows before I forgot, I swiftly diverted her attention away from me and pointed to them. "I was admiring your displays before I came in, Kamini. Who does them?"

"Me," she shyly replied, and then she broke into her native tongue. I glanced around but found no one else in the waiting room except me.

Before long, a short thin man, in his mid-forties, with thick coal-black hair and deep set almond eyes, popped into the outer room. His smart pair of silver-colored wire glasses decorated his tan-skinned face. The husband.

Kamini swiftly turned her attention to the man in the charcoal suit. "Raj, there is someone I'd like you to meet."

"Ah, good," the man with the generous black mustache said, "Our sign on the door is working."

What sign? Where? That dumb blonde dimwit had my full attention before I stepped in here. Since I wasn't a regular customer, I didn't inquire if there was a sale going on.

"No, Raj," Kamini corrected gently. "This is the woman who lives above us."

"Oh, Miss. Zoe, so nice to meet you. Kamini has spoken of you many times."

No, she hasn't. Wrong again.

Raj had picked the right woman for his mate. She had the patience of a saint. Kamini took her husband's smooth hand in hers and said, "This is Mary not Zoe. She's her niece."

"Ah, Mary, the unemployed lady."

I was taken aback. Kamini actually shared that with her husband. *What else had she told him?* "Ah, I'm only sort of unemployed," I explained defensively. "I hope to substitute teach this summer."

"A teacher?" Raj looked through his rimless glasses with wide-eyed wonder. "Kamini, you didn't say she was a teacher. People trust teachers. They listen to what they say." He began to rub his palms together. "A teacher would do nicely here. Don't you agree?"

His wife stroked her extended tummy, wrapped in silk the color of the Caribbean, "Yes, Raj."

"The baby is coming soon," the optometrist hurriedly explained. "We need someone to fill in for my wife."

"But...but I didn't come here to apply for a job. I just want my sunglasses checked to see if they're strong enough." I pulled my prescription out of a pocket.

"Sure. Sure. I will do that." Raj whisked the prescription and sunglasses out of my hands and quickly disappeared to a room beyond the counter.

Kamini and I stared at each other for a couple seconds, and then she finally spoke. "Mary, you must think about working here. My husband is a very practical man and does not put up with nonsense. Surely you can see you have impressed him."

Five minutes later, Raj rejoined us and handed my belongings back to me.

"Is there much of a difference?" I asked.

"Very little. If you want, you can change the lenses after your next exam."

"That's that then. Thank you so much," I said. "How much do I owe you?"

"No charge," Raj assured me, "Just a small request."

Oh, oh. Lookout, Mary. When people say something like that around you, it usually ends up being something major. But what could the man possibly want from me?

"Apply for the job." Well, that definitely was a short and to-the-point request.

"But I don't know the first thing about the optical industry, and I've already committed myself to substituting for summer school."

"No problem," Raj replied as he readjusted his glasses. "Kamini works part-time. Try for a month. If you like, I teach you the optical business."

"Sorry, it wouldn't work for me." I started to leave.

Kamini wasn't about to let me walk out the door without taking one more stab at convincing me to apply for her position. "Before the baby comes, I show you what to do, Mary. It's not hard."

I hated being backed into a corner with no escape hatch. There should always be a way out.

Ah, come on, Mary. This isn't the first time you've found yourself in such a tight spot. You've always been a sucker for people in distress. Just tell Kamini what she wants to hear, and you can escape. "Ah, Kamini."

"Yes?"

"I'll take that application."

~14~

I'd been gone from the Foley, where I lived, for over a half an hour. When I returned, it still didn't look like our caretaker had put in an appearance, but my nonagenarian certainly had.

Even though the elderly woman's back was to me and she was heading to the elevator, her bright pink Isotoner slippers gave her away. They poked out from under her light, beige cotton pants. Since I hadn't run into Mrs. Grimshaw on the way in, I assumed her mission to the lobby had pertained to mail delivery.

"Wait up, Margaret," I called out as I ran to catch up.

The nonagenarian twisted her upper body slightly in my direction. "Oh? Hello, Mary. What a pleasant surprise. Are you coming or going?"

"Coming. I ran an errand."

My theory for Margaret's trip to the lobby proved to be accurate. "I don't know why I bothered to come check the mail," she quietly stated as her tiny fingers squeezed the few items found in her mailbox. "It's all junk."

"But, if you hadn't come down here, we wouldn't have bumped into each other."

A small smile escaped Margaret's lips. "That's true."

Since the elevator was waiting for passengers, we obliged. After I pressed the button for our floor, I stepped back and casually ran my hand across the nape of my neck, hoping my neighbor wouldn't notice.

She did. "I understand it's rather warm out there today."

"That's putting it mildly," I cheerfully replied, swabbing my damp hand across the leg of my jeans. "It actually feels like an oven. Thank goodness it's comfortable in here. So, what's your agenda for this afternoon, Margaret? Baking or dancing?"

"Neither. I'm cutting up vegetables for a dish I'm preparing for supper. How about you, Mary?"

The elevator ground to a halt with a hard jerk. We'd reached our floor. "Nothing much," I replied. "Just laying low. Hey, Margaret, if you have time, why don't you come over later? It will give us three gals a chance to get caught up on the latest gossip." The door slid open. The two of us stepped out and began to tread down the hallway.

"I'd like that. Should I call first?"

I waved my hand for emphasis. "No. Come whenever."

Right before the two of us reached our dwellings, a neighbor of ours, Rod Thompson, popped into the narrow hallway and greeted us. "Hello, ladies."

Good grief. Why did we have to run into him?

After acknowledging the man I least wanted to see, Rod shifted his attention to me personally. "Why, Mary, I don't believe it. You really do own more than one outfit," he sarcastically proclaimed, pointing to the clothing I had on. "Of course, that number you had on the other morning can't be beat. It rates right up there with Fourth of July fireworks."

Just what I need, another twist added to the crazy morning I've had so far: the car, then the job application, and now razzed by Rod Thompson.

Mortified by his comments, my hands flew out in front of me. I felt like Joan of Arc, gearing up for major battle against an enemy. But before war became a reality, I asked myself what sweet Mrs. Grimshaw standing next to me would think if I blew up. With the appropriate conclusion drawn, I hastily reined in my anger.

It soon became apparent I wasn't the only one affected by Rod's thoughtless words. They drew interest from Margaret as well. "What on earth?"

Rod patted Margaret's back. "There's nothing to be concerned about. I'm only passing through. Got a hot date. Can't keep her waiting," and then whoosh, the man vanished into the stairwell like he'd never been here.

"I can't imagine anyone dating him," I said with a sour note, not aware I'd spoken aloud.

Thankfully, Mrs. Grimshaw didn't pick up on my real feelings concerning Rod. "You're right, Mary. He's here and there so much."

"Yes, he's a real flighty fellow."

The old woman permitted a sly smile to escape. "Perhaps, he dates a stewardess."

I grinned. "A flight attendant? Oh, sure. I suppose that would have to be the type."

"Is that what they're called nowadays?"

"Yup. New era. New name." Determined to sidestep any unwanted questions that were bound to come forth now concerning Rod's personal comments to me, I swiftly turned and shoved the key in the lock.

"Mary." Too late. "What was all that mumbo jumbo Rod spoke of?"

Not wanting to share more than I had to with Mrs. Grimshaw, I simply replied, "Let's see. I think he said, 'Hi. I'm just passing through.'"

The petite Italian woman flapped her hands in front of me. "No, no. Before that."

"Before that? Hmm? Oh, he told me liked the outfit I had on."

Margaret fidgeted with her keys but didn't go in. It was as if she was trying to filter the information I'd fed her. "It's nice to see you and Rod getting along so well, especially since Matt and he never saw eye to eye."

"So, I've heard." As I placed my hand on our door knob, preparing to go in, I again reminded Margaret to come by later.

"I will," and then she closed her door.

I strolled into the apartment. How could such a small errand unleash such serious consequences, I wondered as I dropped the optical application and the keys on the tiny entranceway table.

Gracie didn't leave me time to speculate. She came bounding into the hallway and almost slammed me against the door. Darn. I forgot I had told her I'd take her out when I returned. "Cool your jets, Mutt. Let me get situated first," which for me meant finding Aunt Zoe. I thought she'd like to know what transpired at the optical store, but I also needed to warn her about company coming. Since she usually hung out on the couch in the living room, my feet took me there first.

Of course, just when you think you know a person's habits, they surprise you. The words "I'm in here, Mary," burst forth from the kitchen area, and I changed course midstream.

Oh, boy. What am I going to find this time? My stomach tightened. Ever since the burnt toast incident, I haven't felt comfortable leaving my roommate alone with any kitchen device, and I worried something terrible had happened while I was gone. I sniffed the air. Nothing's been burnt. "Surely that's a good sign, right, Gracie?" Inclined to agree with me, the mutt wagged her tail.

"Fixing lun...? Oh, my God!" The kitchen looked like something out of Willy Wonka's chocolate factory. "Auntie, there's chocolate everywhere."

"I know. I just hope I haven't ruined your chef apron for you."

My chef apron? Oh, no! The once pure white apron I was given as a going away present by fellow teachers was now heavily coated with huge splotches of chocolate. "Don't blow a gasket, Mary," I muttered under my breath. "It could've been covered in mud."

"What's that?"

"Oh, I was just saying someone told me a good soaking in Tide can cure any stains."

Aunt Zoe forgot her hands were covered in chocolate and accidentally dragged one across her forehead. "Of course, it can. Why didn't I think of that? Well, I feel much better knowing that's resolved. I suppose you're wondering why I made fudge today of all days. Usually I only make it at Christmas." I kept quiet. "I guess the novel I'm reading spurred me on. The doctor had given the woman a box of chocolate, and before I knew it I was craving it," she revealed. "Besides, why should I wait another six months to make candy?"

She made fudge. Concern about the mess was history. My eyes jumped from the table to the counters. "You made fudge? Let me at it."

"Not yet. It's in the freezer."

"What?" I pounced in disbelief. "Why is it already stashed away?"

Aunt Zoe's head bobbed this way and that. "Didn't have any choice. It's still too runny, Mary."

All right, if you must know, I'm not the greatest cook in the Twin Cities or the surrounding suburbs, but even I know fudge shouldn't be runny. "Did you follow the directions exactly the way they were written?" I hastily inquired.

My roommate suddenly looked like she'd lost a few inches off her height. "Well, that's the thing. I didn't have the right amount of some ingredients the recipe called for, so I... substituted. A lot of recipes say you can do that."

Substituted? How could she ruin such a good thing? My eyes rolled back in their sockets. I stomped over to the freezer, opened the door and examined what was supposed to be fudge. Yup, there it sat. A nine-by-thirteen inch aluminum cake pan filled with what looked like chocolate soup. *Hmm? Chocolate soup. Now, why hasn't someone tried marketing that?*

I closed the freezer door. It was a crime to let so much chocolate go to waste no matter what form it took. Perhaps our neighbor could work her culinary magic with my aunt's creation. I knew I couldn't. In the meantime, the kitchen needed some magic of its own and so did my aunt. I started with my aunt. I dampened a piece of paper toweling and rubbed the mess off her head.

Gracie dropped her paws on my feet, and whined. Obviously, my allotted time to get situated was over.

"Shh, girl. Give me a sec." I wasn't taking anyone for a walk while a messy kitchen begs for help. Suddenly a brilliant idea popped into my head. "Auntie, would you like to take Gracie outside while I clean up? It's such a beautiful day, and you haven't had a chance to enjoy it yet."

"Sure."

The mutt yipped and yipped and spun like crazy.

"Hold on, girl. You need your leash first," my roommate said.

"I'll get it," I offered. I took the dog's blue leash off the lone hook that was mounted on the wall by the fridge and handed it to her.

"Thanks. Oh, Mary, I nearly forgot. You had two calls while you were gone."

"Phone calls can wait," I said, swiftly guiding the two of them to the door. The possibility of the mutt's wild antics putting my mismatched dishes into orbit concerned me more.

*****

Thirty minutes later Aunt Zoe and Gracie returned with Mrs. Grimshaw bringing up the rear. "Good timing, ladies," I announced, stepping into the living room. "I fixed ice tea. Would anyone care for some?"

"Oh, yes, please," the nonagenarian replied.

Since my aunt was too absorbed with unhooking a rambunctious dog's leash and never said whether she wanted tea or not, I repeated myself. "Would you like a glass of ice tea too, Auntie?"

She released a hardy laugh. "You bet. That's exactly what I need after a certain mutt's pushed her walk to the limits." She wound the dog's leash around her hand and then asked if I needed any help.

"No. Go relax. I'll take care of everything." I took the leash from her hand and continued on to the kitchen.

When I returned, I found the two women situated on the couch sharing tales of their travels. Not wanting to disrupt the flow of conversation, I set the tray of filled glasses on the coffee table in front of them, stepped back and said, "There you go."

I shouldn't have spoken yet. The thread the older women had weaved between them snapped. "Thank you, Mary," they said in unison.

"You're welcome. I'd offer fudge too, but I understand it's not quite ready," then, noticing Aunt Zoe's distraction with the glasses on the tray, I shot Margaret a quick wink.

The elderly Italian woman picked up her cue like a real trooper. "Yes, fudge can be fickle. Sometimes it takes several hours to harden."

"See, Mary."

I leaned over and collected my glass of ice tea now before moving to the La-Z-Boy. "Yup. The fudge you made just needs more time to chill."

Mrs. Grimshaw finally took a sip of her tea. "This is very tasty, Mary.

"Thank you. It's not hard to make. Open a can of Lipton ice tea, measure out what you need, and add water."

"Ah? It's not from scratch. I would've never guessed. So, have you scheduled the repair work for your Volkswagen yet?"

Why did that major problem have to be dragged up again so soon? Developments after this morning's phone call, namely the optical store application and the mess with the fudge had succeeded in helping me file it to the back of my brain temporarily. Not wanting to appear rude, I offered a brief response. "Yes."

"Oh, Mary," Aunt Zoe said, "I just remembered I still haven't told you about your phone calls."

I brushed her comment aside. "We have company. Wait until later, Auntie."

"But that's what you told me before I went outside with Gracie."

Mrs. Grimshaw interrupted. "I don't mind, Mary, really."

I held my glass of ice tea in midair. "All right, who called?"

Aunt Zoe leaned more my way. "Mr. Griffin said a major incident occurred last night and suggests we go to Plan B."

The nonagenarian clapped her hands together. "Ooo, sounds intriguing. What's your Plan B, Mary, if you don't mind my asking?"

I didn't have the heart to tell the elderly woman I was as clueless as she. I hemmed and hawed. "Ah. Oh. Hmm. You know, it's kind of hush, hush. How about I explain later?"

"Of course," she meekly replied.

My lips parted to share an appreciative smile. It was nice to know some people in this world don't continue to press you for information especially when you have none to give. And right now, well, I barely had a Plan A put together let alone a Plan B.

Plan B? I don't even like the sound of it. Settle down, Mary. Maybe Plan B can save you from taking the part-time job at the optical store. Maybe, but at what cost?

I set my glass down on an end table next to the La-Z-Boy. "And, what about the other caller? You mentioned there were two."

Aunt Zoe scratched the top of her head. "I think he said his name was Judd."

"Judd from Carmichael's?" I asked, tasting the fear rising up from my stomach and ending in the mouth.

My roommate quickly snapped her fingers. "That's it."

I made a stab at the reason he called. "I suppose he wanted to let me know they got my car to the repair shop okay."

"Nope. I don't remember him using those words."

"Well, what exactly did he say?"

"Something about a tiny hiccup."

"What?" If I hadn't set my tall drink down already, my lap would be covered with two cups of ice tea.

My aunt was walking a fine line with me, and I think she knew it. Her hands and head were shaking. "You might want to call them. I'm… not sure I can explain it right."

Mrs. Grimshaw began to get up. "Oh, dear. Perhaps this isn't such a good time to visit."

"Yes, it is," I hurriedly stated. "Stay put. I won't be on the phone long."

I jumped out of the La-Z-Boy and ran to the bedroom to retrieve my cell phone from the nightstand. The second the phone was in my clutches, I rushed to close the bedroom door. I was afraid the news Judd was about to share wasn't pretty, and I didn't want my swearing to reach the other women's ears. I had a certain image to uphold.

I was right. Closing the door was a good decision. On a scale from one to twenty, twenty being the worst, Judd's news sat right at twenty. *Why did it have to happen to me, Lord?* I felt like tossing an object against the wall, but I didn't know what to grab other than my cell phone, and that cost too much to break. Besides, it was my only contact with the world outside the Foley's four walls.

After my conversation with Judd ended, I hid in the bedroom for another ten minutes before rejoining the others. I needed time to compose myself.

Mrs. Grimshaw's soft, calm motherly tone broke through to me first. "What happened, Mary? You look like you've been hit by a semi-truck."

"That's exactly the way I feel." I grabbed a Kleenex from the tissue box resting on the edge of the coffee table and blew my nose before continuing. "Judd said some idiot plowed into the back of my car when the tow truck was stopped at an intersection light on Highway 95."

"Oh, Mary." Aunt Zoe stood and threw her arms around me.

"You know the irony of it all?" I softly stated.

"What?" our neighbor inquired.

I released a heavy sigh. "The tow truck was only four blocks from Paul's Body Shop when the accident happened."

~15~

I stood in the kitchen doorway and stupidly stared at the taupe-colored western boots I had stashed by a chair the previous night and quizzed myself for the umpteenth time how on earth I had ever gotten myself into this surreal horse mess.

Don't worry. There's no need to explain. I had only myself to blame. I wanted to be a little more like Matt. His line of work was always changing. It never grew stale. In the teaching profession, however, one repeats the same thing over and over year after year.

Listening to Reed Griffin's message on Matt's machine made me think this was my big hurrah, a chance to break loose, do something different and get paid for it. But when I actually spoke with Reed in person, I began to backpedal. Had I flipped my lid? Why did I ever think I could help anyone solve a mystery?

The answer wasn't long in coming. *Heck, yes.* Who fingers the bad guy in a show long before anyone else? *Me.* Who relishes complicated puzzles the most in our family? *This unemployed teacher.* Who did fellow teachers dub Queen of Classroom Mysteries two years in a row due to finding the greatest number of missing objects, including Billy's gym shoes and Sally's trip permission slip? *Little ol' me.*

Too bad I didn't think through the sleuthing deal a little longer. Elementary kids' problems are a walk in the park. Those in the adult world could be life threatening.

"Come on, Mary. It's getting late," Aunt Zoe soberly announced, "You can't afford to procrastinate any longer."

"You're right," I gingerly replied, stepping into the kitchen, pulling out the chair where my footwear rested, and plopping down, "but for the record I still hate these cowgirl boots." I reached for a boot and squeezed my non-Cinderella foot into it.

Aunt Zoe pressed her hands on the back of the chair being occupied by me. "You'll change your mind eventually, niece."

I doubted it. One boot on and one to go rang through my head. "I can't believe this is the only pair of boots Sal's had in my size." I was referring to Sal's Cowgirl Couture on East Lake Street in Minneapolis.

Aunt Zoe bent over to take a closer look. "Oh, my, aren't they darling. I wouldn't mind owning a pair."

"Hmmph. Well, I don't like them. I specifically asked Sal's sales clerk to let me try on four different types: Old West, Navajo Americana, Roper and Justin. Do you see any of those brands gracing my feet?"

My roommate vehemently shook her head.

"Of course not," I pounced pointedly. I ended up with a Durango pair that cost $130 instead. I bet you anything the owner of Sal's ordered that young college gal to push last year's style out the door, no matter what the customer wanted. I mean, who in their right mind wears boots that are decorated with a heart design made from felt that is running up and down the whole upper portion of their boots?"

My aunt's lips split open, but I didn't give her the pleasure of feeding me a response.

"I'll tell you who," I ranted on, "A cowgirl who's on the prowl."

"On the prowl for what?" Auntie innocently inquired.

With both boots on now, I stomped my feet on the linoleum and then stood. "Give it a couple seconds to sink in."

Aunt Zoe's face flushed. "Oh? Ohhhhh."

Ready to face the horse world head on, or so I thought, I grabbed the keys and shooed my roommate out the door. Wouldn't you know, just as my fingers inserted the key in the lock, the phone stopped me cold. "Probably Reed," I spit out, "hope he's not calling to cancel our plans." Internally I was wishing the opposite. I ran back into the apartment and picked up the closest landline.

"*Buongiorno*, Mary. I'm glad I caught you before you left for the Bar X." It was our elderly neighbor Mrs. Grimshaw.

"Hi. What's up? Do you need us to run an errand for you?"

"No, dear, nothing like that. Do you remember the Belgian horse I told you about the day we checked out Matt's apartment?"

"Kind'a. Wasn't her name Ginger?"

"Yes, that's right. Well, something dawned on me from back then that might help your case."

"Oh?" Intrigued, I patiently waited to hear more.

"According to my parents' friends, Ginger was extremely smart. After she watched how the gates opened and closed several times, she started to let the other horses out."

"Whoa! You're thinking Reed Griffin might have a horse clever enough to do the same?"

"*Si*. It's possible."

"Which means there's no human involvement." Hmm? *Easy peasy case, Mary, if that's the real scenario.* My day suddenly felt a lot brighter. All I have to do is uncover which horse is capable of unlocking the gates and jumping high fences. "*Grazie*, Margaret."

"You're most welcome. *Arrivederci*."

*****

Reed's lips brimmed over as he caught sight of us gals clamoring up the hill leading to the horse barn. "Good morning, ladies," he shouted. "My, gosh you two look so charming I hate to see you get dirty."

"We'll be fine," Aunt Zoe gushed nervously. She quickly nudged my elbow and said for my ears only, "You'd better agree with me, Mary, if you don't want Reed to think otherwise."

"It's easy for you to convince him everything's grand," I said above a whisper. "You're interested in the man. I'm not."

She blushed. "How can you say that? I barely know him."

"Ah, come on. Your cheeks are so bright they match your hair color."

"They do not." She fumbled with her purse.

"What are you looking for?"

"My mirror."

"Forget it. We don't have time for that. The client is waiting."

The minute we reached the top of the hill, my stomach lurched forward. It was probably looking for a way out like the rest of my body, but it was too late. There's no escaping. I'm committed to this case, and I'll see it through even if horses scared me to death.

I cautiously threw out the line my aunt wanted me so desperately to give. "Nothing to worry about, Reed. We gals know what we're doing." *Father O'Day is going to be pretty happy hearing my confession when this case is over with. Hopefully, he won't give me too stiff a penance.*

The man standing in front of us was clothed in similar duds seen on our previous visit: Twins baseball cap, Rustler jeans, long-sleeved checkered shirt and dark black boots coated in dry mud. He probably throws down his Fleet Farm card once a year to obtain all his necessities. "So, Miss Malone, have you given any thought to how you're going to proceed?"

"Yes, sir."

"Good. It was bad enough when two of our horses showed up on Clint Russell's property, but now three have ended up there."

Even though my toes felt like they were being squeezed into pretzels and I really wanted to chuck this whole horse sleuthing thing, I tried to exude confidence all around when I said, "I plan to patrol the parameters of your sixty acres until late tonight."

Reed let out a loud snort. "Ma'am, that ain't going to cut it."

I moved back a couple steps now, unsure what to say next. "It won't?"

"Heck, no. You gotta take the bull by the horns—get to know my workers and the people who trust me with their horses. See if I'm reading someone wrong."

My client rubbed the broad jaw connected to his oval face. "I used to pride myself on how well I deciphered people's inner-ticking's, but since this crazy horse stuff began I'm beginning to doubt myself."

Aunt Zoe really had it bad for the man. When she thoughtlessly reached out for Reed's arm, I cleared my throat to stop her. "Ahem." Her guilty hand immediately shot to her side.

Even though my aunt knew I didn't approve of what she almost did, it didn't stop her from digging out another form of acting from her repertoire. She batted her thickly doctored eyelashes at Reed. "Don't fret, Reed. Mary and I are both committed to doing whatever it takes to clear your problem up, aren't we, Mary?"

A thick, sweet "You bet," reluctantly tumbled from my mouth.

"Oh, Miss Zoe," Reed said, "I'm sorry if you misunderstood me. I didn't expect you to work in the barn. Why, you're just a secretary."

She gave the man a questioning stare.

Reed became tongue-tied. "That is, unless you prefer to be in there."

"No, no." She flapped her hand. "I can be as flexible as you want me to be. Where can I help out?"

Lucky dog. I'd give my next year's paycheck to stay away from the horses. That is if I have a job next year.

Hmm? Maybe I don't have to fret. All the horses will be out in the pasture. *Yeah, right.*

Reed kicked up some dirt with his boot and then tugged on the visor of his cap. The man was stalling. Probably didn't have a clue what my aunt could do.

"Well let's see. I think there's plenty of paperwork to be filed and phone calls to be made. And the cook can always use extra hands in the kitchen."

Before I could make a smart remark about Aunt Zoe's kitchen attributes, she kindly offered to help with the office work. *Good choice.* At least she can't poison anyone.

"All right then," I said stalling as long as I could. "I'll just mosey over to the barn and get started. Remember, Zoe, I'm within earshot if you need anything." Hint. Hint.

Aunt Zoe took a while to respond. It appears my client has helped keep her mind off Edward as well as me. Nothing else seemed to matter when he was around. It was like he'd cast a spell on her. "Yeah. Okay," she finally replied. "See you at lunch if not before."

My jean-covered legs switched gears now as they slowly began to maneuver their way towards the entrance to the barn. When I was about halfway there, Reed's voice rang out. Maybe he had something important to share. I quickly tilted my head in his direction. "Yes?"

"Nice pair of boots, Mary."

Yuk. Why couldn't I have been born an ostrich, so I could bury my head?

~16~

The instant I swept through the barn door the intense concoction of hay, manure and wet sawdust wrapped its tentacles around me so tightly I thought I'd lose my breakfast. *Ish!* I would've never agreed to return to the Bar X if it had smelled this badly the first time around. *Flee while you can.* I ground my heels in. "No way. It's not going to be bantered about I'm a bona fide wimp."

I leaned over and inhaled deeply, hoping to find fresh air lingering somewhere. Stupid move. The mixture of delicious barn odors latched on to my respiratory system and hung on for the ride of its life. *Oh, crap.* I put on a brave front, pulled my body to full height, and surveyed the surroundings like a soldier deep in the midst of danger.

Truthfully speaking, acting like a soldier wasn't all it was cracked up to be. Twenty pairs of huge, soulful eyes bore into me. The scene should've invoked laughter, but I found myself scared down to my undies.

There's more than one way to lick a problem.

Ah, yes. How could I forget? Confrontation. "One of you ate Fiona's steering wheel," I boldly proclaimed, swiftly shifting my eyes from one horse to the next, sharing my own mean look. "And it shouldn't take me too long to figure out which of you did the nasty deed." I stayed where I was and kept up the grim look.

A sharp masculine voice, sounding close at hand, managed to interrupt my determination to find the guilty party. "Are you here for a ride, Miss?"

My head snapped to attention. "Huh?" The fellow gaining on me was short in stature and carried a medium-sized belly. "Ah, no. Mr. Griffin said I should report to someone here in the barn."

A heavy head of rusty-colored hair and scruffy matching beard bobbed along as the man examined me from head to toe. "That would be me. So, you're my sidekick for the day," he muttered under his breath. "I wasn't expecting a woman."

"Is that going to be a problem?" I inquired cautiously.

He flipped a hand in the air. "Nah. Not with me." The man around my brother Matt's age— mid-forties— wiped the same thick, sweaty textured hand on his jeans and offered it to me. "I'm Terrence. People call me Terry."

"And I'm Mary."

Terry barely grinned. "Well, that's short enough to remember. Welcome aboard, Mary."

"Thanks," I said weakly.

The man went on now. "Before Reed told me I was getting help, I thought I'd have to do double duty with Jackson out sick."

"What all needs to get done?" I asked, wanting to get on with what I originally came here for.

"Gotta clean the stalls, fill the water troughs, check the feed and do some grooming." The man looked at my feet one more time. "At least you wore the right footwear for the work. You never know what you might step in."

Clean the stalls? Groom the horses? I took a couple steps back. *Uh-uh.* I didn't sign up to get close and personal with any horse. *No. Absolutely not. I'll walk out of here. Go ahead. Try.* My legs stiffened. I was beaten to a pulp, and I knew it. "Ah, is there a certain time the stalls have to be cleaned out by?" I asked wearily.

Terry let go of a belly laugh. "Kinda. We'll do half now, take a break and then finish up."

I rubbed my hands together but didn't move an inch. How could I? There was no broom leaning against a wall, and Terry never said what to do with the horses or the stuff I removed from the stall for that matter.

My so-called supervisor studied my face for a second. He probably was cussing under his breath the fact that he got stuck with a dumb broad like me. I thought about blowing my cover, fortunately I didn't have to. "You look like there are questions swimming around in that pretty little head of yours. Why don't you spit'em out?"

"Sorry. I don't mean to cause any problems, but I was wondering if the horses get upset when we're disturbing their domain?"

Terry let loose with a deep throaty laugh this time. "You're new at this, aren't you?"

I shifted my focus to the hard packed dirt under my feet. "Am I that transparent?"

"'Fraid so, but don't worry none, Miss. I won't have you canned cuz you're a greenhorn. A lot of folks are taking on whatever work they can find nowadays, including some of my own siblings."

Even though this dude's kindness seemed to be genuine, I had to wonder if it was meant to throw me off balance. I lifted my head and flashed a smile. "Thanks. I really do need the income." At least no one could ever fault me for that line. I was in desperate need of money. "What about the horses, Terry? Do they get riled up when someone's messing around in their stall?"

"Nah." He pointed over his shoulder towards the field. "See that group of horses out in the pasture?" I nodded. "Well, they'll graze there until you're done cleaning their stalls."

"Oh?"

*****

"Beep, beep." Yippy. The tiny device hidden in my pocket was about to give me a break, something I've desperately wished for the past three hours while pitching and hauling manure and soiled sawdust to a stinky compost pile surrounded by thousands of flies. "Beep, beep." I hurriedly rubbed off the grit from my filthy, blistered hands onto my jeans before retrieving the phone from my side pocket.

"*Buongiorno*! Have I caught you at a bad time?"

"Sort of," I said in a library setting voice, "but that's okay." I took a quick scan of my surroundings. Terry wasn't visible. Come to think of it, I hadn't seen him since he directed me to the stalls when I first got here. Probably safe to talk, I thought. "Is everything okay, Mrs. Grimshaw? Gracie's not causing trouble is she?"

"Oh, no," the elderly woman readily replied. "I was curious to know what Mr. Griffin said regarding my suggestion this morning."

"I haven't asked yet. Been too caught up in other things." Like tripping over the plastic rake because I forgot where I laid it and getting soaked from juggling water pails to and fro, but she didn't need to know that. No one did.

"That's all right. I understand. I've also been giving Zoe's bad batch of fudge some thought and came up with a couple ideas for you. I hate to see chocolate go to waste."

"Great." I just knew Mrs. Grimshaw would have a solution. "What can I do?"

"Mix it with cookie dough or put it on vanilla ice cream."

Fudge-topped ice cream. "Sounds yummy." I wish I didn't have to wait to indulge. My stomach groaned right on cue as if to acknowledge it agreed with me. Half expecting Terry to reappear any moment, I kept a watchful eye on the barn door while my caller continued to speak.

"Mary, tell me what you were referring to earlier."

I scratched my head trying to remember what I said to Margaret when she first called. "I'm not sure what you're getting at."

"Being caught up in other things. Did you mean digging up stuff concerning your case?"

Oh, Yeah. I've been digging up plenty all right. The darn stuff's been dropping around me like flies. "Not really. Maybe Aunt Zoe has. She's off flirting with our client."

Margaret giggled. "Good for her. So, you're just sitting in Matt's car keeping an eye on the property?"

"I wish."

"What's that?"

"I'm, ah, not in the car. One of Reed's employees has me changing bedding."

Margaret's light tone turned serious. "*Non capisco!* What does changing sheets have to do with the horses on Griffin's property?"

I chuckled. Life would be so much simpler if I was actually doing what the elderly woman thought I was doing. "I'm not changing sheets."

"You're not? But you just said…"

"I was referring to animal bedding."

"Ah? Like straw and wood chips?"

"Yup. You wouldn't believe how much these animals pee and poop, especially the mares."

Her voice raised a notch. "You're working with the horses? But the other day you told me you didn't think it was necessary to be around them."

I rubbed my chin. "You know the old saying 'When in Rome….' Well it's a little hard not to when your client assigns you the task."

"Didn't you explain your plan?"

Someone waltzed through the door and was closing in on me rapidly. It had to be Terry. Luckily my back was to him. I stooped down and whispered into the phone, "If I don't go along with him, he might hire a new sleuth."

"Oh? Well, I better let you get back to work then. *Buona fortuna.*"

Sensing someone was directly behind me; I hastily stashed the phone and stood.

"Are you ready for a break, little lady?" Terry inquired.

My stomach rumbled again. "Does that answer your question?"

"I guess." He pointed to my pant pocket. "I noticed you had your cell phone out. Were you making a call?"

Shoot. This guy doesn't miss a beat. "No. My mother was checking on me," I lied. "I told her I was working and would have to talk to her tonight."

Terry turned ornery after the explanation which I hadn't expected. Perhaps he didn't buy the lie. "Look, we can't afford to be talking during work hours. If you plan to stay here a while, make sure your mother understands that."

Whew! The guy went from angel to devil in two seconds flat. I'm going to have to be mighty careful around him. "Yes, Sir."

~17~

Aunt Zoe thrust herself upon me the instant I entered Reed Griffin's ranch-style house. "Mary," she wailed, "what have you done to yourself?" Before I had the chance to spit out a reply, she tossed me aside like a worn-out shoe. The strong odor seeping from my clothes probably caused the rift. I had noted her nose was slightly turned up when she stepped back.

While I remained glued to my spot, Auntie reached in one of her pant pockets and produced an Avon perfume sample which she tossed to me. "Here. Pat this on your clothing. It might help. But as far as your atrocious hairdo is concerned, you're on your own."

"What's wrong with my hair?"

"Remember the scarecrow in the *Wizard of Oz*?"

Don't panic. Maybe your hair isn't as bad as she's making it out to be. But what if...? Instinctively, my hands shot to the matter at hand, the thick, straight cropped hair that hung loosely over my ears.

Yuk. Sawdust and straw had been added to my locks. The only female remedy for this dire problem was a trip to the nearest powder room. Too bad I required something before I bolted like a colt. I hastily pointed to a hot-pink-and-purple-splotched purse, the size of a kitchen sink, resting on the cream-colored Formica counter by the fridge. The purse belonged to my aunt and usually held anything one needed in a crunch. "Zoe, do you happen to have aspirin stashed in there? My back's killing me."

"Sure thing, Sweetie," then she dashed to her purse and got what I requested.

I took the small Bayer bottle from her. "Thanks. I'll be back in a jiff." Of course, *jiff* had a different connotation today. It meant as fast as I could manage while dragging a painful body to and fro.

Believe me, if cartwheels had gotten me to the nearest bathroom any faster, I would've opted for that instead. But, then again, I doubt it. This thirty-something body of mine hadn't done cartwheels since entering puberty. Besides, who in their right mind did cartwheels when their back is on fire?

The three-quarter bath, set off from the kitchen by only mere inches, offered exactly what I needed: water to wash down the pills and a plain, medium-sized black-metal framed mirror to check out my "A-hem" unique hairdo.

Auntie's comment, along with what my hands touched, should've been sufficient warning for what I'd find once I caught sight of my reflection in the mirror, but it wasn't. Seeing how frightful I looked, I almost jumped out of my skin. "Holy moley!" Good thing no single men my age were lurking in the kitchen when I'd walked through. They would've thought the Bride of Frankenstein had come home to roost.

I tossed the aspirins in my mouth and hurriedly washed them down so I could work with the hair. Without a beautician standing by giving advice, I'd have to rely on myself to correct the mess. I thrust my hands in my pockets. No comb. No problem. I fanned my fingers apart as far as they'd go and ran them through my hair several times. After I finished primping, I glanced at the wood floor. A pool of sawdust and straw formed a close-knit circle, similar to wagon trains preparing for attack.

Great. How do I get rid of that much fallout? This isn't my house. I don't know where anything's kept. I looked down at my boots. They'd work. I toed the mess over to the wastebasket and picked up the container where I planned to hide it. A tiny, square shiny object was lying on the floor. Not knowing if it was important or just trash, I stashed it in my jean pocket until I could ask about it later.

When I rejoined the others at the well-worn oak table, I discovered they'd already been sampling the humongous sugar cookies and strong brewed coffee. My lips trembled. At least they left enough cookies for me to sample. *Look out hips. Make way for the treats.*

Barely ten minutes into my break, Terry jumped up from his seat and threw a serious glance my way indicating he was done. "Ready to get back in the saddle, Slim?"

Is he crazy? I shot a quick look at my half empty cup of java, the only beverage offered with the sweets. Apparently a horse boarding facility doesn't allow for idle chit chat, only enough time to stuff a cookie down one's belly and to scorch one's lips with a single cup of java. Since I'm not a fan of coffee, the amount of liquid rationed out didn't bother me in the least. If I had to leave some coffee in my cup, so be it, but being called *Slim* well, that was something else altogether.

The man will never know how much I appreciated it. Too bad it wasn't true. I'd never had an hourglass figure and probably never would. That's not to say I'll stop trying. There's always a new diet fad ad that catches my interest. As a matter of fact, just the other day I read about one called the Belly Fat Diet. I forced a smile now, and said, "Yup."

Taking her cue from me about getting back to work, Aunt Zoe immediately stood and began to clear the table. "Don't work too hard, you two."

Don't work too hard. Is she being sarcastic or what? How does one not do that around this place? These people aren't dairy farmers. They start at the crack of dawn and work till sometimes eleven at night or later. Stalls have to be cleaned, eats and water supplied as needed and fences repaired. Horses need to be groomed, bathed, shoed, exercised, trained and given pills and shots. *Whew.* Just ticking off that list of work in my head wore me out. There's no way this unemployed teacher ever plans to switch gears and work here full time. Even the thought of substituting is more delightful.

As soon as we left the confines of Reed's cozy country kitchen behind, Terry inquired about my first day on the job. "How you doing? Feel a little more relaxed about what's expected of you?"

His dumb questions ranked right up there with Aunt Zoe's gem a few minutes ago. What did he expect me to say? "*I adore this work. Ever since I was knee-high to a grasshopper, I've dreamt of nothing but scooping up sawdust and horse poop. And now, thanks to you, I know how to do it properly.*" I swung my body to face him, and gave what I thought an appropriate reply. "Okay, I guess. I never realized how much work is involved in caring for horses. It's nothing like owning a cat or dog, is it?"

Apparently Terry thought the last comment hilarious. He started choking so bad I almost had to use the Heimlich maneuver on him. "It sure ain't. And what we did so far this morning, Mary, why that's just a drop in the ol' bucket."

Oh, boy. *"A drop in the ol' bucket for him maybe. I'm the one cleaning the stalls while he's doing who knows what outside of the barn."*

After we reentered the barn and walked a quarter of the way in, Terry signaled for me to stop. "What'dya think, are you ready for another horse task to be added to your day?"

My stomach dropped a couple feet. What could he possibly be thinking of passing on to little ol' me? Surely, he's figured out how scared I am to be around these fifteen and sixteen hand animals; I'd made my concerns loud and clear earlier this morning. While I stood there worried to death about what chore was coming my way next, I noticed the stalls cleaned before break were now filled. When the heck did those other horses come in? Sleuthing's what I'm here for, not grunt work. *I'll tell you one thing, Mary, if this new job requires sitting on a horse's back, you can walk the gangplank.* "I guess. What have you got in mind?"

"The horses need to be groomed after all the stalls are cleaned."

Groomed? Ponies and miniature horses pranced through my head. Unfortunately, this guy wasn't referring to them. He meant those big suckers weighing 1,000-1,200 pounds taking up space in these stalls. I hit the wall. Flipped out. "What?"

The unbridled outburst created quite a stir. The horses snorted wildly while Terry braced his lean body against a stall waiting for the shock waves to settle.

Too late to undo the damage I had unleashed. My hands flew to my mouth. "Sorry," I barely squeaked, "I thought I got stung by a bee." A fib of course. "It's happened to me three times as a kid, and I can't seem to get over it."

The man accepted what I said without reservation. "It was more likely a horse fly, but I understand where you're coming from. The problem is horses are quite skittish. The tiniest thing can set them off. When you're around these big fellas, you just gotta pretend you're in a library setting."

Yeah, right. The day a library is the same as a barn full of horses that's the day I take a rocket ship to Neptune.

"You know, speak in calm, soothing tones."

"Got it."

"Good."

I took a deep breath, already forgetting the first hard lesson I learned when I strolled into the barn first thing this morning. Luckily, I didn't blow out my sinuses, but my reflexes kicked in. I grabbed my nose. It only made matters worse. I began to cough uncontrollably and dropped my hand to my side. Once I stopped hacking away, I managed to say, "Horses are groomed every day?"

"Yup. It prevents skin irritation and chafing. Plus, it helps us pick up on the horses' moods and find any wounds or swellings before they're too serious." He waved his hand towards the back of the barn. "See that black sixteen hand fella in the last stall?" I shook my head. "His name's Cortez. I'll go over the basic grooming procedures for him. Come on."

Sixteen hands? Hmm? I swiftly dug through the recesses of my mind to find out exactly how many inches a hand equaled. It wasn't that long ago this elementary teacher shared the info with her students.

Eureka. A hand is equivalent to four inches. So, Cortez is the height of an average-sized woman. I guess I'm okay with that. If a horse and I are on the same playing field, so to speak, we should see eye-to-eye. "Ah, all right," I rapidly replied, even though my body convinced my mind there was no urgency to get to the back of the barn any sooner than I had to.

When I finally drew close to Cortez's stall, he released the most intense glare just like my mother does when she's upset with me; the only difference was I hadn't done anything to irritate him yet.

I tried not to convey any fear, but that's pretty difficult when you've spent your last thirty years trying to forget a bad incident. Luckily, Cortez also reminded me of *Black Beauty*. He was all shiny and silky too. My lips suddenly parted without me telling them to. "Wow. He's a real beaut."

Terry nodded solemnly. "Yes. Yes, he is."

"How old is he?"

"Five. He was gelded last year at this time."

Good news, Mary. No need to worry. At least I didn't think so. If I'm not mistaken, when Aunt Zoe brought me up to speed on horses, she said gelded ones are calmer.

Yes. That's what she said. Okay, everything is fine. I can relax.

Leave it to good ol' Terry to ruin what calmness I'd just claimed. "This guy still has some feistiness in him though. But we're working on it, aren't we, Cortez?"

Hearing his name, the horse lifted his head and then dropped it.

My stomach went bonkers again. Why did Terry feel the need to pass on that tidbit? Did he want me to squirm even more?

With trepidation uppermost in my mind, my feet tried to make a speedy departure but were blocked by a large wooden box directly in line with the stall. It wasn't the first box I had seen like this. The barn was filled with them. I should've snuck a peek inside one, but I never had the chance.

"Care to guess what's stored in there, Mary?"

I gave a lame reply. "Extra food?"

"Nope. The tack locker holds horse supplies, including grooming ones."

Hot dog! Just what I didn't need to know.

~18~

Once the lid of the tack locker was tossed back, Terry whipped out all the grooming supplies, quickly demonstrated how each was used, and then left them outside the stall for me. "There you are. Pretty simple, huh?" I grinned. *Simple for you maybe.* "All right, Mary, you can finish up with the stalls now and then begin grooming the horses down at this end of the barn."

My throat constricted like it had been placed in a vise. "Are you going to supervise the grooming?"

"Nah. You'll do all right. I got another daily chore that needs attending to, so it's best if I start at the other end."

You know how cats react when they think they're going to be given a bath, they go into panic mode. Well, that scene fits me perfectly. "I...I really don't think I can handle the grooming, without someone overseeing me, Terry."

"Sure, you can. Just remember to never stand directly behind the horse's hind legs, and you'll be fine."

A lot he knows. There's no way I'd be fine around horses. Horses big or small and even in between frightened me. What other daily duty could Terry be so anxious to take care of at the other end of the barn that he couldn't even watch me groom one measly horse?

I gave the man a questioning glance. He had me worried. Was he going to throw another curve my way later? And if he kept this disappearing act up, how the heck was I supposed to find out what makes him tick?

Terry examined my face. "You're going to do serious damage to that forehead of yours, Missy, if you don't watch out. There's nothing to fret over."

"I tend to frown a lot. It's a bad habit. I was merely wondering if whatever you're doing next would eventually include me, is all."

"Heck no. You're what we call a greenhorn. Shooing and hoof cleaning are tended to by special people who have plenty of horse experience under their belts."

Yes! Finally, someone up there's watching over me. I relaxed and permitted a broad smile to spread from one ear to the other. Being confined to the twelve-by-twelve-foot playpen of an animal I was extremely fearful of was bad enough; I didn't need broken toes and bruises to boot.

The minute Terry left me to my own devices, the smile evaporated, and I became jittery all over again. How could I enter the lion's den? Even though I wasn't that familiar with horses, I'd read plenty of novels and seen enough movies in which horses play a prominent role to know they've an uncanny ability to pick up human vibes and react accordingly. "Get a grip, lady," I mumbled with bravado. *What's the worst that can happen when you connect with a horse?* "I'll hyperventilate."

With the brief pep talk out of the way, I returned to cleaning the rest of the stalls, which didn't take long since they weren't as full of poop as the others. The down side—grooming was still beckoning me, and I felt like a train about to derail.

Before beginning my new project, I ran Terry's directives through my mind one more time. "Start on left side, low end of neck. Use curry comb first—brings dirt to the surface. Rub comb in circular motion." Okay. I think that's it. I'm ready.

I gazed down at the various brushes resting at my feet. "Oops." There are too many brushes. That's got to be the soft brush. No, that one is. This one's the stiff brush I think, or is it the mane and tail brush? Soft brush, stiff brush, face brush, tail brush, curry comb. My head was spinning. I know I'm supposed to begin with the curry comb, but which one was it?

I continued to stare at the five items. "It's got to be the soft rubbery circular one that doesn't look like a brush or comb." Hmm. I wonder if anyone's ever thought of using a curry comb to loosen the sand on the scalp and skin after a day at the beach. It could be a hot item at the dollar store. I stooped down now, picked up what I'd figured was the curry comb and entered Cortez's stall.

The horse lifted his star-marked head to medium height and greeted me with a nicker. His ears were relaxed and pointed backwards. I recalled seeing them pricked forward when Terry was demonstrating how to groom him. Should I be concerned?

I forged ahead. The grooming had to get done. "Nice horsey. You're nice, right?" Cortez didn't reply. I stretched out my hand and placed the palm side near his nostrils like Terry had done. It's a get-acquainted gesture. Tells the horse you're not his enemy. "Okay. It's up to you, Cortez."

Cortez took his time sniffing my shaky hand. I didn't blame him. It was vibrating so hard I thought it was going to take off for parts unknown and never return.

Amazingly, with all the hand action going on, Cortez didn't snort or charge me. Surely that was a good sign, right?

When I thought sufficient time had elapsed for the get acquainted session, I dropped my arm to its normal position and inquired how the animal was doing. "Nice Cortez," I said in almost a purring voice. "Got any aches or pains today?"

The horse raised his head slightly and neighed into my ear.

"Nope. Good, because I never intended to give you a massage or rub your legs with stinky ointment when I walked in here. That's what the pros get paid for."

The jet black horse gently nudged my shoulder and then briefly neighed again.

"All right. All right. I hear ya. Let's get to it then. Spruce you up for those mares out in the pasture, shall we?"

*****

"Mary. Mary, come quickly," Aunt Zoe cried as she came charging through the barn door.

Something serious must be taking place outside. Without thinking, I jerked the *stiff* brush. The quick movement wouldn't have been a big deal if the brush hadn't been resting on Cortez's underbelly, an extremely sensitive part, but it was. His hind legs suddenly flew out from under him. Thankfully, I wasn't on the receiving end, but I still shook from my head to my pinky toes.

Aunt Zoe's face took on a deadly ashen appearance. "Oh, my God! Are you all right, Mary?"

"Yes." *No thanks to you.* "What's going on?" I asked, still shaking in my boots from the near fatal encounter I just had with Cortez. "More trouble with a horse or Clint?"

My aunt shook her vibrant red head. "Neither."

What? She almost got me killed, and it wasn't for either of those reasons.

I snapped. "Can't whatever you need wait? I've got a lot on my plate before the lunch hour."

Whoa! Hold on there, partner. Did you hear what you just said? Less than fifteen minutes ago you were looking for the nearest escape hatch, and two seconds ago your life was almost snuffed out.

Aunt Zoe stood her ground. "No, it can't wait," she replied flatly. "You need to drop what you're doing immediately and come with me."

"All righty. I'm coming, but this better be worth the interruption." I hurriedly locked the gate on Cortez's stall and then put the stiff brush with the others before I followed my aunt outside.

As it turned out, my aunt's destination wasn't too far from where we exited the barn. Reed Griffin was already there, huddled over a wooden crate I assumed to be lodged between two barn boards. I wasn't sure what he was up to, maybe searching for an item he'd dropped."

It's so exciting, Mary," my aunt cooed, stationing herself next to our client, "Reed's barn cat, Mini, is having her litter. Three have come so far, but he thinks there'll be more."

That's what all the hoopla was about? A darn cat? My eyes rested on Reed. He reminded me of an expectant father waiting for the doctor to pronounce the good news.

"Well, she had eight the last time," my client shared, "so I figure maybe five this time."

He turned to look at me now. My face had turned to stone. "It's all right, Mary. You don't have to worry about, Terry. I'll tell him you've never witnessed animals being born before."

How did he know that? My stone face cracked. I shook my head to clear my thoughts. *Use your brains, girl. He's crafting a fib. Aunt Zoe's been gone so long she wouldn't know if we've had animals or not.*

"Thanks. I really don't want to get on his bad side." I snuck a peek at the kittens now. "So, how long do you think it will take for the rest of Mini's babies to be born?"

Reed scratched his cap-covered head. "Hard to tell. I think another ten minutes ought to do it."

Without thinking, I reached in the box to pick up a newborn. Mini snarled. Reed's hand instantly flew underneath mine. If he hadn't reacted so fast, I swear Mini would've torn my hand off. "Gotta give her time with her babies," my client warned.

I backed away. "Of course, I wasn't thinking."

"Plus," my aunt continued, "the babies' eyes can be damaged if you touch them too soon, isn't that right, Reed?"

"That's right. The kittens shouldn't be touched for at least five days." He held out his hands for inspection. "The germs on a person's hands can cause their eyes to matt up and never open."

My eyeballs felt like they had been blasted out of their sockets. "Really?" Just what I didn't need to know, I almost blinded a kitten. It's my parents' fault. If they would've let us kids have pets when we were growing up, we'd know what to expect of the animal kingdom.

Reed easily brushed the incident aside. Probably used to seeing other's do the same. "How's it going in the barn? Have you heard or seen anything unusual yet?"

I ran my hands back and forth along the side of my jeans. "To be honest, Reed, I haven't had much of a chance to chat with Terry, and with my lack of horse experience I'm not quite sure what I should be paying attention to. What I really think I should focus on is setting up a lookout near where the other incidents have occurred."

"No one's saying you can't do that, Mary." Now, Reed gave his full attention to the elderly woman in his company. "You know, tonight's one of our many potluck suppers where we sit around the ol' campfire, tell tales, and sing songs with close family members and those who board with us.

"It would be the perfect excuse for you ladies to remain beyond the expected working hours. Don't you agree, Zoe?"

"Oh, yes. Your little soiree would be an excellent screen for what we really plan to do."

Good gravy. Listen to her. I've turned my roommate in to a detective. Well, this gal doesn't give a rip about some stupid cookout. All I want to know is how the heck am I going to be alert for late night activities after working my butt off all day and then being stuffed with heavy grub?

~19~

My back, head, and feet felt like a herd of elephants had trampled over them several times. All that pain and for what? Today's undercover work revealed nothing unless one counted the small scraps pertaining to riding stables.

For instance, rubber mats need to be covered with at least eight inches of bedding. Lime's a great deodorizer. No one will ever ask you out on a date if you've slipped in a stall occupied by a mare. And most importantly, never ever look a horse directly in the eyes.

Since I didn't harbor any future plans concerning horses at the moment, the info regarding them seemed insignificant to me and thankfully not obligatory to retain.

Perched on a crazy canvas camping stool, I was the epitome of grace under fire, watching each new arrival as they joined the cookout. *Yeah, right.* Strands of unkempt hair swept across my smudged face, sweat oozed from every pore, and my grungy stinky jeans were as stiff as a board.

Too bad I hadn't been invited to a masquerade ball instead of a riding stable cookout. No one would know who I was, and I wouldn't have to mingle with all these horse-loving people. They'll recognize the fake among them as soon as my lips parted.

On the other hand, Aunt Zoe seemed to find an element of comfort in this gathering. Maybe it reminded her of safari treks taken with Uncle Edward. "Isn't this fun, Mary?" she said, stabbing her hot dog with a long, two-pronged fork and then holding it over the open fire.

I had just bitten down on my hotdog bun and was more concerned about ketchup dribbling down the front of my shirt than any question my aunt might have pertaining to the stupid cookout, but I complied. "Yeah, a real dilly. I wouldn't have missed it for the world. Right up there with jumping in a Minnesota lake on a cool summer day."

My sarcastic remarks zipped right past my aunt and disappeared into oblivion. "I'm so glad Reed included us. All we'd be doing at home is watching some dumb summer reruns on TV," she said as she backpedaled a few paces from the fire.

I nodded, wondering what time it was getting to be. "What about the big bowl of chocolate fudge ice cream we'd be pigging out on too?" I glanced at my wrist. Darn. Nothing there. "Zoe, I can't seem to find my watch. Any idea how much longer before it gets dark?"

"Nope. Where did you stash your watch? You were wearing it this morning, weren't you?"

A yawn slipped out. "I thought so. Maybe I left it in the glove compartment along with my license."

"Let's hope so. You don't want to shell out any more money. She was referring to Fiona. Her eyes bounced to her covered wrist. "If you can wait, I'll check mine when the hotdog's ready."

"No big deal. I'll wait. So, where did Reed disappear to?"

"Don't know. He didn't say."

"Got a phone call," Terry swiftly interjected real casual-like, poking his fork into the fire pit flames near Aunt Zoe's. "I'm betting it was his wife. After he heard the voice on the other end, he got snarly as a snake."

"His... his wife?" Aunt Zoe stammered. In nothing flat, she went from a happy-go-lucky gal swinging on a star to a woman who had her favorite toy yanked from her. Her exasperating smiley face smashed to smithereens and became a sour one.

Shoot. If that's what heartbreak's all about, I don't need a man that bad, Lord. I cupped my mouth with my hands and whispered condolences to my companion.

Unfortunately for my aunt, Terry wasn't through. "Yeah. She's a real piece of work that wife of his." His harsh words led me to believe he didn't take kindly to Reed's wife. "She lives in Georgia now. Dumped Griffin about two years ago."

I couldn't think of anything short of a miracle that would make my aunt feel better, so with my tush still hanging half-off the crappy canvas seat I'd use what daylight we had left and mix it up with the boarders. The first victim I intended to quiz was the guy across from me. "So, Jim, which horse is it you own again?"

Forty-year-old, thin-as-a-rail Jim Savage, hotshot loans and acquisitions banker with a supposedly eleventh-floor IDS Tower panoramic view of downtown Minneapolis, immediately stopped shoveling food in his mouth. "Silver, the only Arabian in the stable right now." His chest puffed up like a rooster's. "Pretty proud of him. He's won several competitions around town. Got another serious one coming up soon."

Terry barged in. "That's out of town, right?"

"Yup. South Dakota."

"Ah, yes. Silver's the chestnut rabicano. I groomed him this afternoon. Pleasant fella. Sure likes attention." Jim smiled proudly. "What types of competitions do you enter him in?" The man's smile became a questioning frown.

"Mary's new here," Terry shared, yanking his fork out of the fire and displaying hotdogs that looked like soft tar. *Hope those are for him.* "I haven't had a chance to fill her in on anything other than caring for the horses so far."

"Ah." Jim took a slow sip of beer from his can and then set it on the ground. "I enter Silver in Arabian Hunter events mostly. Have you ever had the chance to attend one of those shows, Mary?"

I shook my head. "Afraid not."

"You should. You'd enjoy it."

No, I wouldn't.

I swiftly rewound events that had occurred before today until I found the part where I examined Reed's fence and its height. "I understand a horse in an Arabian Hunter show would be expected to jump around three feet?"

"Yup. And Silver does a darn good job of it." *I bet.* "Terry works with him whenever he can during the week and then on weekends I take him over to the nearby riding arena."

Interesting tidbit. My client had neglected to fill me in on Terry's horse training background. I wonder why? I turned now to the young woman, mid-twenties with dishwater blonde hair bound in a ponytail and a bod about the size of mine, stationed on the other side of Aunt Zoe. She was stirring her food around and around on her paper plate. Her body was there, but her mind wasn't. *What was racing through her mind?* "Hey, there, Sally."

"What? Oh, hi." She stopped playing with her food.

"Nice evening for a cookout, huh?"

"Yeah. I haven't been able to make many of these events Mr. Griffin holds for us. Too busy with home life and caring for Cinnamon."

Aunt Zoe finally got some spunk back in her, albeit a flicker. "Cinnamon? Is that the name of your horse?"

"Yes."

Ah, no wonder she's so distracted. "She's the Tennessee Walker with the hoof problem, isn't she?"

"Ah huh."

"I haven't worked with her yet," I explained.

Sally Sullivan tossed her long ponytail over her broad shoulder so it was behind her. 'We're hoping it's not laminitis."

Aunt Zoe nudged my elbow. "What's laminitis, Mary?"

"Some kind of inflammation of the hoof, I think."

"Oh, dear. What brings it on?"

I shrugged my sore shoulders.

The young woman quickly filled us in. "Overeating of grain usually."

My aunt remained silent for a second and then said, "Is that type of inflammation real serious?"

Sally laid her hand on her neck. "Yup. Progression of the disease can cause perforation of the sole."

"From what I've learned," I offered in a caring tone, "the inflammation's just in one of Cinnamon's hooves so far, isn't it?"

Sally shuffled her booted feet back and forth in the dirt. "That's right. Terry's been real good about keeping me abreast of Cinnamon's problem. I would've been a basket case without him."

I dropped my head and stared at the ground. "Good thing Terry's working for Reed then, huh?"

"Yeah. Supposedly a neighbor bordering Reed's property offered him a better paying job, but he turned it down."

Since Terry had moved on after my discussion with Jim, I figured it was safe to ask who made the offer. Could it have been Clint? "You wouldn't happen to know which neighbor, would you?"

"Nope, Terry never said."

"Is Cinnamon the first horse you've ever owned?" Aunt Zoe inquired.

"No. I kept a quarter horse at my uncle's ranch in Wyoming when I worked there during the summer months." She ran her fingers across her forehead. "You know, that's what so strange."

"What is?" I queried.

"All the years my uncle's boarded horses not one of them ever got laminitis."

My aunt placed another raw hotdog on one of the cooking forks. "His workers must be very vigilant about what the horses eat."

"Extremely."

"Well, we wish you all the best," I said, and I truly meant it.

"Yes," Aunt Zoe added, "You're much too young to worry about such dreadful things."

When Sally suddenly leaned closer to us, I thought perhaps she might be preparing to reveal a deep dark secret. "Having a sick horse is just the half of it. My mother requires around the clock help too. She's dying of cancer."

At that unexpected disclosure, my roommate set a hand on Sally's shoulder. "Oh, I'm so sorry."

"Thanks."

With a few crumbs of new info safely stashed in my brain, I left Aunt Zoe with Sally and brought my paper plate and napkin over to a trash can where two other boarders happened to be conversing. It sounded like they were discussing the latest news regarding another horse.

"It freaked me out George," the older woman said, grounding her cigarette into the earth with the heel of her boot. I hadn't been introduced to her or her companion yet. "Shooting a three-year-old horse and leaving him for dead. Who could be so cruel?"

The man in his mid-twenties was still puffing on his cigarette. "Happened in Stillwater, right?"

The woman threw her arms up in the air which made her slender torso even more slender. "Yes. Less than thirty minutes from here. Poor family. The news reporter said they were on vacation at the time. I just hope they catch whoever it is and string'em up from the rafters."

"You and me both, Nat," the man responded.

Nat produced a pack of cigarettes from her shirt pocket and jiggled one loose. "Dammit. Why are so many horses being purposely injured?"

That's what I'd like to know too. Perhaps there's more to Reed's horses showing up on Clint's property than one would suspect.

"This makes the fifth incident."

Nat's voice displayed anger. "I know." She flipped her waist-length salt and peppered hair over her shoulders. "My mind still becomes numb when I think of the last two."

George shook his thick, caramel-colored head. "Horrible deaths. One doesn't forget that. The show horse from Hastings had his throat slashed—"

"Yes. And the two-year-old filly from Bloomington had been given penicillin even though she wasn't ill. Tell me if I'm being silly, George, but should I be the least bit concerned about how secure our horses are out here?"

He took the woman's free hand in his. "You're not being silly. After the first horse incident occurred, I called Reed and spoke with him regarding the security system he has. He assured me that every precaution has been taken to protect our horses."

The woman referred to as Nat pulled her hand free of George's grip. "Well, let's hope so. Horse insurance is sky high these days."

*****

A few minutes after ten the evening sky fully cloaked us in its royal mantle of darkness, and with it came Minnesota's most beloved summer insect, the mosquito. If you want to make an early night of it, just drop a parachute of those blood sucking varmints on an unsuspecting crowd. The exodus of guests from Reed Griffin's cookout was swift to say the least. Personally I was ecstatic. I could finally do what I wanted to do ever since arriving this morning, a thorough search of Reed's property.

Since Aunt Zoe's and my names weren't included on the roster for cleanup duties, we strolled back to the parking lot with the rest of the departing guests and said our good-nights.

Of course once seated in the Topaz, I had to make it look like Aunt Zoe and I would be leaving as soon as the other cars near us backed out, so I revved up the engine, set the air conditioning on high and then positioned my hands on the steering wheel, making things as realistic as possible.

"Mary, did you ever get a chance to ask Reed if he thought any of the horses he's got on his property were smart enough to open and close gates?"

"Nope. The one and only time I had to question him was when we were looking at the kittens, and I completely forgot."

Aunt Zoe yawned. "That's too bad. Maybe if you had, we wouldn't be pulling this all-nighter."

"Perhaps."

"Any idea how long you plan to have us wait before we hit the back forty?"

Her question regarding the both of us didn't deter my eyes from remaining glued to the rear window and watching the cars slowly depart from the grounds of the Bar X. "You're not going anywhere. You're staying put."

"What?"

"I said you're staying in the car."

"But…, but I thought I was a part of this sleuthing team."

Frustrated, I turned around and faced my aunt. "You are." I leaned across her now, dug in the glove compartment and pulled out a pair of walkie-talkies. They were cheap ones I had absconded from a naughty second-grader who never claimed them at the end of the school year. His parents probably replaced them long ago. I thought I'd pass them on to one of my siblings' kids, but I hadn't seen any of them yet.

I shoved one set in my aunt's hands and demonstrated how to use it. The process was fairly simple. "Remember, if either of us is in trouble, we're to say 'Yankee Doodle'. Got that?"

She nodded her noodle. "Got it. Yankee Doodle."

After the other cars had vanished, I opened the windows and turned the car off. "Pretty quiet out there."

"Dark and spooky too. Reminds me of the many evening hunting safaris Edward and I went on in South Africa. All you could hear were the creatures of the night."

I opened my door as quietly as possible and slid out, taking only a walkie-talkie and the billy club I discovered under the driver seat the other day. "Well, here's hoping the only creature call I'll recognize is an owl's."

"Me too," Aunt Zoe said.

Not wanting to be seen by Terry or any other worker who may still be hanging around, I hugged the property line as best I could while making my way to the exact spot where the horses had previously disappeared.

When Reed first showed me the lay of his land by truck, I had set no timetable to begin sleuthing, but at least I was wise enough to leave a marker of sorts for myself. Now, I was thankful I had done so. I was also thankful for the dark clothes I was wearing. The moon was far enough into its waning mode that I shouldn't have to worry about the white-washed fence giving me away.

After leaving the car and stumbling a bit on rocks that had recently made their way to the surface, I finally reached my destination and let Aunt Zoe know the coast was clear. "Okey, dokey. Ten-four."

"This is Big Bad Mama. Ten-four back at you."

Big Bad Mama? Aunt Zoe must've had one too many beers, or did she even have any? I shook my head to clear the cobwebs. Darned if I could recall. Maybe it was me that had too many. I finally left the security of the fence and moved behind a clump of aged oak trees I thought offered the best hideout possible and hunkered down for the duration. Hopefully, the wait wouldn't be too long.

After squatting among the oaks for roughly an hour, I began to feel like I had been resting on my haunches for several days. My legs were cramping up on me, and my ankles burned like crazy. I thought about standing to relieve my lower extremities of their undo stress, but as I did so, the stillness of the night was shattered by the not too distant barking of dogs.

Some neighboring property must've let them out for the night. Since I was only familiar with one mixed-mutt's bark, Gracie's, I wasn't able to discern whether the dogs were part of the attack-and-ask-questions-later variety or simply the teeny Chihuahua-type. I guess it didn't matter as long as they weren't sent to hunt me down.

A few minutes later, the dog barking ceased and was replaced by human voices. Unfortunately, they weren't floating towards me from a distance.

Holy cow. "Big Mama, do you read me?" No response. "Big Mama, come in." Nothing. I gave it one last shot. "Big Mama, if you're out there, please reply."

Apparently she's zoned out. So much for letting Aunt Zoe know something's amiss. Probably dreaming about her last big safari adventure.

"We're almost there," a young adolescent voice said. Later, if someone were to ask me to recall whether the voice belonged to a boy or girl, I'd have to say it most definitely belonged to a boy going through puberty.

"I know that," the hard toned mature male voice said. "It doesn't look like anyone's been this way since we were last here."

"That's a good thing, right?"

"Right. Come on, Big Fella. Only a couple more steps. That's it. You're almost there. Whoa!"

"I still don't understand why we need the darn horse," the younger voice said.

"Cuz he's perfect for what we need done. Now, stop talking and just direct the flashlight at the fence like you did the last time."

The last time? Yippy. I've got those horse-nappers right where I want 'em. Too bad Aunt Zoe's missing all the action. The flashlight popped on, and I swiftly twisted my head in the direction of the light, but before I could make out anything, I was whacked on the head with an extremely hard object. As I sunk to the ground, I sputtered, "Yankee Doodle."

~20~

At the Crack of Dawn

"Reed, I think she's coming around. Are you all right, Mary?" Aunt Zoe asked, her voice showing strain.

I could barely manage to lift my head off the pillow, let alone answer her. My head ached so bad it felt like a five-ton truck had just run over it. "Just give me a 2 Ginger Whiskey straight up, and I'll tell you in a couple hours," I said, trying to make a joke.

"Always the silly one even when you're hurting." She brushed my bangs aside and kissed my forehead. "I'm glad we found you. When the sun popped up and you still hadn't come back, I thought the worst." Her voice grew shriller. "Why didn't you say Yankee Doodle? I waited all night to hear those two little words."

My speech as well as my thought process was slurred. "I did... I tried to contact you."

"You did?"

"Ah huh. But you didn't respond."

"Oh, dear. I guess I dozed off."

I clutched her hand. "It's okay. I don't blame you. I was having a hard time staying awake too."

She swiped some loose strands of hair away from my mouth. "Reed called a doctor. He should be here shortly."

"For what? I only got conked on the head."

Aunt Zoe pulled her hand from my tight grip. "Don't worry."

"Easy for you to say. I don't have any insurance, remember, Zoe?"

The owner of the Bar X quickly joined Aunt Zoe by the thick, deep-chocolate-brown leather couch I was resting on. "Mary, don't be upset with Zoe. After I saw how jangled her nerves were, it was me who suggested calling a doctor. He just lives down the road. If he feels you need to go to the hospital, my property insurance covers it."

"Oh?"

"And," Aunt Zoe added, "I'm sure Troy won't charge much, he just treats horses."

My mouth flapped shut the instant that news flash sunk in. Wonderful! Another man to see me at my worst— an equine veterinarian at that. Why couldn't the vet at least have been a woman?

*****

Doc Taylor, a single, cute as all get out nerdy thirty-something guy, responded to Reed's call almost immediately and eventually confirmed what we three already presumed. I was fine except for the lump on the back of my head.

In a lame attempt at practicing his professional skills on a human being, the man with the thick head of pale-blonde hair and ocean-blue eyes flashed a bright light in my orbs before asking me, the patient, if I'd been vomiting. Once he received a response, he prescribed an acetaminophen product like Tylenol and predicted I'd be on my feet in no time. Hopefully he wasn't referring to four feet. "You're darn lucky, Mary," Doc Taylor stated. "Your accident could've been worse. Sally Sullivan's dead."

"What?" I took my aunt's hand and squeezed it. "How? When?"

"I think you've been through enough already," Doc Taylor said, smooth as glass, "Let's let your questions ride, okay? Now, getting back to your head injury, there's always a chance for a concussion. I want someone keeping an eye on you for the next twenty-four hours."

Aunt Zoe generously offered her services. The perfect nurse. She was trapped too. Without me she couldn't escape either.

Reed slapped the doctor on the back. "Well, thanks, Doc, for coming on such short notice. How about if I walk you to your car? I've got something else I need to discuss with you."

"Sure." Doctor Taylor excused himself with a nod and the word, "Ladies."

I tried to offer a smile, but it was impossible. It hurt too darn much.

"Looks like we'll be at the Bar X longer than we anticipated," my aunt said quite gleefully when the men had left the room. What a turnaround. Last night she was twisting in the wind when she found out Reed had a wife and today she's ready to kiss and makeup. Did somebody invade my aunt's body while I was knocked out?

"I can't stay here another minute," I nervously announced," and then I tossed off the light blanket that had been covering the lower half of my body and swung my legs over the side of the couch.

Aunt Zoe rested her hand on my shoulder. "Oh, but you must, dear. You heard the doctor."

It's imperative I remain calm. If I don't, my heads going to shatter into tiny pieces. "No, Auntie. You don't understand."

"Don't understand what?"

"I can't stay in this room."

"But why not?" she asked, as she strolled to the living room window, pulled back one of the curtain panels, and looked out at the yard. *She's definitely stuck on Reed.*

"Because we can't afford to have the help asking questions."

She let the curtain panel fall back in place and returned to the couch. "Ah, I see your point. Maybe Reed can help us with that little problem."

"What little problem?" Reed inquired as he reentered the room and handed me a glass of water and two tiny white pills.

"Mary thinks we should be out of sight. Otherwise, the help will become suspicious. Do you have a spare bedroom we can use?"

"Sure. Sure. Come on little lady; I'll fix you right up." Then Reed told me to lean forward so he and Aunt Zoe could get a good grip on me before moving me to the other room. "You just relax, Mary. We'll keep you steady on your feet."

I promise to be good, Lord. Just don't let me slide to the floor.

The double bed in the spare room was covered with a lovely heirloom quality off-white embroidered bedspread, the kind a matronly relative passes on from one generation to the next. Was it from Reed's side of the family or his wife's? Knowing I didn't dare broach the subject of his wife with Aunt Zoe present, I gave my thoughts over to the dirty jeans I'd had on since yesterday morning instead, and suggested someone remove the antique coverlet before they plunked my bod down to rest.

"There you go. Are you comfortable enough, Mary?" Reed anxiously inquired as he and Aunt Zoe positioned two thick pillows behind my head.

"Yup. I'm fine. But I'm sorry I've disrupted your routine."

"No problem. Right now, it's your safety and comfort that are of the utmost importance." The furrows on Reed's forehead froze as he stepped away from the bed a bit. "I know your head is really throbbing, Mary, but did you happen to recognize anyone before you got knocked out?"

I desperately wanted to shake my head, but it was out of the question. "Nope. Too dark."

"That's okay. Try to rest. We'll talk later."

"Fine. But I need to know something before you leave."

"What's that?" He asked.

"Did you find Sally's body in the pasture or the barn?"

"The barn. Why?"

"Just curious."

So what would make Sally return after the evening get-together? She'd already seen her horse. There's definitely more going on here than even my client suspects.

Aunt Zoe picked up the plum-and-cream afghan thrown over the top of a rocking chair and laid it on me. "Mary, dear, you probably won't appreciate my saying this, but one good thing came from your mishap in the woods."

I stared at my aunt like she was the one knocked on the head, not me. "Oh, yeah. What's that?"

Reed's eyes stared straight ahead. "Yes, fill me in too, Zoe."

"Mary planned to ask you if any of the horses were capable of opening and closing gates, but she never had the chance. Now, I guess it doesn't really matter."

"Jumping the fence was included in that equation too," I said as I weakly addressed Reed, "but you had stated the height of the fence would make it impossible for your breeds to do that."

There was no reason to challenge my client concerning horse facts right this second. The head pain had control over me. But I'd done my homework, and it will come in handy down the road. Crossed Arabians and American Quarter Horses don't need to be spooked to clear the fence. They're up to the challenge anytime if trained properly.

Reed rubbed his calloused hands together. "Damn it! So, basically we're back to square one. I know I didn't say anything earlier, but I kind'a hoped one of the horses was getting out on his own too, so I kept my eyes glued on them the best I could. As far as I could tell, not a single stabled horse was interested in the locks." He swiped his hands on his jeans and started to back out of the room. "I hate not being able to figure out what's going on out here, and now Sally's lost her life. Why? What's next?"

My heart bled for Reed. He needed to hear good news, and I didn't have squat to share with him.

"Shoot!" Reed said, stopping short of the doorway. "I almost forgot to tell you, Doc insisted you don't drive anywhere for at least twelve hours."

I flung my hands wildly above my head. "Is the man crazy? I've got things to do and places to go. I can't stay here that long."

Aunt Zoe, ever the peacemaker forced my hands back down to their original resting position. "Calm down, Mary. Remember, Doctor Taylor said not to get excited."

A deep sigh escaped from my lips. "I can't help it. I'm human not a horse."

Reed scratched his prominent forehead. "Look, stay at least until two, and then I'll follow you gals home."

"Fine," I mumbled, not liking the fact that I had to stay even one more hour here.

~21~

The bewitching hour seemed like it would never get here, but it finally did, and now Aunt Zoe and I were back on our own turf discussing the events of last night with Mrs. Grimshaw. The elderly woman had kept Gracie overnight, and it was the mutt who loudly proclaimed our return.

"You know, Mary, I didn't sleep a wink. I was so concerned about your welfare. Yours too, of course, Zoe."

"Thank you. I only wish I could say the same," she said.

"Whatever do you mean?" the old woman asked, selecting a spot to sit. "It sounds like whoever killed Sally and hit Mary was pretty clever. I don't think it would've made much difference one way or the other if you had stayed awake."

My aunt bobbed her head. "Maybe so."

Gracie left Margaret and wandered over to the La-Z-Boy where I was seated and plopped her head in my lap.

The mutt must've sensed I needed some tender attention. I gently patted her head. "That's what I told her, Margaret. She shouldn't keep beating herself up. Besides, knowing you, Aunt Zoe, you would've skipped the cavalry, flew to my defense on your own, and ended up being knocked senseless too."

"And both of you," Margaret interjected, "would still be lying in the woods somewhere."

Aunt Zoe straightened one of the couch's toss pillows she'd brought with her when she moved in. "You're right. I should be thankful you weren't severely injured, Mary. If you had been, I'd never forgive myself."

"So, how's your head?" Margaret asked. "Still hurting?"

"It seems to have quieted down somewhat, but that's probably because I took two more painkillers right before leaving Reed's."

"Too bad my thoughts regarding horses escaping on their own was unfounded," she said, continuing to study my face.

I sighed deeply. "Ditto."

"I suppose with all that's transpired since last night, Mary, you've chosen to end your short sleuthing career and focus on finding a practical, full-time job."

"Nope. Not yet. I'm more determined than ever to figure out what's going on at Reed's."

My roommate seemed surprised by my revelation. "You are? Really?"

"Of course. A little bump on the head's not going to stop this gal."

Margaret stood now. "You'll be better prepared, right?" I nodded ever so slightly.

Aunt Zoe bounced off the couch. "I'm so thrilled you're sticking with the case. I've got a surprise for you."

"Oh? What's that?"

"I begged Reed for a camera, so I could take pictures of the crime scene before Sally's death was reported to the police."

I nearly jumped out of my seat. "Way to go Aunt Zoe."

Our elderly neighbor's lips cracked a smile. "Matt would be so proud of you, Zoe. Did you bring the camera home with you?"

"No. I, ah, left it with Reed."

"Well, that's probably for the best. I'm sure Mary isn't up to scrolling through pictures to find answers at the moment. One needs a clear head." The nonagenarian turned towards the door. "Well, I should be going. I'm preparing a nice Italian meal for supper if anyone cares to join me."

"We never turn down a home-cooked meal," Aunt Zoe said. *Especially when it's her turn to cook.*

"See you two at six then."

~22~

Later That Evening

Aunt Zoe's cell phone urgently plucked her away from her spot on the couch while we were watching an intriguing Perry Mason rerun on TV. Curious to know who dared to disturb our *old folk's* routine, one we had so carefully crafted due to living on shoestring budgets, I lowered the TV volume to barely above a whisper. Five seconds worth of listening is usually enough for me to determine the caller.

Lucky me. Aunt Zoe was barely on the phone two seconds when she revealed the person's identity. "It's Reed, Mary. He insists on speaking to you."

"Me?"

"Ah huh."

"Why did he call you? He's got my number."

She shrugged, meaning I haven't a clue.

I signaled for her to bring the phone to me this instant. It would take me longer to get out of the La-Z-Boy than it would for her to stroll across the carpet to where I sat. Besides, my noggin was still hurting. "Hello, Reed. Yes, I'm feeling much better," I lied. "Zoe said you needed to talk to me about something. Does it pertain to last night?"

"Yeah. The police just finished their preliminary work here about an hour ago and said they plan to call you in for questioning. I thought you'd want to know."

This is clearly a classic slam dunk folks. Now that the cops are involved, my client is calling to say 'Sayonara.' *But how am I going to manage the car payments? Car repairs? The rent? Shoot! How do I explain to the cops what I was doing on Reed's property? I'm not a licensed private eye.* "Did they comment on Sally's death?"

"Nope. They said it would be awhile before they get their answers."

I might as well ask the 64,000 dollar question, I thought. "Suppose that's it then, Reed, huh? With the cops involved you won't need me anymore."

"Whatever gave you that idea? The cops are so backlogged they'll never uncover anything concerning the horses, and who knows when they'll figure out what happened to Sally. I want answers now, not tomorrow."

I swallowed hard. *My butt's saved. I had a chance to hit a home run after all.* Since the sleuthing would remain in my ball park, I explained to my client I'd planned to come out to his property the next evening about nine-thirty. Surprisingly, he agreed to an after dusk surveillance, even though I'd been injured the last time, and horse duties were never mentioned. Our conversation came to a dead end then, and the man asked to speak with Zoe again.

She hadn't gone far. Ever since she announced Reed wanted to speak to me, she had been hovering like a mother bird, afraid she'd miss something of importance I suppose. I passed the phone back to her. She swooped down and scooped it up before I could say, "Here."

"Yes, Reed. Why, I'd love to do that. Just a minute, I need to get paper and pen." She quickly retrieved what she needed off the coffee table. "Okay. That's this Thursday evening, at seven o'clock—line dancing in the back room of Ziggy Piggy's Barbecue Joint on Seventh and Hennepin. Got it. Say, do you mind if Mary tags along?"

I waved my hand signifying I didn't wish to be included in their dancing plans, but Aunt Zoe was so wrapped up in Reed's words she totally ignored me.

I can't line dance. Why does she do this to me? I had already shared I was a klutz when it came to dancing. Hmm? Maybe Kamini could offer to train me that night. The message she left on the landline stated I got the job and how she hopes to train me as much as possible before she goes on maternity leave.

I'd better call her later and see what dates she's thinking of. In the meantime, I have to come up with more safety precautions for my next trip to the riding stable. I don't want a repeat of last night. It bugged me that I hadn't heard anyone come up behind me. I must've been too in tune to the conversation, although that's never been a problem before.

In the classroom, a zillion things buzzed around me. While I used the chalkboard, the teacher aide usually held reading sessions. The students not with her work in groups of four. Amazingly, even with my back to everyone, the commotion coming from the row furthest away could only mean one thing, Joey was annoying Jacob again.

When I was a kid, we thought *all-knowing* teachers were two-headed monsters with eyes in the front and back of their heads. Nowadays kids thought differently—to them we're sorcerers like Harry Potter. As a teacher, I preferred sorcerer to monster.

Leaving my own thoughts behind now, I caught my roommate's final words to Reed and began to seethe. "Great. We'll see you then. Bye."

How dare she? Dad's sister had gone too far. *You have to lambast her with both barrels, Mary.* My eyes bore into hers. "How could you include me in such nonsense? I told you before people make fun of my dancing, so why would I want to be humiliated even more by dancing to the stupidest dance form out there?

"The fun of dancing, Aunt Zoe, in case you've forgotten, is to have some hunk of a guy hold you in his arms, float you around the dance floor, and see all the other eligible men's tongues drop."

There. I'd had said my piece. Auntie looked like she was on the verge of tears, but for once I didn't care. This roommate stuff was for the birds. I was meant to live alone.

"I'm sorry, Mary. I didn't mean to get your dander up, but since you and I have joined forces, you haven't gone out to play, not even once. You need to relax a little. You're too knotted up, like my ball of yarn Gracie got a hold of the other day."

"Wuff. Wuff."

"See. Even Gracie agrees with me."

I could tell my face was in pouting mode, but I didn't feel like rearranging it quite yet. "You're right. I do need to unwind, but I'll do it my way and in my own good time. Okay?"

"All right. I didn't mean to be managing your free time. I'll call Reed back tomorrow and ask him if he can pick me up. I just thought it would be nice to do something fun together outside of these four walls. You know, like we did when we were a lot younger."

Ah, yes. Where did those good old days go? I suddenly felt guilty about my snappishness. "You're much better off without me, you know. A gal doesn't need a third wheel around when establishing rapport with a new man in her life."

Aunt Zoe blushed. "Ah, so this is what it really boils down to, hmm?"

It didn't, but if she felt better thinking my ruffled feathers concerned her and Reed, so be it. I gave her my best imitation of a smile.

~23~

The Next Day

All day long, something concerning horses niggled at the outer fringes of my brain. I tried everything I could think of to jar it loose, including parading around the block ten times with Gracie in sweltering heat that eventually reached 100 degrees, but I got nowhere. Hopefully whatever it was it'll pop into my head before I show up at Reed's. Knowing the way things were running lately, though, it probably won't happen; I had less than a half hour to go.

When Aunt Zoe learned my client was going to be my walkie-talkie buddy tonight, she wasn't happy, but I didn't care. I needed a partner I could depend on, not one who fell asleep at the wheel.

It was pure luck when Reed mentioned he didn't need much sleep. Otherwise, I don't know who I would've dragged with, certainly not fragile Mrs. Grimshaw.

Communication was only part of the plan though. I'm also using night vision goggles I'd found stashed in Matt's upper kitchen cabinets. Why he stored the goggles there instead of a closet was beyond me. Although, an old boyfriend of mine once told me a really good pair can cost upwards of two thousand dollars.

Hmm? I suppose thieves would bypass the kitchen in their hunt for goods like drugs and high-end stuff since those types of items are usually stashed in closets and medicine cabinets. On the other hand, if I were a hungry thief, I'd raid the fridge first. One thinks better on a full stomach.

Shortly before I left the Foley's underground parking to head to Reed's, I received a call from him requesting I push back my arrival time by a half hour. Apparently, a boarded horse was under the weather and Doc Taylor was dropping by to check on the horse's condition. I wish I would've had my sleuthing antennae on. I'd forgotten to ask which horse.

Too lazy to return to the apartment, I buzzed around downtown instead, looking to see if I'd missed any new shops that might have cropped up. I may not be able to spend a dime in them, but there's no harm in a gal filing the info away for future reference, right?

The first thing I caught a glimpse of wasn't a shop but a younger man and an older woman linked arm in arm exiting the Local, an Irish pub I've frequented with many a girlfriend. The food is exceptional, as well as, the Jameson and ginger drink they brag about. *Why couldn't that be me on his arm? Did she meet the hunk in the bar or before?*

The lady looked like Nat, the cougar who was chewing the fat with George at the Bar X cookout. Tonight though, Nat, or whoever she claimed to be, was lighting up the town quite generously with a different fella.

You know how sometimes you wish for something, and it happens? Well, it did. I wanted to see the man who was with the woman, and behold, he turned towards the street for a split second to light the woman's cigarette. I'd swear on my Uncle Edward's grave, although he doesn't have one since he was cremated, the guy looked like Clint Russell.

That man could chew me up and spit me out anytime, but he's not with you, Mary. He's with her. I don't care. If it wasn't so darn hot, I'd put the window down, and then I'd know for sure.

While I tried to decide to tune in or not, someone honked, and I moved forward. *Darn.* Now I'll never know whether it was Clint or not. If it was him, why was he with Nat? Were the two of them up to no good? Maybe Clint was up to his eyeballs in debt and was creating this problem with the horses, so he could sue Reed for tons of money. People had been known to do worse things, but where did Sally fit in? Did she overhear a plot?

I continued to crawl along for a few more blocks, watching the evening crowd disperse from theaters, restaurants, bars and other downtown venues before a particular shop caught my eye, and I pulled over to the curbing to gaze at the display windows.

"Wow! What a discount." Barbara Bridal was offering thirty-percent off their summer collection of wedding gowns. Time stood still as I pictured what I'd look like in each of the four bridal gowns being shown. Of course, every time I rushed to the altar to the waiting groom, I found, to my dismay, a faceless man.

Right then and there, I begged God to send Prince Charming my way. Hadn't I been single long enough? Naturally, no guy appeared. I wasn't surprised. My connection to God was low on the totem pole.

Enough wishful thinking, gal. I sucked in the air-conditioned air and shifted gears. "Yikes." The Topaz's tiny clock showed my spare time had flown the coop. "I need to get rolling." Without giving the flowing traffic a second thought, I swung away from the curb and almost got creamed. *Crap. I didn't need another dented car.*

The car coming alongside me quickly swerved to the left, and as it did so the driver sent a generous message my way. "Watch where you're going, you blankety, blank stupid broad."

Anger flared within. No one calls me a stupid broad. Not even my brothers. I stepped on the gas and flew towards the freeway, leaving the downtown hysteria behind.

*****

By the time I reached the riding stable, cute-as-a-button Doc Taylor was long gone. That was a downer. I had hoped we'd bump into each other again, so I could gaze into his yummy emerald eyes and thank him for his wonderful bedside manner. Maybe another day. "So, what did Doc have to say?" I asked as soon as I knocked on my client's back door.

Reed slipped outside and joined me on the porch. "He thinks Shadow's lungs may have been irritated by pine sawdust." Shadow was Reed's newest boarder. The three-year-old colt was one of two horses owned by Peter Hughes, a Woodbury dentist.

"But Terry told me sawdust is one of the best bedding materials around."

"It is. Occasionally, though, it stirs up problems for an overly sensitive horse."

I folded my arms. "And Shadow happens to be one of them."

"That's what Doc figures, and he's the vet. Now, it's just a waiting game." Reed pointed to the barn as he continued to explain things. "I've already cleared out what was in Shadow's stall and replaced it with recycled paper. Tomorrow morning, I'll make an urgent plea to friends for whatever recycled paper they can spare. That should give me ample time to round some up by other means."

"Couldn't there be another explanation for the respiratory problem? You know, like humans with allergies? For some, its perfume, others smoke."

"Sure, there's plenty that can cause lung problems for a horse, but we try to eliminate them one by one."

Something suddenly popped into my head. "How about medium-sized stones in the food?"

"Are you referring to Cherokee's feeder?"

"Yup."

Reed tugged on his baseball cap's visor. "Those stones were added to the feed on purpose. It helps to slow down a horses eating and keeps them from getting colic."

"Oh, I never thought of that. I guess caring for horses isn't for everyone, is it?"

My client swiped his head from side to side. "You got that right. You have to be on track day and night if you don't want to lose even one of those costly creatures. When my wife split," he said, "she blamed the critters, and rightly so. There's just no way around it."

The lull between spoken words alerted me that the night air had cooled off since leaving the Topaz. I jammed my hands in my jean pockets and thought about what questions I might ask the man now that he'd mentioned his wife. Was it possible she had a vendetta against Reed? If so, she could ruin him from afar, and Aunt Zoe could be tied up in a stinker of a mess. She didn't deserve that. "Say, Reed, I'd like to discuss your wife."

His gentle voice changed dramatically. "If you don't mind, I'd prefer not to discuss her tonight."

Touchy. Touchy. "Fine, but I want to get back to her in the near future. It's important."

"We'll see," Reed fired back as he started up the steps to his house. "Now, get crackin' and see if you can find out what's going on in my woods out yonder."

"Yes, sir." I emptied the tote bag's contents as fast as I could and dropped it on the porch. Then, I slipped the strap holding the night googles over my head and clicked the walkie-talkie on. Ready for another night in the woods with the mosquitoes now, I gave a brief parting message to my client before he went inside. "Set your digital camera aside for me, Reed. I'll pick it up when I head for home."

"Sure thing. I'll leave it in your bag on the porch."

~24~

"How did it go at the Bar X Ranch last night?" Aunt Zoe asked, bursting into the kitchen to join me for a late lunch consisting of frozen Aunt Jemima waffles warmed in the toaster, outdated Hostess Twinkies, and green tea. "Did you catch the outlaws? How about Reed, did he mention me?"

"Nope and nope."

"That's all you've got to say?"

"Ah, pretty much."

Not ready to give up quite yet, Aunt Zoe tried one more time. "Are you sure?"

"Let me think." I let Auntie's hopeful yearnings dangle in the wind a while as I pretended to dig through the crevices of my mind for a worthy tidbit to share. "Oh, yeah, I do recall something else."

My aunt fiddled with her hands. "Out with it, Mary. What can you tell me?"

"Well…"

"Yes, Yes. Go on."

"It was boring last night."

She giggled. "You're nasty. I thought you were about to tell me something of major importance."

"It was important."

"Ah huh."

The bottle of syrup I held in my hands was too sluggish. It could take another few seconds for the syrup's viscosity to kick in to overdrive and by then my breakfast would be cold, so, I boldly took over. I unscrewed the cap, stuck a knife in the bottle and shoved the syrup on out, managing to saturate three waffles with two inches of sticky goo.

"Mary, isn't that a trifle much? You said you were going to start counting calories."

"Did I?" I took a good look at the syrup bottle still in my hand. It was full when I first placed it on the table, now there was barely any left. "I think you misunderstood. I said next month."

While Aunt Zoe thought that over for a moment, I ate a bit of waffle to fortify myself. I had a feeling she'd come back fighting.

"No, I know I didn't misunderstand you. After we shared those last sweets with Margaret, you said you planned to start *this* week."

"Hmm? Had I already had a couple glasses of wine when I stated that?"

"No. We had tea with the coffee cake, not wine."

"Well, it's too late," I said, taking another bite of waffle and savoring the maple flavor lingering on my tongue. "I'll have to start tomorrow or the day after that."

"Suit yourself. Just don't complain about your pants being so darn tight."

"I never do that."

"Of course not." Aunt Zoe finished with her lunch, so she carried her dishes to the sink and began to run water to wash them. "I'm really nervous about going out on this date tonight, Mary. Maybe I shouldn't have agreed to go."

Feeling stuffed from overeating, I finally put my fork down, pushed my chair back, and cleared the remaining dishes from the table. "You'll be fine, Auntie." I handed off what I held and stepped out of her way. "Dating's like riding a bike. You never forget." *At least I hope not. My own dates have been so far and few between.*

"Hmm. I wonder…"

"Yes?"

"Oh, never mind." Aunt Zoe held out a canary-colored dish towel that had been lodged in the cupboard's door handle hidden from view by her legs. I took it. Evidently, we weren't going to let the dishes air dry this time. "So, have you made plans for tonight," she asked, scrubbing and rinsing off dishes as she went, "or are you just going to sit home and watch reruns of *Murder She Wrote?*"

I picked up a plate and dried it. "No reruns for me tonight. I thought I'd examine the pictures you took, take a walk around Loring Park with Gracie, and then maybe chill out with a good book unless a fire alarm interrupts me."

I should've never mentioned I was thinking of taking Gracie for a walk. Upon hearing her name and the magic word for outside, the mutt left her meager Milkbone scraps behind on the kitchen floor by the fridge and zipped over to me. I acknowledged her presence and then motioned for her to sit.

"You don't have to keep reminding me of that toaster incident, Mary."

"You're absolutely right. Why do I want to be reminded of Rod Thompson's rude behavior? He's such a jerk."

"Now, now, you're being mean-spirited. I found Mr. Thompson to be quite a pleasant fellow."

"Humpf. Him pleasant? He's nothing but a chauvinistic know-it-all."

My aunt fanned her wet hand at me. "Whatever you say, dear."

*****

I was bored to death. It'd been a good hour since my aunt had left on her date. My eyes surveyed the living room. One of Aunt Zoe's romance novels had been left on the coffee table. I took a peek. Six pages were all I could swallow. "Such rubbish. How can women read this stuff?"

I tossed the book aside and went to the kitchen to use the landline. The situation brewing between Reed Griffin and my aunt made me nervous and I thought if I discussed the issue with someone I trusted, namely Margaret Grimshaw, maybe I'd feel better about their growing relationship.

"Yes, he seems to be extremely nice. Yes, yes, I understand all that, Margaret. She's definitely old enough to take care of herself, and if she really wanted me there she would've asked me again. I just don't want to see her get hurt. You saw how upset she was about her stepsons getting all her possessions because her thoughtless husband didn't think of writing a new will. What if Reed doesn't share something he should?"

"What's that? Divorced? I have no clue. "I found out through the grapevine his wife moved to Georgia two years ago." I ran my hand across my forehead. "I feel like the parent here. The man could be stringing her along."

"Why don't you go to Ziggy Piggy's and check things out for yourself, Mary."

"No way. I told Aunt Zoe line dancing was stupid."

The listener on the other end of the phone line said, "You'll come up with a logical excuse for showing up. Teachers are good at thinking on their feet."

"Where did you hear that?"

"I don't recall. Just fill me in tomorrow."

"If I go."

"Oh, you will. *Arrivederci.*"

I placed the kitchen phone back in its receptacle and took a peek at my wristwatch. Eight o'clock. *Time is fleeing. You've gotta make up your mind fast, Mary.*

I spun around without being mindful of what might be around me and almost stumbled over Gracie's elongated body stretched between the kitchen doorway and the hallway. Evidently our walk wiped her out. I wish it would've wiped me out too. I glanced at the coffee table from where I stood. There were a few educational magazines I could read, but my mind wasn't in it; it was jammed with concerns for my roommate. "What do you think, Gracie? Should I go?"

Her ears flapped wildly. "Wuff. Wuff."

"Okay, I hear you. You want me out of your hair."

"Wuff."

I jumped over the lazy mutt, picked up my purse and quietly exited the apartment, or so I thought.

"Mary, what a coincidence," Rod Thompson said, strolling over to my entrance as I locked up. Darn. I shouldn't have taken the time to lock the dumb door. Gracie was security enough. "I've been thinking about you a lot lately," he continued. *Ditto, but not the way you think.* "Especially in that morning getup you were modeling. What was it again?"

How could anybody in her right mind fall for this guy?

I began to twirl the chain with my keys round and round while I thought of a good comeback. The best I could come up with at such short notice were the words *get lost*.

While I struggled to keep my sanity, an ingenious plan popped into my head, one in which I wouldn't have to use those two magic words. I'd have to act fast though. Lay on the Malone charm as thick as possible. *No. It won't work. He's an FBI agent. He'll see right through you. Those guys are trained to read facial expressions and body language. Yeah? We'll see about that.*

"Why, Rod, how sweet. I can't believe you're still thinking about that morning. So where are you headed? Any place special tonight?"

"Not really. Did you have something in mind?"

"Yeah, I was kind'a thinking about Ziggy Piggy's. You know tossing back a few beers, chowing down a greasy barbecue sandwich and maybe doing a bit of line dancing. What do you think?"

"Sounds good to me. Did you plan to walk, or do you want me to drive?"

"Silly man. What a question. You see these keys?"

"Ah huh." I tossed them to him.

"You drive. Two beers and I'm wasted. Besides, who's going to stop an FBI agent?"

Rod laughed smugly. "Right."

~25~

"One Killian's Irish Red and a Ziggy Piggy's famous Hot as Hell barbecue sandwich." Rod shouted to the waitress over the noise coming from the dance floor, and then he faced me. "Go ahead, Mary, your turn. You did say we were going Dutch, right?"

What a gem! A perfect gentleman would override a decision to go Dutch and pick up the tab. Proves what you've been thinking, he's not nice. I swallowed hard. *Say goodbye to the last of your discretionary income.*

"You got it." Our waitress spun halfway on her worn-out black oxfords in order to look me in the eyes. "Make sure we get two separate checks would you please. We don't want anyone to construe that we're in some sort of relationship when we're not."

The haggard looking mid-forties waitress kept her droopy lips sealed as she tapped her pen on her order pad and continued to wait for my order.

"Sorry. I guess I'll have the same brand of beer he's having, but throw an olive in it, and I'd like a Dagwood barbecue sandwich on the mild side. Oh, and curly fries."

"Is that it?" the waitress asked before she grabbed our pig menus and dragged her weary body back to the kitchen.

"Ah, add a salad to that too, would you." A slimmer me and dining with a man binged in my noggin. I ignored the message. I wasn't going to starve myself just because a man was sharing my table. Besides, I was paying for the meal.

"Wow, my type of woman, a gal who lives on the wild side. I love the fact you ordered everything but the kitchen sink."

I tapped my chin. "Exactly what are you trying to say, Rod?"

"You know, you've got a hearty appetite. Most women I take out barely let the food skim their thin lips."

"Hmm. I bet that makes for a rather dull evening."

"You got it. Why, when I get them to their doors, they're ready to collapse."

The picture he portrayed was too scary to think about, and I didn't even have a witty comment to bounce back with.

We'd reached an impasse. Silence ensued now. Rod quietly drummed his fingers on the bare table top while my eyes flitted here and there, making it appear as if I was checking things out. *Our order better be up in a flash, or this fake date is history.*

Rod coughed. I think it was his lame attempt at starting the conversation up again. After two more coughs, he said, "I understand you're unemployed. What do you do with yourself all day? Sleep?"

What a Bozo.

If I wasn't so worried about blowing my mission, I'd kick his butt. "Who told...?" *Aunt Zoe of course.* "Actually, Rod, I'm doing a little sleuthing on the side."

Our waitress showed up at the table with our beers, making conversation useless until she left.

When she finally did, Rod picked up the thread concerning my employment. "You're filling in for Matt while he's out of the country? Tell me you're joking."

"No, no. It's not what you're thinking."

Previous diners had left crumbs on the table and no one had bothered to wipe them off. Where's a wet rag when you want one? Known by my friends as Miss Neat Freak, I brushed the mess onto the floor. At least I wouldn't notice it there while I enjoyed the martini beer and food that followed.

The tall lean Nordic man raked his hands through his thick blond hair. "Well, that's good. Every time Matt got into a jam I told him to back off and let the cops and FBI agents do their jobs, but he never listened."

Such a jerk. Matt has more smarts in one finger than Rod will ever have in his whole head.

Imaginary steam oozed out of my head. I didn't know who I felt sorrier for myself or the people in the surrounding tables. When the explosion occurs, which it undoubtedly will, look out. "You're a piece of...."

Incredibly, Rod was saved from strong verbiage about to spew from my mouth by a rude interruption. "Mary," Aunt Zoe said, "I'm so glad you changed your mind"

Noticing who I was with now, my roommate gave her nod of approval before acknowledging him. "Rod, it's nice to see you again. I'll never forget what you did at the apartment for me. I mean us."

The FBI agent greeted Aunt Zoe with a warm smile. "Nice to see you too, Zoe. Mary never mentioned you were down here."

My fingers flew to my lips. "Oops. I guess it slipped my mind."

Rod didn't buy the explanation for a second. His flirtatious eyes turned deadly.

Luckily, Aunt Zoe didn't notice Rod's wonderful charisma had evaporated. "I know you don't like line dancing, Mary, but you and Rod should give it a whirl. *Thanks Aunt Zoe. You just blew my plan wide open.* "Well, I'd better run along. My friend is probably wondering where I am."

"Okay, Zoe. We'll make sure to kick up our heels later," Rod promised.

"Good." She spun around and pranced off in her newest pair of rusty-colored cowgirl boots that matched the crinkle skirt and sleeveless top she wore.

Even though my roommate drives me crazy most of the time and I wished she lived far, far away, for once, I wasn't anxious for her to leave. Rod gave every indication he was about to pounce, and I wasn't ready for his outburst.

"Spill it, Mary. You were pretending to hit on me when we met in the hall, weren't you?"

My eyes shifted from Rod to the half-drunk beer that sat in front of me. I might as well fess up. Continuing to lie wouldn't accomplish anything. "Guilty as charged."

Rod banged his fist on the table. "I can't believe I fell for your feminine wiles."

If the man was trying to scare me, he was barking up the wrong tree. Small kids have temper tantrums all the time. "My suggestion to you, Mr. FBI agent, is to take a break from computers and get out in the real world more."

The macho man sitting opposite me blew his lid. "For your information, I get out plenty, and unlike you, I don't need to fake an interest in someone to have a date for the night. You're pathetic."

I took a deep breath and counted to ten. "It wasn't like that."

"Yeah, right."

"No, I mean it. You've got it all wrong. I swung my hands out. Well, partly."

"See! I bet you can't even explain our night out in the simplest words possible. Women have a habit of going on and on forever."

Plenty of men out there do the same thing, Mr. Know it all. Wanting to dodge the bullet for a while longer, I said, "How about if I try after we eat? I'm famished."

My escort examined the table and then scanned the floor under it. "What do you plan on eating?"

"That." I pointed to the waitress approaching with our tray.

Rod took a quick glance over his shoulder. "Fine. But as soon as we're finished eating, you're going to explain what's going on in the least amount of words possible, whether you like it or not."

"Oh, joy." I moved my order in front of me, picked up the messiest barbecue sandwich this side of Louisville, Kentucky, and bit into it.

~26~

I'm fried. Once I explained the reason for my deception, I thought Rod would let me off the hook. No such luck. Turned out he grew up on line dancing and preferred it to twirling a partner anytime. Go figure. At least no one will ever catch the two of us waltzing together.

"What do you mean you've never line danced? Have you been living in a cave, Mary?"

"Of course not, I'm a teacher. I just prefer old-fashioned dance steps, a polka or the butterfly."

"You said you came down here to keep an eye on your aunt, right?"

"Yes, but—"

"No buts. Take it from me this is the perfect setup for spying. Just follow my lead." Rod pulled me towards the dance floor.

I'm going to make a fool of myself, and he'll be the first one rolling on the floor laughing. I just know it. How do I get out of this? *Fake a stomachache. I did over eat. Nope. He won't swallow another fib. You're stuck then.*

"Come on, Mary; stand next to me," Rod insisted. "You won't learn anything by playing bashful."

I suppose it was better to watch him then trying to follow the moves of ten strangers. "Okay, okay," I replied, inching closer to him. Hmm? I hadn't noticed the great cologne he was wearing. Tommy Bahama if I'm not mistaken. I gave my brother Mike a bottle for Christmas last year. There's no denying that manly scent could heavily influence a gal's attraction to the opposite sex. I shook my head. *But not you. You don't like him, remember? Yeah, yeah.*

Once the next piece of country music started up, the floor filled with several parallel lines. Rod immediately began shifting his feet this way and that. I found the only way I could possibly copy the same step patterns was if my eyes were totally focused on his feet. Even then it wasn't easy keeping up. The steps seemed to be changing faster and faster. Grape vine, turn, heel toe, heel toe.

There's no way I can stay on this dance floor. I'm a disaster waiting to happen. And then, as if on cue, all I'd been trying to do flushed down the toilet. When I should've been pivoting, my feet were still vining. I tripped and landed on my fanny.

Fortunately, I wasn't sitting there too long before somebody rushed to assist me from behind and hoisted me to my feet. "Are you all right?"

Too mortified to look the do-gooder in the face, I kept my eyes focused on the wall in front of me instead, and brushed off the back of my jeans. "Yup. Thanks."

The brief comment I shared didn't ward off the stranger as I'd hoped. "Are you sure? It looked like you hit the floor pretty hard. Maybe you could use something to drink."

Something to drink? What planet is this dude from? Give him the old heave ho. You didn't come here to find a boyfriend. You're here to keep track of your aunt.

The longer I remained silent the harder it was going to be to turn the guy down, and I hate disappointing anyone. Disappointment sucks. I think it's the looking the person in the eye that makes it so tough. *Just get it over with.* I slowly turned around. "Look, thanks but—" *Oh, my God, it's him in the flesh.*

"But what?" Clint Russell asked, standing a mere six inches from me.

"I'm ah, not here by myself."

"I know. You're one of Reed Griffin's employees. I never forget a face."

What a news flash. Scribble that down when you get back home. "Me neither," I barely managed to get out as the music played on, totally forgetting the nasty comments he made when he first saw me at the Bar X Ranch.

Clint shoved his hands in his pant pockets. "It doesn't really matter who you work for if you need something to take care of a hard jolt you received, does it?"

The man made me nervous. "I guess not."

He tried to lighten the mood even with all the commotion surrounding us. "Next time you come out here try to remember a wood floor isn't a trampoline."

I chuckled. "Believe me I've no plans to line dance in the future.

"Good. So name your poison."

"Oh, I don't know. I really shouldn't. If Mr. Griffin sees me fraternizing with you, he may can me."

Clint took my arm. "Then let's hightail it over to the restaurant side," he kindly suggested in my ear. "Your boss won't see us there."

I know what you're thinking. How could I go anywhere with this man who treats my client like dirt? Well, for one, how often do you think a woman like me gets the chance to be near a man like him? Two, a really good sleuth frequently sleeps with the enemy. Okay, forget Perry Mason and Miss Marple. "All right, let's go. By the way, my name's Mary Malone."

"Clint Russell."

A few seconds later the two of us found ourselves in a comfy corner booth on the restaurant side. "So, did you come to Minneapolis just to line dance tonight?" I inquired.

"No, I had a business engagement earlier in this part of town and thought I'd stop in and see what Ziggy Piggy's all about. Several of my friends have mentioned the place." The man's reply was doable, but he also might be spying on Reed for some reason.

I was about to ask another question, but a college-aged waitress stopped me dead. I hadn't seen her before. She must've just come on duty. So full of energy, not like the gal I had earlier. "Hi. What can I get you?"

"Go ahead, Mary."

"Long Island Tea."

The young waitress couldn't get enough of Clint. She was drooling all over him. "And, you, sir?"

He offered her a tiny smile. "Make mine an Irish Coffee."

As soon as she skedaddled out of range, Clint said, "Now, where were we?"

I fidgeted with my hands. I had no clue where they'd wander if they were set free. "You were telling me why you came in here tonight."

"That's right. So, do you live around here, Mary, or in St. Paul?"

My motto in life is never give out information you don't want the enemy to know. Sticking to that now, I said, "Champlin."

"Oh? I've never been to that northern suburb."

Congrats, Mary. Good choice. "Really? Well, the population's only about 24, 000." Continuing to draw on a fellow teacher's hometown now, I fed him another line about the community. "The flour mill and ferry service begun in the 1800s kept the town rolling along."

"Interesting."

"Yeah, I like to dabble in Minnesota history in my spare time." That was true. "What do you do with your free time, Clint?" It was a dumb question since I already knew he harassed his neighbors, but I wanted to hear something flow from his sweet lips.

"Not much." *Hmm. This guy's going to be one tough cookie to crack.* "Where did you work before the Bar X Ranch, Mary?"

Why did I suddenly get the feeling Clint was fishing for info just as much as I was. Well, if he could be vague so could I. "Oh, here and there."

Our drinks were finally delivered. But before I could get my billfold out to pay my share, Clint said, "Charge it to this card, please." Who was I to argue? I needed to save every dime and nickel I had. Besides, Reed had implied the man had money to burn. I wonder which card someone with his wealth preferred using. American Express?

The waitress winked and said, "Sure thing. I'll be right back," and then she disappeared in the crowd.

Alone again, Clint's thoughts went straight to my beverage of choice. "That ought to take care of any pain in your derriere."

"You think?" I picked up my glass. "Cheers."

The cold glass touched my lips. But the Long Island Tea never went down my throat. You see, Rod Thompson appeared out of the blue and charged up to our booth. Why the heck did he have to spoil the moment?

"There you are, Mary."

"Yup. Here I am."

He eyeballed Clint. "Sorry to interrupt the two of you, but I've been looking everywhere for her."

"I fell, and Clint was kind enough to help me off the dance floor."

Rod switched to the type of macho persona I've seen my brothers display over the years when another male's caught ogling their women. His hand quickly claimed possession of my shoulder. I tried to flick it off, but he persisted. "That's nice. Thanks for helping her out, but we need to get back on the dance floor. I've got more moves to show, Mary."

Clint wasn't about to let me leave. "Is he your boyfriend?"

"Not that I know of."

"Then back off," he demanded. "The little lady will join you as soon as she finishes her drink."

Matt always said Rod didn't like losing, so I wasn't surprised when he didn't walk away. "Look, Mr. Hotshot, she's coming with me, or she won't get home."

"Is that so?"

"Yeah."

Even though it was fun having two men fighting over me, I knew it had to end. I didn't want to see either one get thrown in the slammer. I picked up my drink and eased out of the booth. "He's right, Clint. I have to go. He's driving my car. Thanks. See ya."

Clint's face shattered.

Oh, my, gosh! Don't tell me he was truly disappointed this female had to depart, or was it simply a matter of potential questions never being asked? I guess I'll never know unless I create another reason for running into him. *And that, girl, shouldn't be a problem. Your creative side's always coming up with zingers.*

"You were giving off strange vibes back there, Mary," Rod said after we moved a few feet from Clint.

I played dumb. "I don't know what you're talking about."

"Yes, you do. Fess up. The bit about his coming to your aid, there was more to it than that, wasn't there?"

Toss him a bone or he'll be riding you ragged the rest of the evening. FBI agents don't give up easily. "Research," I swiftly volunteered.

Rod's sapphire eyes examined me from head to toe as if he'd only met me a second ago. "So that's what they call it nowadays."

~27~

Morning had come too early, and I wasn't the least bit chipper about it. Not only did I have a headache the size of Lake Superior, but my arms were stiff. They'd been locked in the same position on the kitchen table for over an hour, trying to keep the noggin in midair. At this point, all I could hope was Aunt Zoe wouldn't prance in here with her usual good cheer.

Despite my wish, it didn't get granted.

The minute my roommate, clad in a silky neon-pink bathrobe, waltzed into the kitchen humming loud enough to wake the dead and began slamming cupboard doors, in the wake of foraging for breakfast essentials, I knew my quiet interlude had been irrevocably shattered. "Auntie, please lower the noise level." I softly begged, as I massaged my head.

The request went unheeded. Drawers banged as she opened and closed them.

Maybe her hearing's shot. Although she caught every word I said yesterday at that noisy dog park even when she was more than two feet away from me. I raised my voice a tad and tried one more time. "Aunt Zoe, cut the noise."

She swiftly obeyed. "Rough night, huh?"

I barely managed to pop one eye open. "You could say that I guess. I mixed drinks."

"What are you talking about? You only had a beer at supper and water when you finally joined Reed and me." I ignored her thought process. I was in no condition to explain. Maybe it will dawn on her or maybe it won't. I didn't really care.

Her hand suddenly flew to her face. "Oh, my goodness. Don't tell me Rod spiked your water?"

Spiked my water? Where does she come up with this stuff? I forced my other eye open now. "No! Someone bought me a Long Island Tea." I didn't dare tell her it was Clint, or she'd accidently blab the news to Reed.

She seemed fine with my answer or so I thought.

Without another word she readily returned to her breakfast plans that had been scratched momentarily. It entailed calmly filling a small pan with water. But as she finished that task, a significant change came over her. She took the filled pot, slammed it on a stove burner, and asked, "What sort of man buys a woman a drink that strong?"

"The type who asks what poison she prefers after she almost knocks herself unconscious on the dance floor."

"You fell on the dance floor?" The water on the stove finally hissed. My roommate fell silent again while she completed her breakfast preparation. She removed the pot from the stove, added a half cup of raw oats and stirred.

"Yup. That's what I said." Gracie had been quietly lying under the kitchen table by my bare feet since I'd come in here. Now, she began whining. "Hush," I demanded.

"I seem to be missing something here."

"Sorry. I'm in no shape to help you."

"It's not the oatmeal. What aren't you telling me? Rod was your date. How could an FBI agent let you slip through his fingers like that?"

I shrugged my shoulders. "Gee, I don't know. You'd have to ask him."

In between our two-way conversation, Gracie continued to do her bit, letting me know how unhappy she was. "Wuff. Wuff. Wuff. Wuff."

My hands shot from the jaw to the ears. "I can't stand it anymore, Auntie. You're going to have to take the mutt out."

My aunt didn't argue. She left her cereal behind, buzzed off to put street clothes on, and then hastened back to the kitchen to fetch Gracie. I'd made things simple for her. The dog's leash was already attached to her collar. "Thanks," she said. "Can you do me another favor, Mary?

I dropped my hands. "What's that?"

"Take something for that headache so you'll be in a better mood later."

"Sorry I'm so cranky, but I've downed several aspirin already."

"Oh? Well, in that case I guess I can put up with the crankiness for at least the next hour."

"Why the cutoff of an hour? Is there someplace we need to be?"

She tightened her grip on Gracie's leash. "Not me. You."

"Where?"

"The Singis' optical store."

I threw my hands on my grungy hair. "Oh, crumb! How could I have forgotten?"

My roommate's plump face instantly lit up, a sure sign she was enjoying my misery. "My dear, drinking too much causes many a memory lapse."

~28~

"So, you see," Kamini said, "this job is not hard, Mary. I think a couple more visits with me before you take over will do the trick."

I shook my head to clear it. Stupid move. The pressure on my noggin still hadn't dissipated. *How long is this dumb headache going to last? It's not like it's the first time I've ever mixed drinks. When I go to a house party, I'm always sampling a little of this and a little of that. Maybe Aunt Zoe was right. Someone spiked my drink. But who and why? It's such a dumb adolescent prank, something I could picture Rod doing, but surely not Clint.*

Someone was speaking in a soft voice now. It sounded like Kamini. "What?"

"Don't you agree, Mary?"

I assumed she was speaking of the job. "I don't know, Kamini. It's more duties than I envisioned."

The very pregnant woman patted my hand. "A teacher has many duties, yes?"

"Of course. Some days more than others."

"All right then. Don't worry. You'll do splendidly." She dropped her hand.

Either the woman had a lot of confidence in me, or she was really desperate. I couldn't decide which, but I was leaning towards the latter.

"So, basically my responsibilities are receptionist in nature, nothing more, right?"

"Exactly. Greeting people and such. Of course, you'll be expected to help customers if my husband is occupied."

"In what way?"

"Reattaching a bow to a frame and selecting frames."

"Screwing a bow back on sounds easy enough, but, without any expertise, helping someone select glasses could be quite challenging."

Kamini suddenly winced and then her hands shot to her wide tummy. "What do you mean?"

I gave the pregnant woman a concerned look. When no explanation came forth concerning her behavior, I figured her baby was making adjustments, and I quickly released a reply. "Well, I only started wearing glasses two years ago."

"That may be, but the choice you made frames your face beautifully."

Before I could tell her a friend helped in the decision making process, my cell phone interrupted us. I jerked it out of my pants pocket and glanced at the number. Reed. *What could he want?* Worried that my client might have another crisis on his hands, I said, "Excuse me, Kamini. I need to take this call."

She waved like she was loosening dirt from the floor. "Go. Go. We can talk more another day."

"Thanks." I left her and strolled out to the street to talk. "How's your foot, Reed?" I was referring to his right one which I'd stomped on while line dancing.

He laughed. "Just fine, Mary. Whoever came up with steel-toed shoes was a genius."

"I bet the inventor got the idea after his toes got stepped on too many times by klutzy dancers like me."

"Now come on, little lady, cut yourself some slack. According to Zoe, last night was the first time you've ever line danced."

"Yup."

"Well, that takes guts. Not everyone is willing to try new things." If he only knew.

"So, how are things going at your place? Have they settled down yet?"

He blew into the phone. "Everyone's on edge. Trying not to talk about Sally's death is impossible."

"Who seems to be taking it the hardest?" I asked.

"Terry. He hasn't been worth a plug nickel since it happened. I suggested he take a day or two off. But all he did was counter back with, 'How's all the work going to get done?' So, yesterday I called Jackson, the guy you filled in for, to see if he felt up to coming back to work yet. Said he could give me a couple hours this morning and see how it goes."

The headache was finally subsiding enough to where I could actually think more rationally, thank goodness. "Is anyone else going to be around this afternoon besides you, Reed?"

"Nope. Don't have anyone scheduled. Why? You got something in particular tumbling around in that head of yours?"

"Yeah, as a matter of fact I do, and Terry's absence makes it a whole lot easier."

"Well, then hightail it over here. Unless someone shows up unexpectedly, it should be as quiet as a gentle rain." Then he took a break. *Probably gathering his thoughts. The man uses such delightful words. I can see why Aunt Zoe's so crazy about him.* "Say, Mary."

"Yes."

"Why don't you ask Zoe to join us."

I should've seen that coming. Darn. Now, I'll have to make sure my aunt's paws are kept clear of me while I tend to the investigation. Of course, Reed can help with that.

*****

Not too many people know this, but I am a CSI junkie and proud of it. I was hooked the minute the first crime scene investigation show hit the airwaves, and like the average Joe, I've swallowed every scrap of information shared with the boob tube audience since then. I loved seeing the investigative team poking in this crevice and that with their tiny flashlights, looking for God knows what; tearing cars apart bit by bit for some elusive evidence; hitting the streets, guns in hand, flashing badges as they go from house to house.

Guess what? Most of what television CSIs do doesn't fit the bill. Real life crime scene investigators go out to the crime scene, collect evidence and then scurry back to the lab to analyze what's been found. Period. End of story.

But I didn't learn that fact till I spoke to Matt after this case was history. So naturally when I arrived at the Bar X, gullible me expected to see yellow tape and teeny colored flags spread across the landscape. Instead, I discovered Reed's property had been barely impacted by the Woodbury police department's visit.

It wasn't until I stepped into the barn that I actually saw any evidence the police had come and gone. The warning tape was minimal and only blocked the area enveloping two stalls on the left at the back of the barn, one of which belonged to Sally's horse Cinnamon, the other to Reed's Angel.

The owner of the Bar X guided Aunt Zoe and me forward. "I hope you can figure out something soon, Mary, I don't know how much longer I can keep Cinnamon and Angel out of their stalls."

I glanced at the section he was referring to. "I understand. Where are they being kept in the meantime?"

"The big shed behind the stable where the hay's stored."

Aunt Zoe jumped in with a question before I could ask another. "Any idea what's going to happen to Sally's horse, Reed?"

"Haven't heard from the family yet."

"Are you aware that her mother's seriously ill?" I inquired.

Reed glanced down at his scuffed boots. "Terry mentioned something in passing."

"She's dying of cancer." Aunt Zoe tossed out morbidly.

"Hmm. Maybe I should drive out to her house."

I tore away the tape strung across Cinnamon's stall, swung open the gate and cautiously tiptoed in, being careful not to destroy what previously occurred before today. "Well, if you decide to go, I'd like to tag along. I think it would help to know what was going on in Sally's life the past couple of weeks."

Aunt Zoe scrambled up closer to see the crime scene. "Mary, aren't you going to tell Reed what you noticed on Sally?"

"Noticed on Sally when?" Reed asked.

"In the pictures Zoe took," I shared. "It wasn't much. The scratches I saw on her hand could be from anything."

Reed put his hand to his forehead and bowed his head. "Even the killer."

Aunt Zoe stumbled backwards. "Oh, my. You mean I took something worth noting? Mary, what if the killer finds out and comes after us?"

I let loose with great charismatic charm even though I was shaking in my boots when I thought about a killer watching our every move. "Zoe, a person never puts the cart before the horse until you have to. You know that. Now, if you two don't mind," I said, turning my back on them, "I'd like to get on with it."

"Of course," my client solemnly replied.

"Reed, why don't we go back to the house," Aunt Zoe nervously suggested. "Mary will let us know if she finds anything. Besides, I'm dying to taste the freshly baked French Apple pie we picked up at Ralph's Market on the way out here."

"Just apple pie? How about I throw in a scoop of vanilla ice cream and a cup of strong coffee?"

"A wonderful idea. That's the only way one can truly enjoy pie."

Enough already. Get lost you two. I can't keep a clear head when food is the topic.

Reed must've read my mind. "Mary, are you okay being left here by yourself for a while?"

I waved them off. "Go on. I'll be fine."

"Okay. Dig away," he said as he escorted Aunt Zoe towards the exit. "We'll be up at the house if you should need us."

Digging away? Why didn't I think of that? I peeked
in my small plastic bag of tricks I'd brought this morning.
Not much—camera, flashlight and magnifying glass. Not
exactly digging tools. I should've brought a garden spade
or at least rubber gloves. Mrs. Grimshaw was the only one
who was thinking when I shared my plan. She offered an
old measuring scoop once used in her kitchen. Dumb me. I
said, "No, thanks."

The lovebirds' chatter soon diminished and was
quickly followed by a loud clunk. Good. They were finally
gone. I hastened to the storage closet where I remembered
the plastic forked shovel was kept. It'll pick up more
sawdust then a can or a scoop, but I was also aware I might
miss something because of that fact.

~29~

Remember how desperate I'd been for work? Well, forget that. Looking for the tiniest bit of evidence on an extremely hot July day in two stalls filled with sawdust, pee, and poop that hadn't been touched since being roped off a couple days ago wasn't even close to what I was willing to do for a job, including being blasted by the barn's bug spray mister.

But wait, I haven't covered all the disgusting facts yet. Angel and Cinnamon, the mares whose stalls I was sifting through, don't neatly deposit their waste in the corners of their twelve-by-twelve-foot enclosed areas like geldings do. They drop it wherever they darn well please.

I examined the ceiling and floor surrounding me, and then scanned the length of the barn. Shoot. There was nowhere for this coward to seek asylum.

You're going to have to do the decent thing, Mary, whether you want to or not. Bite the bullet.

I whipped out Aunt Zoe's mighty blood-red bandanna from my back pocket, spread it across my face bandit-style and tightly secured it to the back of my head. *Once again a bandanna rescues a fair damsel in distress.* And if it didn't, well I'd suffocate, and the stench wouldn't matter.

I inhaled slowly. Darn. Disappointment was my buddy today. The mask did the job. I guess I'd better get motivated and do mine. Now, if only I had a pair of gloves.

When I stepped back into Cinnamon's stall to begin the tedious task of scooping up small layers of sawdust, I soon learned a forked shovel could only do so much. The hands would have to do the rest.

What a mess to play with. Too bad it wasn't like sitting in a sandbox making mud pies with preschoolers. My body would have appreciated it. Instead, I had to keep shifting between Indian-style sitting and marionette movements. Before long, I determined neither was comfortable. Although, the half bent over position, waist down, did stretch muscles I'd forgotten existed, primarily because I'd given up on exercising a couple months ago.

When Aunt Zoe and Reed returned to the barn after approximately a half hour, I was still filtering through Cinnamon's stall, with a quarter left to do. "How's it going, Mary?" Reed asked, displaying deep-rooted furrows in his forehead.

"Extremely slow, I'm afraid."

"Sorry about the strong odors, but I can't throw lime down until you're done."

"Ah, it's okay," I fibbed. "The smells not as bad as I thought it'd be."

My client shook his head. "I can't believe I'm hearing a city slicker say that. Are you sure your nasal passages aren't blocked? Maybe you need them checked."

Aunt Zoe slickly got her two cents worth in. "I see you borrowed one of my bandannas. It looks mighty stylish looped around your neck like that."

My lips curled up as I touched the bandanna. "Thanks." Skip the WD-40, folks. A noisy door is worth its weight in gold.

Reed's eyes momentarily drifted to the floor and what I'd been sifting through. "Time consuming, isn't it?"

I nodded.

"Perhaps you'd like some help when you're ready to work in Angel's stall."

"Actually, I think it's best if one person goes through the sawdust. Two people crawling around would cause problems. We'd keep bumping into each other."

"Okay, but if you change your mind let me know."

"Don't worry; I will."

"Meow. Meow."

"Oh, Reed, look," Aunt Zoe said as she rushed to the barn door, "Mommy cat wants to get out. Is it okay to open the door for her?"

"Why don't you wait for me, then we can check on the kittens too."

"The kittens, of course. That's why Mini's in here."

Reed caught up to my roommate. "I rather doubt that. She only came in here to hunt for mice."

"Ick! Mice!" Aunt Zoe bellowed, bolting for the door with Reed swiftly following behind.

And peace reigns yet again. Thanks to mice.

My aunt may have left the building, but I still didn't get the much needed break from her I sought. I couldn't erase from my head the sight of her charging out of the barn, making it difficult to get back to the task at hand, searching for clues. Of course, once the stench from the stalls hit my nose again, I knew I had to get on all fours.

Right before I did though, a soft mewing sound came from somewhere near my feet. I quickly cast my eyes downward. "Well, I'll be." Reed was wrong. Mini was in here looking for her babies. I squatted near the kitten. "Meow to you too, little one. What have you been up to, Kitty? Don't you know you're too young to chase after mice yet?"

"Meow."

"Aren't you a cutie? But I can't give you attention right now. I've got more important things to do." I ran my hand across the kitten's soft charcoal-and-white back, "Besides, you need to get back to your mother. She's looking for you."

"Meow. Meow."

The kitten's beautiful short-haired fur sucked me in even though I preferred dogs at this age. "All right, I give up. You can stay until I'm finished with Cinnamon's stall, and then it's off you go." I pulled the bandanna around my face again and then moved to the section of stall not checked out yet.

Mini's baby continued to cry.

I tried to ignore it, but that was impossible. "Kitty," I said, sifting through another forkful of sawdust, "you're darn lucky the horse who resides here is spending a couple days elsewhere. This area isn't usually a safe haven for small animals." Whoa. *Hold on, Mary. I think you might be on to something.* "The stalls aren't safe for tiny animals."

What if the scratch on Sally's hand was made by a cat? Could it lead me to her killer?

While I remained glued to my spot tossing thoughts around in my cranium concerning Sally and her killer, the kitten quietly squirmed on the ground.

"Hey, who said you could mess with the sawdust?"

I reached over to swat the pesky animal on the butt for making more work for me, but before I managed to do it a shiny object caught my attention. "Well. Well. What did you bring to the surface, you little rascal? It's certainly not a mouse."

I moved to the left of the ball of energy in order to get to the object it had uncovered. The tiny square piece of metal looked familiar, but I couldn't place it. Maybe it had broken off a bridle.

I picked up the sharp object being careful not to shred my jeans as I eased into a back pocket and then I marched out the door to inform Reed about the loose kitten. Having never owned one, I had no idea if it was still too soon to handle it.

~30~

We happened to be finishing up with Reed near the stable, when who should parade up the hill puffing on a cigarette but Nat Newman. *Why was she here?* Earlier my client had mentioned it was too hot today for anyone to ride his or her horse.

I let the owner of Bar X greet her first. "Hi, Nat. Just out driving around?"

She smiled and waved. "Something like that."

Aunt Zoe and I acknowledged her with nods.

"Nat," Reed said, "have you met these two ladies? They were at our last evening get-together out here."

"No." She tossed her finished cigarette on a bare spot and ground it out with her heel. "I didn't stay that long."

I took it upon myself to make the introductions, giving out the most minimal information called for. "Hi, I'm Mary, and this is Zoe."

"You both board horses out here too, huh?"

I made quick eye contact with Reed. He understood the message. "The ladies came by to pick up their paychecks. Mary filled in for Jackson while he was out sick, and Zoe helped me get caught up on bookwork."

"Oh? Yes, I suppose you do need extra help certain times of the year," she replied. "So that must be your Topaz I saw down there." She lifted her arm in the air and pointed to Matt's car at the bottom of the hill. "I owned one a few years back. They're a pretty reliable car, aren't they?"

Aunt Zoe interfered with my response, but that was okay. If she hadn't, I would've blown our sleuthing wide open and told the woman I had no idea. Of course the wording she ended up using wasn't much better and would need to be rectified. "It most certainly is. I don't know what Mary would do without it."

Not wanting Nat to assume we were related in any way or lived together, I made up another yarn. "Well, we'd better get going Zoe. If we don't get you back to your apartment as soon as possible, your place will look like a tornado hit."

Poor Aunt Zoe had no clue what I was up to, but she stood there bravely waiting for the other shoe to fall.

Nat on the other hand, reacted like a cop when one first arrives at the scene of a crime. She slapped her feet together, hunched her shoulders and then tilted her head to one side. "What do you mean she might find her place torn up? Is someone threatening you, Zoe?"

"I, ah," my roommate blubbered, extending her hands in front of her, "I, ah... Mary?"

I displayed a grin. "You misunderstood, Nat. No one is threatening to harm her."

Aunt Zoe's orange-red penciled eyebrows and hairdo matched the coloring of her face. "That's right."

"The reason she needs to get home is a big black furry mutt called Jebb," I explained. "If Zoe's gone too long, the dog tears the place apart."

Nat's shoulders immediately relaxed "Oh?"

"Yes," my roommate confirmed, "I'm babysitting my brother's lab. He's not house trained yet, so if I'm away for more than two hours he destroys everything he can get his paws on."

"I understand completely," she said, digging in her white pant pocket for another cigarette. "My friend's German Shepherd behaves the same way. What you need, Zoe, is a kennel to keep the dog in when you're not there," She tapped a cigarette in her palm before putting it between her lips and lighting it. "Well, have a nice day. Maybe I'll see you two again sometime."

I slapped my leg. "Yeah, you too." Then my roommate and I walked briskly down the hill.

"Nat seems real nice, don't you think, Mary?"

"Are you joking?"

"No." Aunt Zoe opened her bucket-sized aquamarine-colored purse and dug through it. "What's wrong with her? She seemed nice."

"The lady reeks of bad vibes."

"How can you tell?"

"It's the teacher in me. You'd be amazed at what you pick up on at parent-teacher conferences."

I was relieved to be leaving the horse stalls behind as we drew closer to the Topaz, but then it dawned on me I wouldn't be going anywhere. I was keyless.

Shoot! I must've left them up at Reed's house, or they were in the locked car. Well, I'm certainly not going to climb back up that hill and beg Reed for another ride if they're in the car, especially in front of Nat. Now if dad's sister went back up there, that's a different story.

I soon discovered my key worries were unfounded when Aunt Zoe dangled them under my nose like a carrot. Ah, yes. I'd handed the keys to her for safe keeping when we first arrived.

I put my hand out to catch them and unlocked the door. "Do you feel like listening to music on the way home, Auntie, or do you prefer no noise?"

The passenger door swung open. "Doesn't matter to me," she replied as she slid in.

"I'll leave it off then. I'd rather get back to Nat anyway." I poked the key in the ignition, locked my seatbelt in place, and shifted the car into reverse.

"That's fine with me."

"Didn't you think it a bit odd for a rider to show up wearing a dressy blouse and white pants on one of the hottest July days ever recorded in Minnesota history?"

"I did. What about the heavy makeup?"

"That too."

"But if she wasn't out here to spend time with her horse, Mary, then what motivated her to show up?"

"I wish I knew. Whatever her reason was it must've been pretty important."

"Mary… oh, never mind."

"What?"

"You don't suppose there's anything going on between Reed and Nat, do you? Because, well, you see I'm starting to have feelings for him."

No kidding. I let her question brew in the air for a split-second. "Nat and Reed? Nah. Absolutely not. But, have you forgotten about Reed's wife?"

"No, I haven't. But since learning about her, Reed and I've had a chance to talk and he said there's nothing more between them, and I believe him."

Keep your trap shut, Mary, until you get the facts from the horse's mouth. There's nothing like putting a damper on romance before you have to, especially when it's coming from someone who has a poor track record in the romance department like yourself.

The car came to a grinding halt. As usual the Bar X's gates barred our departure. My aunt quickly resolved the problem and we set off for home supposedly. When the Topaz's tires hit the street though, someone started honking at us.

Not wanting to get Matt's car dinged up, I immediately stopped and waited for a car to appear and swerve around us, but none ever did. Obviously, I hadn't missed anything in my blind spot. I glanced in my rearview mirror. A car was sitting on the shoulder of the road a short distance from me. I didn't recognize it. Maybe the person's elbow accidently hit the horn while he or she was talking on their cell phone. I ignored whoever it was, but it didn't help. The honking began anew. "Aunt Zoe, do me a favor. Turn around and see if that car looks familiar to you."

She undid her seatbelt and turned to face the back of the car. "I've never seen it before. You sure you don't know who it belongs to? Maybe it's one of your fellow teachers."

I shook my head. "Don't think so."

The owner of the black Ford Focus finally pulled up alongside of me. I glanced in the car. Thankfully, the passenger window was rolled down which made it easier to recognize the person.

Aunt Zoe leaned over to my side, so she could catch a glimpse of the driver too. "Oh, no. It's Clint Russell," she breathed out excitely, "What does he want with us?"

"I don't know."

It was hard to remain calm when my emotions had just spiked to new highs. I crossed my fingers hoping Clint's sexy mouth wouldn't blab about Ziggy Piggy's, and then I rolled my window down. "Hi. Can I help you?"

"Yeah, I have a quick question for you. Oh, sorry, I see you're with someone."

I shot a glance at my aunt and then focused on Clint. "Pull in front of me and I'll meet you at your car."

"Okay."

"Are you crazy, Mary? If Reed finds out you're speaking with him, he'll fire you."

"Look," I said as I closed the window and parked, "How else am I going to find out what the enemy is thinking if I keep ignoring him?"

"Well, since you put it that way."

I left the comfort of the car and approached the Ford Focus where Clint sat. "Whatever you have to say, make it quick. I don't want my passenger to report back to Reed."

With my piece said, I waited for a response from him and soaked in what the hunk was wearing. Too be honest I was a bit disappointed in what I found today.

Instead of shorts and shirts screaming Tommy Bahama, the scrumptious dude was clad in what looked like your basic blue jean shorts and a navy and white striped, short-sleeved knit shirt, the kind of apparel that sells for twelve bucks a pop at any discount store.

Well, well. I guess what they say about the wealthy is true. The more money they have the more pennies they pinch.

"No problem," the suave Clint Eastwood look-alike finally said. "I just wanted your phone number. The guy you were with at the barbecue joint tore you away too soon."

"Oh?"

*This definitely works into your grand scheme, Mary.
You've been trying to figure out how to meet with him
again. The dude actually wants your number. How cool is
that? Real cool, girl, so don't blow it.* My heart skipped a
beat *Wait a sec. What if the guy's playing you? Nah.
What's in it for him?*

Clint Russell snapped his fingers. "Hey, I thought
you wanted to hurry this up."

"Ah, yeah. I just realized I don't have anything to
write my number on."

"That can be arranged." Clint offered me a pen and
an envelope addressed to him that had been sitting on his
passenger seat. "I believe in being prepared."

You would, you handsome devil. "Thanks." I took
what he was holding and quickly scribbled a number and
then double-checked it, making make sure I hadn't given
him Matt's landline by mistake. "There you go." I handed
his pen and envelope back. "Don't make me wait too long
for that call," I gushed, as I started towards the Topaz.

"I won't."

With our private chat done, Clint rolled up his
window and made a sharp U-turn. Returning to his
property I suspected. As for me, I slipped back in Matt's
car. "Ready to roll, Aunt Zoe?"

"Where to?"

"Home of course. Didn't you tell Nat a mutt was
waiting for you?"

~31~

Aunt Zoe was extremely antsy all the way home, and I knew it was only a matter of time before she boiled over and coerced me into telling her what my private meeting with Clint Russell was about. I just didn't expect her to pounce on me the moment she crossed our apartment threshold.

"All right, Mary, out with it," my roommate said, lightly tapping her newly purchased crimson-colored boot to an imaginary tune," I think I've waited long enough."

I played hardball. "For what?"

Upset with my question, she tapped her booted foot harder. "Enough stalling, Missy. I'm not some acquaintance you can play games with. You forget I watched you grow up. Tell me what that schmuck wanted?"

Geez, Mary Colleen, what kind of sleuth are you? You were in the car for over twenty-five minutes and you never thought up a good yarn for your roommate.

"The jerk wanted me to know I had a cracked taillight."

The foot tapping stopped abruptly. "That's it? Why couldn't he have shared that when he pulled alongside of us?"

Matt's mutt came running out from wherever she'd been hiding and eagerly pressed her body between the two of us, expelling gas in the process. "Gracie, how could you?" Even though I didn't appreciate what the dog had done, she'd unknowingly helped me. Her action cut off further discussion of Clint Russell's so-called behavior.

I gently nudged the mutt out of the way and moved to another spot with Aunt Zoe. "I'd better get Gracie outside pronto. I don't need another stinky mess to clean up."

"Forget the dog I'll take her out, Mary."

"Are you sure?" I said not very convincingly. "It is my turn to walk her you know."

"It doesn't matter. I haven't done anything all afternoon."

Other than flirting with Reed. I yanked my filthy boots off. "Okay. I'll do double duty another day."

Once the mutt and Aunt Zoe left, I stepped in the shower and stood there a long time, scrubbing away the filth and stink of the barn with apple-scented body wash and shampoo.

Focus on your case instead of your body. What did the kitty uncover? Why did Nat show up today? "Don't forget the encounter with that rich dandy." Why am I on his radar? I checked my body. Nope it isn't that yummy. "There's got to be a common denominator, but what is it?"

The warm water flowing from the shower head kept up a steady beat. Practice what you preach to math students. If the answer doesn't work, start over.

The problem is where to start from? Should it be when the first horse ended up on Clint's property?

I got out of the shower, threw on a scruffy two-piece summer lounging outfit, and combed my hair. The answers are out there. Maybe my scope has been too narrow. I need to go beyond Reed's horse realm. "Brilliant idea." Start with Clint Russell. "Why not? It beats working around horses."

Feeling as fresh as a daisy again, I left the bathroom behind, charged into the bedroom to retrieve my cell phone, and then moved on to the kitchen. After I pampered my stomach with comfort foods, I'd make a few phone calls.

I opened the fridge and scanned its contents. What's it going to be, macaroni and cheese or the juicy blueberry pie? Both I decided. I grabbed the two plastic storage containers and set them on the table. Now all I required was eating utensils, but a light knock at the door stopped me from getting any.

Shoot! Why is it whenever I'm ready to succumb to the ranting of my stomach someone has other plans for me.

I shut the fridge and scrambled to the door. "Margaret, what a surprise. Come in."

"I hope I'm not interrupting anything, Mary?" the elderly woman inquired, crossing the threshold a little slower than usual. Maybe she had over taxed herself dancing this week. Matt said she sometimes dances five days in a row. It just amazed me that someone her age could still twirl up a storm when I couldn't even make it through one evening of dance without falling on my fanny.

"Not at all." *Unless you consider plans to stuff my teeny body with tons of food before supper. Pigging out probably doesn't count in my neighbor's world.* "Are you having trouble with one of your crossword puzzles?"

Margaret rested her frail hand against her chest. "Me? Good heavens, no. I was curious to see how today's events unfolded."

"Ah, yes. Well, your timing couldn't be more perfect."

"How so?"

"Aunt Zoe's out walking Gracie." I ushered our neighbor to the living room couch and sat.

"Oh."

"It's hard living with her, Margaret. She gets so excited about the littlest thing."

"Are we talking about your aunt or the mutt?"

I shook my head. "Oh, sorry. I assumed you knew who I was talking about. I meant Aunt Zoe."

"Yes, she does seem to get frazzled easily, doesn't she?"

"You, on the other hand, are always so calm."

My neighbor immediately covered her mouth. "I have my moments too. You're just not around when it happens."

I shoved my damp hair over my ears. "Ah, I don't believe that. Anyway I'm glad you stopped by. I need to chat with someone other than my roommate about the case. Get some decent feedback."

Margaret's boney hands formed a steeple. "I'll do my best. You know, Matt used me as a sounding board whenever a case was giving him problems too."

"I kind'a suspected that. Besides, they say two heads are better than one, right?"

My neighbor laughed lightly. "*Si.* Definitely. So what's your problem?"

"Problems," I stressed.

I leaned against the back of the couch. "I'm not really sure where to begin."

"Towards the beginning is usually a good place to start, dear," Margaret sweetly suggested.

"Did anyone ever tell you that you'd make a great teacher?" I asked, reaching out and clutching one of her tiny hands.

"No. Not that I can recall."

"Believe me, you would. Remember my second trip to the farm when I had to fill in for one of Reed's employees?"

The elderly woman nodded ever so slightly. "That was the same day you got knocked on the head by some kook."

"Yes. Well, I never told you what happened when I went into Reed's house for the morning break."

"And what was that, dear?"

"Aunt Zoe told me how scary I looked."

My neighbor's soft eyes opened wide. "She didn't?"

I raised a couple fingers. "In front of two men no less. Embarrassed, I ran straight to the bathroom."

"To make yourself more presentable, of course."

"Exactly. Aunt Zoe doesn't know it but she actually did me a favor that morning."

Margaret's thin brows peaked considerably. "She did? How so?"

"If I hadn't been forced to use the bathroom for emergency primping, I never would've found a small, square metal object on the floor."

"Did you ask anyone what it could be?" she asked, moving her body a smidgen.

"Nope. I forgot about it. Coffee and cookies were uppermost in my mind at the time. I'm sure glad I stashed it in my jeans though instead of tossing it."

The elderly woman leaned closer to me. "Why's that?"

"This afternoon I found another one."

"You did? Where?"

I scooted off the couch and paced excitedly. "In Cinnamon's stall. A pesky little kitten uncovered it."

"Any idea what the metal pieces are from?"

I paced some more. "My hunch is a bridle, but I could be wrong. The only way I'll know for sure is to connect with someone who sells horse equipment. Hopefully, it doesn't entail driving to Wayzata or Buffalo."

"Is Bloomington close enough?"

"You mean there's something out there besides the Mega Mall and Ikea?"

My neighbor laughed. "Believe it or not there most certainly is. A man from my church owns a saddle and harness shop a short distance from the mall. I can get his number from the church directory for you if you like."

"Great. That will be one less thing to scratch off my list."

"Mary, you mentioned problems as in plural. What else did you want to run by me?"

"Well, a boarder showed up right out of the blue before we left Reed's property."

The elderly woman rested her hands on her lap. "Are the boarders expected to call before they come out to Reed's?"

'No. But it was too hot to take a horse for a ride, and the woman never explained what she was doing there. I'm hoping her appearance didn't mean she was making a play for Reed. Aunt Zoe would be devastated." I took a short breather before I continued. "Hey, you'll never guess who else I bumped into while we were in Cottage Grove."

"Who?"

"Clint Russell."

"He's the man who complained about Reed's horses getting on his property, right?"

"Yup." My stomach rumbled loudly now. "Sorry. Are you hungry, Margaret?"

"A little."

"Come on, let's move to the kitchen. I've got blueberry pie waiting to be eaten."

"I'll agree to a piece of pie as long as you don't keep me hanging too long regarding Mr. Russell."

"I won't."

When we entered the kitchen Margaret noticed the two containers sitting out. "It looks like you were planning to have more than pie."

"I was but the pie will be plenty."

I motioned for the elderly woman to sit before I placed the container of macaroni back in the fridge and gathered the utensils and plates for us. "Here we go. I'll dish up the pie. While you're eating, I'll finish up about Mr. Russell, okay?"

"*Si.*"

"I was flagged down the minute I pulled out on the road running in front of Clint's and Reed's property."

The elderly woman broke off a bit of pie crust with the fork. "By Mister Russell I assume?"

"Yes. He said he wanted to ask me out on a date but didn't have my number. Can you believe it?"

"Oh, dear. Sounds like there might be a conflict brewing." With that said, my neighbor got a decent taste of the pie on her plate.

"Could be, but I have a hunch there's more to this hunk of a guy than meets the eye."

"You mean you think Mr. Russell is somehow involved in what's happening at Reed's?"

"There's something about him. I don't know. Call it a gut feeling." I set my fork down hard. It banged the plate. "I wish there was a way I could check his background before I go out with him."

Finished eating, Margaret gently pushed her empty plate out of the way. "I always lean towards playing it safe, especially these days. Perhaps the police could be of help."

"I don't know. They're so busy with major crimes. Besides I'm not a licensed private eye. I'm only an unemployed teacher. Why would they give me the time of day?"

The nonagenarian flapped her hands on the table. "I hear a box of donuts goes a long way with Sergeant Murchinak. He's just down the street in one of the police substations."

I sighed. "And you know this how?"

"Your brother Matt knows him quite well."

"Terrific. So how do I convince the cop I need help?"

The elderly woman pointed to her forehead. "Use your imagination, Mary. You're a teacher."

"Unemployed, but thanks all the same. Hmm. Let's see. Oh, how about this? I'll tell him Matt thinks the guy I'm dating might have a criminal record and doesn't want to see me ending up dead."

Margaret's eyes twinkled with delight. "*Si*. That ought to get his attention."

~32~

I escaped to my bedroom the second Margaret left, not to take a nap but to make a private phone call. I didn't want to chance my roomie walking in on me and overhearing the conversation.

"Hello, is Sergeant Murchinak there? Oh, I see. He's already gone for the day. Do you know what time he reports in the morning? Ten? Okay, thanks."

Talk about timing. As soon as I put the phone back in its cradle and opened the bedroom door, Aunt Zoe's voice rang out. "We're back."

"I'll be right there," I said, and headed to the kitchen. When I got there, I found Aunt Zoe and Gracie panting. "Looks like the walk wore you both out."

"It did, but we're hungry, aren't we, Gracie?"

"Wuff. Wuff."

"I'll tell you what; you two get a drink, and I'll scrounge up some grub. How does pizza sound?"

Aunt Zoe dampened a paper towel and then wiped the sweat from her brow. "From Crazy Harry's across the street?"

"Nope. Good old Berkley's from the freezer."

"Oh?" My aunt's lips clearly displayed her disappointment. "What time will it be ready?"

I pulled the pizza out and flipped the carton over. "In twenty minutes if all the cheese is melted."

My roommate took a glass out of the cupboard and filled it with ice and water. "I think I'll watch TV since you don't need any help."

"Sure. After I get the pizza in the oven and Gracie's chow ready, I'll join you." Little did I know it would be sooner rather than later.

Aunt Zoe had been in the living room less than a minute when she hollered for me. "Mary, you gotta come in here this instant."

"I'm not done yet."

"It's important."

Right. Just as important as the day she wanted me to see the kittens I suspect. Well, at least I'm not grooming a horse this time.

I left the frozen pizza on the counter and headed to the living room to see what the big deal was. "What's up?"

My aunt jumped up from the couch. "I just got a call from a gal on the third floor. Kamini's gone into labor."

"What? No. That's impossible. I'm not ready to fill in for her yet."

She grinned. "Apparently Kamini thinks so."

"How am I going to put all my energy into the case if I have to work half days there?"

"You should've thought about that before you filled out the application."

I clenched my hands. I couldn't believe what rolled off my aunt's tongue. "I had no choice. I took the job for the two of us."

"What do you mean?"

"How do you think we can afford to live here without extra income coming in? My teaching salary was divided into nine months not twelve." Good thing my cell phone vibrated in my pocket right then otherwise the seams of my jeans would've separated. "Excuse me. I'm going to take this in my bedroom," and then I stomped off.

It was Clint. The call couldn't have come at a better time if I had planned it myself. The hunk wanted to know if I liked to bowl and if there was a night yet this week that I'd be free. Oh, brother. I didn't even have him checked out yet.

You're crazy not to set a date with him. You wanted to dig deeper. Yeah, Yeah, but I wanted to know who I was dealing with first. For all I knew he could be a serial killer.

"I guess that's a chance I'll have to take."

"What did you say?

"Ah, yeah. Sounds fun." He didn't need to know the majority of my balls end up in the gutter. "I have a slight problem though. I don't know my schedule yet for my other part-time job. I should know by tomorrow. Can I call you later in the day?"

"Yeah. If I don't pick up, leave a message."

"All right. Talk to you then." I pulled the handheld mirror off the dresser and looked at my reflection. "Way to go, Mary. You can talk to Murchinak in the a.m. and speak to the hunk in the p.m."

~33~

All my fretting last night was a waste of time. Have you ever had plans jerked out from under you while you were still snoozing? I did. Within the last twelve hours to be exact.

At 6:15 this morning I was awakened from dreamland by none other than my lovely cell phone. The principal of Washington Elementary called to ask if I could fill in for one of the teachers who had a family emergency. I wanted to say "No" and go back to sleep, but I couldn't. Money talked. Besides, I needed to keep my foot in the door. Teachers, who end up out of the school loop for too long, are eventually forgotten, and I didn't want that happening to me.

When the call ended, I remained on the edge of the bed trying to figure out how I was going to manage today's agenda. Let's see. Summer school runs until about two-thirty and I'll probably have to be at the optical store by four. Not much wiggle room for a stop off at the police substation, supper or the phone call to *chick magnet,* Clint.

Oops. You forgot the trip to Bloomington. "Oh crap." That'll have to wait. I glanced at the alarm clock. "Better get moving, Mary. You don't want to be late your first day of subbing."

I dragged myself out of bed and pulled the sheet and blanket taut. As much as I liked Gracie, I wasn't about to let her sleep under my covers. That honor was being reserved for Mister Right.

Finished with the bed, I then gathered appropriate clothing for the classroom and headed to the shower. After I'm fully awake, I'd follow through with breakfast and dig through my teaching stuff to see what fun filler work I could bring to school. It never hurts to be overly prepared. Kids could be overbearing with subs.

I spent more time than I thought in the shower. The minute I got out Aunt Zoe banged on the door. "Are you all right, Mary? You don't usually get up this early."

"I'm fine. I got called to sub at Washington Elementary."

"Oh? Would you like me to throw a couple waffles in the toaster for you?"

Toaster! The scene of Rod Thompson in our apartment the day Auntie burnt toast and the alarm went off is stamped in my memory bank forever.

How could I forget the look on his face when he saw what I was wearing? There would be no repeat of that day if I can help it. "No, no. That's all right. I'll fix myself a bowl of cereal."

"How about if I pack you a lunch?"

Enough already. I opened the bathroom door a quarter of the way and poked my head out. "I appreciate your trying to help, Auntie, but I'm not sure what I want for lunch yet. I don't usually think about that until after breakfast is out of the way."

My roommate waved a hand at me while the other held a cup of steaming coffee. "I'll leave you be then," and she started to walk towards the kitchen. "Oh, by the way, Mary, I'll be busy most of the morning too."

Worried my aunt planned to practice her culinary skills again while I was gone, I sprang back the door that was almost shut. "Really? What are you doing today?"

"Why, I volunteered to watch the Singis two little ones until the grandparents show up."

Whoa! She's in for a rude awakening. As far as I knew my aunt hadn't been around little kids since I was born. "Good luck," was all I could manage to say without bursting out laughing before I shut the door and finished primping for school.

Thirty minutes later I charged towards the fourth floor elevator with a canary-yellow canvas bag dangling from my arm. About halfway there, Rod Thompson intercepted me. He was dressed to the nines as usual and carrying a small suitcase.

"Well, aren't you all dolled up today, Mary. Rushing off to get married in Vegas?"

"Very funny," I snapped. "You're the one carrying the suitcase, Mister."

He lowered his voice. "Shhh. Calm down. I didn't mean to get you riled up, at least not this early in the morning."

"Oh, so now you're admitting you like to upset me."

"No, no. I was just trying to have an adult conversation."

Like he knows how. I drew in a deep breath. "In that case I've got a job to get to."

My Nordic neighbor ran his free hand through his blond hair. "Oh, the sleuthing one you mentioned?" *So much for him thinking he knows everything.*

"Wrong again."

"Give me a hint," he mildly joked.

The elevator door slid open, and we marched in. Perhaps I was being too harsh with him. After all, he did help me out at Ziggy Piggy's. I started over again. "I'm subbing. How about you? What are you up to today?"

"Leaving for Texas."

"Work or vacation?"

"A little of both." The door opened for the lobby level. Rod waited till I stepped out. "Say, how would you feel about a repeat at Ziggy Piggy's?"

"Oh, I don't know, Rod."

"It's okay. I get it."

"Get what?" I asked nonchalantly, shoving the straps of the cloth goodie bag on my shoulder.

"I'm referring to the guy I pulled you away from at Ziggy Piggy's."

My hand flew to my forehead. "Seriously?"

Rod leaned against his suitcase. "Look, maybe I am a computer geek, but I saw what I saw. You seemed to be pretty enthralled with the guy when I found you in that booth."

"We were," I blubbered. *Stupid mistake, Mary. Why did you admit that? For all you know Mister FBI agent was laying a trap.*

"I rest my case," Rod said, as he quickly shifted gears and wheeled his baggage towards his car. "See you around, Mary."

"Rod, wait! I need some answers."

Too late. His car door had already slammed shut.

My head bobbed back and forth as I stood by the Topaz and watched the FBI agent flee from the garage. Did he know what I was really up to, or did he innocently pick up on the vibes going between Clint and me?

If it was the latter, I was seeing a whole new side of Rod Thompson I never knew existed. Maybe he wasn't such a bad guy. He just didn't know how to relate to women. Supposedly, it took one good woman to turn a man around. *Don't go there. Remember you told Mom you don't date FBI agents. Besides, you two don't mix, you're like oil and water.*

*****

As soon as I took off for North East Minneapolis, all thoughts about Rod Thompson evaporated and only summer school remained.

Even though I had enough on my plate before the sub job came along this morning, I was truly looking forward to a day with kids. Honest. Time spent with the little rascals would be a piece of cake compared to living with a menopausal roommate who's so behind the times, doing a job that scares the bejeebers out of me and being taken off guard by an FBI agent down the hall.

Unfortunately, when I arrived at school nothing followed through the way I had envisioned. The principal informed me I'd be nurturing fifty-some rambunctious kindergarteners and first graders in math and remedial reading throughout the course of the day, not teaching classes in the computer lab as he suggested on the phone. Hmm? *Who showed up before me and forced his hand?*

After one hour with the little darlings and the noise level seeping in from the science class next door, I had a splitting headache, one even the knock on my head couldn't measure up to. Hmm? I wonder how Aunt Zoe was faring with the two she was watching. Deep down I had a feeling the rest of my day would play out the same. Kids the world over have always taken advantage of substitute teachers.

I felt like such a failure. Why couldn't time leap forward enough so the students could go to the cafeteria for their morning break?

At the end of the day when the school bell rang for dismissal, I grabbed my belongings and flew out the door with the little darlings. Wouldn't you know one chatterbox, a walker, managed to keep up with me all the way to the Topaz. His non-stop talking almost caused my head to explode. "Miss Malone, what are you doing with that box of Roll'n Donuts?" the boy asked while his eyes begged for a sample.

"It's a gift for a friend," I kindly replied, hating to disappoint the kid. Hearing the bad news, his head fell to his chest. I needed to say something to cheer him up. "I know I feel bad I don't get to eat any either. I love donuts."

He shuffled his foot back and forth on the blacktop. "I understand Miss Malone. It's okay. I'm sure my mom has a snack waiting for me," and then he ran lickety-split down the street.

If only I could move that fast in tennis shoes. Since walking wouldn't get me to where Sergeant Murchinak was supposedly waiting for me, I jumped in the car, put the keys in the ignition, and tore off down the road to Highway 65 and eventually on to Hennepin Avenue and a police substation.

"Thanks for the chocolate donuts," Sergeant Murchinak said, displaying an uneven grin the second I handed them over to him. "How did you know they're my favorite kind?"

"Telepathy."

The big cop chortled. "Matt, huh?" Now, he turned his back on me and placed the box containing the donuts on a bookcase directly behind his sturdy chair.

"Something like that," I replied.

"So, you're really Matt's little sister?" I nodded affirmatively. "Well, how about that. I didn't think I'd ever meet any of his siblings."

I gave him a cheesy smile. "We try to obey the laws."

The cop stuck out his beefy hand. "Well, it's nice to meet you, Mary. Have a seat," then he shoved the stack of papers sitting in front of him to the side of his desk where a lamp and a framed picture of him in uniform rested.

I pulled a lone, side chair away from one of the enclosed walls and set it by his well-worn desk. "As I explained on the phone earlier, I won't take up too much of your time. I know how busy you guys are."

Sergeant Murchinak waved his hand at me. "Don't worry about it. You said it was important to Matt that you see me."

"Yes, especially since he can't look into it." I fumbled with my hands. I couldn't decide if they should be closed or opened when lying to a cop.

The cop leaned his belly over the desk slightly. "Your brother's a good guy. I'm glad you listened to him. So, what's your problem?"

Here we go. I sure hope the guy can't read between the lines. "Well, it all started the minute I mentioned the new guy I've been dating. Matt went ballistic. I begged him to tell me why he got so upset."

Murchinak pulled his body up tight now. "What did he say?"

"My boyfriend was bad news. Matt said his name cropped up while he was working on a prior case and made me promise to ask you to run a check on the guy. He didn't want to find his baby sister in the cemetery when he stepped back on U.S. soil."

"Holy sh.... What's the guy's name? I'll run a check on him as soon as I can."

"Really? Oh, thank you, Sergeant." I stood and clasped my hands together. "Clint, my boyfriend, is such a nice guy. He can't possibly be the criminal my brother's thinking of."

"Don't let his demeanor fool ya. Some of our worst serial killers appear to be as peachy as pie." He grabbed a pen and paper. So what's his last name?"

"Russell."

"Got it." Murchinak dropped his pen on the desk and stood. "Where can I reach you at, Mary?"

"Matt's. I'm staying there with my aunt until he gets back."

~34~

I had exactly a half hour to take care of personal needs, make that stomach demands, before I showed my face at Singi's Optical, and I knew Milt's hamburger joint across from Loring Park could make that happen. I grabbed the fun-filled bag I dragged to school this morning, pulled my cell phone out, and punched in Milt's number.

"Milt's, what can I get yeah?" the high-pitched youthful voice asked.

Hmm. The kid's voice sounds vaguely familiar. Where did I hear it before? Maybe the same person took my order the last time I was here, or he lives somewhere in the Foley complex.

Realizing the guy was still waiting for the order, I quickly summed up what I wanted. "Yeah, I'd like an order-to-go."

"Ready when you are."

"All right. Extra-large fries, small coleslaw, a triple Milt burger with plenty of cheese and a chocolate shake."

"Is that it?"

"No. Throw in a couple chocolate chip cookies too while you're at it." This working girl required more than a skimpy can of tuna and carrots to hold her over. Besides, there's always tomorrow to start dieting. The cabbage one someone shared in the teachers' lounge sounded interesting.

Ten minutes later I paid for my order at Milt's, traipsed back to the car and stuffed my tummy with the goodies. After I dusted off the last remaining evidence of what I had devoured from my dressy pants and blouse, I fled to the underground parking at the Foley and dropped the Topaz off. I wouldn't need it to get to my second job.

Wouldn't you know the second I approached the building's exit to take off for the optical store, my cell phone rang. Thinking it might be Mr. Singi calling to confirm I was still coming, I pressed ANSWER.

"Mary, I thought you'd want to know one of my horses died this morning," Reed reported in a no nonsense tone. "I don't think there was anything malicious about her death, but even so."

My stomach jumped ship at the thought that I might be responsible for the death of such a costly creature. "How terrible. It wasn't the horse who ate my VW's steering wheel, was it?"

The man stumbled with his reply. "No. It was Angel the one you said you felt most comfortable with."

"Yes, I remember. The golden-colored quarter horse. I saw her only that one time when you had me work in the stable with Terry. But I inspected her stall after Sally died. I'm so sorry for your loss."

"Yeah, it's real tough. She'd been with me for about five years. I planned to enter endurance races with her later this summer."

"Did you discover the dead horse?"

"No. Terry found her when he was making the rounds."

Terry? Sally mentioned someone had offered him a job, and the man never seemed to be in the barn when I was. Maybe someone wanted Reed destroyed and hired Terry to help him or her. "What did Doc say?"

"He said she hadn't been dead long."

I rubbed my forehead. This mess at the Bar X was getting hotter by the minute. "Was Troy able to figure out what happened?"

"Not really. Angel never had any underlying health issues."

I glanced at my wristwatch. Every second wasted on the phone would make it that much harder for me to arrive at work on time. "So, what's the standard procedure when a horse dies, Reed?"

My client didn't answer immediately. "Well, when the cause is unknown, like in Angel's case, we usually ask the University of Minnesota's Equine Center to figure it out for us."

"Is that what you've chosen to do?"

"Yeah. Terry offered to take the body there for me; I was too shaken up."

Terry again. If he did something to the horse, it would make perfect sense to get rid of the evidence when no one was around. "Look, Reed, you did the right thing by calling me. Angel's death could be just a fluke, or it could have been planned by someone who is very devious. Either way, I feel we need to talk further. Is it okay to call you later? I'm on my way to another job right now."

"Sure, I ain't going anywhere."

*****

I waltzed into the optical store sweating profusely. Hopefully I wasn't late. The nearest clock was two feet in front of me. Good. Five minutes to spare. I swiped a tissue off a table and wiped my moist hands.

Raj Singi came out from the room beyond the counter and greeted me warmly. "I'm pleased with your promptness, Mary. I told Kamini hiring a teacher was a good idea."

I let the comment slide. He didn't have to know I was almost tardy. "Congratulations, Raj," I said, extending a hand to him.

"Thank you." He reached for my hand.

"How are Kamini and the baby doing?"

"As good as can be expected," he said, displaying a proud smile when he released my hand. "We had a girl. That makes three."

"I suppose you were hoping for a boy."

"Yes," he sighed, "what father wouldn't want a son, but we are blessed all the same."

"She'll make you proud one day."

Raj laughed. "I have no doubt."

The optometrist continued to share tales of the newest addition to his family, which I enjoyed hearing until a customer rushed through the door and interrupted us. "Sorry, I'm late for my appointment," she said.

I recognized the woman immediately. I had run into her several times in the laundry room at the Foley. She was impossible to forget. Every time I saw her she was color coordinated from the mound of her ratted hair right down to her toenails. Tonight, the two-hundred-pound woman's choice of color was bright yellow like a toy duck. Too bad the dark Star Wars tattoos covering both arms, the neck and one side of her face didn't match.

Raj didn't flinch at the sight of the woman. Apparently, she had previous history here, or he was the type of guy who didn't let weird sights distract him from his work. "Gertie, nice to see you. Let's go back to the exam room, shall we?"

"Sure thing, Doc." She gave me a good hard look before she took off with Raj, but her eyes didn't seem to register recognition.

Since my boss hadn't given me any orders before he took flight, I made myself busy with little things around the office, straightening magazines, picking up toys in the kid's corner, placing frames back on the wall racks and restocking lens cleaner. It wasn't until I was finished with my tasks that the phone rang for the first time since clocking in. Remembering what Kamini said about trying to answer the phone before the third ring, I scrambled to answer it.

"Singi's Optical, how may I help you?"

The caller wanted to set up an appointment for next week. I could handle that. When I turned my back to the counter to search for available openings in the black, leather bound appointment book, I caught the reflection of the next person about to step into the store. Nat Newman?

Was her appearance a coincidence? I shook my head. I doubted it. I had a funny feeling she was stalking me, but why? Maybe I was wrong about her. She was cozying up to Reed and thought I was the competition.

I ended my conversation with the caller and quickly hung up. Then I put on the best surprised face I could muster and spun around. "Why, Nat, how nice to see you."

"Oh? Hi. I didn't know you worked here. I thought you were just involved with horses."

I bet. I work a little here and a little there. Right now I'm filling in for the gal who's on maternity leave. So, what brings you out this way? Do you have an appointment with Doctor Singi?"

Nat Newman's smile was full of charm. "No, I just happened to be at the bookstore down the block and noticed a screw had fallen out where the front piece and the earpiece are supposed to connect." She whipped her glasses out of a soft covered case and showed me what she meant. *What a lame excuse. If she had said her dog had got ahold of the glasses, I might have bought it. At least there would be teeth marks to prove it.* She droned on like I required further explanation. "I would've tightened the screw myself, but I don't carry tools like that in my purse," she neatly added.

I glanced at the small straw purse hanging from her shoulder. "Not big enough, huh?" I joked. "Good thing we were close by." I reached for her plain, brown plastic-framed glasses and looked for the company who designed them. "I don't remember seeing you wear these. Are they new?"

"Ah, fairly. I just have to wear them for close up."

What a bunch of hooey she was spewing. Even I know glasses can take a lot of beatings before a screw comes loose. "Well, why don't you have a seat by the window while I go in the back and work my magic. There are tons of magazines to peruse."

"Thank you. I'll do that."

When I went to the back room to search for a tiny screwdriver, I found one by a sample card patients are asked to read from when picking up new bifocal prescriptions. It only took me a second to decide to check out Nat's tale. If the lenses in her glasses were for close range, they would definitely magnify the words on the card at some point. I tested my theory. "Just as I thought," I muttered. Yup, the woman's here to check up on me. I set the card down and then went about connecting the earpiece and frame, making sure not to strip the screw.

Raj entered the back room just as I'd put the tiny screwdriver and glasses on the counter. "Are you almost finished, Mary?"

"Yup." I picked up a bottle of lens cleaner, squirted Nat's lenses with the liquid, and wiped them dry with a cloth.

"Good. Gertie is done with her exam and I'm expecting another patient in about five minutes," he explained, turning back to the doorway leading to the outer area. "So it's up to you to help her select a frame."

"Okay. I'll take care of her." I finished putting the things I used away, washed my hands, and then strolled out front. "Here you go, Nat."

"How much do I owe you?" she asked as she skirted up to the counter and opened her purse.

"No charge."

"Thanks. So, will I see you again at Reed's?"

"Depends on him," I said, letting her draw her own conclusions.

Gertie must've been listening to Nat's and my conversation and assumed we were done. She moseyed over to where we were, pressed her ample girth against the counter, and waved a yellow polished finger in my face. "I knew you looked familiar. You're the new tenant on the fourth floor who does private eye work."

After hearing the stranger's sudden revelation, Nat's light-colored eyebrows arched severely, giving me the impression she was on the fringe of asking a question.

Damage control was definitely in order. There was no way I was exposing my secret to anyone connected with the Bar X other than Reed. "Sorry. You're mistaken," I said, squashing Gertie's comment as swiftly as it came.

"My brother's the PI, but he's been out of the country for a while."

"But, but," Gertie muttered. "I was positive that's what someone told me." The guilty party she was referring to was Aunt Zoe obviously. There's no way Margaret would have blabbed.

"They got it wrong. I usually work with horses and teach, but the rest of this summer I'll also be filling in for Kamini who's on maternity leave."

Nat Newman snapped her purse shut and then she peeked at her bulky silver watch. "Thanks again. I'd better get going. I've got a meeting down the road in fifteen minutes."

I waved her off. "Have a nice evening," and then directed my attention to the other woman. "Sorry you had to wait, Gertie. Are you ready to pick out some frames?"

The woman planted her thick hands on her chunky hips. "Look, honey, I just want you to know I don't blame you for denying you're a PI. I can smell a cop a mile away."

I thought about what she had said. *Nat Newman, a cop? Nah, she doesn't fit the profile.* "Gertie, I'm really not a private eye. Honest."

"Okay, have it your way. You probably aren't licensed and don't want to get in trouble. I understand these things. I did a short stint in the slammer myself. But if you ever can spare the time, my cousin's in a dilly of a pickle."

~35~

After Gertie left, Raj had three contact lens patients waiting to see him, so I took advantage of the long stretch and began to think about how I was going to handle Clint. He needed to be taken care of first before I even allowed myself to worry about my client's problems. The best option was to lie. Tell Clint my boss hadn't had a chance to work out a schedule for me yet. That would give Sergeant Murchinak more time to get back to me. I put down the *National Geographic* I had been reading and reached for the phone. It rang before I even had a chance to enter Clint Russell's number.

"Good evening. Singi's Optical, how may I help you?

"Mary?"

"Yes, this is she."

"It's Margaret Grimshaw."

"Oh? Hi. I suppose you're wondering how it's going for me?

"Well...."

"I don't mean to brag, but I'm doing all right."

"That's nice to know, dear, but it's not the reason I called. I ran into Zoe in the lobby. She filled me in on your busy schedule. From what she said, I gathered you didn't have time to visit my friend in Bloomington."

"Nope. But tomorrow isn't going to work either, I've got other fish to fry."

The elderly woman cleared her throat. "Don't fret, Mary; I took care of it."

"How could you? You didn't have the object I wanted to show him."

"*Si.* But Tom agreed to stop off here on his way home."

"Oh, you shouldn't have bothered."

"Now, now, it's no problem. The two of us haven't seen each other in a while, and he's never turned down a plate of my lasagna yet. Just pop in as soon as you get home."

"That's not as easy as it sounds. How do I bypass Aunt Zoe without her getting suspicious?"

"Simply tell her I need to borrow a cup of sugar. *Arrivederci.*"

Worried Raj might appear any second and I wouldn't have a chance to speak with Clint, I quickly dialed his number. It rang and rang. *Come on, pick up.*

"Mary, could you... Oh? I'll wait," Raj whispered.

Darn interruptions. As I set the receiver back in its cradle, someone on the other end said, "Hello." Hopefully, it was Clint's voicemail.

"I didn't mean to rush you," the optometrist said.

Feeling guilty about making a personal call, I didn't dare look at Raj, instead I settled for the bottles of lens cleaner sitting on the counter. One seemed to be missing. "That's all right. It was a wrong number."

*****

When Raj's last appointment scheduled for this evening called to cancel, he told me I could leave whenever I wanted. Pleased to hear the news, I tidied up and then ventured out into the cool night air. Just the way I liked my summer evenings. Too bad I couldn't enjoy it longer, but Mrs. Grimshaw and her friend were waiting, and I still needed to call my client back.

The instant my hand tugged on one of the Foley's heavy entrance doors my cell phone vibrated. I jabbed a hand in my pocket, pulled out the phone, and pressed ANSWER without looking to see who was calling, like I had done earlier. This time I assumed it was my roommate. "Auntie, you don't need to check up on me. I'm a big girl."

A masculine voice replied, "Well, I'm glad we got that straightened out. I certainly wouldn't want to be dating a little girl."

It's him. It's him. I shook so badly I almost walked through the lobby's second set of doors. "Oh, my gosh. Hold on a minute." I fumbled with my ring of keys, found the lobby entrance one, and let myself in. "Okay, Clint, sorry about that."

"Not as sorry as I am," he rattled on, "You never called to tell me which day you could go bowling."

"Actually I did try, but I got interrupted." I pressed the elevator button and hoped no one would be joining me when it arrived.

"Oh? That must've been what I thought was a crank call."

"Probably."

"Well, what day works for you?"

I inhaled deeply and let out a heavy sigh. "I still don't have an answer for you."

"Are you putting me off?"

"No. Why would I do that?"

"I don't know. Maybe you have a boyfriend tucked away you haven't told me about?"

Not him too. Are all men cut from the same cloth?

The elevator dropped me off at the fourth floor, but I didn't dare finish this conversation in the apartment. Instead, I got off and remained by the exit door. "As far as I know, there's no one waiting for me around the corner, so do you want to get together or not." I crossed my fingers. It was imperative I got under Clint's skin. He held the key to this case. But what?

Clint backpedaled now. "Yeah, yeah. I just didn't want anyone beating me up."

I released a nervous laugh. "You've got enough neighbors upset with you. Why would I bother sending a henchman too?" *Although if I found out he was a wanted man, I may have to.*

"That's extremely thoughtful of you."

"Look, Clint, the only reason I put off calling you was because I never got my schedule from my boss. He was too wrapped up in his work and his newborn baby. Why don't we just plan to go Sunday evening?"

"Sure, why not. I'll pick you up at six."

"Nope."

"Too early?"

I cleared my throat. "No. it'd be easier if we met at the bowling alley. You know, halfway between my place and yours. Less chasing for you." *And I don't want you finding out where I live.*

"You got some place in mind?"

"Yeah, Bowlarama.

He hesitated long enough to probably *Google* it. "That's in West St. Paul, right?

"You got it. See you there." I put the cell phone away and rushed to my abode.

"Home already, Mary?"

"Yes," I replied short of breath, "but I have to dash over to Margaret's. She needs a cup of sugar." I took a couple deep breaths as I dropped my bag and purse on the table in the hallway and sprinted into the living room. "What the....?"

"Are you surprised?" Aunt Zoe asked. I didn't respond. "I hoped you would be. The material's just been sitting in one of my trunks all this time."

And that's just where it should've stayed, I thought. "Moroccan isn't it?"

My roommate beamed. "That's right."

The mutt jumped off the couch, raced over to me and whined.

I know exactly how you feel. I stroked her head while I soaked in the redecorated room. Bright tangerine-colored sheer material softly cascaded down from ceiling to floor encasing Matt's old couch. Matching striped fabric followed through on the couch's enormous tossed pillows which were no longer on the couch but had been haphazardly delegated to the floor. The coffee table had been bedecked with Moroccan do-dads and placed between the couch and La-Z-Boy. And my beloved chair, well, it was draped in an outlandish shade of pink.

"How did you get the fabric strung up?" I asked flatly not really wanting to hear the reply.

"Our caretaker, Mr. Edwards." She took a good look at all she had done. "You know, I think I've outdone myself, Mary."

I bit my tongue. "You sure have." *Good thing I'm going to Margaret's. I can blow off steam there.* "Well, I'd better get the sugar." I left my aunt stranded on the couch, amid the Moroccan hubbub, ran down the hallway to retrieve the metal object tucked in my top dresser drawer and then traipsed to the kitchen to toss it an empty sugar bowl. Once I had what I needed, I marched out the door.

~36~

I had barely bopped back into our abode when Aunt Zoe quizzed me about our neighbor. "What's Margaret making, Mary?"

I should've expected to be drilled, but I hadn't. Stepping into the newly decorated Moroccan living room at this moment in time, or even the next day or two, was at the bottom of my list. This gal can only manage to keep her feelings corked if she steers clear of what's upsetting her. You know, out of sight out of mind. When I left Margaret's, my intention was to bypass the living room and finish out the evening in the kitchen. But as I began to flee in that direction, I remembered the promise I'd made to myself regarding yelling between rooms and hastily surrendered. I strutted into the living room like a turkey, looked my aunt in the eye, and woodenly stated, "Banana bread."

"Yum. That would go good with coffee in the morning. Do you think we'll get a sample? We did share our sugar after all."

She's got you cornered. Better pull out a whopper. "I hate to disappoint you, Auntie, but Margaret told me the bread's for the upcoming bake sale at her church."

My roommate's mouth dropped a mile. "Oh? Well, we can make our own bread tomorrow."

Fire alarms went off in my head. Thankfully, I remembered Reed's latest message and felt better. I know it wasn't nice to use Reed as an excuse instead of saying we didn't have the right ingredients in the house, but it worked for me. "One thing at a time," I said. "Reed called when I was on my way to the optical store."

She smiled. "He did? What did he want?"

"He called to tell me Angel had died."

Aunt Zoe's hands flew to her mouth. "The poor man. He must be devastated. I need to call him."

"I plan to phone him in about a half an hour. You can talk to him then."

"We should make a pie for him, Mary. I bet he'd like that."

"I hate to be a party pooper, but depending on what type you decide to make we may not have all the ingredients. What recipe did you have in mind?"

Aunt Zoe remained on the couch and stared into space.

My stomach complained angrily while waiting to hear from her. *Be patient.* . Knowing Auntie's recipes always come from the food containers she's bought rather than from the books she's collected, I swiftly broke through the silence. "Is your recipe handy?"

She shook her red spiked head. "I use the pumpkin one on the Festival can."

Ta da. Score one for Mary. There were no cans of pumpkin in our nearly bare cupboard which meant there would be no charred mess to clean up or smoke to inhale.

"I'm pretty certain we don't have that on hand. I guess we'll have to get a pie from Cub's bakery on our way out to Cottage Grove tomorrow," I said, and promptly turned in the direction of the kitchen to fix myself supper.

"There's still chow mein left from the other night. You might as well eat it," Aunt Zoe said as she followed behind.

"All right." I love it when I can microwave a meal and not have to scrub pots and pans. I dug in the fridge and pulled out the chow mein and soy sauce.

Aunt Zoe sat at the table and waited for me to place the food in the microwave. "Oh, Mary, I forgot to tell you the landline rang just as I stepped out to finish the laundry. Maybe someone else needs help."

"Either that or it's one of Matt's buddies. He left on such short notice he probably didn't get around to telling everyone what his plans were."

The minute I finished supper, I scrambled to the bedroom to see if any messages had been left. Gracie was lounging on the bed hiding the machine from view. "Ah hah. This is where you've been. I thought it strange you didn't greet me when I got home." I shoved her over and sat down.

There was one message. "This call is for Mary Malone." I recognized the voice. It was Sergeant Murchinak. "Mary, I barely scratched the surface, but I wanted to share what information I have so far regarding what we talked about earlier. Matt was right. John Doe does have a history. He was brought up on a drug charge a few years back, but it was tossed out on a technicality." The cop probably meant *daddy dear* pulled strings and got him off. "Colorado's Department of Transportation faxed me a copy of his license. I'm expecting more specifics.

Hopefully I'll be able to share them with you when you come by to verify the picture."

Clint Russell got caught up in drugs. Huh? What kind? And what's with the Colorado license? As far as I knew he was a resident of Minnesota.

Too bad Clint wasn't my only problem. Margaret's friend, Tom, who has been around saddles and harnesses for well over fifty years didn't have good news for me either. He didn't recognize the thin piece of metal I'd found. "There are always new buckle designs being flaunted," he told me, "Perhaps I just haven't caught it on the Internet." He did, however strongly recommend I talk to a vet who works with large animals. "They see so much more when they visit ranches than I do with what comes into my small shop."

I flipped my hair behind my ears. Huh? That's something I hadn't thought about. Visit a vet. Aren't I lucky? I knew just the one. I could spin my wheels around, and he lived right here in the metro area. Of course, I was referring to cute-as-a-button Doctor Troy Taylor. Hmm? His bedside manner for humans does leave one wondering, but, hey, if I hung around him, at least he wouldn't stab me in the back. *Another thing, Mary, doctors don't hightail it out of town on a whim.* That's true. Surely Mom would get off my back about dating the minute she learned I was seeing a doctor. *A win-win for everyone. Why not?*

Good thing no one has asked me to sub tomorrow; my dance card's already full. I changed into shortie PJs, and then went to find Aunt Zoe. It was time to call Reed.

~37~

"Well, look at you, Mary," Aunt Zoe said as she greeted me in the kitchen doorway with her hair rolled up in juice-can-size rollers again. How did Uncle Edward manage to stay married to her all those years? Maybe it's one of those unexplained miracles. "Did you sneak out after I went to bed?"

"Why?"

"You look like something the cat dragged in."

"Ouch. You really know how to hurt a girl." I swiped away the gunk surrounding my eyes left by the sandman and fluffed my hair. "There. Is that better?"

She laughed. "Maybe a tad. So, are you going to reveal who your *hot* date was?"

I pulled out a chair and yawned. "There was no *hot* date unless you're referring to the weird dream I kept having."

Aunt Zoe tightened the belt on her neon pink bathrobe before offering me a cup of freshly brewed coffee. "See. I was right. A man was involved." After she handed me the java, she returned to the counter to pour herself a cup.

"Men," I clarified as I locked my elbows on the table and picked up the steaming cup sitting in front of me.

"Men? Ooo. This gets juicier by the minute." Aunt Zoe zipped back to the table with her java and sat. "Fill me in, niece."

Darn. I hadn't anticipated going down that road. You'd think I'd know better. You can't say anything about the opposite sex around her. If only she'd stop reading those dumb romance novels. *Oh, well. One man will just have to remain anonymous.* "In my dream I was on a Ferris wheel and couldn't get off. It just kept going around and around."

Aunt Zoe took a couple sips of coffee and then set her cup down, "Go on, get to the good part," she demanded, "I want to know who was with you."

"One time it was Rod, the next Doc Taylor."

"Oh, my," she gulped. "Maybe we should've had tea instead of coffee. I could've read your tea leaves. Tell me, who were you with when the dream ended?"

"I, ah, don't know." *I did, but I wasn't sharing.* "Everything got fuzzy real fast." I got up from the table and poured myself a bowl of cereal now before my aunt tried to analyze my crazy dream.

The break did the trick. Aunt Zoe lifted her coffee cup to her lips and held it there for a time. "Mary, exactly how soon are we leaving for Reed's? I'm concerned about his welfare."

I set the filled cereal bowl on the table, and then gripped my roommate's shoulders. "I am too, Auntie. If I didn't have an errand to run this morning, we could've been out there already." I released her shoulders and sat. "I suppose I could drop you off at his ranch before I go to a meeting out that way."

"About what time will that be?"

"Twelve-thirty."

"Why didn't I ever learn to drive? I could've already been consoling Reed at the Bar X." She slapped a gob of raspberry jam on her toast and spread it around. "Oh, I hope you haven't forgotten about getting a pie at Cub."

"I haven't. I'll pick it up after my errand."

The second Aunt Zoe devoured her toast she rushed to the living room. I presumed to call Reed and tell him when she'd be arriving.

When she left, Gracie got up from her spot by the fridge, meandered over to me, and put a paw on my lap. I hugged her. "Well, that worked out splendidly, girl. Don't you think?"

"Wuff. Wuff."

"Yup. She never asked about the meeting or the errand."

*****

For some reason, the instant I stepped into the police substation this morning I felt like I was playing a scene in one of the old Perry Mason shows. Paul Drake, the usual detective, was out of the picture and I was filling in. Sergeant Murchinak had replaced Lieutenant Tragg.

"Can I help you, Miss?" the young officer at the front desk asked.

I was just about to tell him what my mission was when Sergeant Murchinak popped into the lobby. "I'll take care of it, Cal. She's here to see me," and then he led me back to his office.

"Sorry I didn't call beforehand," I said, drawing up the nearest chair. "I haven't been thinking too clearly ever since Matt first mentioned Clint might be a criminal." I wrung my hands for emphasis.

"No need to apologize," the heavyset cop said. "Your timing's perfect. My departmental meeting doesn't start for another twenty minutes." He pushed his swivel chair in the opposite direction now, grabbed a folder off the shelving unit where he'd put the box of donuts the other day, and then spun back towards me. "There isn't too much more on Russell then what I stated, but at least we have a picture of him." He let go of the fax he had received and slid it across his well-worn desk.

This is it, Mary. It all boils down to one lousy picture. My fingers were sweating so profusely I didn't think I'd be able to lift the paper off the cop's desk. Did I want the guy I knew as Clint Russell to really be him or not? I wasn't sure. Maybe in some perverse sort of way I did. Loneliness could be dangerous. I held the fax in my moist hands and stared at the photo. The man looking back at me was shockingly similar to the one I've come face to face with several times this summer, but I knew without a doubt this was not the Clint Russell I've been with. He was lacking Clint Eastwood's fine chiseled lips and prominent Adam's apple like my guy had.

"Well, what do you think?"

"Could be the guy," I said, "except you said he has a Colorado license."

Sergeant Murchinak cleared his throat. "That's true, but it doesn't mean he couldn't be living up here." He pulled more info out of his folder. "According to our sources, Clint Russell is supposed to be managing a hotel in Denver for his dad, but he hasn't been around for some time. When the employees were asked why they hadn't reported his being AWOL to daddy yet, they said it was because Russell's quite the playboy and skips town whenever he pleases. Sometimes he hit the casinos. Other times he jets off to a clandestine location with a top model in tow."

More bad news. The real Russell doesn't even remotely sound like the guy I have the hots for. I dropped the dreaded fax back on Sergeant Murchinak's desk.

"Are you okay, Mary? You look a little pale. I suppose it's the shock of finding out the guy you've been dating has been in trouble with the law?"

Not quite. What's shaking me up is discovering the guy I have a crush on isn't who he says he is and may be a worse criminal than the real Clint Russell. Speaking of him, where is he? Being held for ransom? "Yes, it is," I replied, "but I'll have to move past it somehow."

Sergeant Murchinak scooped up the information he had shared with me and stuffed it back in the folder. "Look, Mary, if this Russell guy ends up giving you any grief when you let him loose, feel free to dial my number and I'll straighten him out."

"Thanks. I'll remember that."

~38~

I pulled up to the Bar X's massive gates to let Aunt Zoe out, waited long enough for her to adjust the gates so she could squeeze through, and then handed her the pumpkin pie. "Now, don't forget to tell Reed I'll be by in about a half hour to pick you two up. Sally Sullivan's mother is ill, and I don't want to keep her waiting."

"I'll remember. Have a good meeting."

"I plan to." Before I took off down King's Trail for Doc Taylor's, I made darn sure the coast was clear, no oncoming traffic. I didn't need Matt's car in the shop too.

The good-looking veterinarian was getting out of his deep blue Toyota pickup when I pulled into his driveway behind him. He stared at the Topaz for a split second, and then he waved.

I rolled down the car window to check if it was okay to keep the car where it was or park somewhere else.

"It's fine. Leave it there," the casually clothed doctor replied as he walked around to the truck's passenger side, opened the door and grabbed something off the seat.

When his right hand finally emerged from the truck, I saw a medium-sized black bag which I presumed held veterinarian equipment. Doc seemed to struggle with the bag when he shifted it to his left hand to close the truck door and wave me over. "Come on up on the porch where it's cooler. We can talk there."

"Big place you've got here, Doc," I remarked as I followed him up the wide steps leading to an old-fashioned country style veranda furnished with down-home furniture. "How do you have time to take care of it all?" *And how can you afford it? According to my information, you haven't been practicing all that long. Hmm? Maybe he got lucky. A family member left him a ton of money or he won the lottery.*

The vet grinned sheepishly. "Hired help. Besides the upkeep of the house and land, there's a barn where I stable my two horses as well as others I'm asked to tend to from time to time." He plopped his bag by the front door as if it was insignificant and then ushered me over to the white rocking chairs, a southern influence, one sees on many porches in Minnesota and elsewhere during the summer months. "Care for anything cold to drink?" he asked.

I should've milked my visit for all it was worth, but something stopped me. At the time I blamed it on being too jittery. I quickly claimed a chair and sat. "No, thanks, but if you're thirsty go right ahead." I looked beyond him and noticed a small fridge at the end of the veranda. At least he didn't need to abandon his guests if he had a craving for a beer or wine while enjoying the outdoors.

"Actually, I'm fine too. So, what brings you by?"

"I've been curious about a strange object I found a while back and thought I'd show it to you."

Doc Taylor's tanned well-toned six-foot body instantly tensed up. "Oh? How does it concern me?"

I took the small metal object out of a pant pocket and held it in my fist until I was ready to hand it over. "I showed this to a guy at a harness and saddle shop. He didn't recognize it, but suggested I talk to a vet involved with large animals since you guys see a lot more than he does."

He uncrossed his arms. "I see." He held out his hand. "May I examine it?" I passed the object to him. The second his eyes caught a glimpse of it he sucked in too much air and began to choke.

I jumped out of the rocking chair. "Are you all right, Doc? Do you want me to get you a glass of water?" Before he could reply, I headed for the front door.

"No... wait!" he said between coughs. "Don't bother, Miss Malone. I'm fine. It's only my allergies kicking in."

"Are you sure?" *Because I don't mind waiting on a hunk like you.*

"Yup. Positive." He bent his head and stared at the narrow whitewashed floorboards surrounding his feet.

"Something wrong?"

"I dropped the piece of metal you gave me when that coughing spell kicked in." He got up from his chair and looked around. At least he gave me the impression that's what he was doing.

"Oh, I think I see it," I lied.

"You do?"

I got down on my hands and knees but didn't see a thing. It didn't matter. I still had my wild card to play which was hidden in my pant pocket. While Doc Taylor had his head turned in another direction, I pulled the other piece of metal out and pretended to pluck the object in question off the faded floorboards. "I got it." I stood and handed him the piece of metal. "Does this go in a horse's mouth, or is it off a piece of horse equipment?"

The veterinarian acted like the tiny metal object was burning a hole in his hand. He tossed it back to me after about two seconds. "I, ah, don't recall ever seeing anything like that when I've been out and about. Most likely it came off of a piece of farm machinery. Might as well toss it," he casually suggested.

"Yes, you're probably right." I shoved the unidentified object back in my pocket and moved towards the steps. "Say, Doc, have you ever met Reed Griffin's wife? People say she was pretty nasty?"

"Yeah, I think sometime last year. She treated me okay."

Interesting. Either Terry's wrong about when the missus flew the coop, or she returned to do some sniffing around. Which was it? "Huh? Well, maybe those who don't speak highly of her just rubbed her the wrong way," I said, dangling my best smile in front of him, hoping he'd pick up on the cue and invite me to chat longer.

"Could be." Darn, he didn't follow through. Maybe he'd had too strenuous of a morning.

I turned my back to him and marched down the steps. "Thanks for your time."

"Sure. Sorry I couldn't be of help."

You hit pay dirt, Girl. Wait till Mrs. Grimshaw hears what you have to tell her. I put the keys in the ignition and buzzed off.

~39~

I happened to fall a little short of my destination after leaving Doc Taylor's all because of a teeny glitch. The gas tank registered empty. The fault lies with me, of course. I had been too busy to notice, but it also doesn't help that the supply symbols for the Topaz are hard to read on a sunny day. Thankfully, help was only a cell phone away. I opened the glove compartment and dug it out. "Crap." The phone's battery was depleted, and I had no way to recharge it.

That's what you get for telling your aunt you're going to start exercising. Now, you'll have to hoof it.

I climbed out of the car and immediately walked to the front of it to put the hood up. I didn't want some idiot plowing into it, and later state he never saw anything indicating the car had broken down.

Little did I know how hard it would be to get the Topaz's hood to release. Nothing happened even after I threw all my weight on it.

"Having a bit of car trouble, lady?"

I glanced at the car that had just pulled up alongside of me. Great. I wasn't planning on running into him today. *Stay calm, Mary. Russell doesn't know you've got something on him.*

"Oh, hi Clint. Yeah, I ran out of gas and was just trying to put up the hood before I hiked over to Reed's and asked for help."

The man gave me an easy-care smile. "Must be your day to help out at the Bar X again, huh?"

"Yup," I lied, "and I'm running late." I looked at the clothes I had on. Oops. How do I explain what I'm wearing, the outfits too nice to be working in the barn? "Reed's got me helping out in the kitchen. He's throwing a whopper of a shindig this weekend."

"Oh, what's the celebration?"

"I don't know. He didn't elaborate. Just said he needed extra help."

"Well, let me get that hood up for you, and then I'll drop you off."

I swiped the sweat from my forehead. "Thanks. That would be great."

Clint backed his car up behind me and left it running. Then he got out and strolled over to the front of the Topaz. "Give me a little room here, okay?"

I swiftly moved aside, inhaling his intoxicating cologne as I did so. *You've got it bad, Mary. I don't know what you're going to do if this guy turns out to be working for the mafia or something just as sinister.*

Clint laid his hands on the hood, yanked on something I couldn't see, and presto the hood flew up.

"Nice job."

"Glad you think so." He pulled his filthy hands away from the car and brushed them on his stylish jeans.

"Come on. We better get going. You don't want to make your boss mad."

*****

"You were lucky to run out of gas close to the Bar X," my client said as we drove off his property and headed towards the home where Sally Sullivan was raised. "Afternoon temperatures in the summer can be a bear."

I nodded. "That's for sure. Just hiking those four blocks was a killer."

Aunt Zoe examined me closely. "I don't understand why you're not all sweaty after being out in the heat. You usually are. If I didn't know better, I'd say you've been in an air-conditioned room."

"I do feel comfy," I whispered. "It must be that new deodorant I started using the other day."

"Mary, have you given any thought to what you want to ask Sally's mother when we get there?" Reed asked.

"A little," I replied, leaning over my aunt a bit. "I think the rest will come naturally. Once she starts talking, I'm hoping it'll lead somewhere. I just don't want to tire the poor woman out." Now, I positioned my body tightly against the seat again leaving my aunt with room to spare.

She took advantage of the situation and tapped our driver on the arm. "Reed, when do you plan to share your surprise with Mary?"

"What surprise?" I queried.

The owner of the Bar X took his eyes off the road briefly to glance our way. "It's Zoe's idea actually. I'm throwing a party at the ranch this weekend to raise money for Mrs. Sullivan. Hopefully, we'll make enough to cover some of Sally's funeral expenses. They can be quite costly."

"Wow." *How prophetic is that? Here I thought I was making up a big fat lie for Clint and it ends up being true.* "That's very generous, Reed, especially with you just losing Angel."

"It's the least I could do. Besides, we horse people are known to be very generous when it comes to donating to a good cause."

My aunt waved her hands in front of her. "I knew you'd love my idea, Mary. That's why I told Reed we'd like to help him. We don't have any plans for this weekend, or do we?"

I didn't want Reed and my aunt to know about my bowling date with Clint on Sunday evening, so I nonchalantly asked, "Which day? Saturday or Sunday?"

"Saturday," Reed and my aunt replied in unison.

"Perfect. That day is wide open."

Twenty minutes later, Reed turned off the main highway. We had reached Fish Lake in Oakdale. According to the directions Mrs. Sullivan gave me, she resided around the bend from Louie's Bait and Tackle shop which came into view as Reed progressed along the lake frontage road.

"There it is, Reed," I announced dryly. "See the little white clapboard cottage-style cabin tucked in among the pines?"

"I do now. I'm glad you gals came with. I would've driven right past the place."

Aunt Zoe spoke up. "It's a cute yard. I half expect Bambi to prance across the lawn looking for his friends, Flower and Thumper."

I felt the same way, but I wasn't going to admit it. "Oh, I'm sure there are plenty of deer, skunks and rabbits when no one's poking around."

"Don't forget snakes," added Reed.

After we stepped out of Reed's truck, we paraded up a gravel path that led to the front of the house where Mrs. Sullivan, pale as a ghost, sat in a lawn chair positioned on the narrow wooden landing at the top of the steps. "I'd ask you inside," she said weakly, "but since Sally died there's been no one here to pick up after me." She pointed to the right side of the house. "There's lawn chairs in the shed if you'd like to sit."

"No, thank you," the three of us replied.

I moved in closer. "We just have a few things to discuss, and then we'll be on our way."

"I'm so sorry for your loss, Mrs. Sullivan," Reed added. "Sally was such a sweet gal. I looked forward to her visits at the Bar X."

Mrs. Sullivan grabbed a Kleenex from her pant pocket and dabbed her nose. "She spoke very highly of you too, Mr. Griffin. I just wish she hadn't been caring for me, so she could've spent more time with Cinnamon. I don't know what I'm going to do with the horse."

Reed sat down on the edge of the landing. "We can discuss Cinnamon in a bit, okay?"

"All right," the woman replied as she brushed tears off her cheeks.

"I know Sally was pretty upset about Cinnamon being diagnosed with laminitis," I said. "Did she share anything concerning that with you?"

Mrs. Sullivan shook her head. "No, not that I recall. She probably didn't want me to worry. You see, I grew up around horses as a child, and I know what kind of damage laminitis can cause." She shook her head again. "I still don't understand whatever possessed her to drive back to the Bar X that night."

"Could she have been meeting someone?" I asked.

Mrs. Sullivan's thin eyebrows arched severely. "You mean a guy?" I nodded. "With school, the horse and caring for me, she didn't have time for anything else."

Well, that didn't get you anywhere, Mary. I tried another topic. "Has anyone else spoken with you about Sally's death besides the police, neighbors and family?"

Sally's mother thought for a moment. "A few classmates, and there was a message from a man who was interested in purchasing Cinnamon. He didn't leave his name or say how he knew about the horse."

Reed bent his head foreword and shook it, signifying he wasn't the one who contacted her. Could it have been Doc Taylor?"

"I suppose you didn't happen to save the message about the horse?" I said.

Sally's mom dropped the damp Kleenex in her lap. "No. I just thought they'd call back since they didn't leave a number."

Aunt Zoe couldn't stand being on the outer fringes collecting dust any longer. "Do you think you'd recognize his voice if you heard it again?"

"Maybe," Mrs. Sullivan replied, reaching for a glass of water sitting on a table next to her, "I don't get that many calls."

Aunt Zoe turned to me. "You've got a tape recorder, Mary."

I shared a smile. Thankfully, I knew exactly where my aunt was going with her sly comment. With a plan in mind now, I quickly ushered my aunt off the landing so Reed could talk to Mrs. Sullivan privately. Whatever he discussed with her was none of our business. I was only hired to find out why the horses were going over the fence. If Reed wanted to share later, so be it.

~40~

The minute we arrived home I dashed to the computer in the bedroom and sent a picture of the metal object I'd found at the Bar X to the U of M Equine Center, positive they'd recognize the item. Once that was out of the way, I discarded my dress clothes, changing into shorts, tank top, and scruffy tennis shoes. Then, with another mission in mind, which no one could stop, meaning Aunt Zoe, it was off to the kitchen to retrieve the mutt's leash.

I like using Gracie as an excuse to get out of dodge. Oh, I'd walk her all right, but first we'd meander over to Mrs. Grimshaw's. The visit there was twofold: bring her up-to-date on the case and glean sage advice to boot.

"You can unhook Gracie's leash now, Mary," the nonagenarian said as soon as Gracie and I stepped into her apartment. "She's used to my place."

"Thanks. I wasn't sure how long I could restrain her."

"Pretty bird. Pretty bird."

Gracie's ears peaked, but she stayed by my feet.

"Who is that, Gracie? Is that your buddy, Petey?" the elderly woman asked, pointing down the short hallway. "Go see what he wants." The mutt obeyed and dashed out of the living room.

"I know it's impolite to not give someone notice before stopping by," I said, "but I didn't want Aunt Zoe interfering."

The Italian-born woman clapped her hands. "Ah, you've come to discuss your case. Don't you ever fret about showing up unannounced on my doorstep, Mary. Matt did it all the time. How about a glass of ice tea? I was just getting myself some."

I set my tush in her aged rocker, a family heirloom. "No, thank you. I have to stay away from liquids."

Margaret's face looked perplexed. "In this heat?"

"Of course not. Only when I take the mutt for a walk. There's no place I can leave her if I have to, you know, stop some place along the way."

"*Si.* Parrots don't cause that sort of problem, do they?" Margaret left me be for a few minutes to get her tea, and then ambled back to the living room with glass in hand and ensconced herself on her couch. All right, dear, tell me what's going on. I'm all ears."

"What a day this has been," I said, pushing loose strands of hair off my face. "I've been chasing information all over town, and I've got tons to sift through. It all began with Sergeant Murchinak this morning. He wanted me to see a photo of what the real Clint Russell is supposed to look like. Guess what? The guy I've been talking to doesn't fit the bill, and I have a date with him on Sunday night." Some hair cascaded over my face again, and I pushed it aside. "Then, this afternoon, Doc Taylor, the veterinarian my client uses, told me he had no idea what that piece of metal was I'd found. He did let it slip though that he's seen Reed Griffin's wife within this past year. According to Terry from the Bar X, she's been gone two years." I took a brief break, I'd run out of breath.

"My, you certainly have a real mess to muddle through."

"That's not all of it," I added. "The final stop, in Oakdale, produced even more info."

Margaret lifted the tea to her lips but didn't taste it "Who did you see there?"

"Mrs. Sullivan."

"Why of course. She's the deceased girl's mother?"

"Yes. Reed and Aunt Zoe came with. I needed to ask her a few questions about her daughter, and Reed wanted to talk to her about daughter's horse."

"What did she have to say?" My neighbor greedily inquired.

I inched forward on her couch. "Some man left a message saying he was interested in buying her dead daughter's horse."

"Well, that would certainly help with the bills."

"The strange thing is," I continued, "the obituary never mentioned the horse, and the caller never left his name or number."

"Hmm?" Margaret sipped her tea and then set the glass back down on a scenic coaster residing on her light-maple coffee table. "That is odd. How do you plan to follow up on the call?"

I rubbed my hands together. "You're not going to believe this, but Aunt Zoe actually came up with the perfect plan. She thinks if I innocently record voices of those involved at the stable, Sally's mother might recognize who left the message."

"I guess it's worth a try. Just be careful."

Gracie wandered back into the living room, plopped down by my feet, and whined.

"I haven't forgotten about you, girl. We're almost finished."

"Mary, what do you plan to do about Mr. Russell? He could be an outlaw?"

"I'm thinking I'd better call in the big guns."

She frowned. "Who might that be?"

"Matt."

"Yes, that does sound like the sensible thing to do."

I got out of the rocker and hooked the dog's leash to her collar again. "Tell Margaret goodbye, Gracie."

"Wuff. Wuff."

~41~

My head was spinning out of control, and the only way to solve the problem at 3:00 a.m. was to get up and head to the kitchen. Of course, when I got there, I was greeted by a singular Post-It note plastered to the fridge door with a message written in my handwriting. *Mary, remember you promised to start your diet today.*

"How about next week?" I tore the note off the fridge and tossed it in the wastebasket like worn-out sandals. My motto has always been what you can't see you can't feel guilty about. I swung the fridge door open and contemplated what to devour.

Before I could pull anything out, Aunt Zoe waltzed in wearing a knee-length silk nightie past its prime that would put the original meaning of chartreuse to shame. True to form, her face was again painted with that putrid looking African concoction, and her head was covered with those crazy juice-can size rollers that always look like they're ready to explode. "Couldn't sleep either, huh, Mary?"

"Nope."

"Why don't you open that Marshmallow Graham Cracker ice cream we bought the other day. I'm dying to try it."

I slapped my leg. "I can't believe I forgot about it." I closed the fridge and yanked the freezer door open. The ice cream was in plain view. I pulled the carton out, set it on the counter, and then gathered spoons and bowls. "How many scoops would you like, Auntie?" I asked over my shoulder.

"Two. No, make that three."

I scooped out the desired amount of ice cream she requested, and then gave myself the same portion plus a little extra. I know what you're thinking, but don't worry. I packed down my ice cream so Aunt Zoe will never be the wiser. Besides, where was it written gaining weight while pigging out on a dairy product's a crime? It's not like eating a double burger and fries.

After I put the ice cream carton away, I brought our bowls to the table, and set my aunt's in front of her. "Why did you get up?" I finally thought to ask. "I hope it wasn't because of me."

My aunt's ice cream-laden spoon stopped just before entering her open lips. "My waking up had nothing to do with you. I'm worried about Reed. He's still keeping his thoughts on Angel's death bottled up, and that's not healthy. If he doesn't open up soon, I'm afraid he might do something drastic."

I had eaten the first helping of ice cream too fast, and was suffering from brain freeze. "Like what?"

Aunt Zoe set her spoon in her bowl. "That's just it. I haven't a clue. I wish…"

"Wish what?"

"I knew the secret of getting him to open up. The problem is we haven't been together long enough for him to feel he can trust me yet." She picked up her spoon and stirred her ice cream round and round like she was trying to make a shake. "I'd bet anything he'd spill his guts to that woman who split on him."

"You're referring to his wife," I stated, and then devoured the last bite of evidence that proved my dieting vow had been broken and then some. After the cool cream slid through my esophagus, I continued. "She's a very intriguing person. Oh, I forgot I didn't share the latest scoop on her, did I? Doc Taylor told me he saw her this past year, but Terry said she'd been gone two years. I believe you need to get the story from the horse's mouth, Auntie. Ask him straight out."

She pressed her hand to her cheek. "Do you think Reed's been lying to me?"

"No, but you really don't know that much about him, do you?"

Aunt Zoe braced her elbows on the table and rested her bowed head in her hands. "You must think I'm a foolish old woman. But is it so wrong to think I can find another man to love me?"

I reached out and put my arm around her shoulders. "Of course not, Auntie, everyone deserves happiness no matter how old they are."

She lifted her head and dropped her hands in her lap. "You really mean that, Mary?"

"Sure. If Mrs. Grimshaw found love at her age, I'd jump on the bandwagon and help her plan the wedding." I carried the used bowls to the sink where they would sit until I washed them after breakfast in about five hours, and then I grabbed a wet dishrag and brought it to the table to wipe it off.

"Mary, why were you roaming around this time of night? Did it have to do with Reed's problems?"

"Yup." I finished cleaning the table and tossed the dishrag in the sink. "I've got so much info concerning Reed's ranch swimming around in my noggin it's looking for an outlet. Why and how are horses jumping over a neighbor's fence? What prompts a young woman to return to a ranch after hours? Why did a healthy horse suddenly die? Could all three events be connected?"

Aunt Zoe stretched her arms out and shook her flame-curled hair. "I don't know. You're the sleuth. Figure it out before we both go nuts," she said, and went off to bed.

I will. Right after I speak to Matt about another problem.

~42~

Friday

I was sitting at the kitchen table deep in thought trying to figure out which scenario worked best for what's been happening at Reed's ranch when Aunt Zoe quietly treaded into the room. She probably thought she'd catch me enjoying a snack right after finishing breakfast. I held up a pen and immediately put her at ease. "No food in front of me. See. I'm jotting stuff down."

"Honestly, Mary. You make it sound like I'm spying on you. Can't a person come in here to get a cup of coffee?"

"Sure. I don't control anyone's coffee intake," I said tongue in cheek.

"Okay, you got me. I did think you might be sneaking a snack." She walked over to where I sat and leaned over my shoulder. "What are all those squiggles on your paper?"

"People who might have it in for Reed."

"And the lines?"

"I'm using them to show which squiggles might be working with each other."

"Would I be correct in assuming the letters of the alphabet you're using stand for different people, like A for Jackson and B for Terry?"

"Good deduction. So far, I've got Terry connected to Jackson and Reed's wife, but I'm thinking Nat and Clint might play a part in it there somewhere too." Not knowing how long I'd been sitting here trying to connect up people, I took a quick look over my shoulder at the wall clock. "Yikes. I didn't realize it was so late. I need to call Matt. Would you like me to give him a message?"

"Why are you calling Matt? Asking him for advice about the case?"

I waved my hand. "Heavens no. Matt doesn't know about it. Remember when I begged to use the Topaz?"

"Yes."

"Well, he made me promise to let him know how it was running, and I haven't done that yet." I tried to scoot my chair back now, but Aunt Zoe blocked my progress.

When she finally realized my dilemma, she moved to the side. "Just tell that brother of yours we miss him and his mutt's doing fine."

"I will." Since I was still keeping my involvement with Clint Russell a secret in regards to my aunt, I left the kitchen, ventured off to the bedroom which offered absolute privacy, and dialed the contact number I had for Matt. "Hi, I didn't wake you, did I?"

Matt let out a loud yawn. "Nope. Got a few things to do before I can get any shut-eye."

"Are you in Ireland?"

"I was in Dublin last week, and I head there again next week. How are Mom, Dad, and Gracie?"

"Mom and Dad are doing fine. They've been traveling a lot this summer, so Aunt Zoe and I volunteered to have Gracie with us. She's been great. Of course, Mrs. Grimshaw's thrilled she's here again."

"How are you and Aunt Zoe?"

I laughed. "Some days I'm ready to kick her out and let her fend for herself. Then other days she surprises me with ideas I would have never thought of."

"Sounds promising. How's the Topaz been working out for you?"

"So far, it's going where I want it to go."

"Great. So, what's up, Sis? This is only the second time you've chatted with me since I left Minnesota. I've a feeling this call pertains to more than the car. Is Rod Thompson giving you a hard time? If he is, I'll have someone back home kick his butt for me. You wouldn't believe how many people owe me favors."

"In your line of work, probably a small army, but you can cool your jets. Rod's in and out of town too much to make trouble for anyone in this complex. I'm calling about a friend of mine. She's dating a guy who says he's a certain person, but when I checked him out I discovered he isn't really that person. When I told her he was lying about his identity, she was adamant he wasn't a criminal."

"Ah, Mary, this friend doesn't happen to be you, does it?"

Darn. Why does he always see through things so easily?

"Me? No way. I'm not dating anyone at the moment." Which is the truth. My date's not till Sunday. "The person I'm referring to is actually another teacher. *Now, I do have to get to the confessional.* "Who besides a teenager or a criminal would use a fake identity?

"A married person for one. I've seen a lot of that in my line of work. Then there are police informants and people in the witness protection program. Of course, the person your girlfriend is associating with could also be a famous person just trying to stay out of the limelight."

"Believe me, he's not anybody famous."

Matt yawned over the phone lines again. "Look. You could talk to my buddy Sergeant Murchinak and see what he thinks. He's at the sub-station nearest the apartment."

"That's a thought. So, there's nothing else you can think of?"

Silence filled the phone wires for a second, and then, "How long has your friend known this guy?"

"Not long. Is that important?"

"Could be. Somebody working undercover wouldn't want anyone knowing his true identity either. You know, like an investigator, a cop, an FBI agent or someone with the CIA."

"Hmm? You've certainly given me plenty to chew on. I especially appreciate your suggesting I talk to your cop friend. I wouldn't have thought of that. Oh, before I hang up Aunt Zoe sends her love."

"Tell her ditto."

"I will. Good luck with your work in Ireland. Who knows, maybe you'll find time to look up our long lost Malone clan while you're there."

"Maybe. Good night, Sis."

"Good night."

Finished with the call now, I went to the living room. Aunt Zoe was sitting on the sofa, romance book in hand and Gracie snuggled next to her. "Hey, my stomach says it's time for lunch. How do you feel about going to Milt's to get one of their juicy California burgers?"

Aunt Zoe marked the page she was on with her hand and then looked up. "I'm fine with that. It's you who's dieting."

"Ah, phooey, grapefruit doesn't spoil that fast. Let's go. You too, Gracie."

~43~

When I chose to eat at Milt's Hamburger Joint, I didn't realize what a terrific decision it would turn out to be. As soon as the skinny, pimple-faced teenager opened his mouth to take Aunt Zoe's and my orders, bells and whistles blasted away. Unfortunately, the sound I picked up on had nothing to do with being the millionth customer to walk through Milt's doors and winning a free meal. But something just as exciting happened that didn't include food. Memories stashed in my cranium from the night I got knocked unconscious at the Bar X had finally been jarred loose thanks to our waiter's voice.

"Mary. Earth to Mary," Aunt Zoe said, waving her hand in front of my face to make contact. "The waiter wants your order. Are you having that hard of a time deciding?"

"What? Oh, sorry. I guess I was daydreaming."

"That's okay," the waiter replied, "Take your time. We're not that busy."

I held the menu in front of me pretending to peruse it even though I already knew what I planned to get. "I don't remember seeing you here at Milts before," I slyly said to the waiter. "Are you new?"

"Nah, I've been here a while. I work part-time."

I smiled. "I see. I set the two-sided menu on the table. "I guess I'll have a double cheeseburger, onion rings and a chocolate shake."

"Okay, thanks, ladies. Your orders shouldn't take too long. Do you want a bowl of popcorn while you wait?"

"I don't know," Aunt Zoe said. "What do you think, Mary?"

"Sure, why not."

When the teenager moved out of range, Aunt Zoe questioned my behavior. "What was that malarkey about? You knew what you were going to order before we even left the underground parking at the Foley."

I leaned in closer to her and cupped my mouth. "I know. I just wanted to hear the kid talk."

She gave me a sharp look. "What were you smoking before we got here?"

"Smoking? Speak for yourself. Your eyes are burning a hole in my head, Auntie."

"Can you blame me? You aren't making any sense."

Look who's talking! "Yes, I am. I haven't lost any marbles yet."

Aunt Zoe drummed her nails on the plastic tabletop and gave me her not-a-happy-camper frown. "Then please explain."

"I can't." If told her something right now, I'd jeopardize the case I was hired for. You see our waiter was rapidly approaching with the popcorn and beverages.

"I don't understand," she blubbered. "I asked a simple ques—"

"Shh," I warned. "He's coming."

"Who...?" she asked, whipping her head to the left to see the person walking towards us. "Oh?"

Within seconds, the snack and shakes were plopped on the table. "There you go, ladies. The cook said your order will be ready in five minutes. Is there anything else I can get you?"

"Nope," I replied, taking possession of my chocolate shake.

"Okay," and then our server trotted back towards the kitchen.

The moment he was out of sight, I let my aunt know what was going on. "I recognized that kid's voice from the night I got knocked out."

"Are you positive?"

I poked a straw in my shake and had a sip. "Yup. The cracks and faltering in his voice gave him away."

Auntie mimicked my movements. After she swallowed what had come through her straw, she said, "What are you going to do about the kid?"

"We'll watch for him to go on break. If he's anything like teenagers working at other fast food places, he'll head to his car and listen to his favorite music."

Aunt Zoe got wound up. "And, we'll trap him in his car."

I shared a smile. "Exactly."

*****

It was late afternoon when we invited Margaret Grimshaw to join Aunt Zoe and me in our Moroccan-style living room as we relived our lunchtime escapade in the alley behind Milt's.

"I can't believe you two surprised that youth the way you did," Margaret said, trying to persuade her body she could get down low enough to sit on one of the covered cushions resting on the carpet. "Weren't you afraid he'd pull out a knife? Or worse yet, run you down with his car?"

I put off the elderly woman's questions for the time being. Right now, it was more important to resolve her struggles with our housing accommodations, and in order to do that I'd have to give up the La-Z-Boy. I jumped up. "Margaret, take my seat. You'll be more comfortable," then I sat where she'd originally planned to.

Being of the old school, our neighbor hastily questioned my interference in the seating arrangements. "You don't have to give up your chair, Mary, you know. I'm perfectly happy to sit wherever."

"Yes, I do," I firmly stated. I didn't relish the thought of sitting on the floor either, but unlike the much younger generation coming up, I highly respected my elders. Besides, it would be easier to help the nonagenarian out of the recliner than it would be to get her off the floor.

Margaret didn't say another word. She straightened out her aged-body and slowly padded her way to the large chair.

With the seating arrangement finally settled, I was ready to answer our neighbor's previous questions concerning the teenaged waiter at Milt's, but Aunt Zoe didn't give me a chance. She beat me to the punch. Since I didn't feel like causing a ruckus in front of our neighbor, I let it slide.

"Mary and I didn't think about the danger involved," she said. "We only wanted answers."

The elderly woman clapped her hands. "Bravo."

Wonderful! Margaret thinks we're some kind of super heroines. If I don't set her straight, she'll be spreading the wrong message around the Foley. "Ah, we weren't alone. Gracie was with us too."

"Oh?" She put a hand to her chest and then just as suddenly took it away. *My, God. I hope she's not having a heart attack.* Luckily, that wasn't the case. "I'm so relieved to hear that. Gracie's very protective. So, did the teenager tell you whose idea it was to have Reed's horses jump over the fence?"

"It wasn't Terry's according to the description he gave," Aunt Zoe announced, slowly melting into a cushion pressed against Gracie's body.

"What name did he give you?"

"Mr. Smith," I said. "How original is that? What's wrong with Mr. Zorba or say Mr. Rogers?"

"Yeah," Aunt Zoe agreed. "I wouldn't have questioned those names."

Our visitor steepled her fingers and then slowly flexed them back and forth. "Think a little harder about the youth's description, Mary? There's got to be someone at the Bar X who fits the bill."

I shook my head. "I've tried. I can't think of anyone. The only person I haven't met is Jackson."

"He's the one you filled in for, right?"

"Yup, that's one day I'll never forget."

Aunt Zoe stood up and began to move around the room. "Maybe if we're lucky, he'll be at the party Saturday."

"According to Reed, he's quite the ladies' man," I added.

"A party?" Margaret said excitedly. "Where?"

Aunt Zoe blushed. "At the Bar X."

"Of course, another possibility," I stated, "is that Reed's wife is involved with what's been happening at the

Bar X. If that's the case, the guy working with the teen could be her boyfriend."

Gracie got up and wandered over to the woman in the La-Z-Boy. "I know they're both ignoring you, aren't they?"

"Wuff. Wuff."

Margaret tilted her head and began rubbing Gracie's noggin. "It wouldn't surprise me if Jackson was both the boyfriend and the mysterious horse man."

"Me neither," I chimed in. "It takes two to tango."

Aunt Zoe stopped pacing. "Tango? Why, I thought you didn't like to dance, Mary?"

~44~

Saturday

The reflection of me viewed from the bathroom mirror was downright scary. I was beginning to take on the shape of a few familiar balloons in Macy's Thanksgiving Day Parade, and I didn't like it one bit. Several pounds needed to be shed, but it wasn't going to happen tonight, not while I was being tempted by generous portions of free food served on a zillion different plates at Reed Griffin's party. Why, it's downright rude to turn down goodies offered by the host. Besides, when I'm nervous, I need comfort food, and there was plenty to be nervous about. I was hunting down a killer or two.

"Mary, will you please stop wiggling. I'll never get the recorder attached to your vest, and it was your idea."

"I can't help it, Auntie. This mirror makes me look like an elephant."

"Don't drag me into your weight problem. You know what you can do. Now stand still."

I sighed. "Why, couldn't I have been born to be a size eight like my mother's side of the family?"

"I'm not the one to ask. Perhaps your Mom ate too much before she delivered you."

"Boy, if only I could blame it on that, I'd feel a whole lot better." I moved too sharply now.

"Ow! That's it. If I prick myself one more time, Mary, you can just get someone else to finish the job."

"I'm sorry. I'm worried about the recorder. Are you positive I'll be able to reach it?"

"Here, give me your hand and see for yourself." I shot my right hand behind me and my aunt set it where she had partially sewed the recorder in place. "See, you'll be able to reach it, and no one will ever be the wiser."

"That's for sure. If I was doing this spy gig a couple years ago, the only thing you'd spot floating over my pants would be the vest. Now, no one cares what rides over his or her pants as long as they can tug on whatever upper covering they're wearing to hide their humongous derrières and underpants."

"Just remember you're hiding more than that tonight," my aunt stressed, "so don't raise the vest too high."

"Gott'cha."

*****

Reed was all thumbs when we arrived at his backdoor carrying the bakery treats he requested for tonight. "I'm glad you gals came so early. I haven't a clue what I'm supposed to be doing. Terry usually handles everything when we have the cookouts."

Aunt Zoe immediately took his hand and led him inside to the kitchen table. "Don't fret, Reed. Tell us what needs doing and we'll see to it. But first I'm going to get you a cup of coffee."

"That would be nice. I haven't poured myself one since early this morning."

I pulled up a chair and sat down next to my client. "Zoe managed to sew the recorder to the inside of my vest. Wasn't that clever?"

Reed gave my aunt a quick wink. "Yup, she's quite a clever filly that secretary of yours, and a smart dresser too."

Wild and crazy perhaps, but not smart.

Aunt Zoe deposited his mug of steaming coffee in front of him and then joined us. "You're too kind, sir," she remarked using a sultry voice.

Reed rapped his knuckles on the table, causing a bit of coffee to spill out of his cup. "I mean every darn word. Roy Rogers wouldn't have given Dale Evans a second glance if you had been available. Why, you're the only woman I know, Zoe, who is brave enough to wear a full-fledged fire engine red cowgirl outfit from head to toe, besides his wife."

Auntie went gaga on us. *I'll have to borrow a page from Reed's script the next time her jabbering is driving me crazy.*

I dug out a pen and paper from my miniature bluish-green woven handbag before my aunt woke up from whatever corner of her mind she had escaped to. "Okay, Reed, tick off what still needs to get done around here."

"Let's see. Put plastic tablecloths on the metal tables; paper plates and other eating accessories should be set on the card table. Folding chairs need to be set out. And figure out where the hamburger and hotdog buns should go on."

"Got any trays?" I inquired.

"Not that I know of."

Aunt Zoe finally regained her senses. "How about cookie sheets?"

"Yup. We've got tons of those."

"I figured you would," she sweetly replied. "I know how much you like chocolate chip cookies."

Loud growling came from my stomach. Mentioning cookies anytime is bad. "Hush. I'll get plenty for you later."

Aunt Zoe poked me in the arm. "What did you say?"

"Oh, I was wondering about condiments. Reed, you're going to offer mustard, onions, ketchup, and relishes, aren't you."

"Sure. Sure," the master of the house said as he gulped his last drop of coffee. "Meat doesn't taste right without those garnishments." He pointed to the pantry. "I buy in bulk so you ought to find everything in there you need, except the onions, they're by the fridge."

"Roughly, how many people are you expecting for this fund raiser?" I asked, concerned I wouldn't be able to keep track of the main characters, namely those who boarded or worked on Reed's property.

He scratched his bare head. "About fifty."

Whew, you've got your work cut out for you, girl. I picked up my pen and scribbled *slice fifteen large onions* as my mother's culinary words came back to me, "Always slice enough onions for more than you think will eat them."

While I busied myself with notes, my roommate scanned the various counters in the kitchen. "I see the buns, but I don't see any hamburger thawing, Reed. Did you forget to take the meat out of the freezer?"

The owner of the Bar X pushed his chair out and stood. "Terry should be along shortly. He's in charge of picking the meat up from the market and cooking it." He plucked his mug off the table and set it by the coffee pot. "By the way, Mary, I thought of a few other things. Watermelons need to be cut up; chips, pretzels and such need to be put in serving containers, and pop and water bottles can be stashed in the metal coolers on the porch after a bag of ice has been dumped in each one."

"I noticed the grills when we walked up to the house. Are they charcoal or gas?

Reed swiped his brow. "Oh, crap! That's another thing I have to do. Hook up the gas tanks."

That answered my question. I put my pen down, picked up the list, and moved away from the table. "Okay gang, if we divvy up these tasks I jotted down, we might be able to relax before the guests arrive."

"Sounds good," Reed said.

Aunt Zoe got out of her seat and marched over to Reed and I. "Wait a second. Aren't we're rushing things a bit?"

"What do you mean?" I replied, "We've only got two hours."

"I know that, but before you divide the chores up you'd better put down cutting cake and putting bars and cookies on serving plates too."

Thanks for catching that Zoe." I patted my stomach. *How could you let me forget about the cookies?* "Now, who wants to do what?"

~45~

"Pruning time has arrived, Aunt Zoe," I announced, as we stepped into the party crowd filling the grounds nearest Reed's house.

For once, it didn't take her long to figure out I was speaking figuratively. Her head bounced in agreement. "Yes, some trees around here could definitely use some reshaping. Which ones do you think you'll start with?"

"I was thinking those tall oaks near the barn where Cinnamon's tied up."

"Looks like there's quite a bit of work to be done, but you can handle it." Aunt Zoe caught sight of Reed and waved. He returned the wave and then motioned for her to come over by him, so she did. After a couple minutes with him, she returned carrying a small object in her hand. "You forgot your cell phone in the kitchen. Will it fit in a pants pocket?"

I took the phone from her. "Nah, but that's all right. I'd rather have it out, so I can take pictures of people when they least expect it. Come on."

We slowly sauntered over to the intimate group of ten we had been referring to earlier. I didn't know a soul, but I went ahead and inquired about the horse saddled up and tied to a post.

While I was trying to collect an answer, Nat Newman arrived on the scene with cigarette in hand at precisely the right moment. "It's Sally's horse. Terry and Jackson thought she should be out here with us. You know to honor her owner." She lit her cigarette now.

"That was very thoughtful of them," I said, and then proceeded to prepare my phone camera for usage. "Does anyone mind if I snap a few pictures?"

"Depends on what you're going to do with them," the tall, skinny guy with a black cowboy hat resting at an angle on his head said with a serious air about him. He looked like death warmed over. Either the 100 degree day or a recent illness was taking its toll on him. Since I didn't know him, I wasn't sure which.

"Sally's mother is too ill to come tonight," I explained, "and I thought she'd appreciate seeing what took place."

Unfortunately, the man who questioned me never had a chance to react. "What a nice gesture. Go ahead, take all the pictures you want" the rest of the group replied, moving closer together and posing for me.

George Owen, who I'd seen with Nat the night of the cookout, stepped out from behind me after I finished the first click. Either he had just arrived, or he had been visiting with a different circle of people. "Make sure to take a picture of Cinnamon's hooves while you're at it."

"Why would I want to do that, George?"

Aunt Zoe, who had steadfastly remained by my side since joining this particular cluster of people, glanced here and there before nonchalantly moving a few inches behind me. I waited till she cleared her throat, our signal for all is fine, and then pretended to tug on the back of my frilly white shirt. But you and I both know differently. I'd flicked on the recorder my aunt had so painstakingly sewed to my vest, and George was my first subject.

He shook his head. "You must be fairly new to horses. Otherwise, you'd know it's an honor to have a horse's hooves painted."

Terry joined our group now. "She's a greenhorn, but she's learning fast."

"Terry, I'd like a shot of you standing next to Cinnamon, is that okay." I said.

He didn't hesitate for an instant. "Sure." As he sauntered closer to Sally's horse he somberly explained the significance of painted hooves. "The horses that are chosen to pull the black artillery caisson holding a fallen soldier's casket for burial at Arlington National Cemetery get special primping for the occasion, one of which is painted hooves."

"Where do the horses come from?" someone in the group asked.

"Mainly Illinois, Texas and Virginia. They, as well as, the riders train in Fort Myer, Virginia." Cinnamon dropped her head slightly and playfully nudged Terry. Terry still had his mouth open when I snapped the picture.

It was the way the man and animal were together that made me realize Terry had nothing to do with Sally's death. Sally had a strong bond with her horse. If this man killed Sally, there's no way Cinnamon would tolerate his nearness.

I had one more question for him though, before I caught up with another group and captured their voices and pictures. "What kind of paint's used to cover the hooves?"

Terry patted Cinnamon's neck and then drew out a carrot from his shirt pocket. "Gosh, I don't know. You'd have to ask Jackson. He was here just a minute ago."

"He headed towards the house," Nat shared enthusiastically.

I studied the group of people I had been hanging out with for the last few minutes and noted the only person missing was the dude who had questioned me about the picture taking. Darn. I couldn't remember if he had shied away from view before I snapped the first pose or not. I peeked at my watch now. *Better mosey on, Gal. If you didn't get him this time, you can always catch him off guard later.* I slickly slid my hand under my vest and promptly turned the microcassette recorder off.

Aunt Zoe had disappeared right after Terry explained about horses being used for military funerals, but she must've sensed I was ready to change my focus because she suddenly appeared at my side again. "The grubs finally ready, Mary. Should we go chow down?"

"Okay." And so we meandered off towards the tables holding the grub, staying a safe distance from the others when we reached our goal. "Thanks, for rescuing me. I was trying to think of a way to cut loose."

"That's all right. I'm famished. So, how's the sleuthing going so far?"

"According to Terry, Jackson had been among those we were just with."

"Really? "What did he look like?" She raised a hand to her mouth and started chewing on her bright red painted nails.

I yanked off the cowgirl hat I wore in honor of Sally and ran my hand through my damp hair. "Did you see the skinny dude with the black Stetson?"

"The one who looked like he was about to die?"

"Yup."

"Wow. I can't believe you found him so fast," she said, dropping the hand she had been chewing on to her side.

"The problem is I didn't know it was him until after he skedaddled so he may not even be in the photos I took. And if I don't catch him later, I might not have anything to show the waiter."

"But you got him on the recorder, right?"

"Nope. I didn't flick the microcassette on until after he asked what the pictures were for," I said, arriving at the table with grilled meat and picking up a paper plate.

"I've got an idea. Reed can invent a reason for Jackson to meet him by the barn, and you can hide nearby."

I placed a burger on a bun and filled it with condiments. My stomach appreciated being fed, but revolted against Aunt Zoe's plan. There was always the off chance it could backfire. Like Jackson's partner in crime catching me in the act. "I'll think about it," I stated politely without hinting at how I actually felt. "The party hasn't been going all that long yet, Auntie, so there should still be an opportunity to catch him chewing the fat on the sidelines with someone else."

"All I'm saying is plant my suggestion in your head, and if you need to go to plan B come find me." After she piled an assortment of goodies on her plate, she said, "I'm going to see if anything else needs to be put on these tables," and left me to fend for myself.

"I knew I should've invited Mrs. Grimshaw along to keep me company," I muttered under my breath, "or Gracie for that matter." When I had finally filled my plate beyond recognition, I glanced over my shoulder to see if anyone I had seen earlier was still by the barn. Nope. Jim

Savage whom I had met at the last cookout was standing there by his lonesome using the barn to brace his back as he scarfed his food down. He must've just gotten here. I snapped on the recorder and waltzed over to him.

*****

I roamed the grounds for another hour after I finished the stint with Jim, but I never did run into Jackson. Discouraged, I returned to Reed's house and looked for Aunt Zoe.

The second I rounded the back of my client's house, I caught sight of Doc Taylor with Reed. Hmm? When did he arrive? From the way Doc's tall, muscular figure was leaning into Reed's shorter stature it looked like the two were having a meaningful discussion, one that shouldn't be interrupted, leaving me in a quandary whether to advance or not. A minute later, I turned the recorder on and proceeded forward. If the men wanted a private conversation, they should've taken it inside behind closed doors.

"I know what you're saying, Troy, but I haven't made up my mind yet."

About what?

"Oh, hi, Mary," Reed said. "Look who just got here."

I grinned and hastily nodded to acknowledge Troy's presence, forgetting for a moment that I had put the stupid turquoise cowgirl hat my aunt had loaned me back on. Of course, the hat slipped and partially covered my face when I'd bent my head. *Great! Why do I always end up looking like such an idiot around him? If you want to capture someone like the vet, Mary, you have to train yourself to be on your toes all the time. The heck I do. Not on a scorcher of a day like this.*

"I gotta tell you this party wouldn't have been a success, Troy, if Mary and Zoe hadn't helped out."

Doc lifted a can of beer to his lips. "Is that so?" *So, he's a beer guy. Huh? All this time I had pegged him as a wine connoisseur. Well, at least we have one thing in common.* "I thought your work here at the Bar X was a one-shot thing, Mary. You know, filling in for Jackson like you did."

My eyes swiftly darted to my dusty boots. "What can I say? Obviously, Reed likes my work ethics."

Reed swiftly backed me up. "These days it's hard finding last minute help you can depend on, and Mary is definitely dependable. Why, the minute I call her, she drops everything and zips on over."

"I'll have to remember that," the vet said, "when I need help with my next shindig."

How about inviting me to the party instead, dude? "What kept you from getting here sooner, Doc, trouble at your place or somewhere else?"

The innocent interrogation seemed to make him on edge. *Why?* "My place," he replied hesitantly, "but I got the situation under control," and didn't elaborate further.

"Too bad you didn't get here earlier," I continued, "You missed seeing Cinnamon saddled up in honor of Sally. Jackson painted her hooves like they do for the horses carrying the casket of fallen soldiers at Arlington National Cemetery. Actually, I was kind of surprised to see the painted hooves."

"Why?" Reed asked.

"Cinnamon has laminitis."

Doc's normally sedate voice boomed. "What? Who said that?"

"Sally Sullivan."

Reed looked shocked. "When did she tell you?"

"At the last cookout you had."

The owner of the Bar X turned on the vet. "Why didn't you inform me, Troy? I want to know these things."

Troy's mouth clamped shut. Darn. The only way it will ever come loose is if we get a crow bar to pry it open or if the Doc himself comes up with a reasonable doozie to weasel his way out of the doghouse.

Seeing as he was getting nowhere with the young vet, my client finally gave up on him and shined the spotlight on me instead. "Mary, do you know who informed Sally of her horse's problem?"

"As a matter of fact—"

"Mary, there you are," Aunt Zoe bellowed from the porch before she trotted down the steps to join us. "I was beginning to think you had wandered out on the trail and had gotten lost."

"Afraid not. I'm right here."

"Sorry to interrupt the two of you," Reed said, "but Mary was about to reveal something of major importance."

"She was?" Aunt Zoe buzzed straight to my side. *Why couldn't she move that fast when Gracie needed to be walked?* "Go ahead, Mary. You and I can chat later."

Before I breathed another word, I readjusted the stupid cowgirl hat. It was bugging me. "Sally said Terry told her."

Doc Taylor grew red in the face. "What the heck have you hired me for, Reed, if you're going to allow your workers to diagnose and treat ailments without consulting me?"

"You mean you didn't know about it either?" Reed said.

"Of course not."

"Then why didn't you just come out and say so?"

"I didn't know what kind of rebuttal you expected."

What a wimp. Maybe I should reconsider establishing a relationship with this guy even if it meant mother would continue to harp about who I was dating.

"When this fund raiser is over tonight, Terry and I are sitting down and having a long chat," Reed fumed, and then stormed up the steps leading to his back door.

After the screen door slammed shut, shy Doc shared a lopsided grin. "Well, if you'll excuse me, ladies, I'd better get some grub before it's all gone," and off he went, never to see him again that evening.

~46~

Aunt Zoe folded and unfolded her pudgy hands "I suppose I should check on Reed. He seemed mighty upset. By the way, did you ever find Jackson?"

"Nope. He seems to have vanished."

I probably would've hightailed it too if I thought the game was up. Tell me the truth, Mary. Do you really think Terry's been helping Jackson stir the pot?"

I stretched my hands out in front of me and stared at the broken nails. "He could be. Both men work side by side from sunup to sundown. The real question is what did Terry hope to gain by telling Sally her horse had laminitis and then hiding the information from his boss?"

My aunt tapped her red-booted foot. "It doesn't make sense, does it? Remember the day you and I ate lunch here, and Terry bored us to death with all the ranch details he shared with Reed."

I released a long laugh. "How can I forget? You were so looking forward to having a nice, relaxing luncheon with Reed, and then, pow, Terry took over the show. Your eyes rolled back in their sockets."

"I was disgusted with that man," she said, spinning in the direction of the house now. I'd better go in. Where will you be if I need to find you later?"

"I wanted to take another look at Cinnamon and Angel's stalls just in case I missed anything, but I probably should take the recorder off my vest first. No reason to wear that extra weight if I don't have to."

Aunt Zoe locked arms with me as we walked up the narrow wooden steps together. "Mary, promise me you'll be careful when you go out to the barn."

I held up my hand. "I swear, Auntie."

*****

Once the recorder was safely tucked away in a cookie jar on Reed's kitchen counter, I gravitated towards the barn, a good thirty feet from the house. Too bad I didn't sense I'd hit a bump in the road before entering the barn.

Two feet from my destination, Terry, one of the few people I had hoped to avoid, quietly approached from behind catching me totally off guard. "Hey, where are you headed, cowgirl?"

I stopped dead in my tracks. "Terry, I had no idea anyone was behind me."

"Sorry. The garbage bags were full, and I thought they should be dropped in the dumpster before the dogs and other critters start messing with them."

"No need to apologize. With all the people wandering around here today, I should've expected someone to come up behind me without knowing it. "So, what were you saying to me?"

"I asked where you're going."

"To spend time with Cinnamon before she gets sold."

We reached the dumpster now, and Terry tossed the two bags in. "You know, Missy, I think you've gotten a lot braver around here since you filled in for Jackson."

His comment sounded like a compliment and I thanked him. But then, without regard to my client personally wanting to rake this man over the coals, I did an about face and went for the jugular. "Why tell Sally that Cinnamon had laminitis, but not share the info with the vet or Reed?"

"What?? They didn't know? Dam!" He balled his hands into fists. I stepped back worried he might take a swing at me. "Do I have to do everything around here? Jackson said he'd report Cinnamon's condition to the boss."

The fear I had of this man a moment ago swiftly disappeared. "Are you saying Jackson's the one who discovered Cinnamon had laminitis?"

"That's right. Look, I've worked around horses here and there, but there's no way my experiences will ever match Jackson's. He has farrier experience, and I don't. So, when he tells me one of the horses has health issues, I'd be crazy to question him."

All roads kept winding back to Jackson, but my gut tells me there's still someone working behind the scenes. Who is it? Nat? Clint? Reed's wife? I hadn't heard back yet from the University of Minnesota Equine Center regarding the picture I faxed them of the metal object, but what the heck, as long as Terry was right here and no one else was around I might as well get his input. I whipped the piece of metal out of my jean's left side pocket.

"Terry, have you ever used this before?"

His scruffy jaw dropped. "Where did you get that?"

Oh, oh. I hadn't expected that reaction. Aunt Zoe's warning flashed through my head. Hopefully, I'm not going to regret the can of worms I opened. *You're okay, Mary. You're out in the open, and there are still plenty of people milling around.* "I don't remember where I found it," I lied.

"Oh, God, don't tell Reed." He took his cheap straw cowboy hat off and twisted it in his hands. "The man's got enough on his plate with Sally's and Angel's death and his ex-wife bullying him."

Just then my cell phone binged. Someone had texted me. I pulled the phone from my other front pocket now and began to read the message from the U of M as it floated across the screen. The timing couldn't have been more perfect.

According to the message, the foreign object I held in my hand had been used five years ago on Run Great, a thoroughbred, owned by a rich Polish gent. The horse was disqualified at the Grand National in England after it was discovered that a hidden charging device had been inserted in one of his hindquarters. Since then, the illegal device had been pulled from the market.

Having been armed with extremely important information, I put my phone away and focused my attention once again on the man with the rusty-colored hair. "Why did you use this metal device on those three horses that were retrieved from Clint Russell's yard? Are you and Russell running a scam, or were you trying to prove something to someone? Come on, Terry, which is it?"

"Just tell me this," he grunted, "Are you a private eye?"

"Do I look like one?"

"Not really."

"Well, you're right. I'm merely a substitute teacher," I explained, "but Reed's been good to me, and I don't want to see him get screwed."

Terry glanced over his shoulder to make sure no one else was around. "Hey, you don't have to worry; I'm not screwing anybody, not even his wife."

"What's that supposed to mean?"

"Stay here awhile longer, and you'll figure it out."

I dragged my foot in the dirt. "You still haven't answered my question concerning the horses."

"All right. You want the scoop? Here it is, Miss Goodie Two Shoes. I don't know how you got ahold of that charging device, but I swear I never sent any horses over Clint's fence with it. I only use it when training horses to jump. That's it." He glanced at his watch like he had a heavy date. "I gotta go. The supply of grilled hotdogs and hamburgers is running low."

"Just one more question, Terry. How hard would it be for a person to obtain this device?"

He crossed his arms and thought for a moment. "I purchased mine before it was pulled off the market," he said, "but I suppose anyone with a police record wouldn't have trouble getting one," and then he spun on his heels and started back towards the grills he'd been manning.

"Wait a second! I hate to see you get fired for no reason. Your boss is out for blood. Cooking meat can wait. Find Reed and tell him what you told me about Cinnamon's condition and your thoughts on the metal device I found. He needs to hear it from your lips as soon as possible."

"If you're not a PI, why the heck are you getting so involved in ranch matters?" Terry asked. "And don't feed me that bull about it's because he gave you a job, again. You owe me the hard truth."

I placed my hand on my hip like a teacher or a mother does when being confronted by a little one. "I'll explain later. Just do as I suggested."

~47~

If Terry wasn't the one using the metal device on the horses Clint complained about, it had to be Jackson. Of course, Doc Taylor had easy access to the horses too, and his excuse about dropping the metal device, I first handed him the other day, seemed a trifle lame. Then again, what did he have to gain from messing with the horses, unless he's got a thing going with my client's soon-to-be ex-wife? That would put a different spin on the picture. Come to think of it, Doc did mention he saw Reed's wife last year. Maybe she's been using him to help her squeeze every last penny out of Reed and cause chaos to boot. Men have been known to do crazy things for the fairer sex. The only thing is I don't think Doc kills for love. Could he be Jackson's partner in crime?

My thoughts switched back to the guy I filled in for as another scenario made itself known. If Jackson was hooked up with Reed's wife, there might be a reason for him to intentionally lie about a horse having laminitis. But what was it?

Finding no definite answers for the recent actions around here, I pulled back the heavy barn door and went inside. Nothing had changed. Strong smells still permeated the air. I hesitated briefly by the door before proceeding further. Did I really want to check out two horse stalls tonight? There wasn't much light to see beyond my nose. *Stop being so childish, Mary. Everyone's busy visiting. No one's going to come in here, especially Jackson. He's long gone.* The gate for Angel's stall was open. I'd start there.

The floor was bare which made sense. Why waste sawdust if no horse is going to occupy the twelve-by-twelve foot area? "But more importantly, why would a healthy horse die so suddenly? What actually happened here?" I muttered. I slowly strolled from one section of the stall to the next looking for a clue.

When I reached the corner where Angel's feed holder was mounted, I discovered whoever cleaned up had forgotten to empty the remaining remnants of her last meal. Did anyone think to have this food tested? The day I worked with Terry he told me there were many toxic plants and such that can invade a pasture causing horses to get brain disorders and liver damage: maple leaves, chokecherries, yews and acorns. And, recently I came across a newspaper clipping detailing the poisoning and death of fifteen bucking horses from gopher pellets.

I pulled out a plastic gallon baggie from my jeans I'd brought from home. Aunt Zoe thought it was a silly idea, even after I mentioned bringing leftovers home from the party. With bare cupboards at home, did she think tonight's late snack would magically appear? I opened the gallon bag and quickly swept some remaining food into it with my free hand. When I was finished, I stuffed the half-filled baggie between my shirt and jeans and then traipsed over to Cinnamon's stall.

Cinnamon must've heard me coming; she poked her head over her stall gate. "I brought you a treat," I said in a melodic tone. The horse dropped her head and sniffed the air. "It's coming." I stuck my hand in my shirt pocket, pulled out a few carrots, and offered them to her. "Here you go, girl."

"Ain't that sweet," a rough baritone voice said from the other end of the barn.

I looked in the direction of the speaker, but I couldn't make out who it was. "Who's there?" I asked as my knees knocked together.

The man laughed. "Oh, come on. Don't tell me you don't know who I am? You know everything that's going on at this ranch. Reed hired you to spy on us."

Oh, crap. It's Jackson. Where did he come from? I pressed my back up against Cinnamon's wood stall while I tried to figure out how to get out of this jam. I had no mace on me or anything else I could defend myself with. "Look, Jackson. Your boss never hired anyone to spy on you. Why don't you stop hiding and we'll talk."

"Sure, Sweet Cakes, anything you say." He sauntered towards me. "You've been a busy little gal today, taking all those pictures and nosing around in Angel's stall. Oh, yeah, and let's not forget the sneaky way you tape-recorded all of us."

Shoot! I thought I had been so careful. I shook my head. "I wasn't tape-recording anyone."

Jackson grabbed the back of my vest and pulled it up, "What's th—?"

I was sweating bullets, but for once I had done something smart. What are you looking for?"

"You know damn well what I'm looking for," the man grunted. "Where did you stash it?"

"Stash what? Why are you so upset, Jackson?"

He twisted my arm and then pinned me against Cinnamon's stall. "Things were going fine until you showed up. Now, everything's falling apart." He ran a sweaty hand through my hair. "Why couldn't you mind your own business? What are you? A cop? A PI?" I didn't answer. "Never mind. I know how to take care of people like you."

That's what I was afraid of. When Jackson let go of my hair, I noticed the scratch marks on his hand. They were identical to Sally's. Fear crept through me, but I spoke anyway. "Have you been feeling a bit under the weather?"

"Why?"

"Well, when I saw you earlier, you looked like death warmed over."

He shoved his hand in a pocket. "Is that so?"

"Yeah. Apparently it only takes seven days for cat scratch fever to make you feel really sick."

Jackson growled. "What the hell are you talking about?"

"Sally's hands and yours look alike. You must've tossed one of Mini's kittens at Sally to distract her, making it easier to kill her."

The man ran his hand across his forehead. "I've never felt better."

"Glad to hear it," I said, trying to squeeze out of his control, "but if cat scratch fever isn't taken care of properly you could die."

"Stop with your mumbo jumbo," he shouted in my ear. "Your scare tactics aren't working. You're the one who should be shaking in your boots."

I was already trembling internally so I figured I go full throttle. "Why, because you killed Sally and made it look like Cinnamon kicked her in the head?"

"That little mouse had to be stopped," he blurted out. "She caught me inserting a device on Cinnamon and threatened to have me fired. I wasn't harming her horse. I was just proving to my partner how well horses could jump if they were encouraged a bit."

I twisted some more, but it didn't help. "Your partner wouldn't happen to be Reed's soon-to-be ex-wife, would it?"

Jackson's voice spiked. "I'm not filling in any blanks for you, Missy. Just shut your trap."

Too bad he didn't know me very well. When someone tries to silence me, I keep plugging away. "You got rid of Angel to increase your odds of winning a horse race, didn't you? Well, it's not going to work. It's illegal to use that metal device of yours. By the way, which of Reed's horses were you planning on using?"

Jackson had enough. He jerked me away from Cinnamon's gate and wrapped his arm tightly around my neck. "Shut up and move." I did as he requested since there weren't any other options. When he had me stationed where he wanted me to be, he opened Cinnamon's door.

I squirmed. "What are you doing?"

"Weren't you listening?"

He hadn't threatened me with a gun or a knife. If I had a chance, maybe I could kick him in the you-know-where and tear out of here. Unfortunately, the moment never came. Jackson never left himself open for any fight on my part. He dragged me into the stall, tossed me on Cinnamon's back and then forced me to put my hands behind myself so he could bind them together. I wanted to scream, but I remembered Terry's warning of how that would drive the horses crazy, and I didn't need that. "You don't want to do this, Jackson. Please, I beg you take me off this horse."

"No can do. You know too much."

My stomach turned over and over. I became nauseous. The one thing I was afraid of was finally coming true. I never wanted to be on another horse as long as I lived, and I was sitting on a saddle on the back of a sixteen-hand horse with no way to control her. "Don't do this, Jackson. You'll regret it."

"I don't think so." He led Cinnamon and me out of the stall, opened the barn door, swatted the horse on the butt with a crop and yelled, "Trot, Cinnamon."

How could I stay on the horse with no hands? The only thing that came to mind was to squeeze my knees as fiercely against the horses belly as possible. Little did I know that was the signal for Cinnamon to fly off deep into the woods at forty miles per hour.

~48~

Apparently, the metal charging device had been inserted in Cinnamon more than once because as soon as we reached the fenced area where the horses had been known to jump over, Cinnamon took one huge leap and landed in the fake Clint Russell's pasture and kept on going. I, on the other hand, lay crumpled on the ground waiting for a hero from the old west to come and rescue this damsel in distress. But, who knew I was here?

As minutes seemed to tick by and the pain in my arms and legs kicked in, I wondered if this hellish nightmare would ever end. *Dear God, just send someone. I'm not fussy who it is.*

Five minutes later my ears picked up the sound of a lone horse galloping towards me. Could it be Cinnamon? I glanced over my shoulder. Nope. Cinnamon's reddish-brown. This horse was black and white, and someone was riding it. Maybe it's Clint's caretaker. Oh, no! What if it's Clint? I don't want him to see me this way. I'm a mess.

Save your complaining. You prayed for help, and you're getting it.

"We've really got to stop meeting like this, Mary," Clint said. "Whoa, Charley. Whoa." The horse stopped, and he slid off. "In case you're worried about your horse, I rounded her up and tied her to a tree. How's your neck feel?"

"All right, I guess."

He stooped next to me. "How about the other parts of your body?"

"I feel like crap all over. If you untie my hands, I could check things out."

Clint whipped out a jackknife he'd obtained from his back pant pocket and sawed through the rope. "Someone needs to show you the proper dismount technique. If you want to stop a horse to get off, you pull back gently on the reins and slide off."

"Thanks. I'll try to remember that the next time a horse is running away with me." When I finished commenting, I accidently jerked my body and Clint's knife grazed my skin. "Ouch. Be careful. I'm not a pin cushion."

"Sorry."

The rope finally fell away. I rubbed my sore wrists, said a silent prayer, and then tried to stand. I failed miserably. *Shoot!* "My legs feel rubbery. There's no way I can get up without help."

He put his arms under me and carefully scooped me off the ground. "Legs feel that way after you've smacked the ground hard. You're lucky you didn't break your neck or back. "Hopefully, you haven't broken anything."

"Me too." Do you realize this is the third time you've rescued me, Clint?" I placed my arms around his thick neck. It felt good.

"No. I hadn't been keeping track." He carried me over by a huge boulder and leaned me against it. "You know you're a day early, Mary."

"What are you talking about?"

"Our bowling date."

The guy sure knows how to lighten things up. I might as well go with the flow. "Oh, darn. I forgot my bowling ball. I need to go back home and get it."

"I can fix that. Just let me collect your horse, and I'll saddle you up again."

My hands started shaking uncontrollably. "Oh, no you're not," I screamed.

"Calm down. I'm only kidding. I'm going to ride back to the house, get the four-wheeler, aspirin and a couple bottles of water. Can you handle my absence?"

"Sure, now that I'm on your side of the fence." Clint blushed. He had taken my words the wrong way, but I didn't care. It was nice having him take control. I felt safe with him. *Like one does with a cop.* That's it! Nat and Clint were undercover cops. Nat must've seen me fly off and called to warn Clint. That's how he showed up so fast. So, the two of them are running a sting operation. But what's involved? "When you get back though," I continued, "we need to have a long overdue talk."

"Whatever you say, sweet pea. You're the boss."

Five minutes later, Clint came tearing back through the pasture with his red and black four-wheeler shouting, "I let your friend know where you were."

"And how did you do that?" I yelled, watching him turn his noisy vehicle off. "Did you buzz your cohort, Nat?"

Clint hopped out of the vehicle and carried the items he promised over to the boulder where he had settled me. "Did I hear you say something about 'Nat and me'?"

"Yes, you and that gal. I've seen you two together before, but I couldn't figure out what you were up to."

"Have you now?" he asked real casual-like as he sat down on the ground next to me.

"Yeah, I've put some of the pieces together."

He unscrewed the bottled water and then passed the bottle and a couple aspirins to me. "Like what?"

I tossed the aspirins in my mouth, quickly washed them down, and then ran my hand across my mouth. "You're not Clint Russell. I've seen a copy of his driver's license."

Clint pretended to yawn. "Is that it?"

I shook my head. "No." A sharp pain cut through my pelvic region and I winced. "Clint or whoever you are, I don't think the aspirins are going to cut it. How about we finish this discussion on the way to the nearest emergency room?"

"I had a feeling you were going to say that." He stood, whisked me off the ground, settled me in the four-wheeler, and then hopped in on the driver side. "Fasten your seatbelt, sweet pea. You're in for a real treat." We tore through the pasture lickety-split, reaching the Ford Focus in nothing flat, and then Clint immediately transferred me to the car, and we took off for the freeway. "Okay, so where did we leave our discussion at?"

"I said you weren't Clint Russell, and you asked if I knew anything else."

He lifted his right hand off the steering wheel for a moment. "Oh, yeah. So, do you?"

I swept a hand through my grungy hair. "Yeah. I'm betting you and Nat are undercover cops. And since the real Clint Russell got busted on drug charges a couple years back, I think it's safe to say your sting operation pertains to drugs."

"Wow," Clint said with a tinge of sarcasm, "You amaze me. You thought of that all on your own?"

"Pretty much." I wasn't about to tell him a fellow cop helped a little.

His fiery blue eyes searched my face. "So, Mary, is your story any better than mine?"

"You betcha. I'm the real deal, Mary Malone, hired to solve Reed's horse issues."

He chuckled. "Ah, but you're not a licensed PI."

"Found me out, did ya?"

"Didn't take long."

"Yeah, especially when you have help."

Clint's eyebrows almost marched off his forehead.

"Don't deny it. I know Nat's been spying on me and reporting back to you."

His face relaxed now. "Okay. You're right. So, who tied you up at Reed's and sent you on your merry way?"

"Jackson. I figured out he killed Sally, and he wasn't too pleased about it. By the way, I'm sure he's the one who has been sending the horses over the fence. Don't ask me why."

"You got any proof to back up your allegations?"

"Plenty." I raised my shirt a smidgen and pulled out the baggie. "This is part of it. Have it analyzed. The other is stashed in a pig cookie jar in Reed's kitchen."

"A cookie jar? Couldn't you think of a better place to hide it?"

I gave him a cold stare. "That's where Stephanie Plum hides her gun."

"Who's Plum?"

"A fictional character in one of Janet Evanovich's mystery novels."

"Good Lord!" Clint ran his hand through his sandy-colored hair. "Let's forget about Plum for a minute, okay? Do you believe Jackson's messing with drugs too?"

"Could be." Another pain shot through me as Clint turned a sharp corner, and I wondered how much longer the ride would be. Just then, St. Agnes Hospital came into view.

Two minutes later we pulled up to the emergency entrance, and a fifty-something bald male hospital attendant immediately rushed over with a wheelchair. "What happened?"

Before I could spit the words out, Clint explained I'd been thrown off a horse and was suffering severe pain in the upper portion of my right leg.

"Has she taken any pain medication?" the male attendant questioned, assuming the man speaking for me was my husband. Of course, I wouldn't mind if he was.

"Yeah, I gave her a couple aspirins about twenty minutes ago."

"Okay, well let's get her in there and see about x-rays."

Now I knew how Rita Sinclair, Matt's ex-girlfriend must've felt when she broke her ankle this past winter in Puerto Vallarta. The injured person gets bypassed as if he or she can't function. Well, no one was going to get away with that if I could help it. I cleared my throat and said, "Look, I don't know if you're going to be with me through this whole ordeal, Mister, but you can talk to me from now on. This man and I are in no way related. You got that."

"The name's Dean," he replied softly.

"All right, Dean, let's see how fast I can get out of here."

~49~

Once I was safely ensconced in the ER, Clint said he'd better skedaddle before he blew his cover. I wasn't happy about his departure and being left to fend for myself. "You won't be for long," he said. "Nat texted and said she was on her way with Zoe." Right before he departed, he made me swear to say one of his employees found me out in the pasture if anyone asked. Not wanting to be featured on the Most Wanted list anytime soon, I agreed to stick to the dude's story.

While I sat idly by twiddling my thumbs in a freezing hallway waiting for someone to come and take me to the x-ray room, I noticed the big red warning sign about cell phones: usage was prohibited in this particular area. Shoot. I'd forgotten about mine. It had been safely tucked in a pant pocket when I entered the barn. After the fall I took, it's probably busted, but I'd better turn it off anyway. I dug it out of my pocket and looked it over. Still in one piece, but did it work. Maybe I should check.

My timing was off. Dean, the hospital employee, showed up and wheeled me off before I could make a call. "Hope your little gizmo there's turned off," the short statured Oriental man said, pointing to the sign by the water cooler. "Can't have them on in this area."

"Yup. I just noticed the sign." Darn. I held down a button on the cell phone until the screen went blank. "Okay, Dean, let's do some pop-wheelies."

"Whatever you say." And then he rested his slim hands on the handles at the top of the chair and began to push me forward.

We hadn't traveled very far down the corridor, when a familiar voice rang in my ears. "Mary! Where is he taking you? Please tell me you aren't having surgery." Aunt Zoe asked, rushing towards us looking like a fire engine chasing a fire.

"He's only taking me to the x-ray room," I calmly explained. "I'll be right back."

Dean glanced at Aunt Zoe. "Are you family, Miss?"

My aunt threw her hands on her hips. "I most certainly am."

"You'll find a lounge around the corner where you can wait."

"Thank you." She pressed my shoulder. "Everything will be all right, Mary. You'll see."

I crossed my fingers and forced a smile.

When I got back to the lounge a half hour later, I found Nat with Zoe, and shared that I was good to go.

Hearing the news, Aunt Zoe jumped out of her seat. "What does that mean, Mary? They didn't find anything wrong?"

"Oh, yeah, they found something."

"Well, what is it, niece? What's wrong?" my aunt's face coloring suddenly dimmed to a dull pink. "I'm sorry, Mary. I wasn't thinking. It just slipped out."

"It's all right, Auntie. Nat's not really who we thought she was either."

"That's right," Nat said. "I'm not mixed up with whatever you gals are working on."

Aunt Zoe stared at Nat like she was seeing her for the first time. "You're not?"

"No," Nat and I both chimed in.

"That means you must have the hots for Reed too."

Nat laughed. "Sorry. He's not my type."

"Then…"

I grabbed her hand. "I'll explain later." I tilted my head up to view Nat better. "Can you give us a lift home?" I inquired. "I just downed a pain pill for my fractured pelvis, and the nurse said I'm not supposed to drive."

"Sure, I have a good idea where you live."

*****

"I still can't figure out how Nat knew exactly where we lived, Mary," Aunt Zoe said as she helped me off the elevator and we progressed down the fourth floor hallway.

Each painful step I took required me to press down on the cane the hospital staff gave me to use for support the next several weeks. Not wanting to expose the real truth that Nat was an undercover cop, I said, "I must've mentioned it when she stopped by the optical store to have her glasses adjusted."

"Ah?"

Aunt Zoe didn't have the keys for the apartment handy yet when we reached our door, so she began digging through every crevice in her huge purse looking for them. While she continued to look, out popped Margaret

Grimshaw clad in a white-and-blue stripped apron, blue pants and a white blouse. "Oh, good, you've returned," she said in a high-pitched tone. "I'm anxious to hear about your adventures, but I also have wonderful news to share. Your brother Michael stopped by, Mary. He had found out Fiona was ready to be picked up so he thought he'd surprise you and bring the car around to the Foley." When I slowly turned to respond to her news, she said, "Mary, what happened? Why are you using a cane?"

"I'll tell you about it as soon as we get inside."

"I found them. I found them." Aunt Zoe dangled the keys in front of my nose.

"Well, perhaps you should put the one you need in the lock," Margaret kindly suggested.

"Yes, of course." She shoved the key in the hole and unlocked the door. "I'll go in first, Mary, you know how excited Gracie gets."

"Good thinking," I said. I already had one fractured bone, and I didn't need another.

Sure enough, Gracie flew at Aunt Zoe the second she stepped in the door as anticipated. But the minute she saw me she calmed down and sniffed me from my knees down. Evidently she didn't like the odor she picked up on. She turned and scrambled off to the bedroom.

"Must be the smell of the hospital," I said, I limping into the living room. "It probably reminds her of her visits to the vet. The vet!"

"What is it, Mary?" Margaret asked, squishing her fragile body to conform to a pillow on the floor.

"Something just dawned on me," I replied. "Auntie, can I use your cell phone?"

She reached for her purse. It was sitting on the coffee table. "What's wrong with yours?"

"I had it on me when I fell off the horse."

"Oh? Do you think it might be busted?"

"It's possible." I held out my hand. Just lend me yours, please. It's an emergency."

She yanked her cell phone out and handed it over.

I tried to remember Clint Russell's number as I took a spot on the edge of the couch and set the cane down. *Was there a two in it or not? Come on. It wasn't that hard a number to remember.* I finally recalled it, pressed the digits, and hoped he was available. "Clint. It's Mary."

Aunt Zoe marched over to where Margaret sat and said, "I can't believe she's talking to Clint Russell. When Reed finds out, he'll fire her for sure."

"Shh, Zoe," Margaret ordered. "I want to hear what she has to say."

"You do?"

"*Si.* Aren't you interested?"

"I suppose."

"I think you'll find what you're looking for at Dr. Troy Taylor's home," I said, "Don't forget to let me know how it turns out."

Either the pain pills or the umpteen x-rays had finally loosened up my brain cells. Of course, it could've been plain hunger pains, but everything seemed to gel all of a sudden. The day I visited Doc Taylor he had acted mighty strange. I know he purposely dropped the metal object I gave him, but why had he been so determined that I not enter his house even though he was choking? I also recalled the loud thud his vet bag made when it smacked the porch: too noisy for a few instruments to make. Probably packed with cocaine.

Aunt Zoe pounced the instant I ended the call. "What's going on with Doc Taylor? He left the party right after he ate."

"One thing at a time," I said. "Don't rush me."

The pain I felt must've registered on my face because Margaret hastily intervened on my behalf. "I made a French apple pie today. I think we could use a bit of nourishment. Zoe, would you mind running across the hall and getting it? It's sitting on the kitchen counter."

"It's been awhile since I've eaten," I added. "I'd enjoy a slice of pie. How about you, Auntie?"

"I suppose it wouldn't hurt to have one more sweet after all that's happened today. I can't believe how crazy those horses are at Reed's," she said, and then traipsed out the door.

"Thanks, Margaret. She was coming on too strong."

The elderly woman shared a knowing smile. "May I ask why you're using a cane?"

"I've got a fractured pelvis." I tried to make myself more comfortable on the cushion-less couch, but nothing I did seemed to help.

"Oh, my. How did that happen?"

"A horse threw me." Before I could manage to explain the events surrounding the incident further, my aunt waltzed back in the apartment carrying a nicely browned crusted pie in a glass dish. It looked so yummy I was ready to tear it out of her hands.

Aunt Zoe must've sensed how desperate I was. She only stopped in the living room doorway long enough to tell us her plans, "I'll slice it up, add vanilla ice cream and bring it in here, so you two don't have to get up," and then she went on to the kitchen.

I looked at the nonagenarian. "Margaret, you don't need to be so uncomfortable. When Zoe gets back in here, have her help you up, so you can sit in the La-Z-Boy."

"I'm all right where I am. How much longer do you think your aunt will keep up this Moroccan style living of hers?"

I flipped my palms up. "Your guess is as good as mine."

A couple minutes later, Aunt Zoe buzzed back to us and handed out the dessert. "I bet you gals don't know how pie a la mode came about." Margaret and I shrugged. "John Gieriet from Duluth came up with the name and idea in 1885."

I bobbed my head. "Thanks, just what I wanted to know. People will be thrilled to hear me brag about another Minnesota tidbit besides Paul Bunyan, 3M and our 10,000 lakes."

Margaret giggled.

Aunt Zoe chose to sit on a cushion by our neighbor and found it hard to manipulate her dessert plate and squish down at the same time, but eventually she managed. "Do you feel like talking yet, Mary?"

"I suppose. Let me taste this luscious dessert first." I pressed my fork into the flakey crust and ice cream and shifted everything to my lips. "Yum. The apple pie is delicious, Margaret. You'll have to show me how to make it someday."

Our neighbor nodded. "I will if you continue to keep me in the loop regarding your case."

It hurt to laugh, but I did. "I promise. Now, about today's events..."

~50~

Two Weeks Later

"You did a fine job, Mary," my client said, hoisting his second cup of strong java in the air over his kitchen table, "for a newbie sleuth."

I gave my aunt a disgusted look.

Her cup trembled in her hand. "I'm sorry, Mary. The night of the party the two of us were talking about so many things, I accidently blurted it out."

Reed didn't waste time coming to Aunt Zoe's defense "It's not a bad thing, Mary. You should be darn proud of what you've accomplished. Although, I'm still having a hard time believing Jackson killed Sally. He doesn't seem like the type."

"Well, he definitely did," I said.

Aunt Zoe cleared her throat. "And don't forget about his decision to join forces with your ex, Georgette, to end Angel's racing career by poisoning her with Maple leaves. What did he hope to gain from that?"

"The same thing he got from smuggling cocaine with Doc Taylor," I answered, "Money. It is the root of all evil. He and Georgette wanted Angel out of the way, so they could enter another horse that matched her speed, a horse that's right here in Reed's stable."

"Which horse is it, Mary?" my aunt asked. "You never told me."

I poured myself a second cup of coffee from the pot sitting on the table. "Think back. Which horse was supposed to have laminitis, but didn't?"

"Cinnamon?"

"Yup."

"That was pretty clever the way you snapped those pictures at the picnic," Reed stated. "Why, if it weren't for those snapshots, the young fellow at Milt's would've never been able to identify Jackson."

"I still wish I had gotten his voice on the recorder, so Misses Sullivan could have heard it," I said, reaching over and grabbing one of the chocolate chip cookies Margaret had sent along with us this morning. "Reed, I never asked how much money you raised for Sally's mom."

He wiped crumbs from his jaw. "Almost three thousand dollars and money's still rolling in. That article in the local newspaper after the police arrested Jackson, Georgette, and Doc Taylor made a huge impact on the community."

Aunt Zoe collected our plates and then carried them to the sink. "There's no possible way Jackson will ever earn a *get out of jail* card," she said. The U of M's vet department can prove the toxic substance Mary found in Angel's feeder was the same as that discovered in Jackson's storage locker. And, the man was stupid enough to admit to Mary that he'd killed Sally."

Even if he doesn't fess up," Reed said, "I think Doc Taylor will soon be crowing like a rooster now that he's been offered a reduced sentence."

"I imagine so. I still can't believe how greedy Jackson was being involved in two money making schemes like that." With that said, I drew silent.

"What's wrong, Mary?" Reed inquired. "Is your fracture bothering you?"

"No," I said with a tinge of sadness. "I'm wondering what will happen to Cinnamon?"

My client drained the last drop of coffee in his horse-head mug. "That's right I never told you. She's been bought and will be staying right here at the Bar X."

"Oh, Reed, that's wonderful news," Aunt Zoe said, rejoining us at the table. "Which of your boarders purchased her?"

Reed threw back his head and laughed. "None. You're looking at him. Since my ex and Jackson illegally entered Cinnamon in the endurance race, I'm going to follow through in Sally's honor and see what she can do. Who knows, we both might be standing in the winner's circle real soon."

"Speaking of surprises," Aunt Zoe remarked, "Reed's got another announcement to make," then she winked at him.

Oh, my gosh. Don't tell me they're going to tie the knot? What will I do without a roommate? I know I've said Aunt Zoe drives me crazy, but still... I held my breath.

"Jim Savage is getting hitched and wants the wedding held on my premises."

I heaved a sigh of relief. *Thank you, Lord. Evidently I've been a pretty good gal the last several days.* "What fun. Has he set the date?"

"Yup. He wants it to take place in three weeks."

Aunt Zoe rested her fiery-red head on her hands. "And, guess what, Mary? Jim wants you and me to help plan the wedding. What do you think of a horseshoe-shaped cake?"

My hands flew to my forehead. *Oh, crap. I thought I was finished with horses.*

~51~

"Didn't Jim and Stephanie luck out with a beautiful September day?" Aunt Zoe said. "Not one teeny cloud in the sky." She didn't realize it, but she could've been a storm cloud with all the dark green cowgirl paraphernalia she had on, including the parasol she was holding. She must've run out of bright colored outfits.

"Yes," I replied, "but then September is supposedly the driest month of the year."

Rod Thompson, who I had invited to be my escort for the festivities, joined me now. He had been chatting with Reed. I sure hope the owner of the Bar X hadn't filled his head with too much of what had happened around here. I'd never hear the end of it. "Did I tell you how spiffy you look, Mary?"

"Ah huh, but you can tell me again if you want."

"Where did you find your getup?"

The outfit he was referring to was a soft, white sheer short-sleeved blouse, a turquoise fringed vest and matching broomstick skirt, a brand new white cowgirl hat and stupid boots that pinched my toes. I waved my hand in the air. "Oh, you know, here and there." He didn't have to know most of it was from Bargain Suzie's Recycled Clothing.

Rod tossed his head back and let out a rip-roaring laugh. "No, I don't know, but that's all right." He slid his royal blue long-sleeved shirt up and peeked at his watch. "What time is this shindig supposed to start?"

"Anytime," Aunt Zoe said. They're just lining up the horses."

Rod's mouth flew open. "Horses?"

"Didn't you tell him about the wedding, Mary?"

"Yup. All except the part about the horses."

"What's going on? Rod asked. "Don't tell me everyone has to ride a horse?"

"Not everyone."

Rod swiped his forehead. "Phew. That's good."

"Just the bridal party," I continued, "the minister, the wedding planners and their escorts."

The tall, blonde Norwegian stepped back. "Whoa! You're one of the wedding planners, Mary, which means I've got to get on a horse too."

I batted my thick-glossed eyelashes and smiled sweetly. "Yup."

"No way, I'm not doing it."

"But Rod, have you forgotten how you made me line dance?"

"That's different."

"No, it isn't," I argued.

He swung his head from side to side. "I can't do it, Mary. I really can't. I had a traumatic experience with a horse when I was a kid."

Hmm. The FBI agent isn't so different from me after all. "Pretty please," I begged, "we'll put you on the slowest horse Reed's got."

"Leave him be," a male voice said from behind us. It was Clint. Well, not really Clint. It was David. "I'll ride with you, Mary."

I spun around. "I didn't think you'd show. You never sent a reply."

"Rod, you remember Clint." I gave a quick wink to David.

Rod sidled up alongside David and I. "Yes, we ran into him at Ziggy Piggy's. Great place to eat and dance, but I haven't been back there since." He gave me a dirty look which I ignored.

"Come on Mary and Clint," Aunt Zoe said as she waved to Reed. Apparently, he was signaling for us to get over by the horses. "You can chat with Rod later."

Before we walked away, the Norwegian squeezed in one more comment. "Don't forget, I'm dancing with you later, Mary. You know how I love to line dance."

I had a feeling Rod was worried I'd leave him in the dust now that David had come on the scene, and he was right. "Sorry. Jim and his bride requested nothing but waltzes and polkas."

David put his arm around my waist and led me off to the horses. "I'm glad I was able to make it. I was scheduled for another sting operation, but everything wasn't in place yet."

"And, I couldn't be happier to see you. By the way, how did you get the U of M's veterinary diagnostic lab to move so swiftly on Angel's necropsy and the bag of goodies you delivered for me?"

"I told them if they didn't get right on it there would be more horse deaths, and I didn't think they'd want that hanging over their heads, especially with all the donations they receive from animal lovers all over Minnesota and beyond."

"Wow. Now, it's my turn to be amazed."

"I've got some other news I can share too."

"Oh?"

"Doc had interned a year in Colorado. That's where he first got mixed up with drug trafficking, but he never met Clint so he wasn't suspicious of me."

"I was told they caught him at the airport as he was boarding a flight for Switzerland."

"Yeah, our guys are good."

We had finally reached Reed, and David asked him to point out which horses we were supposed to get on. "I want you two to ride on Cortez and Cinnamon. They get along great together." David and I shared a smile.

I took David's hand and led him over to the horses. "Did you know years ago there were several cities in the United States where married men weren't allowed to ride by themselves until they had been married longer than a year?"

"No kidding? Well, I guess it's a good thing I'm not married then."

"You better believe it." After I gave the signal for Reed and David to put me on Cinnamon, they gently hoisted me up and left me in sidesaddle position due to my recent injury. It was interesting to note, now that I was seated on the horse, I wasn't shaking in my boots, although I thought I would be. Perhaps the reason was Prince Charming remained by my side this time.

David mounted Cortez as the guitarist began strumming *Cowboy Take Me Away* by the Dixie Chicks. Luckily, we were near the tail end of the horse procession giving David a chance to ask me a serious question. "Do you plan to keep your sleuthing career, Mary?"

I picked up Cinnamon's reins and tossed a similar question his way. "Do you plan to continue your work as an undercover cop?"

Book Club Questions
For
Death At The Bar X Ranch

1. What motivated Mary Malone to take on a case meant for her brother? Should she have told Reed Griffin her brother wasn't available? What would you have done if you had heard a similar message and were unemployed? Would you have informed the person who the message was originally meant for?

2. What was Mrs. Grimshaw's underlying motive for getting Mary to the Foley? How do you think she felt when Mary actually moved in?

3. Did you honestly think the cohabitation of relatives, one in her thirties and the other past retirement age, would work out in a one bedroom apartment?

4. Do you think Aunt Zoe was rushing her feelings for Reed a bit or had she gotten through her mourning stage? What amount of time do you think a widow or widower should take before becoming involved with someone else? Do you know someone who dated after their spouse died? How long was it before they started dating?

5. When Mary first got behind the wheel of Matt's Topaz she was scared silly. If you had to borrow another person's car would you feel the same way? Why or why not?

6. Should Mary have warned Reed Griffin she had a severe fear of horses before volunteering to take the case? How about opening up to her aunt?

7. Do you think Mary's first contact with Clint Russell may have made her more determined than ever to work on the horse case? Would you have let a good-looking guy affect your job decision even if a great fear factor was involved?

8. Was it appropriate for Reed to expect Mary to fill in for an ill employee when she knew nothing about horses? Have you ever had to fill in for someone out sick and knew nothing about their job? How did it go? Were you glad when the day was over?

9. Do you think Terry was being too tough on Mary, being it was her first time around horses? Why or why not? Did you think he might be the one causing Reed's horse problems? If so, what led you to believe this?

10. If you had a fear of horses and didn't have previous experience around them, would you have ventured into the stalls by yourself and groomed the horses?

11. When reading chapter 18, did you sense any of the characters at the cookout could be responsible for Reed Griffin's horses jumping over Clint Russell's fence? Why or why not?

12. After the Bar X cookout, did you think Mary would run into trouble out in the woods by herself or did you think her walk in the woods would be a waste of time? Did you suspect Aunt Zoe might fail Mary if she required help?

13. Do you feel deception is acceptable at times in order to get your own way, like Mary deceived Rod in order to spy on her aunt at Ziggy Piggy's? What were the consequences of Mary's deception? When you were involved in a minor deception, what were the repercussions if any?

14. When the cats were first introduced in a barn scene, did you sense they might be used in a sinister crime further along in the story, or did you just think about cuddly kittens and how nice it would be to own one?

15. Nat and Clint kept popping up no matter where Mary went. Did you suspect they were red herrings like Terry or did you think they were plotting against the Bar X Ranch?

16. Which of the three males Mary seemed to be interested in did you hope she'd end up with? Why? Were you satisfied with the ending?

17. If you were working on a project and needed some input, would you reach out to an elderly person, or would you steer clear of them and seek a person your own age? Why?

18. Do you think Mary would have eventually solved this case without seeking answers from other reliable sources? Why is it important

to get all the facts before jumping to conclusions? Have you ever rushed headlong into a situation without getting enough information beforehand? What were the consequences?

Made in USA - North Chelmsford, MA
1308642_9781986182249
03.17.2022 1502